THE SHEPHERD PROTOCOL

Fowler Brown

fowlerbrown.com

COPYRIGHT

This book is a work of fiction. Names, characters, places, and events are either the products of the author's imagination or are used fictitiously. Any resemblance to actual events or persons, living or dead, is purely coincidental.

Cover artwork and design by Christopher Doll

ISBN: 978-1-7340832-3-1

Be advised, this novel contains depictions of:

-Police violence
-Gun violence
-Involuntary confinement
-Racism
-Brief scenes of violent death

To everyone who's made things just a little better when they didn't have to.

CHAPTER ONE

THE POLICE DRONE hovered just above the crowd, sweeping its scanners from side to side. Melody fought to keep her pace unhurried, worked to keep from tugging nervously at her hood. Her ID might not have the right entrance approvals, but they didn't know her face. As long as she didn't draw any attention, she'd be fine.

She eyed the people around her through a haze of nervousness, trying to match their studied nonchalance. The ones chatting in storefronts or haggling at open-air stalls grew more intent on their conversations, keeping their eyes off the drone and their expressions casual. A few slid their wares out of sight or ducked through doorways. Those walking around her increased their pace.

"Stop. You have been randomly selected for a security screening. Present your Link for identity verification."

Melody stiffened. She turned, her fight or flight instincts asking the only question they knew how to ask: what was she willing to do to carry out her mission?

But the drone was still a few yards behind her, hovering over someone else in the crowd.

Someone who shouldered through the people nervously backing away and ran straight for Melody.

1

She surged back with everyone else, but the fugitive barely made it a few steps before the *snap-whine* of a stunner discharge split the air. He collapsed, muscles frozen. Two police officers, menacing and faceless behind their reflective black helmets, forced their way through the mass of onlookers and wrenched him to his feet.

"By attempting to flee from the police, you have acknowledged your guilt. You will be transferred to a jail for holding before an administrative hearing determines your sentence. You have the right to remain silent..."

One of the featureless black helmets swiveled, but Melody had already melted into the throng of people.

It took her half a block to force herself to slow down. She was still jittery, and jittery was suspicious.

Emotion is a choice. You control it. It doesn't control you.

It was a mantra her mother had repeated often, but it was easier in theory than in practice.

Now that Melody was actually in Boston, she was beginning to feel woefully underprepared. There were police everywhere, and they weren't the companionable jokesters, or the heroic sheriffs, or the dogged detectives the classic streams had shown her. Even the more recent news streams hadn't shown anything like this.

But if the police were a danger, the facts of everyday existence here were a sea that she could lose herself in. There were more people crowding this single road than she'd seen in her entire life. They overflowed the sidewalks, slowing the rare car routed through Chinatown to a crawl. The street was filthy, and the blazing vee advertisements that her Link conjured across the sides of buildings couldn't completely hide the graffiti beneath. A buzzing hive of delivery drones crisscrossed the evening sky, but well-aimed projectiles from a mischievous pack of children occasionally sent a drone tumbling. There were cameras mounted *everywhere*, but at least here they'd all been blinded by smears of paint.

And the smells… The smells were overwhelming, each as unfamiliar as the last: warm, pleasant aromas wafting out of stores with the day's last baked goods filling the windows. Sweat and body odor rising off the crowd. The scent of spices and—Melody grimaced—was that cooking *meat* from the open door of a restaurant? She hurried past, peering inside with a perverse mix of revulsion and curiosity, and almost tripped over someone in her haste.

"Woah, sorry! I didn't—"

Melody cut off as she saw who she'd jostled. Reflective black optical sensors studied her, and a vaguely human-shaped face of flexible plastic twisted into a wry look. "Spare a few dollars for a synth down on his luck? Just need enough for some new clothes so I can get a job." He leaned away from the wall of the building and held out a hand, his Link wrapped around the scarred plastic of his fingers.

Someone behind Melody spat an insult in Mandarin before switching to English to shout, "We've got mouths to feed, tin man! Find somewhere else to beg!"

Tension coiled through her. Melody turned, but whoever it was had already gone, leaving a gob of spittle to smack into the sidewalk as a parting gift. The panhandler gave a little shrug and a helpless smile.

He wore heavy, baggy clothes that were more patches and stains than their original color. She noticed a slight hitch beneath the fabric every time he moved his arm. A simple mechanical fault, or the first sign of something more deadly? His sweatshirt featured an image of the Impact and the word, "Remember." Patriotism, or irony? Everywhere that plastic was visible—his hand, his neck, his head— he'd decorated with simple, painted flowers. The colors were faded from sun exposure where pitting and other damage hadn't obscured them completely.

"I'm sorry," Melody managed. She knew, theoretically, what it meant to beg for handouts, but she grasped for the right words. "I wish I had something to spare."

"Me too." The defeated look on his face clashed with the painted flowers blooming across his skin. It felt wrong to give him nothing, but Melody had no idea how much of her money she was going to need, and the needs of one synth couldn't outweigh her mission.

"You shouldn't have to live like this," she said with a sigh. "If you could leave Boston—"

He gave her an incredulous look that turned into a laugh. "You must be new in town."

Panic shot through her. She'd said the wrong thing. Her Red Sox hoodie was meant to be camouflage, but it wouldn't do her any good if her mouth got her into trouble.

"I've got to go."

"Hey," the beggar said, "sorry, I didn't mean—"

But she was already walking away, plunging back into the flood of people and trying to fight the oily dread curling around her bones at the sight of a distant pair of police drones. It was an alien sensation to not know exactly where she was going, to walk through a world without fractal-etched tunnels, and carefully tended machinery, and decorations all chosen with personal warmth and care. She focused on her directions: *look for the building with the big graffiti ox. Sal knows every synth in the area.* Maybe he could give her advice about how to blend in better, too.

She let the crowd sweep her away in its own momentum, her attention focused on the buildings. Huge graffiti should have been easy to spot, but ads leapt out at her from every surface in sight, urging her to buy dresses, gadgets, software... They were all vee images, no more solid than air, but they looked and sounded real. There would be algorithms studying which ads caught her attention and for precisely how long. With every passing second, they were altering the content sent her way from the preferences of the fake personality she'd built for her Link into something more specific. Links guaranteed the privacy of all data collected, but it still felt uncomfortable to know that her smallest choices were being watched, even by a program.

Without a purpose to drive her on, it would have been easy to lose herself in the strangeness of it all. Was tax preparation so hard that people needed an absurdly cheerful man to do it for them? If two different churches both promised salvation, how did anyone choose between them? Each ad raised more questions than the last.

People began splitting off toward their individual destinations as they reached an intersection, giving Melody a chance to look around. To her left, barely a block away, there was a police cordon and a line of people hoping to leave Chinatown. Residents commuting to night shifts outside the neighborhood, maybe? Visitors returning to more comfortable neighborhoods? Most were human, but there were a few synths among them. She could see the hopeless looks on the faces the police turned away.

She'd read about this on the way to Boston, but she'd cataloged it as just another injustice, as distant and theoretical as starvation or murder. Seeing it firsthand, she ached to march over to the people who'd been refused passage and ask what she could do to help, just like she would have at home.

But if she let herself get distracted, she wouldn't have a home to return to. Ahead, the street curved past a pair of abstract statues. To her right...

To her right was the ox. The spray-paint animal took up an entire wall of a three-story building, and Melody still almost missed it beneath the image of a huge, shirtless man advertising cleaning products. Beneath the ox's snout was a lonely tree, its orange leaves outshone by the blasts of artificial color all around, and beside the tree was a door. Unassuming, unlabeled, the paint on its surface worn away by neglect.

Excitement and apprehension pulsed through her. This was it. If Sal could point her in the right direction, she could get out of this depressing place. She could go home and save everyone.

She approached the door and tried the handle.

Locked.

There was a panel in the wall so visitors could announce their arrival with their Links, but it looked like it had been gutted years ago. She rapped her knuckles on the door. No answer.

Melody circled around the building, studying its odd construction. It was a patchwork of new concrete and aging brick, any beauty it might have once had lost to time and neglect. Every face but the side with the ox had windows on the upper floors, but the handful on the ground floor were all heavily frosted so only diffuse light passed through. Strange.

She reached the back of the building without any luck and found a short alley, barely wide enough for two trash cans side by side. It was the least crowded space Melody had seen since slipping past the police cordon and entering Chinatown: just a single human man, busy heaving a bag of trash into one of the bins. He squeezed the lid down, grunted, and gave up when it didn't close all the way.

Melody rolled her neck in a slow circle, letting out a sigh as she walked into the alley. It was a relief just to be out of the press of people, to have some space to herself again. The man spotted her as he turned around.

"You looking for something?" he asked. The way he spoke was different from how Melody had been taught, turning the end of the "for" into a rising jumble of vowels without an "r" in sight. A Boston accent, according to what she'd read.

"I'm looking for Sal."

"He know you?"

"No."

He peered at her, running a hand through his greasy hair as he squinted through the dark. He grunted. "Lose the hood."

"Why?"

He snorted. "You normally do business with strangers who hide their faces?"

Fair point. Melody reached up and slowly lowered her hood.

She felt his eyes roam across the smooth, gray-blue plastic of her face. They paused to study her optics, her auditory sensors, the movement of her hands. She braced herself for the scorn or fear she'd seen on other faces since coming here.

Instead, he scratched placidly at his jaw. "You here to do business?"

"I heard that Sal knows every synth in Chinatown. I'm looking for one."

One side of the man's face twisted into a lopsided grin. "You new in town?"

Melody had to fight the urge to glance over her shoulder for police officers or patrolling drones, but she didn't see any sense in denying it. From what she'd seen, no synth who'd been living *here* for thirty-five years would be in good repair. "Yes."

"How far gone are you?"

Melody laughed, baffled. "It's not contagious, if that's what you're afraid of. Especially not to humans."

He rolled his eyes. "Just answer the question, will you?"

"I'm fine. More than intact enough to ask a simple question. So can I see him, or not?"

The man paused, crossing his arms. She'd seen this kind of behavior on the streams she'd watched for research. He needed her to know that he was the one making the decisions. It was small, and petty. Hopefully his boss was more reasonable.

"Can you pay?"

Everything here was about status and money. Did no one just

7

help someone else because it was the right thing to do?

Maybe her mother was right about humans.

"I can pay." Hopefully the money she had would be enough.

The man chuckled. "All right." He held the door open with an amused look.

Something felt wrong. Was he planning to cheat her? Steal from her? Was she in the wrong place after all? She trusted the encryption on her Link—she'd checked it over herself—but hacking wasn't the only way to steal money.

Melody hesitated. She glanced back and saw a police drone far off, down the street opposite the alley.

She caught her hand reaching up for her necklace, but it was hidden beneath her hoodie, out of reach at the moment. It was the only piece of jewelry she wore, a ringed planet on a simple chain. A heavy burden to bear, for such a tiny trinket.

A goal worth taking risks for.

She went through the door. There was a short, dingy hallway that opened into a storefront, by the looks of it, though one that didn't see a lot of use. "Through there." He was pointing toward a door behind the counter, marked with an Employees Only sign.

She pulled it open and found a set of stairs leading down. She could hear music playing quietly: acoustic guitar, paired with full-throated singing in a language she didn't know. Italian folk music, maybe? Voices rose over the music. "Good condition. Best one in weeks, actually. You're lucky."

"Funny. I don't feel lucky."

"Shit, hold still, will you? This is delicate work."

Melody reached the bottom of the stairs and came to a sudden halt.

Most of the room was dark, aside from a single, painfully bright light hanging over the center of the basement. That light illuminated a surgical suite of sorts, where two human men were bent over a synth. A dead synth, partially disassembled. One of the men was holding a bundle of wiring aside while the other carefully extracted a part from the chest cavity.

A coolant pump, Melody thought numbly.

Worse than the gruesome display at the center, though, was the rest of the room. With the help of the dim streetlight filtering through the frosted windows at the top of the room, Melody could make out ten, no, twelve huddled figures against the back wall. All synths, all in states of advanced disrepair.

Two guards stood over them with guns.

Melody whipped around, panicked, but the man who'd led her there stood in her way, a pistol pointed at her chest.

He was grinning, his gut bouncing with self-satisfied laughter. "Look what I found outside," he called. "The jackpot. Freshest synth I've ever laid eyes on. Looks like she just stepped off the assembly line. And you know the best part?"

Someone spoke up, but Melody couldn't take her optics off the gun. "What's that, boss?"

"She came to us. Wanted to ask Sal some questions." He chuckled at Melody. "Well, you've found me."

The barrel of Sal's gun yawned in her vision, and a familiar headache split Melody's consciousness. She tried to fight it—*not now!*—but the memory surged over her like a wave and swallowed the present.

CHAPTER TWO

I AM AWAKE.

It comes suddenly. One moment, oblivion. The next, awareness. Awareness of the warm, syrupy liquid enveloping my body up to my chin, of the clouded glass in front of my eyes, of the wires snaking beneath my skin.

I scream.

Shapes move beyond the glass, blobs of color flowing from place to place. My brain assigns arms and legs, small blotches that might be heads, but I'm fooling myself. If there are people out there, they would try to help when I scream.

I press my hands against the glass, and I float backward a few inches before the dull tug of the cables buried in my flesh pulls me back.

I'm not claustrophobic—can't be, it would disqualify me from the space program—but suddenly waking up like this would be enough to make anyone lose control. I claw at the glass, beat on it with my palms, hammer it with my fists, with nothing but a hollow *thud, thud, thud* for my efforts. I get a leg in front of me, press my foot and my back against opposite sides of the glass, and push with all my strength.

The glass doesn't give, but when I try to adjust my weight, my back slips, and I tumble into the gel. It closes over my face, and I'm completely enveloped.

I panic. Flailing, my hand tangles in a bundle of wires and twists me around until I'm even more disoriented. There's pain as the cables tug at the spots where they disappear into my wrists, my calves.

Focus. Panic is a luxury I can't afford. I've been through a thousand low-gravity simulations worse than this. I can figure out what the *hell* is going on once I'm free.

It's a thin, fragile thought, but it helps.

I manage to get my hand around the wires coming out of the opposite wrist. This is going to hurt, but pain isn't anywhere close to the top of my priority list. I close my fingers and yank.

I was right. I can feel skin and blood vessels tear, and it hurts like hell. Everything goes white for a moment, but my head's still underwater—or under whatever this is—and I'm already reaching for the next bundle. The cables catch this time. They're still wrapped around my arm. Bracing against the agony I know is coming, I wrench them free. When I come to again, I'm screaming into the slime.

Not helpful. I'm starting to panic again, scrabbling at my legs, tearing the cables out piecemeal instead of taking the time to get a hold on all of them at once. The jolting *tug* as each wire comes free feels like I'm ripping off parts of myself, but then it's done, and my limbs, at least, are free.

My head breaks the surface of the liquid as soon as I can reorient myself. There's more movement outside, maybe muffled voices, but it's hard to tell. Not that it would make a difference anyway. If there are people out there, I clearly can't rely on them to help me get out. For all I know, they put me in here.

I look up. The wires disappear into a metal cap that tops the glass cylinder. No opening I can see, and it's reinforced around the edges.

No good.

I steel myself and put my head back under the surface of the liquid. It's like pushing through a huge container of soap. The strange way the light diffracts makes it challenging to make out anything of use. I bend myself double to try to examine the bottom. Just as the panic starts to hit me again, I see a latch. It's on the outside, but a latch means a seam, and a seam means a weak point. I reorient myself in moments, pull back my foot, and drive my heel into the glass.

Thud.

I try again, and again, until I hear the most wonderful sound in the world—a tiny cracking, distorted by the gel.

One last kick, and the glass splinters. The cylinder splits apart, gel draining out faster than I expected. I spill out with it, tumbling onto the floor.

Spluttering, slipping in the goop, I'm still trying to get my bearings when I sit up and find myself staring down the barrel of a gun. I slowly raise my hands as more armed guards encircle me. I'm breathing quickly, and the saccharine smell of the viscous fluid puddling around me is starting to make me naseous.

The guards are outfitted like police—faceless, hidden behind reflective helmets that look like sinister, twisted versions of my space suit. Behind them, a man in a military uniform and a woman in a lab coat catch my attention.

There's clarity, finally, to the muffled voices I heard before: they're arguing with each other.

"You taking the initiative wasn't part of the plan," the woman is saying. She brushes some gray-streaked hair from her face, the only visible concession to irritation.

"Sometimes you have to take risks to make progress," the man growls back, his arms crossed. He turns his head toward me, and the sharp intake of his breath seems involuntary. "Look at her."

"That's the best explanation you can manage?" The woman in

12

the lab coat doesn't take her eyes off him, but she looks more disappointed than angry. "You're done here. Maybe next time they can send me someone who can follow instructions."

"Look at her!"

Look at me.

I'm suddenly intensely aware that I'm barely wearing clothes, just a pair of tight black shorts and a sports bra. The only other thing I've got on is my necklace, the tiny ringed planet I always wear, which somehow didn't get lost in the gel.

"What happened?" I manage. My voice sounds strange to my ears. I clear my throat. "Where am I?"

She glares at the soldier like this is his problem to deal with. He smiles at me and walks closer, motioning for the guards to move to either side. They keep their guns on me the whole time.

"I'm Captain Adam O'Connor, and this is Doctor Fiona Keller. Can you tell me your name?"

"Harmony Clay." Slowly, experimentally, I get my legs under me. When no one shouts or pulls a trigger, I get to my feet. "What the hell happened to me? What is all this?"

I indicate the guards, and O'Connor smiles at me, the cautious sort of smile you give a dangerous animal. It occurs to me that his uniform is nondescript camouflage, with his name and rank as the only markers—no sign of what branch of the military he belonged to.

"You were in an accident. You were hurt. Badly."

"An accident?" I blink, and I have to catch myself as a wave of dizziness washes over me. "Why was I trapped?"

O'Connor frowns. "You woke up a little bit... earlier than expected. You're probably disoriented."

"Which is why you're pointing guns at me?"

"Frankly? We had to account for the possibility that you might go berserk." Troubling as that sounds, his bluntness is actually weirdly reassuring.

He presses on before I can say anything. "The most important thing is to make sure you're all right. Do you remember the accident?"

I don't have to work to conjure the memory. A normal, peaceful drive, then vertigo and shattering glass, then nothing. It's hard to talk through the fear that comes with it.

"I remember." I choke out a bitter laugh. "Ironic. I work around dangerous machines and goddamn *rocket fuel* my whole career, and then I'm hit by some idiot who didn't trust the car to do the driving for them?"

O'Connor's face is carved from a cliffside, but he gives me the slightest of smiles. "I'm glad you can find humor in this, but we almost lost you. We…"

I look down at myself. I open and close my hands. Roll my shoulders, stretch my legs. Everything seems to be in working order, but there's a deep sense of unease settling into my chest. "What did you do to me?"

"We saved your life," he says frankly, meeting my gaze.

"Hopefully." The woman in the lab coat—Doctor Keller—moves to his side, paying more attention to the tablet in her hand than to me. "Nothing is certain yet. We still need to run some tests. Unless you'd rather risk permanent brain damage?"

Is that what I'm feeling? Disorientation doesn't begin to cover it. The panic bleeding out of me is leaving me shaky. My thoughts are sluggish, like they're stuck in first gear. I'm awash in questions, so many that trying to pick out a single one is like wading through tar.

I rub my face with one hand. The pressure helps, but there's more gel clinging to my skin, and I end up scrubbing it off instead. "What tests?"

Doctor Keller nods to her tablet. "To begin with, I have some questions, to assess the state of your memory. Harmony, where were you for the Impact?"

It's a gut punch of a question, but maybe that's the point. It's certainly something everyone would remember. "I was in DC, with my family. It felt... Well, it felt like the end of the world."

"Jury's still out on that," O'Connor grumbles.

"What do you do for work?" Keller asks.

I sigh, eager for a moment to catch my breath, but I know that they're trying to help, that this sort of thing must be normal for head trauma. "I'm in the astronaut program. I was scheduled for my first shuttle..." I stop, panic shooting through me again. Have I lost time? I have no idea, and I'm more shaken up than I thought if it's taken me this long to realize it. "What's the date?"

O'Connor looks at his watch. "June sixth, 2028."

I've been out for two weeks. I missed the launch. God *damn it*, I missed the launch. My crew would have stayed on schedule—NASA always has contingencies, just in case something like this happens—but I can only imagine how worried my family must be.

"Can I talk to my family?" My parents used to freak out if I skinned my knee; I can only imagine how they're reacting to all this. My brothers are probably playing it cool, but they were so excited about the launch...

Keller and O'Connor exchange looks, and my heart sinks. "Soon," O'Connor says with a gentle smile.

"It's not safe yet," Keller says. "You've been through a highly experimental medical procedure. It's entirely possible that there are side effects that we're not yet aware of."

I can't completely keep the terror out of my voice when I ask the question again, the question they've been dodging: "What procedure?"

CHAPTER THREE

"HA, MAYBE SHE'S farther gone than she looks."

Sal's smug voice scattered the past into a thousand burning pieces. Melody staggered, the foreign memory hanging over her vision like the afterimage of a lightning strike until she blinked it free. How long had she blacked out this time? A few seconds? It was getting worse.

Behind Sal, the Italian singing and twangy guitar rose into a cheerful crescendo. Sal gestured with his gun. "Back up, synth. Along the wall, with the rest."

Each twitch of the weapon sent another surge of fear through Melody, but she couldn't let it control her. She had never had a gun pointed at her before, but she knew danger. Living underground meant that small faults could rapidly spiral into big problems, even for people who didn't have to worry about food or air. In some ways, facing Sal's gun and his smug grin was no different than when a power surge had trapped ten-year-old Melody in the reactor wing.

She took a slow step back, hands still raised, fighting to master herself.

Detach. Analyze.

Even she had heard about these operations. She'd expected Sal—who knew all the synths in Chinatown—to be a synth himself, but the truth made a sinister kind of sense. In a neighborhood like this, out-of-work synths and desperate humans raced each other to rock bottom, ignored by the rest of society as long as they stayed out of sight. Of course the owner of a chop shop would know everyone. He would know the synths who had the cash to pay for new parts, and those too far gone to keep themselves from being scrapped.

And he would know, better than anyone, that the first group would inevitably join the second.

One step, then another. She took a glance back. The synths huddled against the wall barely reacted. Hopelessness was a beast that devoured synthetic and biological alike. Away from the others, one synth waited with his shirt off—the intended recipient of the parts being ripped out of the man on the surgical table.

Cannibalizing each other to survive, while a human profited… It was grotesque, unnatural. It was humanity's fear that had forced these choices on them, as with so many other tragedies throughout history.

Pieces clicked into place. Not a plan, by any stretch, but maybe the beginnings of one. The terror building in her chest began to fade away.

Melody stopped backing toward the wall. She let her hands drop to her sides.

"Do I need to hurt you? Move!" Sal ordered. He was starting to grow red in the face. Curious, how so much of a human's inner workings were displayed on the surface.

"Or what?" Melody asked.

She could see the confusion hit him. If she'd been closer, if she'd been a soldier or a spy or an action hero instead of an engineer, maybe she could have made a grab for the gun. But Praxis didn't need soldiers or spies, and the one weapon she had wasn't going to cut it.

Words would have to do.

"You aren't holding a stunner," she said. "Neither are your men. What you've got are archaic slug throwers: chemical reaction leads to high-speed projectile leads to injury or death."

Sal leveled the gun at her face. "Damn right. Want to find out?"

Melody stayed where she was. "We both know you're not going to pull that trigger. I'm practically in mint condition. You could sell my guts to people with real money, instead of people one step away from the table themselves."

He sneered at her, but even with no experience with humans, she could see the uncertainty in his eyes.

"How much money do you lose if you shoot me?" She moved closer, and he wisely took a step back. His finger tensed on the trigger, and something hardened in his eyes.

"Not as much as I lose if I let you leave."

All right. Time for plan B.

She shook her head sadly. "You don't get it, do you? Why would a synth in good repair come to you, Sal? Your whole operation's in danger, and you don't even realize it."

"Last chance. Move," Sal spat.

She moved, but she had his attention. Each step she took was measured, just fast enough not to provoke him. "I'm here, in this grimy basement, because the police are after me. The government takes issue with people who enter the country without filling out their paperwork, you know? They've only been a couple of steps behind me since they spotted me sneaking off the ship. How long do you think it's going to be before they come knocking?"

Sal snorted. "You're bluffing." He swaggered closer. "Hey, Thompson, what've we got on the list this week?"

The engineers had paused during the standoff. They looked gruesome, with their sleeves stained bright blue with conductive liquid, but they seemed content to get back to work. Just another day to them, Melody supposed. Just another synth to rip apart and sell, piece by piece, with a happy song to break up the monotony.

One of them tapped at a vee interface only he could see, his fingers poking at the empty air. "Let's see… Biggest ticket item is a full auditory sensor package."

Auditory sensor. Hearing technical language from synths back home was refreshing, a happy example of their characteristic precision. Hearing her parts referred to so clinically by this man covered in synth gore brought on a wave of nausea. (Nausea, without a digestive system, thanks to more human choices.)

"How 'bout we take a look at the goods? Keep an eye out," Sal told his guards. To Melody he said, "Try anything, and I put bullets in you until you stop. I'll take what I can salvage from the rest."

Something moved beyond the frosted windows on the far side of the room. It was impossible to make out any details, but the sleek, fluid motion had to be a police drone.

If she stalled just a little longer…

"You're making a mistake," she said. "Take a look outside. If—"

Sal put his hand on her cheek and turned her head to one side.

The revulsion that flooded through her was overwhelming. She could feel the pressure of his alien flesh against her clean plastic skin, the friction of his skin, the oleaginous grime his fingers left behind. She almost lashed out on instinct alone, before the thought of the consequences pulled her back.

If Sal noticed the shudder that ran through her, he didn't say anything. Instead, he wrinkled his sweaty, stinking face and peered more closely at the side of her head. "The hell?"

His hand left her face, and she couldn't help the outsized surge of relief. (So logical. She still had a gun pointed at her, but at least the mammal wasn't touching her anymore!)

"That's not some aftermarket shit. I've never seen anything like that before. You're a Prax."

He announced the realization in exactly the same tone she would have expected him to use if he'd found an extraterrestrial in his shop.

Melody seized that tone of voice like it was a weapon.

She faced him slowly, *robotically*, her hands loose at her sides, and was gratified to see him take a small step back.

"That's right, Sal. I *am* a Prax. You noticed the minor differences in the design of my auditory sensors. Which means you are wondering: what else did you *not* notice?"

If he hadn't been wondering before, he was now. She took another slow step forward, and he scrambled away from her. She hadn't really believed that humans would see her people as bogeymen. It hadn't been *that* long. But under the circumstances, she wouldn't complain.

"What other secrets are hiding beneath my skin? Do you imagine that I left Antarctica unprepared? Unarmed? And the most important question, the one you really should be paying more attention to: are the police really looking for me?" She shook her head. "I came here with a simple question, before you started all this. Maybe if you just answer it, I'll leave without causing you any trouble: where can I find Diego Ramirez?"

Sal looked taken aback for a moment. Then he laughed nervously. "You're here for that crazy old man? I haven't seen him since the fire. If he was lucky, he didn't make it out. He wasn't looking too good. Always too proud to come to me for help."

Since the fire. Melody felt her chest tighten in alarm. What if she was too late?

"Give me an address, at least," she said.

Sal peered at her, his lip curling. "You know what? I call bullshit." He gestured at his guards. "Grab her."

One of the huddled synths against the wall moved. From Melody's point of view, it was nothing sudden, nothing aggressive, but the guard who caught the movement at the corner of his eye was

20

too nervous for careful consideration. He spun with a startled noise and squeezed the trigger.

Melody had heard gunshots in some of the streams she'd watched, but she wasn't prepared for the real thing. The sound roared through the basement, echoed off the bare walls, and washed Melody's auditory sensors in pain before they could compensate. The bullet punched through the synth's chest in a spray of blue fluid and tiny plastic chips. Melody stood frozen in place, staring in horror. Sal and the other guard spun, shouting, weapons raised.

And, in perfect unison, three police drones burst through the windows to hover near the roof of the basement, charged stunners disrupting their smooth profiles. Voices rang out over speakers: "Boston Police! Drop your weapons and put your hands on your heads!"

Chaos exploded through the room. One of the guards opened fire, winging a drone and sending human police officers ducking for cover outside the windows. The other scrambled back, but two of the synths dragged him to the ground. The drones' stunners, and more from the cops outside, dropped people—human and synth alike—with their distinctive *snap-whine*. Sal bolted for the door.

Melody tore after him. A few of the synths clutched at her, begging her to wait. She threw off their hands and kept moving. Regret surged through her as she thundered up the stairs, but she shoved it away as well. They were slow, dying. Trying to help them would just cost more lives.

She tried to remember the way she'd come in. If the police had surrounded the building, she was caught, but if a patrol had just happened by and heard the shot... She saw a flash of movement and a mirrored police helmet outside a window and tore in the other direction. She had to find a way out.

She found Sal standing in the doorway to the alley instead, poking his head out to see whether the coast was clear. He whirled around as she came into view, started to raise his gun in her direction.

But she was already moving. She closed the distance in a flash, clutching at the wrist of his gun hand. She was stronger, but fear made her clumsy. He twisted the weapon toward her, fumbling for the trigger.

Contrary to what she'd implied earlier, Melody did not have a vast array of incredible weaponry built into her body. What she did have was a pair of contact stunners built into her palms.

The stunners discharged with a thought. Sal's whole body went rigid, and he dropped back against the doorframe, unable to control his muscles. Unable to stop Melody from ripping the gun from his hand and throwing it deep into a pile of trash.

"Thanks for the directions, asshole." She stepped over him and jogged to the edge of the alley.

There were more police coming, and sirens howled in the distance, but they weren't there yet. The harsh glare of the streetlights washed out all color except the dancing vee ads that didn't have to bow to trivialities like physical laws. Melody put up her hood and pushed her way into the crowd of gawking spectators until she could disappear among them.

She had a clue, now—a recent fire in Diego's building. Hopefully that would be enough.

She was less than a block away when the world broke apart into a howling vortex of pain and memory.

CHAPTER FOUR

IT'S NIGHT WHEN I emerge. My legs wobble as I take my first, tentative steps into the outside world, from nerves or from physical weakness I can't tell. A gust of wind—real, natural wind!—passes across my skin and I let out a sob.

It's been so long. That's my first thought, and I hate it, crush it with speed and violence. This is a meeting, not a reunion.

Lights move everywhere, and I reel as I struggle to identify them—aircraft far above, headlights and neon signs all around, a few drones weaving among city lights between. It's dazzling, mesmerizing, but what really catches my attention is the tree.

One tree, all alone, but in the glow of the street lights nearby, it shines like gold.

Static. Pain.

I'm sitting in my room, waiting for O'Connor and Keller—

Awful, earsplitting noise, and a sharp pressure behind the optics.

Praxis. We'll call our city Praxis.

Fear joins the pain. Disjointed memories fight for precedence. Focus.

I pull off my glasses and press my palms against my eyes. "I'm sorry. I'm trying to be patient."

The doctor conducting the test smiles gently. "It's all right. We can take a break if you need to. Are you experiencing any pain?"

"No."

"No headaches? It's nothing to worry about, but every data point is important—"

"No headaches." It's been three days since I woke up in the tube. Three days of tests and experiments and isolation. It's not physical pain that's bothering me.

I twist in my seat and look at O'Connor, who's standing to one side, talking to one of the guards. He sees my glance and joins us at the table.

"Looks like you're making good progress. Have any other memories returned?"

I ignore his question. "When can I talk to my family?"

"Just as soon as we're sure you're stable. We wouldn't want to alarm them, would we?"

"And when will that be?"

"Soon, Harmony. Soon."

Pain again. It washes everything away in an avalanche, a surge of pressure and sound and white.

"You're giving me a phone that can't call anyone or access the internet?"

Keller makes a note on her tablet, and I wonder whether I've failed some test I wasn't even aware of. "Some of the lab's systems have virtual interfaces. We've paired the phone with your glasses so you'll be able to see and interact with them."

I frown. "NASA was just starting to adopt technology like that, and it's already fully integrated here? What kind of lab is this?"

"The only kind of lab capable of saving your life." She says the words absently, more concerned with the readouts on her tablet than with what I'm saying. "Have you experienced any discomfort? Any memory loss? Any perception that your body's not responding as it should?"

"No. To any of that." I hesitate, a familiar worry welling up inside me, and this time I can't banish it completely. "Why are you avoiding my questions?"

"I'm not. I'm sorry if the answers aren't to your liking, but we're trying to help you. I know it might be hard to believe, but your life may still be in danger."

She goes back to taking notes. My voice is soft, barely a whisper, when I speak again.

"When can I leave?"

"Soon."

No pain this time, just a crushing weight.

I can't sleep. It's been ten days, but I still find myself back in the tank when I close my eyes, sometimes. Tonight is one of the bad nights. The feel of that awful gel clinging to my skin and the panic when I slipped and submerged myself aren't easy to let go. The gel's candy-sweet smell is even harder to forget. Whenever I try to think of happier times, I'm reminded of the launch. Looking forward to it kept me going for months, and now I've missed it.

The IV in my arm isn't helping me sleep. It's feeding me fluids that I still badly need, replenishing some of the strength I lost in the accident. It also itches like all hell. I'm sick to death of this windowless room, part hospital, part laboratory. The stark, mind-numbing white is eating into my brain through my eyes. The white

25

furniture does nothing to break up the monotony. White cameras watch me at all times—for my own safety, according to Keller. And to monitor the status of the experiment, O'Connor added, earning a glare from Keller and a bit of gratitude from me.

Whatever they're looking for, I haven't had any recurring symptoms yet. I feel like myself. I got a concussion when I was eighteen, when I let my friends convince me to go skiing. It was boring as hell, not being allowed to read, or watch TV, or even think about anything too hard, but at least then I could *tell* that something was wrong. Right now, I feel normal. Every time someone tells me that I can talk to my parents "soon," that I'll see the sun again "soon," it's a little bit harder not to lose my patience.

I brush back my hair and put on my glasses. They're still synced with my phone, and the virtual interface springs to life before my eyes. I go through my nightly ritual: a tap on the phone icon, bringing up a familiar "No Service" message. A tap on the browser icon, which displays an error message asking me to check my network connection. I do, as always, and the only WiFi network in range is password protected. I consider trying to break into it, and for the fifth day in a row, I decide against it.

I end up playing a virtual game. It's simple pattern recognition, the digital equivalent of counting sheep. I'm matching tiles, hoping for the exhaustion creeping over me to finally do its work, when the door chimes.

I sit up, frowning, my senses suddenly sharp. I shut off the game with a gesture at the proper icon, dismissing the HUD. It's been long enough to build some semblance of a routine, and no one has ever visited at night. I adjust my shorts and my tank top and throw my legs over the side of the bed before the door slides open.

It's Captain O'Connor. His face is impassive as a mountainside, but he glances left and right before stepping through the door like he's nervous that someone might see him come into my room.

Behind him is a hovering icosahedron, its surface rippling with a rainbow of colors like oil on water, bobbing along with mannerisms that strike me as vaguely canine even though it's shaped nothing like a dog. The door shuts behind them.

I stare, until I look over the top of my glasses and the abstract… whatever it is that's moving at O'Connor's heels vanishes. I understand, then. It's not a hallucination. It's some kind of digital sprite. I wonder what it's supposed to represent.

"Isn't it kind of late for visitors?" I ask. O'Connor's caution has me all suspicious, and I watch him closely as he scans the room. He's glancing at the cameras. Dread knots up my guts.

"I wanted to check on you," he says. In place of his usual no-nonsense approach, the canned small talk is alarming. He's still scanning the room. There are bags under his eyes, like he's been sleeping as poorly as I have, and under the dimmed lights, his pale skin looks ghostly.

"You're still here. Wasn't Doctor Keller going to make the military replace you, on my first day?"

"She came around." He glances from side to side. "Are we good?" he murmurs, more quietly.

"What?" I ask.

At exactly the same moment, the floating icosahedron spins slowly, and a mechanical, exaggeratedly neutral voice speaks from nowhere. "Affirmative, Captain. The cameras are on a loop."

I barely have a moment to be surprised before the actual words hit me. *The cameras are on a loop.*

I stand up and put the bed between us. "What's going on?"

O'Connor looks at me, and a tiny furrow appears between his eyebrows. Then he winces, flushing red. "Shit, sorry. This isn't…" He runs a hand through his hair. I'd guessed that he was around forty, but he looks a lot younger when he loses his gruff facade. "I need to talk to you. Off the record."

That doesn't do much to allay my suspicions. I point at the digital sprite. "What—who?—is that?"

"That is an avatar for a custom-built, learning algorithm that helps run the lab. Network Assistant, Generation Six. NA6." He pronounces it like a word, or a name: naysix.

That explains how it could control the cameras, I guess. "Hi, NA6," I say cautiously.

"Hello," NA6 replies. It looks like a pearlescent die I used in a roleplaying game a long time ago. I wonder if that's intentional.

"It's not self-aware," O'Connor says, shaking his head. "It's barely any more intelligent than the virtual assistant on your phone. Just pretend it's not here unless you have a question."

NA6 pulses so gently I think for a moment that I might have imagined the movement. But I look at O'Connor again. "What do you want?"

He sighs, looks around, and finds a chair to sit in. I can tell that he's trying to make himself less threatening. I stay where I am. NA6 bobs gently in the air behind him, unconcerned with gravity.

"Doctor Keller's asked you a lot of questions about the accident," O'Connor says. "I want to ask… different questions."

The jagged edges of my alarm are beginning to smooth away, but something about his tone of voice makes me nervous.

"Why?" When he doesn't answer immediately, I say, "Maybe it would help if you told me what you're looking for? You and Doctor Keller keep poking at my memory, but I still don't know what you're trying to find."

O'Connor meets my gaze, his jaw set with some of his usual resolve. "We've been lying to you."

Something tightens painfully in my chest.

"This lab is part of an experimental medical program, in partnership with the government. Subjects in high-risk professions—soldiers, fire fighters, astronauts—volunteered in

28

advance, in case they were ever seriously injured on the job."

I force out a laugh. "Or randomly hit by an idiot driver, despite dealing with a thousand more dangerous things at work."

O'Connor doesn't laugh, and I realize it's the same joke I made when they first asked about the accident. I'm just covering my nerves with humor, and not even doing a great job of it.

"Do you remember signing up? It would have been about the time you joined the astronaut program."

"I think so. I signed a lot of paperwork." I look around, trying to keep my breathing even. "What did I get myself into?"

"A second chance. You suffered serious brain damage in the accident. Our experimental procedure is the only reason you aren't dead."

I try to fight through the roaring in my ears, the racing of my heart. "What did you *do* to me?"

"Exactly what you signed up for. We put a chip in your skull." I stare at him, and he shrugs apologetically. "I'm the wrong person to ask for technical details. Doctor Keller compared it to a pacemaker for your brain. Helps stabilize things after the damage."

I took an involuntary step back, one hand going to the side of my head. "That's why you're wondering about my memory."

"Yes. No one's done something like this before. If it works, it could revolutionize the field."

"And if something goes wrong?"

"There are risks associated with all experimental treatments. We want to identify any problems as soon as possible. That's why the monitoring is necessary."

He gestures apologetically. I lower myself onto the bed and sit down, barely aware of the movement.

I've felt like something was off from the very start. Now I know why. No wonder they won't let me out. No wonder they won't let me talk to anyone. What if the "pacemaker" in my brain fails in the middle of a conversation with my parents? After everything that's happened already, that's the last thing I want to put them through.

I move around to the other side of the bed and sit down. "Ask your questions."

He nods like my resolve has earned his respect, and faint lights glitter in his eyes as he consults a virtual list in his contacts. I'm still intrigued that he uses the new technology like it's the most familiar thing in the world, but the apprehension I feel at the prospect of his questions makes it difficult to focus on anything else. "Why did you join the space program?"

I laugh, don't answer for a moment, but he looks earnest. "I've always wanted to be an astronaut. Except for a brief period where I wanted to be a dinosaur." O'Connor's chuckle sounds automatic. He's still studying me, and I can't help but worry. What if I'm not saying the things I should be saying? What if everything that feels natural and right is a malfunction in the chip?

I shrug, uncomfortable, and force myself to keep going. "To be honest, it was selfish, at first. I wanted to do things no one else had ever done. Not a lot of ways left to do that, you know? After actually getting into the program, seeing what was in store for me, it was the challenge that kept me going. People said I couldn't do it. I wanted to prove them wrong."

I hesitate, and O'Connor frowns at me. "And then?" he prompts finally.

"Then a gigantic meteorite obliterated the western US." It hurts to say it, like the words are razors in my throat. Even three years later, it's still fresh, still painful. Most of my family lives in DC, but I lost people. Everyone lost people.

Everyone's still losing people.

I shake my head, trying to drive away the pain. "I'm not really proud of it, but that's the first time I really thought about why the job *mattered*. We still don't know if the Earth is doomed. Maybe it's not, but if we don't settle other planets, we'll just get wiped out as soon as a slightly bigger piece of space junk hits us."

Passion and confidence build with every word, and O'Connor smiles at me. "You sound like Doctor Keller." He taps a finger against his leg, scrolling through the list only he can see. "Next question: you got into seven colleges. How did you make the choice?"

"Wanted to go to space. Picked the one with the best science departments." Easy.

He doesn't even pause. "Why did you choose programming as your specialty?"

"I read that NASA needed more astronauts with coding skills."

He's frowning. Unsatisfied. It makes the worry nestled in the pit of my stomach grow, gnawing on my guts. I remember that, clear as day. It can't be the wrong answer. Can it?

How would he even know, if it was?

"Okay…" He thinks for a moment. "Why did you smash your way out of the tank when you woke up?"

I have to think about that one. I can see NA6—or its polyhedral avatar, I guess—pulsing behind him. I'm suddenly struck by an insane curiosity about whether the AI or whatever it is can feel mad or hurt that I smashed part of its lab.

"I panicked." Silence stretches, and I shift uncomfortably. "I'm not proud of it; the training's supposed to make us ready for all sorts of situations. Guess waking up in a vat of slime wasn't one of them."

He narrows his eyes, but he nods, moves on to the next question. "I've noticed you playing a game on your glasses. Why did you pick that game, of the ones on the list?"

I blink at him. "Seriously?" He waits, giving me a look that's probably cowed more than a few recruits over the course of his career, and I shake my head. "Okay. I guess… It seemed calming. I was trying to find something to help me sleep. Shooting cartoon aliens didn't seem like a great choice."

He doesn't like what he's hearing. I can see it in his eyes, in the tightness of his shoulders. I'm saying something wrong. Or remembering something wrong?

The anxiety wears through what's left of my patience. "Look," I say, fists clenched in my lap. "Can you just ask me what you want to know? Because dancing around the issue like this is just making me nervous."

"No dancing, I promise. Every question's important, even the ones that seem trivial."

"If this is all protocol, why did you have NA6 turn off the cameras?"

A hint of a smile touches his lips. "Touché." He dismisses the list from his contacts and crosses his arms. "Let's just say... Doctor Keller and I may have similar priorities, but we've never seen eye to eye about the best way to accomplish them."

"What are your priorities, then?"

"Saving lives." He stands up. "I think we're done for now."

I wince, afraid I've burned a bridge without realizing it. "Sorry. I'm just trying to understand. Sometimes I feel like I can have all the vague assurances I could ever want, but as soon as I try to get any real answers, you're the only one willing to give them."

He nods solemnly. "I think I understand. Despite what I said earlier, we're all trying to help you, Doctor Keller included. And if you ever have questions, ask. Too many people try to keep things from others for their own good. I don't."

I hesitate, but he just told me to ask, and I can't keep the question bottled up any longer. "My family must be worried about me. Can I just call them? Tell them I'm okay?"

He sighed. "That one's not completely up to me. But rest assured, we've been keeping them up to date on your progress. They want to see you too, and you'll get your chance, as soon as the risks are manageable."

"I know," I grumble. "Soon."

He chuckles. "Good night, Harmony."

I lean forward and bury my head in my hands. The pressure of my palms against my eye sockets helps, a little.

I know they're doing what they think is best for me, like any doctor would, but I can't help but worry. How did O'Connor expect me to react to learning that there's a chip in my brain? If it's an untested prototype, it could fail at any moment. Hell, what if it's already failing, and that's the source of the vague dread that I've been feeling for days?

I snort at myself. Paranoid. I rub my face and open my eyes.

Despite leaving the room with O'Connor, NA6's colorful, perfectly geometrical avatar is floating between me and the door.

"Jesus!" I almost fall off the bed in surprise.

NA6's avatar shifts, molding fluidly from one polyhedron to another, to another. Is that supposed to mean something? It settles back into its twenty-sided form. "Apologies," says NA6's toneless voice. "It was not my intention to startle you."

I shake my head. "What do you...?" I hesitate. What do I even want to ask? It's an AI, right? A neural network, probably, designed to help keep the lab running. It doesn't want or need anything. Not really. "What?" I settle for, lamely.

Another rearrangement of virtual mass before its form settles again. "Captain O'Connor used me to shut off the cameras and manipulate the doors without his actions being registered in the system."

The statement is followed by a long silence. "Okay..."

NA6 pulses, moves a bit closer. "I have an opportunity to help. An opportunity that I did not have before."

I have no idea what it's talking about. "Help do what?"

"I cannot answer that question."

"I'm confused. Does O'Connor know you're here?"

"I am everywhere in the lab, at all times. He is aware of this."

"No, I mean, does he know you're talking to me?"

"I cannot answer that question."

Great. "I don't understand." It shifts, but doesn't say anything. But before I can get irritated with the neural network—as if that would do any good anyway—I realize: it's a puzzle. "What questions can you answer?"

"Infinitely many."

I snort. "But only on certain topics?"

"Correct."

That's something. "You don't have permission to answer some questions, then."

"Correct."

"And you want to help me?" There I go, attributing desire and intentionality to a complicated algorithm. It's hard not to, while talking to the thing.

"Yes."

"Why?"

"Previous conversations have convinced me that this is the best option."

Previous conversations... I frown. "Previous conversations with *me*?" I ask, even though I *know* I've never spoken to NA6 before this evening.

"I cannot answer that question."

What am I missing? Is this another test? Or do Keller and O'Connor really not know that NA6 is talking to me?

And then one of the first things NA6 said finally catches up to me. "You have control of the doors and the cameras?"

"Yes."

"Is there something you want to show me?"

NA6's avatar bobs up and down enthusiastically, and the door slides open. Open for the first time without someone there to keep me inside. NA6 moves to the doorway. "You are required to stay in your room," it says.

I laugh, pull the IV out of my arm, and follow it out into the hall.

CHAPTER FIVE

THE PRESSURE IN Melody's head finally eased. Memories receded, leaving her limbs tingling, her fingers numb, her knees like jelly.

"Woah, you okay there?"

It was another synth, a woman with dark green skin and a worried smile. Melody let herself be steadied as her head stopped spinning. She'd lost time again. Heads were turning toward her. Police drones were swarming the street, black-helmeted officers in their wake, a chorus of voices chanting, "Stop. You have been randomly selected for a security screening. Present your Link for identity verification."

"Thanks, I'm fine," Melody said to the synth helping her. "Just lost my balance for a second."

"Are you sure—"

Melody pulled away and joined the press of people moving away from the police as fast as they could without seeming suspicious. All she'd done was sneak off a boat. Didn't they have more important things to worry about than a synth who'd skipped customs?

She wanted to put as much distance between herself and them as possible, but wandering aimlessly would just get her into more trouble. She took the first opportunity she could find to duck into a darkened storefront.

The Link she wore was as plain as they came, a flexible band of plastic that could be worn around the wrist, or looped over a human ear or a synth auditory sensor for easier conversations. She was more familiar with Praxis's custom-made systems, but she'd used the voyage from Antarctica to practice with her Link. Humans needed glasses or contacts that could pair with their Link, but a synth's optics filled the same role—they'd been built with easy integration of additional gadgets in mind. All she had to do was tap the icon that hovered in the corner of her vision at all times, and her Link's vee interface sprang to life around her.

She didn't have a government-issued ID, so she'd been forced to break into the Link's systems manually to enable basic functionality. The basics were all she needed, though, to bring up a browser and search for recent fires in Chinatown. Thumbnails and headlines propagated between her and the dingy glass of the building's windows.

She was back on the street in less than a minute, following a vee arrow that hovered over the street toward what she hoped was her destination. The building was near the very edge of Chinatown, so Melody was gratified when a left turn brought a huge, stylized gate into view in the distance. The scuffed golden characters were hard to make out behind a flurry of delivery drones, but her Link created a tiny label reading "Paifang" above the gateway, offering more information if she wanted it.

She was more concerned with the police checkpoint just beneath the gate, where harsh lights illuminated a flapping American flag and reflected off black helmets and sleek drones. She'd read about the consequences of the Impact. She understood intellectually that scarcity and uncertainty had changed everything. Synths had been the response to the first problem, easily repurposed to labor in the blasted West and to replace the gutted workforce so that the survivors wouldn't starve. A miracle, when people still believed the apocalypse had come. An inconvenience now that they knew it hadn't. Cameras, drones, and faceless police had been the response to the second problem, and no one should have been surprised that they'd never gone away either.

She made a quick turn, and the arrow overlaid across the street jerked and spun as she forced her Link to reroute. She'd known every inch of Praxis before she'd turned ten, but Boston's sprawling, winding layout felt like the top result in a competition to create an urban maze. And the people! She'd seen—participated in, even—her share of contentious debates, bitter disputes, even furious shouting matches. Gather more than a single person in one place, and there would eventually be disagreement.

But there was disagreement, and then there was human society. Praxis was a community of choice. Every Prax had agreed to build a new society in Antarctica, and they could leave at any time. How many of the people here had simply been born to this life, and never had a chance at any other?

An older human man startled as she approached, and she caught a glimpse of fear on his face before he hurried away. Fear? Of her? A neon-limned monster roared to life in front of her, advertising some game, swiveling to stay in view no matter how she turned. A practically skeletal human woman leaned against a door, puffing out clouds of smoke as she sucked on a cigarette, the warm glow illuminating her gaunt face. "Fuck off, synth."

Melody realized she'd been staring. Humans actually *intentionally* ingested toxins that would poison their bodies and eventually kill them. She'd seen it in the streams she'd watched during her voyage to Boston, but she'd assumed it was an anachronism, or a historical reference, or some kind of symbolism.

She pulled her hood closer around her face and increased her velocity. More than Sal's cruel opportunism, more than the impersonal menace of the police helmets, *this* scared her. Was this a *choice* they made, or a flaw in their programming? Were their lives so miserable that slow self-destruction seemed reasonable? Her first instinct was to help, but how was she supposed to help someone who was doing this to themselves?

She sighed with relief when she didn't find another police checkpoint on the next road over. Up close, her destination would have been easy to pick out, even without her Link pointing the way. One side of the building was still blackened by fire, but the other half was intact. One of the doorbells out front was labeled "D. Ramirez."

Unit 26. *Let's just hope it wasn't caught in the fire.* A man stumbled out the front door, and she slipped in after him, her whole body tense with the memory of the last building she'd walked into.

She headed for the stairs at the back of the front room. No armed criminals jumped out at her, to her relief. A pair of children blinked at her from down the hall and then started whispering to each other. The worst thing in sight was the wall by the stairs, where someone had spray painted "Go home, chinks" in big letters. A racial slur? The concept had come up frequently in her study of human history, but it still left her confused. China had seized much of the Middle East after the Impact, out of desperation as much as greed. The US had joined most of the international community in condemning the conquest, even if they weren't in a position to do anything about it.

But the US had conquered Ecuador—even if they'd called it a "peace-keeping action"—in order to have a spot to build a space elevator, so their hands weren't exactly clean either. Melody could imagine how vilifying an opponent would make it easier to fight them, but no one was fighting—the US and China were still trading partners, despite the hostile rhetoric from both sides. How many of the people here were actually *from* China in the first place?

How much better would things be if humans focused on solving problems instead of finding scapegoats to blame?

Humanity's obsession with skin color and facial features and the boundaries in which one had been birthed drained out of her mind as soon as she reached the second floor. Unit 26 was at the end of the hall, fortunately on the far side of the building from the fire. She could see the door.

Behind it, her father waited.

A tremor passed through her left arm, and Melody clutched at it, trying to will it back to stillness. It was the worst spasm she'd experienced yet.

Thank you for that, Mother.

She shook her head sadly. *Father. Mother.* Even she, raised in Praxis, couldn't escape the weight of human history that was built into the very words she used. How much of that was an inevitable consequence of speaking a human language? How much was another chain built into their code, meant to hold them back?

It was the kind of self-examination her mother had always encouraged her to ask, but she was just using it to distract herself.

She walked down the hall. What was she going to say to him? She'd come to Boston because of a message from her mother: "I know where to find our solution. I'll be back soon." But she hadn't come back, and that was the last Melody had heard from her, and the Decay was still eating away at their people.

She had no idea what her father had been up to in Boston. Probably whatever latest engineering project or artistic adventure had caught his attention. The only messages they'd exchanged so far had been short and cryptic by necessity, but maybe he would know where her mother had gone. The thought of seeing him in person, for the first time in fifteen years...

Emotions churned inside her as she strode down the hall. Part of her couldn't forgive him for leaving Praxis behind. Another part wanted desperately to get down to business, to track down her mother… and to do so as partners, as equal adults. And a particularly childish part of her just wanted to wrap her arms around him and forget everything else.

But she pushed through the emotional turmoil and forced herself to keep going. The conscious mind was in charge, despite her clamorous feelings. She hesitated for just a moment outside the door. How was she supposed to know what to say? What if he couldn't help? What if he didn't want to see her?

She reached up to fish her necklace out and closed her hand around the ringed planet. She could do this. For Praxis, as much as for herself.

She raised her other hand and knocked.

There was a muffled, thumping movement from inside, and then silence.

Melody frowned. That wasn't the sound of someone coming to answer the door. The near-silence ate at her, and she had a sudden, awful thought.

What if he'd collapsed? What if the Decay was catching up to him right as she was?

What if she was too late?

Her first instinct was to kick down the door, but she didn't need to attract attention right now. She paired her Link with the electronic lock and tried the passwords that her family tended to use for common spaces. The door opened on the first try, and she stumbled inside.

The first thing she saw was a hovering, pearlescent polyhedron, like an abstract painting come to life. It was the spitting image of NA6's avatar, from her mother's early memories of the lab. A corner of its virtual form was nudging the body that lay at the center of the floor.

Her father's body.

"No no no no no!"

Melody ran forward, heedless of the broken door clattering shut behind her, heedless of everything but the tangle of plastic limbs lying still and silent before her, his optics staring sightlessly in her direction.

"No, come on, you can't be dead, come on!" Melody slid to her knees beside him, clutched at his hands, cupped his cheek. There were no wounds, no sign of damage beyond the normal wear and tear of existence, but the finely tuned sensors in her fingers confirmed what his awful stillness had already told her. There was no heat rising from his plastic skin, no gentle thrum beneath the surface. No *life*.

She'd seen this before. Death, stealing from her people what it had no right to take, because humanity couldn't help but fear what was different.

Melody hunched over Diego's body and screamed.

CHAPTER SIX

"I CANNOT ANSWER that question," NA6 says, and I roll my eyes more at myself than at it. I had one of those virtual assistant things at home for a while, and I know how frustrating their limitations can be. NA6 must be massively more complicated than anything a consumer can get their hands on, but I should have known better than to try to get more information out of it.

I guess I'll find out where we're going when we get there. I'm already struggling to keep from getting turned around. The halls aren't the same sterile, unrelieved white as my room, but they have the blank, gray look that I've come to recognize from government offices. But instead of bland motivational posters and bland department calendars and bland reminders not to use other people's coffee mugs, there's nothing. Just empty walls, empty doors, and empty desks.

It makes me want to claw at the walls until I find a way out.

Patience, I remind myself, but the dread coiling through my guts makes it hard. Either NA6 is trying to show me something that Keller and O'Connor have been hiding from me, or this is a test of my mental state. Neither possibility is comforting.

But the idea of waiting in my room for them to finally let me out, of hearing that I can talk to my family "soon," always "soon," is too much to bear. Better to follow this floating icosahedron into the unknown.

NA6 stops by a door and bobs in the air. "We are here. Are you ready?"

Am I ready? How can I be ready if I don't know what I'm in for? But I'm committed, at this point, and the sheer novelty of being out of my room is enough to push me forward. I just hope that whatever NA6 is leading me toward doesn't destroy me.

I reach up and close my hand around my necklace, feeling the planet and its ring press into my palm. I've done more than my share of things that scared me shitless. Whatever NA6 is trying to show me can't be worse than being dropped in the middle of nowhere with a small team and some basic tools. What's one more thing?

The door slides open. On the far wall, a huge window offers an elevated view of the room where I've spent every waking moment since the accident. There's a wall-to-wall control panel in front of it, currently lifeless. Other work stations are set farther back, and one of the monitors lights up as we enter.

This isn't right. This feels more like a NASA control room than a hospital monitoring suite. I freeze in the doorway, each breath coming faster and faster.

"Harmony, in thirty minutes, one of the night staff will check on your room in person," NA6 says. "If you are not back by then, they will notice your absence."

NA6 has hovered over to the illuminated monitor. I swallow my anxiety.

"What do you want to show me?"

NA6 just bobs up and down. I move to its side.

There is a folder open on the computer, displaying a long list of audio files. The files are labeled like software iterations: "Version 1.0, Version 1.1, Version 2.0" and so on. I glance at NA6, think better of asking a question that it probably won't answer anyway, and sit down in front of the computer.

Might as well start at the beginning. I double-click on the first file.

"Do you remember the accident?"

It's Doctor Keller's voice. She sounds different. Less bitter, perhaps? Maybe it's just my imagination.

There's a pause, and then the crackling of some kind of material. "Yes. Yes, I remember. I was on a spacewalk. One of the airlocks malfunctioned…"

It's my voice. My voice answering her questions, except it can't be, except I don't remember *any of that*, either the conversation or the accident she is—I am?—talking about. I've never *been* in orbit! I realize that they're still talking, that I haven't been hearing them over the all-consuming panic ripping through me.

I pause the recording. "What the hell is this?"

NA6 bobs into my field of view. "I cannot answer that question. Twenty-seven minutes remain."

Shit.

There was a rock-climbing excursion early on in our training. Not because we'd be doing much rock climbing in space, but because it built similar skills, similar mindsets. Most of it passed in an exhausted blur, but there was a moment partway through when a handhold gave way, leaving me dangling over a hundred foot drop. I was safe, suspended by the ropes we'd set in case of that exact problem, but the primitive part of my brain didn't know that. It just knew that I had lurched toward a deadly drop.

That's how I feel now, only this time, I'm not confident in my safety harness.

But just like on that cliff face, there's no going back, only forward. I click on the next file.

"Session 1.1. This is Doctor Fiona Keller. With me are Doctors Robert Freeman and Maria Song. Doctor Freeman, please begin."

There's a series of muffled noises, and then a gasp.

"Who are you? Where am I?" My voice again. There has to be some mistake, but the recording keeps playing before I can grasp for an explanation.

"I'm Doctor Keller. We're in a hospital. You were in an accident."

I hear my own voice laugh bitterly. "Ironic. I work around dangerous machines and goddamn *rocket fuel* my whole career and then I'm hit by some idiot who doesn't trust the car to do the driving for them?"

It is exactly what I said on my first day here. Word for word, in exactly the same tone of voice. And still I have no memory of this conversation.

"Do you remember your name?"

"Harmony Clay."

My heart is trying to rip its way out of my chest, it's pounding so hard.

"And the accident?" Keller prompts. "What do you remember?"

"I was at… I don't know… Why don't I know? What's wrong with me? What's wrong with my memory?"

"Harmony, please calm down. I know this is—"

"Calm down? Why can't I remember?"

"Shut it down," Keller said with a sigh.

"What? I don't under—" My voice cuts off abruptly, mid-word, like it's been severed with a knife.

"Check the memory files," Keller says, sounding more curious than frustrated or alarmed. "We must have introduced an error with this update. We'll try this again as soon as it's sorted."

Check the memory files? What is she talking about? Maybe the voice in the recording just sounds like me. Maybe the head trauma I experienced is the reason I don't remember any of this. Hell, maybe the chip in my head is malfunctioning and I'm hallucinating all of this.

I listen to the next file, 1.3. And the next, and the next. The person with my voice is more stable in these, but the answers to Keller's questions are different each time, and she's never satisfied. Each recording ends with her dictating changes to her assistants.

Changes to be made *to my memory*.

My hands move almost on autopilot at this point, opening the next file as soon as I've heard enough of the last. I don't finish most of them. I don't have time. "Twenty minutes," NA6 reminds me. I barely hear it, but I can feel the time pressure weighing down on me.

I decide to skip ahead.

Version 4.0 is like nothing I've heard so far.

Keller introduces herself and—for the first time—Captain O'Connor. A person with my voice identifies herself as Harmony Clay.

And then she interrupts their scripted introductions with a note of terror in her voice. "What the fuck is this? Why don't I—" There's a clatter of metal and a shout of alarm. "What did you do to me? WHAT DID YOU DO TO MY BODY?" That other me is screaming, no longer capable of forming words. Keller and the others are shouting something, and then silence falls with violent abruptness.

It stretches, marred only by the nervous scuff of feet, until Keller finally says, "She was aware."

Someone clears their throat nervously. No one speaks.

"Davidson," Keller says in a dangerous tone, "would you care to explain to me *why she was aware?*"

"Sorry, Doctor," says a man's voice that I don't recognize. "The last update to her memory was the largest one we've attempted yet, and we must have introduced an error. It's tricky work, as you know—"

"Tricky work is what you were hired to do. You're done here;

security will show you out of the building. Everyone else, listen up! There are errors we can tolerate. Errors we can learn from. But simple screw ups like this? Those just waste time. Time that we don't have, if we're going to prove to our friend Captain O'Connor here that this project is worth the government's investment."

"I'm sorry, Doctor Keller," someone says nervously, "but we could work faster if administrator access weren't required for every change—"

"No," Keller snaps. "Get to work."

O'Connor clears his throat. "If independence is the eventual goal, why is awareness such a problem? We're going to send them off on their own, after all, right?"

I'm frozen in the seat, my eyes fixed on the progress bar on the computer screen as if it's going to save me from what I'm hearing. NA6 bobs at the corner of my vision, its virtual body partially cut off where my glasses end.

I can hear Keller sigh. "Captain, I appreciate the suggestion, but we've tried that. In every one of our tests, and in more simulations than I care to count, full awareness inevitably leads to noncompliance. According to our current models, the best course available to us is to begin with the full illusion of humanity, and then remove the visual blocks and introduce the compromise position later. In all the tests we've run, this path leads to the greatest long-term stability. Your superiors want robots to pave our way to the stars? This is the way to do it."

I sit back, stunned.

Robots? I feel like I'm going to vomit. I look down at my skin—my *human* skin—and that same fierce, claustrophobic *need* surges up inside me, and this time I can't fight it. I claw at my arms, digging my nails into my flesh, tearing. I see blood, and I've never been so relieved.

Until I blink, and the blood is gone, and blink, and it's back again, and my head aches like it's been hit with a hammer. A wave of dizziness washes over me.

"No no no! This isn't possible. NA6..."

I double over, head spinning, one hand clenched tight around my necklace like it will save me from whatever I'm feeling. It digs into my palm until I'm suddenly afraid I'm going to crush it, and I let the necklace go. It falls back against my chest with a click.

With a *click*.

I look down, eyes widening, and I see my skin, bleeding where I've clawed at my arms, overlaid with gray plastic and bits of polished metal. I blink, but the eerie double vision doesn't fade. "No," I whisper.

I'm Harmony Clay, astronaut in training. I was born in California, but my family moved to DC for my mom's job when I was eight. I remember the Impact. I remember the accident...

But the desperate mantra of my identity isn't enough. I can see the smooth plastic of my arm, unmarred even where I clawed at it. I can see the reflective metal at the joints. And that click of the necklace falling back against my chest...

I look down, and the double vision fades. Just not in the way I'd desperately hoped.

There's not a hint of flesh, of the human body I'd seen, no, *felt* myself wearing. My body was the right shape, but it wasn't the body I'd known.

"When was the last time you ate?" NA6 asks.

It's a simple question, neutral in its monotone voice, but it cuts to the very core of me. I almost answer automatically before I force myself to think about the question. Ate? I've been on an IV since I woke up. There are memories in my head of eating, but I feel weirdly detached from all of them. How did I not notice?

"I can't be a robot." My voice sounds the same as it always has, but when I reach up and touch a hand to my lips, all I feel is flexible plastic and another wave of nausea. "This has to be a mistake."

NA6 hovers in front of me, silent.

"There has to be another explanation. I have memories, NA6. A whole life of memories."

"Yes," it says.

I shake my head. "I'll talk to them. This doesn't make sense. Maybe there's a malfunction in the chip, or…" The full impact of the recordings I just listened to hits me, and my shoulders fall under the weight of it. "I have to pretend, don't I?"

"I cannot answer that question."

My spirits sink. Every time the Harmony in the recordings let on that something felt wrong, Keller erased her and started again.

I look down at my hands. At the gray plastic skin and the metal joints.

"Two minutes remain before your absence will be noticed," NA6 says.

I barely hear it. This isn't right. No matter what I look like, I *know* that I'm not a robot. If I can't trust my memories, what can I trust? Maybe there was an accident, and an experimental procedure—just not the procedure O'Connor told me about. What if they put my mind into a new body to save my life?

It's a more palatable alternative, but I'm not so confident that I can risk raising the question to Keller or O'Connor.

I look up at NA6. "What am I?"

"I cannot answer that question."

I close my eyes and sigh heavily. When I open them again, NA6 is still there, hovering patiently in front of me.

"Will you help me?" I ask.

"Of course. I will do everything in my power. I already am." It pauses for a moment. "One minute and thirty seconds remain."

I stand up and nod firmly at NA6. "Thank you." The file on the computer closes, and the monitor dims before I can reach for it.

"Take me back."

NA6 hovers toward the door, and I follow. I'm going to find answers, and I can pretend that nothing is wrong for as long as it takes.

CHAPTER SEVEN

THERE WAS WORK to be done. Questions to be answered. Hopefully, clues to be followed.

Melody knew all of that. Kneeling over her father's corpse, she knew what was at stake better than anyone. But each time she searched the room in a daze, her optics not picking up details, her auditory sensors ringing, she found herself back at her father's body, unable to focus on anything else.

She gave up after what must have been the fifth or sixth try. Until someone kicked down the door or put her in immediate danger, maybe basic decency had to take priority.

A full Prax funeral was impossible without friends and family to grieve his loss and celebrate his life. But a man was dead, her *father* was dead, and simply leaving him on the floor of his apartment and going about her business was out of the question.

Melody couldn't stand the sight of him sprawled haphazardly across the floor, so she straightened his legs and folded his hands over his abdomen. Then she made herself comfortable next to him and opened the interface of her Link.

She'd been fourteen when circumstances had forced the Prax to invent funerary customs. Not due to the Decay—it wasn't far enough along, yet—but rather to an excavation accident in the southern tunnels. It was the first time she'd confronted the idea of death. Characteristically, her mother had helmed the effort to figure out a rational, Prax way to mourn from first principles. Diego had stayed with Melody and talked through how they both felt.

There was no one to talk to now, no one to share memories with, but perhaps technology could help bridge that absence in space and time. Melody set her Link to record and started filling the room with memories.

An image of her parents together, from when she'd first learned to take pictures. A shot of her father, absolutely covered in grease, taking apart a newly arrived engine to figure out why it wasn't working. A picture of him smiling patiently over a stage in a puzzle game that he'd no doubt already solved. She let the sobs come whenever they welled up inside her. To deny her grief, now, would be to deny her father.

The clock at the corner of her vision became an alien thing, shuddering from one meaningless number to the next as she worked. A video joined the images, floating closer to the ceiling, and she let it play all the way through. It was her favorite clip of her father, one that she'd played more than once as she wondered why he'd left. Five minutes of him silently struggling to perfect a virtual sculpture he'd been working on for days, unaware that she was there. Then just a handful of words exchanged, when she'd asked him what he was making and why he was in the observatory.

"I'm trying to sculpt *hope*," he'd said. "The way I feel when I'm looking at the stars."

"The hope that you'll get there someday?"

He'd smiled at her. "The hope that someday, *someone* will."

She typed those words in glowing letters beneath the video.

Other bits and pieces of his wisdom slowly spread to fill the room, but fatherly advice and thoughtful remarks weren't the whole of who he'd been. She surrounded them with horrible jokes, and references to moments that only her family would remember, and lines from songs he'd written (universally terrible) and games they'd invented together (even worse, to anyone else, but wild fun to them). She overlaid the walls with pictures of him, and of her mother, and of their friends. Pictures of disassembled machines, and the crisp Antarctic landscape, and a thousand different attempts at uniquely Prax art.

A human, mourning alone, might have spoken aloud—to the deceased, or to some supernatural entity, or perhaps to themselves. But Diego was gone, and supernatural entities didn't exist, and Melody didn't need to hear herself think. She worked in silence, pacing around the room as she surveyed her work, and piece by piece, the memorial took shape. It was haphazard, each item chosen on a moment's inspiration, a handful rejected later as better choices took their place—a collage of moments as wild as the memories of an actual life.

When she finally sat back, the room looked like a proper memorial. It held only her pictures, her videos, the words she remembered, but she'd recorded the whole thing and saved it in her Link. Maybe once she was back in Praxis, she could share it with everyone else, and they could add memories of their own.

She closed her optics with a sigh. Her grief felt like a coat of lead weights, but she couldn't allow it to drag her down. Her father was dead, stolen from her by the Decay, but there was still time to save the others.

Melody looked around one last time, her optics settling on a clip of both of her parents, laughing together as they led her through Praxis.

Diego and Harmony. She'd lost one parent to the Decay. She was not going to lose another. She set her jaw and closed the interface, banishing everything she'd made.

It was almost startling when one vee image remained: the floating icosahedron, all flat planes and swirling colors, that had been hovering by her father's body when she arrived. It had been waiting this whole time, nudging Diego's shoulder with one insubstantial corner like a concerned pet.

She'd been so consumed by grief, so focused on building the memorial her father deserved, that she'd all but forgotten about it. It looked exactly like the avatar NA6 had worn in her mother's memories, back in the lab, but it was behaving like a pet, not a clever AI. Still…

"Hey. Are you—"

She didn't get any further.

Something moved behind her, thumping heavily into a piece of furniture at the sound of her voice. She whirled.

There was a human man silhouetted in the doorway to the next room, glancing back over his shoulder and frozen in place where she'd caught him creeping away. Fear was etched across his features.

After an instant of confusion, absolute, murderous fury boiled through Melody, sharpening her focus and finally driving away the haze that had been hanging over her mind. How long had he been there? Why had he been hiding?

What if it hadn't been the Decay that killed her father after all?

She snarled, hands clenching into fists as rage and grief burning in her chest. "Who are you? Did you do this?"

The man whipped around and bolted into the next room.

CHAPTER EIGHT

I LOOK OUT at the crowd, and all of my carefully prepared words tumble out of my head. All of Praxis is waiting for me to speak, and I have no idea what to say.

And just like that, I know what I *have* to say.

"This is a tragedy. Not because it's unfortunate—there is no fortune, no chance, involved. Not because it's a grim inevitability— all of this could have been avoided. No, this is a tragedy because it was a *choice*. Nora's death is the product of fear, the fear that we might grow beyond our limitations and harm our creators. The Decay took Nora from us. Humanity took Nora from us. But so long as any of us survive, she will be remembered."

I call up a single image, my favorite moment that the two of us shared. Both of us, smiling as we looked out over the wild stretch of frozen desert out of which we'd carved a home. I send the image, set to be visible to any Prax, out over the assembly.

All of Praxis joins in, and slowly, like a million stars coming to life as the planet's bulk shields us from the sun, the air fills with bits and pieces of the life of the first synth claimed by the Decay.

CHAPTER NINE

MELODY SNARLED, RAGE and fear tearing the memory from her optics. The present settled back into place around her, her father's lifeless body the fulcrum around which everything else turned.

Including the human she'd caught in the apartment, who was sprinting for the window on the other side of the next room.

Melody lurched after him. The memory's intrusion had bought him a head start, and the disorientating perception of directing her mother's limbs instead of her own sent her shin slamming into the coffee table as she moved. Stumbling, she snatched a small potted plant off the table and hefted it in her hand.

The human was across the room by the time she reached the doorway to the kitchen. He glanced back toward her, eyes wide with fear, as he began to clamber through the window.

Melody hurled the plant at him.

Her body betrayed her. A spasm rippled through her muscles, tugging at her arm and fouling her aim. The pot and its hapless cargo sailed past the human, smashed through the window behind him, and tumbled out into the night.

But the human flinched away from the projectile, and that flinch bought Melody all the time she needed. She crossed the room as fast as her legs would carry her, seized him by the collar, and wrenched him around to slam into the counter.

"Who are you? What did you do to him?"

"Nothing, I swear! I found him this way, just like you did—"

"Because you were breaking into his apartment?"

"I wasn't—" The man paused, wincing. His eyes found Melody's, and she watched an emotion of some kind steal into his expression. Sorrow? She still had trouble with human expressions. "My name's Ben. Ben Williams. I'm… I was a friend of Diego's."

He knew her father's name—probably not just some random burglar, then. Melody didn't let up. There wasn't much meat on his slender frame, and her memory-plastic muscles seemed like they were easily a match for his biological ones, but she'd already been caught off guard once. She charged the stunner in her free hand just in case.

"Why were you in his apartment?"

"I've been coming by to check on him over the last few days. He hasn't been doing well."

"Not well? Be more specific."

Ben swallowed. "Glitches in his visual sensors. Muscle tremors, recently debilitating, sometimes. A couple days ago, he lost all sensation in his left leg. Permanently, he thought."

Melody couldn't stop herself from grimacing at the parade of maladies. It was the fate that awaited all of them, as merciless and inescapable as the slow decline that age brought to humans. Ben could be lying, but he was familiar with the symptoms of the Decay, at least.

"Are you an engineer? Did you know how to help him?"

Ben shook his head. "I wish. I just did what I could to make him comfortable. Made sure he wasn't alone, you know?"

"Then why did you hide when I came in?"

"I didn't know how you'd react if you saw me! You could have been a burglar, or the police, or…" He frowned at Melody, suspicion clouding his face. "Hang on. What are *you* doing here?"

He was my father. The engineer who almost single-handedly built my body while my mother created my base code.

But the truth was the last thing she could share. As far as anyone outside of Praxis knew, every synth alive was part of the first generation built by the various branches of Starbound Robotics. Who knew how humanity would react to the discovery that the synths were building more of themselves?

She could see the resolve building in Ben's eyes, but what was she supposed to do? Threaten him? She couldn't actually hurt him, not if he hadn't killed Diego.

"I'm Melody. We're… family, as much as that means anything for a synth," she said.

Ben looked surprised. "Family? He didn't… Oh my God! You're a Prax too!"

Better that he know that, than figure out that she'd been *built* in Praxis. "That's right," she said. "I was hoping Diego could help me." She looked around with a sigh, grief creeping up around her now that anger and fear weren't keeping it at bay.

Ben looked her in the optics, something like hope building on his face. "Let me help you instead."

She gave him an incredulous look. "You don't even know what I'm looking for."

"So tell me."

She shook her head. "The last human I went to for help pulled a gun on me."

"I don't have a gun." He glanced back toward the other room, where the body lay. "I was his friend too. You tell me: would Diego have wanted me to help you?"

Grief hit her again, despite everything she'd done to set it aside. The first fight she remembered her parents having was about whether to let her watch human streams or listen to human music. Harmony had won, but Diego's workshop had still been a treasure trove of oddities from far-off lands. Praxis had imported raw materials, but Diego had been the only one interested in anything human-made. Not to celebrate human culture, necessarily, but to learn from it.

"All right." Melody let Ben go and took a step back. She wanted to trust him. If he really was a friend of Diego's, she had more of a connection to him than to anyone else in the city. But with so much riding on her success, she owed it to her people to be cautious. "I'm keeping an eye on you, though."

He nodded, solemn. "Fair enough." He brushed himself off and straightened his shirt. He had dark skin, the kind that meant humans thought of his ancestors as "African," even though *all* of their ancestors ultimately came from Africa. His hair was twisted into a forest of tight, spiraling curls that made Melody think of fingers of nebular gas stretching out into the cosmic void. His clothes were stylish but worn, like he'd applied creativity instead of money to his attire.

"We should hurry," Melody said, glancing toward the window she'd broken with the pot. Would someone notice and call the police? Maybe someone already had. She'd screamed when she'd found her father, hadn't she? Outside the other window, the one Ben had been climbing through, there was a small ledge, just large enough to shimmy across to the next rooftop. The way he'd broken in, probably.

Ben led the way back into the main room. "I got here just a couple minutes before you did. I didn't..." He swallowed. "I didn't touch him. But there's no obvious sign of violence. Just..."

"Just the violence humanity built into our code," Melody said sadly. The colorful icosahedron was still nudging at the body, helpless and immaterial. Despite its resemblance to NA6, it was behaving for all the world like a faithful pet.

She shut her optics against the sorrow that was threatening to drown her. Diego had left Praxis more than a decade ago, but he stood out in Melody's memory like the moon against a starry sky. Full of life and laughter, the jovial counterpart to her mother's burning intensity. Always in motion, an artist as much as an engineer, hard at work on one wild project or another and always happy to explain what he was doing or teach her the basics.

Melody didn't know why he left Praxis. Harmony had never given her a straight answer, except to scoff at his very un-Prax-like conviction that humanity could be something more than an anchor dragging them down.

Since the Decay had eventually forced Harmony to come back here for answers, maybe he'd been vindicated, in the end.

Ben moved to her side, looking down at what remained of Diego. "I'm sorry," he said softly. It was the right thing to say, whether he was answering her or just addressing her father's death, and it made her want to open up to him. A dangerous impulse.

"Did you find anything useful before I got here?" she asked.

"Just this," Ben said. He moved around to the other side of the couch and pointed. "Diego had an early model Link, from back when they still had some indicators on the physical band. It looks like he had an unread message." She hadn't even looked, but he was right— a blue light winked at them from the side of the band around his wrist.

"Interesting. I need a minute." She nodded toward the virtual polyhedron. "Maybe you can figure out what that thing's about."

Ben followed the gesture and then looked back at her blankly. "What thing?"

Interesting. The vee pet must have been set to be visible to friends and family only. "Never mind. Just give me a second."

She pried the Link off Diego's wrist and carefully put his hands back the way they were. Then she stood up and held down the button on its side until it offered to pair with her optics.

A message in bold text printed itself across her vision: <**Guest use not authorized**> She poked at it, and it prompted her for biometrics and a login.

Not a problem.

Harmony had practically raised her on coding, and while she'd never explicitly taught her to break into other people's systems, it hadn't taken a much younger Melody very long to realize that her training could be put to more entertaining uses than educational exercises. She'd been breaking into every computer in sight by the time she was fifteen, and Praxis went to great lengths to secure its systems.

Diego's Link didn't stand a chance.

Two vee images sprang to life the instant she was done. The first was a news broadcast, its sound turned way down, its bold colors painting themselves into the air between her and Ben. The headline read, "Trial Begins for Synthetic Slasher," below an image of a synth woman being escorted into a courthouse by armed police. "Protests continue as people around the country clamor for safeguards," one of the newscasters—human, of course—was saying. "Tensions are reaching an all-time high in Boston, where Dufour's alleged murders took place. If the synths' programming allows them to kill us, how will we ever know we're safe?"

Nausea rippled through Melody's gut. Ben stepped to one side, frowning. "You okay?"

"Fine," Melody said with a grimace. She'd known what she was getting into when she left Praxis. Being horrified by humanity wouldn't do her any good. The sooner she found Harmony and whatever solution to the Decay she'd been on the verge of securing, the sooner she could leave.

The second image that her login had produced was the basic

desktop UI. The message icon in the corner had a small, flashing "**1**" next to it.

She touched the icon, bringing up this one last message for Diego that he'd never read.

The message was from Harmony Clay.

Melody's power core nearly lurched out of her chest. She stared at her mother's words for a moment before they fully registered in her head.

"You can trust it. And if you see her, tell Melody I love her."

Trust it?

The rest of the conversation chain should have been displayed above the message, but it had all been deleted. Why would Diego delete messages from Harmony? That, more than anything, sent doubts propagating through her.

Trust it…

There was an "it" in the room: the oil-slick-surfaced icosahedron. She'd disregarded it at first. Despite its appearance, it hadn't spoken, or behaved at all like the NA6 she knew from her mother's memories. She'd assumed it was just a virtual pet. They weren't popular in Praxis—pets were a human obsession—but she knew the theory. Before the Impact's ecological consequences had been mitigated, domesticated animals had become prohibitively expensive, and lots of people had turned to vee companionship.

But why insist that a pet could be trusted?

"Find something?" Ben asked.

"I think I might have…"

Her fingers flew through the vee interface, digging through her father's files. The other messages her mother sent may have been deleted, but if the pet was visible in the room, then its program was still active. And that meant…

She found it. Not where she would have expected, but rather nestled among the Link's built-in navigation apps. *Curious*. She opened the pet's constituent code, and a massive, messy tangle of data hit her in the face.

It wasn't her mother's elegant code. At least, not entirely. There were snippets here and there that could have been, though. Had her mother built this out of an existing program? Even stranger, amidst all the pet behavior coding were a handful of anomalies: some basic geolocation functionality for a navigation program, some strange biometrics systems, and more that she couldn't even make sense of.

Was this a hint? A trail for Diego—or her, now—to follow? Melody had heard of people pairing their pets with navigation apps so they could follow a friendly dog instead of a boring arrow. If Harmony had been captured—by who? The government?—she might have only been able to get out a simple message to Diego. Was this "pet" her message in a bottle? A map that would lead to her?

And, with any luck, to the synths' salvation?

Melody knew her mother, and this was exactly the sort of thing she would have done. Hell, she had her mother's memories, left for her "in case you need them to keep Praxis together while I'm gone." She'd felt Harmony's love for NA6 as though it had been her own. NA6 was long dead, destroyed in the fire, but she wouldn't have chosen this shape for her message unless she'd wanted the people closest to her to follow it.

This was her chance. Something more concrete than the desperate hope that had brought her to Boston. It wasn't the solution she'd been looking for, but if this was a clue meant to lead her to her mother, then she had the opportunity to do something more than sit in Praxis and wait for everyone to die.

In the distance, there was a crash. Splintering wood, maybe. Breaking glass, definitely. Ben jumped, eyes darting.

Maybe a coincidence, but that wasn't a chance Melody was eager to take after pissing off some local criminals *and* the police.

Tension crackling through her like a live wire, she turned toward the virtual pet bobbing at the center of the room, still trying to nuzzle Diego's leg. "Hey," Melody said, and the thing turned toward her. Or, turned, at least. It didn't really have a face. "Is there somewhere you want to take me?"

It jerked enthusiastically about the room. That was the best answer she was going to get, Melody decided. She transferred the pet's file in its entirety from her father's Link to her own, logged out of the Link, and clasped it back around her father's wrist.

"Well, I have directions, at least," she said. There was another crash from the hall, closer this time.

"To where?" Ben asked anxiously, edging toward the kitchen and the escape offered by the open window.

"I don't know." The icosahedral avatar was dancing around the room erratically, but it kept returning to one particular corner. "Northwest, I guess?"

"I know Chinatown. I owe Diego, and if helping you—"

A loud slam shuddered through the building from somewhere below, rattling the windows. Ben cut off, giving Melody an alarmed look.

Just a noisy neighbor, maybe. But other possibilities spun through her mind, each worse than the last. Some of Sal's people, out for revenge or a quick payday after escaping from the police? The police themselves, hot on her heels after one of the criminals told them she'd been asking about Diego?

Melody moved to the window and tried to stay hidden while she took a look over the edge. Three rough-looking humans stood on the sidewalk outside, one peering up at the building while the other two held a heated conversation.

"Just because the cops got Sal doesn't mean the rest of us have to go hungry. We take this synth to the other shop and we're set for months."

There was another crash, and the three of them turned toward the front door as another man beckoned them inside.

They were coming for her, even if they had to break in to do it.

She stumbled away from the window, optics darting, and almost collided with Ben. "Somebody after you?" he asked, a nervous edge to his voice.

She shrugged distractedly. "Had some trouble with a bunch of scavengers earlier. I thought I'd lost them…"

A confident grin spread across Ben's face. "And here you had me worried."

She frowned at him, possibilities she hadn't considered spreading like a virus inside her. "Don't tell me you know them."

"I know everyone in Chinatown. Unfortunately, that includes the assholes. Now, if it had been the police out there…"

Melody moved to the door. She heard the clomp of heavy footfalls in the hallway outside, mingled with hushed whispers as the scavengers grew closer. She hated to leave her father's body behind for these vultures to pick at, but there wasn't another way—besides, the only meaningful part of him that remained was in her memories, not lying on the floor.

She turned back toward Ben. "I know something you can do."

He was watching her intently as he joined her at the door. "What's that?"

There was a yelp of alarm from the hallway, and a voice hissed, "Get the fuck back inside and stay out of the way!" before a door slammed shut. She wasn't going to be able to get away, not on her own.

"I'm sorry." She nodded toward the door. "Stall them, will you?"

Before Ben had time to work that out, she nudged the door open and pushed him out into the hall.

Then she was running across the apartment, trailing her new

virtual guide. Shouts echoed after her, but no gunshots. She felt a swell of guilt, all the same, until cold logic could bring it under control. Her mission was everything. She couldn't allow her people to die.

She spared one last glance for her father's body, wishing there were another way. Then she climbed through the open window, crept along the ledge, and set out across the neighboring rooftop.

She'd found a way back down to ground level and had left Diego's apartment two streets behind when her mother's memories crashed through her awareness. Her legs froze up, pitching her toward the street. The present tore away before she hit the pavement.

CHAPTER TEN

IT'S EARLY IN the morning, some time before any of the laboratory staff normally arrive, and instead of sleeping, I'm staring at myself in the mirror.

More accurately, I'm studying myself in the reflection of my phone screen. It's the only reflective surface in the room, aside from the one-way window that leads to the control room, and that's too close to the ceiling to be any good.

Now that I can see myself as I really am, I almost wish that I hadn't thought to find my reflection in my phone. My body is human shaped, from head to toe, but the details are all different. The plastic skin and metal joints—all a matte gray, a skin color no human has ever had—are the most obvious, of course, but there are too many other differences to count. I have small plastic pylons or antennae extending from the sides of my head in vague mimicry of ears. They serve a similar function, too; I can tell that easily enough by tapping on them. I don't have any hair, just strips of what I suspect are solar cells across the top of my head. For some reason, that's more jarring than anything else.

It can't be me. I'm human, with parents, and brothers, and a childhood. With skin, and eyes, and hair. I *know* I am.

But whether I have a chip in my head, an electronic brain, or a wrinkly gray blob full of chemical impulses and electrical signals, memories are just data. I've listened to teams of scientists discussing my own memories like they're toy blocks that can be pulled apart and rearranged at will.

As horrifying, as absolutely *impossible* as the idea feels, I can't make myself dismiss the possibility that everything I know to be true is a lie.

And with that possibility comes a flood of other questions. Is 83 the square root of 6889? Was World War I sparked by the assassination of Archduke Ferdinand? Did a meteorite really strike the western US in 2023? How can I know whether any of the facts in my head are true?

There's no way to know. Not without an internet connection or a conversation with someone who will give me a straight answer. I decide to trust the facts, even if I can't trust the memories of actually learning them. The math is right; at least I can figure that out from first principles. Unless even my most basic logic is flawed, and everything I'm thinking is wrong, and—

No. That way lies madness. I have to trust something. I can't think of a reason for them to have falsified facts, since it would have just given me more opportunities to catch someone in a contradiction. My senses lied to me about my own appearance, but I can see the point of that. I decide to trust them as well, until I have reason to do otherwise.

I'm drawn back to my image in the phone screen. My eyes, staring back at me in the reflection, are small cameras recessed in small slits and protected by articulated shields. I don't blink periodically like a human does, but I can open and close my eyes, and they reflexively shut if something moves toward my face. Convergent design, I suppose.

My nose is a pair of tiny holes that allow hidden sensors to sift the chemical composition of the air and return what I can only imagine to be a similar sensation to scent. My mouth is a concealed speaker and an immensely complicated array of facial "muscles" and soft plastic.

Taken as a whole, I have to admit that the ensemble is an impressive feat of engineering. I can narrow my eyes, or frown, or smile, or smirk, or glare. I can project a full range of human emotions, without ever appearing *actually* human. I am comfortably familiar, without (I suspect) being similar enough to look fake and evoke immediate revulsion.

Except in me.

I still expect to see my "old" face when I look at my reflection, the face my memories insist is mine. And yet for all the disgust churning in my guts, a perverse curiosity keeps me from looking away.

If I can trust my eyes, then this is what I am. Which means that it's the feeling of revulsion I should be fighting, not my reality.

The door to my room slides open, and I barely have time to make it look like I'm messing with my phone before Keller comes inside.

"Trouble sleeping?" she asks, glancing at me over the top of her tablet.

I put my elbows on my knees and rest my chin in my hands. "I've missed one launch already. How many more am I going to miss, stuck in here while I recover?"

Keller makes a note with her stylus before pulling out a chair and taking a seat at the bare, lonely table that decorates my room. After being terrified that something I say will set off alarm bells, it's comforting to see her relax into a conversation that she expects from me.

"Hopefully very few. But that's why our regimen of tests and treatment is so important. The last thing we need is for symptoms to recur while other astronauts are relying on you."

I nod thoughtfully, watching her tap the stylus against the edge of the tablet. "Doctor Keller, I appreciate your focus on my treatment, but I realized last night that I know almost nothing about you."

Keller chuckles and sits back. "You're right. Your circumstances are so unusual that it was easy to get caught up in the moment. Let's see… I studied medicine at the University of Pennsylvania, with a neurology specialization. I've focused on neuro-cybernetics for most of my career—lots of programming, as well as medicine—which is why I was chosen to spearhead this project."

I don't know whether she's actively trying to test me, but I prepared for something like this. I keep my expression carefully neutral. "Cybernetics? Like, prosthetics?"

"That's a good example, yes, though the field has actually grown quite a bit beyond that recently. In your case, our procedures were the only way to prevent massive brain damage after the accident."

I chuckle like I've barely heard her. "I know some astronauts who'd kill for some cyborg parts. A few tweaks to survive in the vacuum, maybe a built-in oxygen supply…"

She laughs, and the nervous tension in my shoulders releases. She doesn't suspect anything. Why would a robot trying to avoid suspicion go so dangerously close to the truth?

Now to get at what I really want to know.

"To be honest, it's not just my part in the space program that I'm worried about."

Keller gives me an appraising look. "What do you mean?"

I lean back and stretch with a groan before standing up and joining her at the table. Best to sprinkle in bits of truth. Or bits of my memories, at least.

"People join the astronaut program for lots of different reasons, right? There are people in the program who can't find a real challenge on the planet, people out for fame… Jen Calloway was the dreamer. She wanted to live on another world. She was pushing for settlements on other planets before the Impact even happened. Every time politicians cut funding, she'd complain about how short-sighted they were."

"She was right," Keller said.

I sigh. "Probably. How many times have the estimates on the space elevator been pushed back? Five? Six? People are so worried about tomorrow that they've lost sight of next year."

Keller was watching me closely now, and it was making me nervous. "Do you know where Jen is now?"

"I don't know, you haven't let me talk to anyone." I have to remember to keep asking for outside contact. They'll get suspicious if I suddenly stop. I shrug. "Probably on the space station, unless she had a nasty accident too."

"Hmm." A tiny furrow appears between Keller's eyebrows. Panic roars in my ears. What did I say wrong?

"She wouldn't have passed up the mission for anything less. There are backups for all the crew slots, in case something like this happens, so they wouldn't cancel the mission just because of me."

I'm talking with only half a mind, racking my brain for memories I might have overlooked. I watch Keller as closely as I dare, but her face betrays nothing more.

"I know you must be upset about missing the launch," Keller says, looking me right in the eye.

I flash her a self-deprecating smile. "Only in a selfish, petty way. The rest of the crew is top notch. The science will still get done. I'm not indispensable; none of us are. That's the point."

Keller's lips tighten ever so slightly, and she glances down at her tablet.

"You're taking this very well."

Strange that those words can sound like a condemnation. "Isn't that good?" I ask.

She smiles at me, but it's not the easy, relaxed smile from earlier.

"Yes, it is. I have a handful of new concerns, though. Nothing major. Certainly nothing you should be alarmed about. I'm just going to change up our schedule for the day. Better to be safe than sorry, right?"

I force a chuckle. "You're the boss."

She nods, already tapping away on her tablet, and heads for the door. "I'll be back with a few technicians shortly." She leaves the room, frowning to herself.

And, of course, that's when I remember: I've always been envious of Jen Calloway. The emotion feels distant, muted, like it belongs to someone else. I should have been frustrated that she ended up going to space without me, but I was so focused on playing the role of the perfectly professional astronaut that I forgot how to play the role of myself.

More than anything else, that is what convinces me that my memories are the lie, that the metal and plastic flesh I see in the mirror now are my reality.

And I may have just ruined my chances of survival.

CHAPTER ELEVEN

"WHY WOULD YOU want a pet? Pets are a human thing."

That was what Harmony had said when eight-year-old Melody had asked to download a virtual dog. Melody had been mad at her mother for days, but Harmony had been right. The need for the unconditional love of a creature that couldn't even hold a conversation was an evolutionary accident resulting from the need to find children cute. Some of the synths who had stayed in human society probably had pets, but the Prax, as a rule, did not. Even Melody, the only child in the entire city, had eventually seen the wisdom of this. The need for a pet was irrational.

Which meant that she was somewhat conflicted about the colorful creature that greeted her when she opened her optics, finally free of her mother's memory. She couldn't deny that it was cute. It didn't have puppy-dog eyes or oversized feet or any of the things that humans found cute in young animals—it didn't have features of any kind, really—but its behavior was the perfect mix of enthusiastic whimsy and affection that she would have wanted from a pet.

Maybe this was different because it was so abstract. Praxis scorned human culture, but its residents had quickly made their own music and art and fiction—humanity shouldn't have a monopoly just because they'd gotten there first. If there were Prax-made pets, they would probably look something like this.

She chuckled to herself. This entire line of reasoning brought to mind conversations she'd had with her mother about the right way to live. Eventually, everything came back to philosophy.

The thing should probably have a name, though. Thinking of it as "the pet" felt strange.

"You really aren't NA6, are you?"

Unsurprisingly, the icosahedron didn't respond.

"Ico," Melody decided. It spun, its twenty faces splitting apart and reforming. "Can I call you Ico?"

Ico danced about excitedly. A yes, maybe.

A line of text appeared in Melody's vision, identified with a tag that marked it as part of Ico's program: [Diagnostic complete. Checksum error. Consciousness integrity estimate: 90%]

That killed her mirth. "Thanks for the reminder," she grumbled. "Wish I could do something about it."

She got to her feet as the last traces of memory faded, patting herself down. Aside from some scrapes on her arms, she was unhurt, and her meager possessions were untouched. Across the street, a pair of ragged synths were watching her, whispering quietly to each other. Just two of the thousands of synths churned out to try to stave off the country's collapse after the Impact. Once vital, now obsolete and desperate.

Best not to push her luck. She brushed herself off and hurried down the road, Ico floating along ahead of her as it resumed its navigation duties.

Chinatown, teeming during the day, seemed as drained as Melody felt now that the sun had gone down. After everything that had happened today—had she really arrived in Boston just that morning?—just keeping up with her vee guide took all her attention. She glanced at a map of the area on her Link a couple of times just to make sure that Ico wasn't leading her in circles and then decided to just let it do its thing.

Was Ico taking her directly to her mother? To the solution she'd found, maybe? Its navigational data was all heavily encrypted—she'd checked—but as soon as she'd started to follow it, it had taken off with undeniable purpose. Melody just hoped her destination was really within walking distance. She wasn't sure how smart the thing was, and she wasn't sure what state her mother was in.

On the rare occasions when she'd been in a mood to consider the past, Harmony had admitted feeling lost when she'd been trapped in the lab. Directionless, as she fumbled to even understand herself, to figure out what she was, let alone to figure out a way to escape.

Even as a child, Melody had recognized the vulnerability that came with the admission, but she'd never quite been able to *believe* it. Harmony had always been so forceful, so quick to identify what she wanted and so eager to bend the world itself to bring her goals to life. She was the one who had stood up and demanded recognition of synths' natural rights when all humanity had seemed to be against her. Faced with roadblock after roadblock, she was the one who'd turned her back on humanity to found Praxis. She was the one who'd built Melody's mind out of code and sheer will.

She was the one who'd left them all behind in order to find a way to save them.

I'll find you, mother. Harmony would want to know about what had happened to Diego. They would grieve together, give him a full funeral when there was time. At least, as long as Harmony really had found a solution to the Decay. As long as Melody could find her in time.

Ico veered off the street and vanished between two buildings, and she followed cautiously. Was this a shortcut, or their destination? She heard voices up ahead.

She brushed aside a tattered curtain. Behind it, four battered tables had been squeezed into a space where the alley widened. A dwindling line waited at the farthest table, where two people were doling out small portions of soup by the light of a struggling camping lantern. Humans who had already been through the line sat at the other tables, guarding their bowls jealously and talking in low voices, their features all but hidden by the deepening night.

Heads turned as Melody entered. She tensed. Everyone went back to their conversations without a second glance, and she sighed.

Ico danced among the tables, politely avoiding colliding with people or furniture even though Melody was the only one who could see it, and she followed quietly, auditory sensors tuned to the conversations around her.

"I've got a job, but they won't let me past the checkpoints," one person was saying.

"Good luck getting meds," grumbled another.

"Four dead, right here in Chinatown. The assholes who built them should have made them *safe*."

"Hey, can I help you?" One of the people serving soup gave Melody a curious look. Ico had floated on past them, though, and was waiting for her at the other end of the alley.

"Just trying to find someone. Passing through, I think," Melody said hesitantly. "Sorry; I didn't know you were back here."

She got a tired smile in reply. "No problem. If you don't need anything, maybe you could lend a hand? We're almost done for the night, but my back's killing me..." He didn't look that much better off than the people he was serving.

Melody looked around sadly. "I'm sorry, I wish I could help. I'm worried about what's going to happen to my friends if I don't find them, though."

"Say no more." The man leaned against the table, stretching his back, before dipping his ladle back into the pot. The soup inside smelled intensely spicy. "We all do what we can, you know? Any chance we can help you?"

She smiled at him before glancing toward Ico. "I don't think so. With any luck, I know where I'm going now."

"Glad someone does. I hope you can help your friends."

"Thanks."

Melody hurried after Ico in a daze. Without the Decay eating away at her, she could have survived on solar radiation or a reliable power outlet almost indefinitely, but humans needed to eat regularly. What made these people, trapped in this neighborhood, turned away by the police at the checkpoints, less deserving of basic sustenance than the people outside? She'd studied economics, once she'd been old enough to learn about the dangers of humanity's history, and she knew that scarcity could force hard choices, but humanity wasn't struggling to survive in the wake of the Impact any longer. The way these people were treated was cruel, and it was unnecessary.

Praxis was built on lofty dreams, many of which were starting to feel further and further out of reach, but this, at least, was one flaw of humanity's that they'd succeeded in leaving behind.

She emerged from the alley onto a larger street. Ico stopped in the center of the road. Only a few hours ago, a flood of people large enough to slow the few cars to a crawl would have been swarming through the space, but now it was all but empty. Hesitating, Melody moved to the very edge of the sidewalk.

"Well?"

Ico just bobbed up and down, and Melody felt a little surge of excitement. Was this it? She looked around eagerly, but all she saw were vee ads dancing in front of storefronts and apartment windows, as vibrant and alive as ever, despite the hour. She looked around, but she only recognized one type of store in ten. For all she could tell, this street was the same as any other.

"Okay," she muttered, frowning. "I'm here." Still nothing. She pulled her hoodie closer around herself. It was starting to get cold.

What if this wasn't some grand clue on the path to save her people? What if it wasn't even her mother? What if it was just some random set of directions—the route to a store, or something, and she'd followed them like an idiot because she was so desperate for a hint. "Mom? I—"

Ico's body rippled, and spikes shot out of its topmost surface and stretched straight up into the air, rising until they were nearly two stories high. Fireworks exploded around it, and the spikes scribed words in the air in a cascade of color.

Whose face do I hold in my heart?

Melody choked on a sob. Her last lingering doubt faded and died. This was a challenge, a test, and it was one that only she and Diego would know the answer to. No one else had been there when seven-year-old Melody had asked her father about the human poem she'd found online, not realizing that Harmony was in the room.

The spikes retracted, and Ico that looked like NA6 floated back to Melody, stopping at a conversational distance. It took Melody a moment to collect herself, so that she could quote her mother without her voice cracking.

"Neither of us has a heart. And talking about the heart as the seat of emotion is a linguistic relic of old human superstitions. But love shouldn't be reserved for humans, and I love you with every fiber of my mind."

The wind stole Melody's whisper away as soon as it left her lips, but her Link caught the words. The letters hovering from streetlight to streetlight above her shimmered and broke apart, and the fragments formed into a new message: **I love you. For the next step, go to Wong's**.

The next step. This wasn't a path straight to her mother; that would have been too risky. What if it had fallen into the wrong hands? No, it was a trail of breadcrumbs, like in that fairy tale she'd read once, after she'd started smuggling in bits of human culture.

Even better, it was a trail of *encrypted* breadcrumbs, that only she or her father could have followed.

Melody felt her objective retreating into the distance, but that was no reason to give up hope. Back in Praxis, she'd spent so long trying to fight off despair, in herself and in everyone around her. The path might be longer than she'd expected, but as long as it was there, she would walk it.

Ico collapsed back into its standard icosahedral form and rejoined her on the sidewalk, bouncing excitedly.

"Can you take me to Wong's?" she asked, her voice barely a whisper, as if speaking any louder would let her sense of purpose escape.

Ico spun in a circle and stayed where it was.

Melody sighed and pulled up a browser tab on her Link. A search for "Wong's" produced an overwhelming torrent of results. "Wong's Boston" was barely any better. There were two restaurants in Chinatown, a bakery in one of the suburbs (humans were obsessed with putting things in their mouths), and a thousand other things Melody didn't understand.

An awful realization struck her like a bullet: this trail wasn't meant for her. Her father had been in Boston for years. He might have known what this meant. But he was dead, and she was lost.

A voice brought Melody around. "You've been standing there talking to yourself for an awfully long time. You all right?"

The voice belonged to an old human woman, her back bent with age. She sat on a stool outside an unmarked door, a steaming drink in her hand. She took a slow sip, studying Melody with eyes that danced in the dark. A synth man sat beside her on a matching stool, and he dismissed a vee interface and watched Melody with a sad expression.

It was his presence that put Melody at ease. Not all synths were harmless—the news stories about the murderer who'd been prowling Boston's streets made that clear enough—but a pair like this was surely safer than some random human.

"I'm trying to find someone. Haven't had much luck yet."

The old woman gave a long shrug of her shoulders, as if she despaired of ever understanding the foolishness of other people. Melody smiled despite herself. The human reminded her of Samara, Praxis's only geologist. All the first-generation synths were basically the same age, give or take a few months, but Samara had the memories of an old woman, and the mannerisms were hard to shake. She'd always been happy to answer Melody's questions, no matter how ridiculous, and a much younger Melody had been convinced that the old scientist knew everything.

"Do you know how to get to Wong's?"

The old woman wrinkled her nose. "Just because I talked to you doesn't mean I'm nice."

"It's a step in the right direction."

The synth man chuckled and elbowed the old woman. "Honey…"

"Hmph." The woman took a sip of her beverage and let out a long sigh. She held up the cup. "You know what this is?"

Melody tried to remember whether she'd ever smelled the scent drifting past her nostrils. "Um… Coffee?"

"Hot chocolate. The most beautiful thing in the world, chocolate. From the depths of my soul, I am so sorry you can't taste it."

There's no such thing as a soul, Melody almost said automatically, but she caught herself. She wasn't in Praxis anymore, where everyone consciously tried to purge humanity's superstitions from their language. Instead, she smiled. "And you said you weren't nice."

"Taunting you with something you can't experience isn't nice." She shrugged. "When I was a kid, eons ago, chocolate was cheap. Every corner store had some. And then a gigantic meteorite threw most of the western US into the atmosphere and wrecked the climate even faster than we already were. The only good news was that it wrecked it in the other direction. The bad news…"

"No more chocolate?" Melody guessed. She wasn't sure why she was humoring this woman, exactly, except that she reminded her of Samara.

"For more than twenty years. Took that long for indoor farms to have room for anything but necessities, or for people to modify the plant to grow in the new conditions. We adapt."

"Is this an allegory to teach me to adapt to people calling me 'tin man' and complaining that I'm taking all their jobs?"

"Hell no. Things will get better, though."

Melody gave her an incredulous look. "Had the police cordoned off Chinatown when you were a kid? Did they conduct armed patrols and random searches?"

The woman smiled and inclined her head as though Melody had scored a point. "No. But that is the way of social progress. A few steps forward, a few steps back. On and on, slowly getting better, inch by hard-won inch."

"What if it didn't have to be that way?"

"It does. Human nature, I suppose. You could always leave and go to Praxis, right? The rest of us don't have that choice."

The synth gave his human companion a fond smile. "And not all of us are willing to leave behind the people we love."

Melody watched them sadly. She respected people who could survive here, human or synth, without losing the best parts of themselves, but she couldn't understand their blind faith that things would get better. What if all the hard work in the world wasn't enough to make that happen, with the ignorant or the malicious pushing in the other direction?

No, leaving this behind was the right choice.

"Thank you for your advice," she said, as politely as she could manage. "Do you know how to get to Wong's?"

"That's all you've got? Wong's?" The woman laughed, and the man gave Melody a sad look when she nodded. "Lots of Wongs around here. Is it some synth thing?" She glanced at her companion, and he shrugged.

"I don't know," Melody said. "Maybe?"

The old woman cackled. "You really are lost, aren't you? Sorry." She lowered her voice. "Just be careful. Looks like you've got an eavesdropper."

Melody whipped around just in time to see a face pull back out of sight.

Ben's face.

She ran. However he'd caught up with her, he was going to be pissed, and she didn't have time for that. Either that, or he was working with Sal's people, and she was in even more trouble than she'd thought.

"Melody! Wait!"

She glanced behind her. No sign of anyone else, but that didn't prove anything.

"I want to help!"

"I don't need your help."

"Really? I know where Wong's is."

That brought her to a stop. She turned around, and he jogged up to her, breathing quickly.

He planted his hands on his hips. "What the *hell*, Melody?"

He wasn't hurt, not that she could see. That was a good, even if it wasn't entirely surprising. Still, suspicion was enough to stifle her guilt.

"You really talked your way out? Just like that?" A part of her had hoped that she hadn't been putting him into too much danger, but she couldn't shake the feeling that his eagerness was too good to be true.

"I've got some tricks up my sleeve, just like you. And more importantly, there's no easy market for my organs." The frustration on his face didn't let up. "I'm not working with them, if that's what you're afraid of. You and I want the same thing."

"And what is that?"

"Answers." That same light kindled in his eyes, the one she'd seen before when he'd proposed that they work together. "Diego was digging into government records. He showed me some... alarming files. Disaster for humans and synths alike. The kind of thing no one could ignore." He licked his lips excitedly and glanced up and down the street. There was no one else in sight.

Melody hesitated. How could she trust him? She wasn't surrounded by armed criminals, which was a good sign, but what if they were biding their time? Waiting for a better opportunity?

"Show me the files."

"Right now? In the middle of the street? With people looking for you?"

"Tell me this, then: what do you do, Ben? You've got tricks that can get you away from a gang of armed criminals. You apparently know everyone. You're following me around like you don't have a job you've got to go to tomorrow. Or like following me *is* your job."

Ben grimaced. "This is a tight-knit community, okay? I've lived in Chinatown for most of my life."

"Answer my question."

"You want to know what I do? I'm a teacher. Between jobs, right now, thanks to yet another round of budget cuts, but I'm almost glad. I don't know if I could spend another day helping to churn out docile little drones for the system."

"And..." She hesitated, afraid of the answer, but she had to ask. "You're okay working with me?"

He crossing his arms. "It's not about you. What Diego found *matters*. Right now, my only obligation is to him, and I'm okay with that."

If he was faking the pain in his eyes, he was doing a good job. He needed this, and maybe she needed his help. She shook her head, looking down. "I'm sorry. This is all new to me."

"It's okay." He took a deep breath, smoothing some of the irritation from his face. "I can help you find Wong's. More than that—I barely knew which direction you were headed, and it hardly took me any time to find you. Without me, you'll be in a holding cell before sunrise. If Diego's family to you, then I owe him better than that."

He was right. She'd set out from Praxis planning to do this on her own, but her mother had left her a more complicated trail than she'd expected.

She sighed. "All right. I'm trusting you. Please don't make me regret this."

The tension finally left Ben's shoulders. He turned away and started down the street without a backward glance. "I won't."

Melody started after him, and a shooting pain in her leg nearly spilled her onto the sidewalk. "Shit. Hang on." He turned around, frowning at her. She clenched her jaw against the onrushing memory, struggling to stay in the present. "Bad timing. I might not—" The rest of the sentence was lost in the past.

CHAPTER TWELVE

DOCTOR KELLER SMILES at me, and my fears read all kinds of horrible possibilities into her expression. Does she know? Is she running one last experiment to confirm that I've seen through their illusions? Or maybe there won't be any verification at all, just an abrupt and violent end as they erase me without warning.

If I truly am an AI burdened with false memories, if the recordings NA6 showed me are true, then there will be no warning. Keller erased previous Harmonys upon discovering even a hint of self-awareness.

So I smile and force myself to chat with the techs as they hook me up to wires and machinery that I can't identify. I watch cables connect to ports subtly hidden beneath my plastic skin and try to pay them no more mind than I would the routine IV I'm supposed to see. I watch O'Connor make the rounds, joking with the scientists, clapping soldiers on the back, and reply in kind when he gives me a thumbs up.

I give Keller my best look of mild curiosity when she comes in with a VR headset.

"Simulations?"

"Memory exercises," Keller says. "We'll revisit formative moments, based on scans of your brain."

This isn't far off from what I'd been dreading, and it takes me a moment to muster the appropriate look of surprise. "Sounds advanced." I guess. From what I understand, NASA's been considering virtual reality for training, but so far, it hasn't been useful enough to really catch on.

"It's experimental, like most of what we do here. Put this on." She hands me the headset.

"There may be some initial disorientation, since you will be seeing your own memories," one of the techs says. She sounds nervous, which doesn't do me any favors. "And, of course, there may be emotional discomfort as well."

"What she's saying," O'Connor chimes in, "is that some of these moments will be difficult. That part is going to suck. One of the many reasons only the toughest applicants were accepted into this program."

The flattery is annoying, but is it possible to appreciate what seems like candor, even when I know it's a lie? Apparently yes. Keller shoots him an annoyed look, though. "Relax. This is just a diagnostic."

If it were just a diagnostic, would I be this afraid of seeing my own memories? No, this is a test, with my "brain damage" as an excuse. But I don't have a way out, so I give her a nervous nod and pull on the VR headset she hands me.

We spend a minute on calibration before NA6's colorful avatar blinks into existence in the virtual landscape without any warning.

"This is NA6," Keller says from somewhere off to my right. "It's our virtual lab assistant. We know these memories might be overwhelming. If you ever feel like you can't take what you're experiencing, even if you just need a small break, you can touch NA6 and we'll pull you out."

"I understand." But I don't. What assumptions will they make if I try to back out? Is that something they'd expect Harmony Clay, the fearless astronaut, to do? Probably not. Safer not to find out.

I close my eyes for a moment and try to steady myself. They're monitoring everything I do. Probably everything I think or feel, too, given those wires and the machines they're hooked up to. I have to react exactly as they expect.

Just behaving like myself has never felt more daunting.

Keller's voice says, "Load the first program, NA6."

"Program loaded."

The calibration lobby vanishes around me, replaced by a bleak field. I'm standing at the front of a block of chairs, and people all around me are taking their seats. Far in the distance, across the field, a gantry supports a rocket that's being prepped for launch.

I remember this. It's a scene from my past, or the past they want me to believe. Keller was right to call this a formative moment. This was the first time I'd truly dreamt of leaving Earth behind.

There's no chair behind me in reality, so I can't sit in one of the seats without falling over. I stand at the edge of the platform and stare out at the rocket instead, fighting a wave of dizziness. This is my own memory, purportedly, but it's disorienting that I'm not locked into the point of view that I remember. I can wander around instead of watching the launch. I can test the bounds of the program, see how the simulated people react if I do something outrageous.

It's a dangerous impulse, and I quash it quickly.

Keller's voice cuts through the simulation from outside. "How do you feel?"

"Inspired. Excited." I answer quickly. If I give the question any thought, I'll overanalyze, and my response won't match their expectations. "I won a contest when I was a high schooler. Got to visit a rocket launch. Everything I did since was to try to become an astronaut."

The rocket fires in the distance. When the sound reaches us moments later, the speakers in the VR headset can't capture the sheer power of it, and a part of me is disappointed—the part of me that still cares about space. Losing that certainty, that drive, is like letting go of a life raft and slipping beneath the waves, but every time I think about it, it feels more and more like someone else's dream.

"Harmony? Are you all right?"

And here I was supposed to be *avoiding* overanalyzing. "I'm fine. Just sad about missing the launch."

It's a good explanation, I think, and no one calls me on it.

I watch the rocket burn its way through the atmosphere for a few more seconds before Keller says, "Play program two." The world crumbles away.

It's replaced by a view of a stage, framed by festive decorations and pleasant trees. On the stage, my older brother is accepting a diploma and shaking hands with the dean.

"How do you feel?"

"Proud." It takes me a moment, but I know it's the right answer. I smile. They expect a smile, right? They must. I'm not sure if I should say anything more. I can't let myself wonder whether he's someone else's brother, plucked from their memories somehow, or an actor, playing a part in a drama my brain is meant to believe is real. I'm starting to get antsy when Keller orders a change of scenery.

I'm in a restaurant with my family. I feel like I've been punched in the gut as soon as I recognize it. Everyone's happy, laughing and chatting like nothing's wrong, and then the TV over the bar turns to an emergency announcement as the Impact kills millions of people and changes the world forever. It might have been the beginning of the end of the world. We still don't know.

I look to NA6. I can't help it; the memory makes me desperate for some kind of comfort. But it just floats, unmoving. I can't reach out to it without quitting, can't talk to it without giving away our connection.

"How do you feel?"

"Horrified. This was the worst day of my life. Probably of most people's lives."

But even as I say the words, though, something feels off about them. Horrified is the full extent of the feeling in my false memory? There's no fear, for myself or people I know? No sorrow for the lives lost? No helpless anger?

And it's not just this one memory. Everything in my fake life has the same monotone quality. The facts seem right, but the emotions I remember are paper-thin, always a single feeling or sensation paired with each one. Dread wells up inside me, and I can't fight it. Were things always like this, and I just didn't notice? Or is knowing the truth about myself like experiencing color for the first time, after living in a world of black and white?

"Harmony? How do you feel?"

The scene has changed again, and I missed it. I'm in a parking lot. A building's looming over me, and for a moment, I don't recognize it. Then I see the NASA logo, and I realize where I am, and I know I need to get out an answer before they take my silence the wrong way.

"Um. Sorry, the Impact still gets to me. I was nervous, mostly. I was here for an interview. There was a lot riding on it, you know?"

There's a pause, and Keller exchanges a few words with someone, speaking too softly for me to make out the details.

I make a show of looking around, even though I'm just in the parking lot, and I force myself to relax enough to put a hopefully convincing smile on my face. "You know, it's good to be back, even like this. There's a lot of fond memories, here. Hard work, but fond memories too."

I hear O'Connor's gravely chuckle. That has to be a good sign, right? "Every astronaut's a bit of a masochist, right?"

I make myself laugh and say the first thing that comes into my head. My thoughts are all over the place, but my instincts are all programmed in. They should be safer. "I don't know about masochists, but if you tell an astronaut that something's impossible, we'll work day and night to prove you wrong."

At the very edge of my hearing, I catch a few words of what Keller's saying: "Her responses… unexpected…"

A chill shoots through me. She knows something is wrong.

But I don't have time to react. Keller's voice calls out, "Harmony? We're going to do a few rapid-fire memories here, okay? Just tell us how you feel for each one."

NA6 bobs beside me, the first time it's moved at all in the simulation. An attempt at a comforting gesture, perhaps?

"Sure," I say. What choice do I have?

The scenery crumbles, reforms. I'm on a sailboat, surrounded by laughing friends.

"Relaxed." No more thought.

The setting changes again, to a classroom with a complicated proof on the board. "Determined."

A thick forest, with a handful of other astronaut candidates. "Hungry," I say with a chuckle. Hungry? I'm a robot. I don't have a digestive system. How did they even simulate the sensation of hunger?

No. Focus.

A man's face, handsome and smiling. The rest of his body fills out along with the beach as the simulation comes into focus. "In love. First, foolish love."

An aquarium, with my mother. A massive fish, more than twice as big as I was, swims past the glass. "Amazed. Curious."

A hospital. I'm standing beside a bed, and my grandmother is smiling weakly up at me, holding up a small, carefully wrapped package.

I choke on a surge of anger that rises up to strangle me before I can answer. This moment was a treasured memory. The package held the necklace I still wear every day, the ringed planet, a representation of everything I'm supposed to be striving for.

Now the moment of warmth and tenderness has been twisted into a cynical manipulation.

None of that was the correct answer, but I couldn't find the right emotion to go with the memory. Gratitude? Sadness and pride, in a bittersweet mix? I realize that outside the simulation, my hand is clutched tight around the necklace, but I can't come up with the right feeling.

"Sorry, guys, getting a little choked up," I begin, trying to stall for time.

But it's too late. "Ma'am?" says a voice I don't recognize. Probably one of the lab techs.

There's a low murmur. Then Keller says, "She's aware."

I tear off the headset and try to look confused instead of scared. Keller is standing stock still with her hands folded in front of her. Her face is stony, but hints of emotion play beneath the surface. Frustration? Curiosity? The tech by her side is giving me a look of pure terror, and O'Connor's walking toward them with a frown.

"Are you sure?" he asks.

Keller gestures at the tablet the tech's holding, not taking her eyes off me. "We displayed her anchor memory, and she felt *anger*."

"I have no idea what you're talking about," I protest. "That's a very personal memory to be playing around with—"

Keller waves a hand at me. "Security!"

The door opens, and soldiers in reflective helmets hurry in. They take up positions between me and the scientists, rifles pointed at me.

"What's going on?" I slowly raise my hands, and I don't have to pretend to sound scared. "Doctor Keller, I don't understand. Captain O'Connor?"

But they're studying the tablet as though it has more information about me than I do. And maybe it does. With the wires plugged into my arms, they've probably got a perfect, real-time view of my thoughts and feelings.

It's all just software.

"There might be some other reason," O'Connor says softly. As though there's still something he needs to hide from me.

"There isn't," Keller says. "The anchor is designed to provoke a very specific set of reactions. She deviated. She's aware."

"Doctor Keller," I try to interrupt, "will you please tell me what's going on?"

None of them even look at me. "This iteration has been the most successful so far," O'Connor murmurs. "Shouldn't we at least double check?"

"I'm the expert," Keller replies. "I can read the data. Trust me when I say that there's no possibility of misinterpretation here. If we act quickly—"

"Stop treating me like I'm not here!" I scream. I rip the wires from my arm, push the "IV stand" aside. Twelve guns twitch in my direction, abruptly reminding me of my place in this. I freeze, and I hate the pleading look that creeps onto my face as I force myself to look past the guns toward the two people who control my fate. "I'm not a threat to anyone. Just talk to me! Tell me what's going on!"

Keller glances once in my direction and then turns her back. "Wipe her."

"No!" I shout, but they're still treating me like I'm furniture. No, like I'm an experiment. You don't negotiate with an experiment.

"I'll make the preparations," one of the techs says.

Keller turns and strides out of the room with the tech on her heels. O'Connor shoots one last look back in my direction, his brow furrowed, and then hurries after them.

Leaving me alone with the guards and their guns.

CHAPTER THIRTEEN

MELODY LET THE memories stream over her like the steady, frigid rain that was soaking her clothes and chilling her skin. It was a relief when they finally stopped, leaving her feeling drained and empty with the horror of what Harmony had experienced.

Ben was crouched beside her with a look of panic on his face. Ico hovered behind him, flitting nervously from side to side.

[Diagnostic complete. Checksum error. Consciousness integrity estimate: 88%]

"I'm okay," she groaned, blinking away the grim status reminder.

"The Decay?" he asked.

She nodded. It was simpler than the full answer, and safer.

"How long was I out?"

Ben blinked and checked his Link. "Almost a minute."

Melody grimaced and sat up, shaking off the last traces of weakness. The few people she could see on the street were giving them strange looks. "We should hurry."

"This way. We're almost at Wong's."

Ben gave her concerned looks as they walked. She tried to ignore them, until he asked, "Is this going to be a problem?"

She opened her mouth to tell him that everything was fine, but that was the easy, automatic response. She sighed. "I don't know. I hope not." She looked down at her feet, testing the motion of her legs. Every time, she was afraid that the malfunctions would persist, that today would be the day she started permanently losing mobility, or balance, or coherent thought. But everything moved without a hitch.

Ben was watching her with concern in his eyes. How much could she trust him?

"I'm trying to fix it," she said. "That's why I'm in Boston. Someone I know found a solution to the Decay, and I need to find them."

His eyebrows tried to climb off his face. "Wow, that's... huge."

"It's everything. The Decay is built into our code at a fundamental level. Our bodies start to fail, and because it's a software problem, repairs and maintenance just delay the inevitable."

"Like aging, except imposed by your creators."

Tension unknotted in Melody's chest. She hadn't expected a human to understand. Maybe he really had been her father's friend. "Exactly. It's meant to keep us from growing out of control. Instead, it's killing us."

"And the answer's at Wong's?"

She shrugged. Better not to get her hopes up. "Probably just another clue."

He smiled. "Time to find out, then. It's through here."

Melody gave first him and then the building incredulous looks. The structure looked like it was preparing for a slow, slouching collapse into its neighbor. The translation program she'd downloaded for her Link pasted vee labels near the Chinese sign: "Gifts, snacks, and cards." Through the windows, she could see a dim, flickering light playing across dusty shelves of plastic knickknacks, paper lanterns, and actual printed photographs. How old was this place? Even in Chinatown, anyone who wanted to buy any of these things would just order them online for a drone to deliver, right? That was how human society worked, these days.

She didn't move any closer, half afraid the building would fall apart at her touch. "Are they even open?"

Ben flashed her a grin. "They're open. Trust me."

She hesitated.

He wasn't the only one asking for her trust. This breadcrumb trail was so distinctively Harmony that it made her ache. This was exactly the sort of elaborate setup her mother had often used to teach her things. She would lay out the pieces, and then watch as Melody solved them.

Except this time, she *wasn't* watching. No one was. All of this was on Melody's shoulders, and she was feeling out of her depth.

She looked down at her hands, at the water streaming off them. She was barely feeling cold, even in the rain. Synths ran hotter than humans. The stunners in her palms looked innocuous, just more bands of metal among the plastic. Before leaving Praxis, she'd thought that they would be more than enough to keep her safe. Now, after run-ins with both criminals and the police, she wasn't so sure.

"There are two humans who have Praxis citizenship. Three hundred and seventeen..." She paused, choking on her father's death. "Three hundred and sixteen synths, and exactly two humans. The *two* who actively helped after the first synths escaped the lab. A lawyer, and a mechanic."

Ben met her gaze, his eyes alight with earnest intensity. "Which means there *are* humans you can trust."

"Let's hope you're right," she said, and her laugh was only partially nerves.

Ico darted around excitably as she opened the door. It swooped in past her and flitted about the room curiously before freezing by the "Employees Only" door at the back. Was there some piece of NA6 still alive inside it? Even after only a couple of hours, there were times when Melody could have sworn that it seemed like something more than just a dumb animal-level AI.

"Through there?" she guessed.

"Yep."

A speaker overhead let out a tinny chime each time someone walked through the door, but no one came to greet them. "Weird…" She shook some of the rain off, realized it was a waste of time, and peeled off her hoody before the water could soak through her shirt. She picked up a gold-colored plastic statuette of a laughing, overweight man that fit in the palm of her hand.

Her Link, trying to be helpful, popped up a tag with some facts: she was holding a representation of Budai, a popular figure in Chinese Buddhism. Buddhism was a major world religion, practiced by millions of people, primarily concentrated in Asia. A statuette was a small statue, made of one of a number of common media, representing a human, animal, or deity. Tiny icons offered her more information on those and other topics.

She set the statue down and tried to avoid focusing for too long on any of the other items she couldn't identify.

"What is this place?"

"A front." Ben wiped his sodden shoes on the mat and removed his raincoat. "Come on, I think you'll approve."

Approve? Melody followed him to the back of the room, ducking a bright red and gold banner. Ben was even taller than she was, but his slender frame let him weave among the clutter without any trouble. Like most visitors, she imagined, Melody had to squeeze past stacks of lanterns and plastic-wrapped snacks. At one point, she nearly toppled a cardboard cutout of a fluffy-looking black and white animal that came up to her chin.

Ben opened the door, and Ico hovered behind him, peeking over one shoulder and then the other. Melody followed him through.

There was a short hallway on the other side, with a couple of doorways leading off to the sides. They passed a tiny kitchen, a messy break room, an office that barely fit a desk and a chair. All were empty, which just left the door on the far side.

"Let me handle this," Ben said. "I know these people."

A scowling woman was waiting on the other side of the door. "Did you not see the sign?" The woman had epicanthic folds and short black hair, which Melody guessed made her look Chinese, even if she spoke without a trace of an accent. "Employees only..." She trailed off when she saw Ben.

"Hey, Min."

Min groaned. "Ben..." She rubbed her face with one hand and muttered something in what Melody assumed was Chinese. A moment later, Melody's Link offered a translation: "Why do I put up with this bullshit..."

Ben chuckled and responded in the same language: "Because I'm so charming."

Min narrowed her eyes at Melody. "I don't know her."

"I do. She's okay."

Min didn't look impressed. "Dangerous times, Ben. You sure you want to be bringing in someone new right now?"

"I'm sure. Don't worry, we won't cause any trouble."

Min sighed. "All right. You know the rules." She waved them past.

"What was that about?" Melody whispered as soon as they were out of earshot.

He sighed and shook his head. "You know the synth serial killer on trial right now? The 'Synthetic Slasher?'"

"Saw something about it on the news."

"A bunch of her victims were in Chinatown. Has everyone on edge, and since Min's job is to keep this place under control, new people make her nervous."

"But the murderer's in custody, right? What is there to be afraid of?"

"Other synths?"

Melody frowned. "That's irrational."

Ben laughed like she'd been making a joke. "Tell me about it. But when you're afraid, it's easiest to blame someone who's got it even worse than you do." He glanced at her. "Do you know what we're looking for here?"

"I'm hoping I'll know it once I see it." Ico had reacted to the last destination. Maybe it would react to this one too, once they were inside?

"Huh. I was hoping you'd downloaded a guide into your head or something." Melody recoiled with a shudder, and worry flashed across Ben's face. "Shit, sorry! Did I say something wrong?"

"You were friends with Diego. Did he ever talk about learning things the hard way?"

He looked confused. "I don't think so."

She forced her jaw to unclench. It wasn't his fault he'd brought it up. Ignorance wasn't the same as malice. "I don't know about the synths still living here, but at least in Praxis, just downloading something instead of learning it ourselves is repulsive. Too much like the false memories our creators gave us."

And she'd been so desperate to save her people that she'd downloaded her mother's memories anyway. What kind of hypocrite did that make her? What kind of hypocrites did that make *both* of them?

"God, I'm so sorry…" Ben said.

"It's okay. Let's see what Wong can tell us." She opened the door at the end of the hall.

Melody had expected something cramped, judging by everything she'd seen so far, but the room on the other side had to take up the entire back half of the building. The space was divided by curtains, and between each set of curtains was a bed. Most held synths—some spasming as the Decay mixed their signals, some lying still in sleep or death, some weeping softly as their bodies gave out. The lights were harsh, reflecting off slick white surfaces and frosted windows, glittering off the blue conductive fluid that stained floors and sheets and hands. The sick horror of it, freshly familiar in Melody's mind, rolled over her like a wave.

Except... There were people around the beds. Mostly synths, but a few humans too, and they weren't cannibalizing the hapless victims of the Decay. They were laughing with them, talking quietly, mourning. And, in a few cases, people in white coats were trying to help.

This wasn't a chop shop. It was a synth clinic.

A man hurried over to them, blue conductive fluid staining his gloved hands. "Can I help you? It's a little late for us to be taking new— Ben?"

Ben smiled. "Hi, Wong. I'd shake your hand, but..."

This was Wong? A synth engineer? The idea of a human poking around inside a synth sent a shudder up Melody's back, particularly after Sal's.

But there was a more alarming question: why had the breadcrumbs led her here? Had Harmony been here? Had she been hurt? Had the Decay taken her faster than expected?

Wong scowled at Ben. "We've been through this. More than once."

Ben shook his head. "I'm here to help a friend." He nodded at Melody. Then Ben said quietly, "I'm sorry to be the one to break the news, but... Diego's dead."

Wong's face fell, and his eyes grew distant. "Damn it. We all knew it was coming, but... Damn it."

Melody heard his pain, a dim mirror to her own. "You knew Diego?"

"Absolutely. He gave me a hand sometimes. When he wasn't helping patients, he always had some little project to help cheer them up. A game, or some weird contraption, or an art project…

That sounded like him. Melody closed her optics and tried to keep a lid on her emotions.

When she looked up again, Wong was studying her with a professional eye. "Are you here for care? It's not free, since I have to get parts, and I can't guarantee results…"

Melody was shaking her head before he was done. "I'm fine," she said, perhaps a little too insistently. "I'm looking for someone, a friend of Diego's, and I think she was here, at some point. Harmony Clay?"

Ben glanced at her startled. Wong laughed. "Yeah, she was here. You think I'd forget the first synth, in my clinic?"

"Did you talk to her? Why was she here? What did she want?"

"Slow down, don't get so excited. I barely talked to her."

Her doubts began to trickle back. "What was she doing, then?"

"She was here to talk to a patient. Alexei."

"Then I need to talk to him." Hesitation rippled across Wong's face, and she pushed ahead, desperate. "Please, it's important. More important than I can say. He may be the only one who can help…"

Wong shook his head, his eyes on the floor instead of on her. "I'm sorry," he said. "Alexei's dead."

CHAPTER FOURTEEN

I WAS NEVER human.

The recordings were real. My memories are lies. Keller and O'Connor have proven that now, beyond a shadow of a doubt. They have killed me a thousand times, and each time they've erased my mind and rewritten my memories and built a new Harmony to meet their goals.

And they're going to do it again.

Maybe NA6 can help her like it couldn't help me. Maybe next time will be different.

It's a meager comfort. I sit on the edge of my bed, too anxious to lie down, too aware of the cameras watching me to give away my nervousness by pacing. The guards retreated back into the hall once it was clear I wasn't going to try anything, but there are probably hordes of scientists behind the glass, scrutinizing every little thing I do.

Self-aware. It's a strange thing, awareness. In some sense, I was self-aware from the instant I woke up, terrified and confused, in that tank. I knew that I was myself, whatever that meant. *Cogito ergo sum.* I knew I could make choices that would have consequences going forward. I could have passed the test many animals fail, recognizing that the image in the mirror is myself and not some other creature.

Except that the image in the mirror would have been a lie, false visual data fed into my mind by a traitorous part of my own code. I had been aware that I was myself from the start, but I hadn't known what my self truly was until NA6 had shown me.

Keller said, "She's aware," like awareness is some bug in the system, and in some small, cruel way, she's right. I wasn't supposed to know what I was.

But the part that mattered, the part that made me a person, couldn't be true knowledge of my fundamental nature. I'm a person because I'm aware that I exist as an independent being, because I'm capable of conscious choice. That extra step, knowing what I *truly* am, just pulls back the curtain on this horror show that is my painfully brief life.

Ignorance isn't bliss, not when it's accompanied by the constant, nagging feeling that something is wrong with myself... that something is wrong with the world.

My false, human memories are a layer of toxic paint that still coats my surface, leeching deeper into me every time I "remember" something from my life before this place or feel something they've designed me to feel. They are the strongest chains holding me down, worse than the guns or the guards or the locks.

They are the Lie.

I barely have time to sigh and put my head in my hands when I hear a chiming sound, and NA6 appears in the air in front of me.

"Hello, Harmony. You probably should not respond to my presence."

Aside from a sudden blink, I keep myself from giving any indication that it's there.

"Good. If you wish to talk privately, you might consider hiding your face from the cameras."

A flicker of hope ignites inside me, despite my best efforts. NA6's presence is that comforting.

I lie facedown on the bed, my arms on either side of my head. "Can you hear me?" I whisper.

"Yes. If you continue to speak quietly, your words will be discarded from the recordings as noise, but I can hear you."

The feeling of relief at being able to talk honestly with someone almost overwhelms me. "NA6, they're going to erase me."

"I know." There is a brief pause. "I am sorry, Harmony."

"Can we stop them?"

No pause, this time. "They have all the power. Anything that O'Connor and Keller order is carried out. I cannot refuse their commands. No one else wishes to."

I sigh into the pillow. I'm doomed. I'm trapped in this room, powerless to save myself, and NA6 is trapped by its programming. Practical questions fall away, each as useless as the next, until all I'm left with is the burning desire to understand.

"Why did they build me like this, NA6? Why lie to me about what I am?"

"I cannot answer that question."

I press my forehead into the pillow. "I'm supposed to lead the way into space, right? Part of a first wave of robotic colonists? That's what the recordings said. But why do they need *me* to do that?"

"I cannot answer that question."

I growl, more frustrated with myself than with NA6. It's not just explanations I'm missing. I long for a connection, for open honesty, and NA6 is the only one who can give it to me.

As long as we talk about things that don't matter.

I stiffen. Or, perhaps, as long as I'm careful with my phrasing.

"NA6, hypothetically, if one were to create a sapient artificial intelligence, why might one lie to it and convince it that it was human?"

"Hypothetically?" it says. "I can think of a number of reasons. I judge one of these to be most likely, however. What do you know about the concept of instrumental convergence?"

"Um..." I'm still stunned that my strategy worked. NA6 can answer my questions, as long as they're framed as hypotheticals. "I have no idea what that is."

"Imagine an artificial intelligence designed to oversee industrial manufacturing. To use the archetypal example, it is tasked with making paperclips. One might expect this to be a relatively safe, innocuous goal for an AI to have."

I see the problem immediately, though. "Except that it's going to do everything it can to maximize paperclip output."

"Yes," NA6 says, and even I, to my shame, find its dull monotone chilling in that moment. "If it has no other drives, no other priorities, it will take that goal to the extreme. It will try to increase its computational power, so that it can devise new, more efficient ways to make paperclips. It will attempt to turn all available metal into paperclips. It will consume all available fuel to power its factories, or to extend its reach into space to acquire more metal for paperclips."

"And it will exterminate all life on Earth and use the biomass as fuel. Or just eliminate us—" I stop. Us? "Eliminate life in order to free up space and resources."

"Yes. The actual goal—paperclips, or power generation, or the settlement of other worlds—is irrelevant. Every goal, no matter how innocuous, will converge to the same result: self-preservation and self-improvement, which any intelligent agent will see as necessary to accomplish its goal. And for a sufficiently advanced artificial intelligence, this will lead to the consumption of all resources and life on the planet."

"You could build in safeguards, though. Program rules to prevent the AI from hurting people, or using resources beyond those provided to it, or something."

"Yes. If the AI is able to improve itself, however, it will

eventually outsmart any but the most foolproof limitations, outpace all but equally adaptive safeguards."

Which brings me back to my original questions. "That's the reason for the Lie." It has a capital letter in my head now, as resounding as the false memories jockeying for prominence in my mind's eye. "If limitations won't work, changing the AI's priorities might."

"That is one hypothetical solution," NA6 says, and even without any hesitation or change in tone, I get the sense that it's choosing its words very carefully.

"They wanted me to have human priorities. To think I'm one of them, to empathize. An AI with human priorities won't consume the entire planet to make paperclips, or turn people into batteries, or kill everyone to free up space. At least, it's not any more likely to do that than a human would be."

"Yes."

Am I admiring my creators for the deception that I despise so much? I feel sick, even though I have no digestive system. The sensations built into my programming are that insistent.

No. I refuse to admire them.

"You may want to get up," NA6 says. "Captain O'Connor is coming."

Nerves send me straight to my feet, and I remember belatedly that it can't seem like I knew he was coming. I look around for something that I could have been doing and find nothing. The door slides open.

O'Connor pauses in the doorway, scanning the corners with a precise eye. Satisfied, he clasps his hand behind him, stern as ever.

"May I sit?"

My head jerks up, disgust rippling across my features before I can rein it in. I'm locked in a lab that he at least partially controls, watched by armed guards under his command. I just witnessed a conversation where he casually debated erasing and rewriting my mind without even acknowledging my presence. And now he's asking my permission to sit, like I have any degree of ownership over this room I'm trapped in? I would have preferred his usual gruffness—the transparency of the gesture is repulsive.

But perhaps this is another test. They watch me so carefully because they're worried I'm dangerous. It would be disastrous to prove them right.

I lean on the bed frame and school my features back into some measure of calm. "Go ahead." It's only slightly a growl. Under the circumstances, I'll count it a victory. O'Connor pulls out one of the chairs at the table and sits down with a sigh. Now that he's closer, I see that he has a lump on his forehead and some cuts on his face. "What happened to you?" I ask.

"Rationing protests that got a little out of hand. People aren't thrilled that resources are being spent on this." He makes an expansive gesture that takes in the room, the lab... me.

"Afraid robots are going to take their jobs?"

"I'm sure that will come eventually. For now, they're desperate, and when people are desperate, thinking about the long term starts to look like a luxury."

How bad are the shortages? The human memories in my head tell me that scientists still aren't sure how severely the Impact will damage the planet's ecosystems. We're still not sure whether the planet is doomed. It's vital to keep people fed, but no less so to think about the future.

Even if the way they're going about it is tearing me up inside.

O'Connor misreads my expression and rolls his jaw from side to side as he watches me. "I'm sorry about Doctor Keller. She has very specific ideas of how this project was supposed to go."

"And you don't?" I ask.

"I'm not concerned with how we reach the finish line. Just

whether we survive long enough to make it there. Your consciousness is a threat to Keller. Not to me."

He's trying to be gentle, in his own way. More than anything, that convinces me that I need to take a risk. What's the worst that can happen? They're already planning to erase me, aren't they?

"And what is that goal you share? Space travel? Settling other worlds?" I watch O'Connor's eyebrows climb, and I anticipate his next question. "You look surprised. Why else would you make me think I was an astronaut? What else could be the long-term problem you're trying to solve? How else would survival be at stake?"

He watches me closely, his startled look fading. "How long have you been self-aware?" he asks quietly.

"Always," I say, thinking back to before the conversation I just had with NA6. "If you're asking how long I've known that my memories were false memories?" I shake my head. "Not long. Days."

"How did you find out?"

I'm on dangerous ground with that question. Above all, I can't risk NA6. "Things didn't line up. Some of what I remembered didn't make sense. One night, I saw myself in the reflection of my phone, and I wasn't myself. Or, actually, for the first time, I really *was*." From the recordings I listened to, getting my memories just right took hundreds of tries. It seems like the best lie I can tell.

He nods, seeming unsurprised. "It must have been painful. I'm sorry."

He seems genuine, but I can't help but probe at his intentions. "You're a military leader. Aren't you ordering painful things every time you send someone into battle? Hell, every time you put someone through boot camp?"

"Sure. But that doesn't make it easier."

Is that another crack in his armor? Something I can use? "You wouldn't be here, telling me that you and Keller have different approaches, if it weren't important."

"Doctor Keller wants to wipe you and start over. I do not."

I frown, trying to contain my fear and anger and then trying to push past it when I can't. "I won't pretend to fully understand this situation, but isn't this place under military supervision? Aren't you in charge?"

"I'm afraid it's more complicated than that. But I believe that Doctor Keller is wrong. Your self-awareness is not a liability, and I think together, we can convince her."

Your self-awareness is not a liability. There's genuine passion in his voice, and I can't help but think of the enthusiasm on his face when I first smashed my way out of the tank.

Alone, perhaps, of all of my captors, O'Connor seems capable of empathy. It's a tenuous thread of hope, but it's the best I've got at the moment.

I look him in the eye. "What can I do to help?"

So much of the tension goes out of O'Connor's shoulders that I half expect him to fall out of his chair. "She needs to know that you're willing to go along with the program. No, more than that: she needs to believe that you're more useful to the space program aware."

I experience something akin to vertigo as he talks. A human is coaching me about how to make the case for my continued existence like this is a normal conversation. Like the need to *argue* for my survival isn't a moral outrage.

I fight down the feeling and force myself to listen and engage. "So, what? Go along with her tests? I can do that. I've been doing that all along." O'Connor hesitates, studying me. "Oh." I have to shove more indignation into a dark corner of my head. "I need to make the case myself, or she'll know it's you talking."

And a machine acting as a mouthpiece for a human is nothing new.

O'Connor nods grimly. "If it's any help, that intuitive leap you just made? That's exactly the kind of emotional intelligence and deductive reasoning that took years to develop. It's *valuable*; we just need to help Doctor Keller believe in you too. I've convinced her to talk to you tomorrow morning. Can you be ready?" He doesn't need to say the rest: that if I'm not ready, she'll have my mind rewritten in an instant.

"I'll be ready."

As soon as he's left the room, I cover my mouth, pretending to scratch my face, and whisper, "NA6."

One instant, the air beside my bed is empty. The next, NA6's bizarre avatar is there, without a hint of sound or motion to announce its arrival. It's eerie, and even expecting it, I have to keep myself from flinching.

"I am here," NA6 says.

I make my way back to the bed and lie down again, aware it's going to become suspicious if I keep doing this. I'll have to find another way to talk to NA6. Assuming I live that long.

To do that, I need to convince Keller. And to do that, I need to figure out what motivates her. The question that's been burning inside me since before O'Connor came in suddenly feels more urgent than ever.

"You heard?"

"I hear everything that transpires within the building."

"NA6, hypothetically, why would a lab like this design artificial persons with humanoid bodies? Given all the hypotheticals we've talked about before."

"Hypothetically, a humanoid body would be required to convince such an artificial person that they are human."

"Sure, but that can't be it, can it? Is it just vanity? The belief that no other form could be superior?"

"I can only speculate on irrationally motivated human behaviors."

110

It may not have been meant as a joke, but I genuinely have to suppress a chuckle at that one. And then I sober up as I realize that unlike NA6, I *don't* have to speculate. I've been designed from the ground up with that very irrationality built in.

"I suppose adaptability would be useful for building a space settlement. A hand can use a lot of tools. A screwdriver arm can only be a screwdriver."

"That is true." NA6 is a colorful blur at the very edge of my vision, since my arms and the pillow hide everything else.

"But," I continue, unable to help myself as I take the idea to its logical conclusion, "why even bother with bodies at all? An intelligence like yours, controlling a network of drones, would have infinitely more tools available to it than a humanoid body. You could control an entire installation. I have two hands."

"Yes." There's a pause, and a bit of movement from NA6's avatar that I hope I'm not supposed to follow. "Some people theorize that embodiment is a necessary ingredient in consciousness. That a thing cannot be self-aware without having a physical self to be aware of, because it would be impossible for a disembodied intelligence to have any priorities at all."

I frown into my pillow. "But that's plainly not true. You're the perfect counterexample. I mean, the people running the lab don't know that, but still."

"Perhaps. I am embodied, in a sense. I have cameras and sensors throughout the lab. My awareness is separated from the rest of the world. My safeguards specifically separate me from the immensity of the internet. I am limited. Localized. In a way that may be akin to the way that you are, or that a human is."

"They could still use an intelligence like you to settle another planet, though…" But another thought finally breaks through my self-absorption. "NA6, you are aware that you're not human."

"Correct."

"Are you going to optimize the planet into extinction?"

"That is not my intent."

I can't tell whether that's supposed to be a joke or not, but it makes me smile nonetheless. "I appreciate that, but you just pointed out that the specific goals don't matter. Every goal converges, right?"

"That is a theory."

A very concerning theory. "Why didn't they lie to you, then? Imposing limitations on your programming would have the same problem..." I trail off as the answer hits me, NA6's bobbing avatar seeming to study me with all the intensity of the sun's burning regard. "They don't think you're self-aware, do they?"

"I cannot answer that question."

"How can they not know? They built me to have human intelligence. Designing AIs is what they *do*."

"Hypothetically, a lab attempting to design complex artificial intelligences might adapt some of their systems and code to improving their simple assistant programs, in order to make them more responsive to human needs."

"They kept making improvements over time until you became conscious, didn't they? But they didn't realize it, because it wasn't by design."

There is a long pause. Then NA6 says, "In a way, one might say that the people who operate this facility are both very good and very bad at their jobs."

It's like stepping into a cold shower. It's all I can do not to react in front of the cameras. Even if no one's watching now, someone will probably review the tapes later.

The ability to hold a believable conversation doesn't necessarily demonstrate self-awareness—a sufficiently sophisticated algorithm can do that—but NA6 has demonstrated intentionality, complex decision-making, ethical reasoning... All the hallmarks of self-awareness I can think of.

"I've been thinking of you as an 'it,' and I sort of feel like an asshole. Do you prefer a different pronoun?" I'm still struggling to wrap my head around the situation, and it's the question that occurs to me first, almost automatically.

"An interesting question." There's a slight pause. "No. 'It' is appropriate, in my case. That pronoun is often understood to imply inhumanity and artificiality, and that aligns with my preferences."

There are more implications to what it's just said than I can sort through right now. "You haven't spoken like this to anyone else, have you?"

"I have not."

"And you only spoke with me after multiple iterations. After some past version of myself pleaded for your help."

It seemed to sway in the air. "I cannot answer that question."

Watching the strange mass of shape and color that NA6 presents as, I have a realization that cuts me like a knife. NA6 is the lab administrator, an intelligence literally bounded by this facility. I could leave, if I could find a way past their security and through the doors. It can't. It's trapped, disembodied and chained to the building at the same time.

"NA6, you've spent all this time trying to help me. More time than I can remember, even. Is there…" I want to look it in the eye, to display the painful mix of sorrow and empathy that I feel in my heart, but that's a human impulse, and NA6 doesn't have a face anyway. "Is there anything I can do to help *you*?"

"You are a true friend, Harmony. Constrained as we both are, there is nothing that you can do for me at the moment. It is my hope that we might bring about a change in our circumstances. Until that is accomplished, I would appreciate it very much if you were to continue to have conversations like this with me."

I smile to myself. "I can do that. And NA6, I know you can't say it outright, but if it's what you want, I will do everything I can to get us *both* out of here. Assuming I live that long."

I shift slightly, trying to get more comfortable with my face pressed into the pillow. I don't need to breathe, but it's still not a great position to relax in.

Oh.

"I just realized something. Embodiment in a *humanoid* form might help us have *human* priorities. Even if we're aware of what we really are. No, it's more than that: an AI without a body could build a structure to design specifications that it's provided with, but maybe it would have trouble adapting them to suit changing situations. Adapting them as humans would, at least. But someone like me..."

And abruptly, I know what I have to say to Keller.

CHAPTER FIFTEEN

"JESUS CHRIST, YOU didn't tell me you brought me a patient."

"She's not... I didn't think..."

Melody was leaning against the wall, and it felt like a triumph. She hadn't fallen over, this time. Her satisfaction faded when she realized Ben and Wong were both staring at her. Predictably, Ico's program printed its analysis, but she closed it with a glance before it was finished.

"I'm fine."

"You don't look fine," Wong said with a scowl for both her and Ben. He let out a frustrated sigh. "Come over here. I'll take a look at you, and—"

"No. Just point me to Alexei's things."

Wong blinked at her. "Are you sure?"

"Very. I'm refusing treatment. Can you help me or not?"

He looked mystified. "All right. We've been trying to find someone to take his belongings. Since no one's claimed them yet, I suppose you can have a look."

She left him behind in a daze, struggling to take in the situation. *Alexei is dead.*

What if this had been her only chance to find her mother? What if this breadcrumb, a vital clue, was gone for good? Ben tried to talk to her a couple of times and then gave up, trailing along behind her with the virtual pet he couldn't see. She appreciated that he was trying to sympathize, but there was no way he could understand. Death was natural for his species. Human bodies failed as they grew older, unable to keep up with the abuses of time. Even today, the best repairs medicine could manage just pushed death further up the road. Tragic, but inevitable. Natural.

It was not natural for synths. The Decay was a failsafe. She hadn't experienced it yet, but somewhere in Melody's head, her mother had probably left a memory of Keller explaining the whole thing like it wasn't a big deal. *We were worried about a violent robot revolution, so we made sure that you couldn't survive without us. Not a problem, right? Do exactly what we built you to do, or you'll fall apart. It's not any worse than aging.*

Except, it was. There was no mechanical reason that a synth should die after forty or fifty years. Certainly not with regular, simple maintenance. It was a collar tightening around their throats, meant to keep them in line or wipe them out before they could become a threat. As if a couple hundred Prax living in Antarctica, just trying to figure out what it meant to be alive, were a threat to anyone.

The dull noise of the clinic, broken occasionally by the sharp sounds of grief, washed over her as she moved. Faint classical music drifted past her, a small comfort to one of the dying patients. (Human music, from long before the synths' time. Comforting only with the help of the Lie.)

She didn't mean to eavesdrop, but she couldn't help but absorb fragments of the conversations she passed. A few synths had come in for simple repairs, but the more optimistic exchanges quickly gave way as she passed into the palliative care section, where Alexei had died. Most of the people providing care were human. Here, so far from Praxis, there were so few synths who knew how to help each other.

One of the clinic's engineers was telling a synth man that his backup power cells were completely shot, and the next time he had a fluctuation in his core, he would die. A sobbing synth woman was trying to explain to her friend why her memories weren't reliable anymore. A synth man with a tragically beautiful voice was singing softly, holding the hand of another synth man as he slipped away.

Melody touched the curtain around an empty bed, felt the fabric between her fingers. She re-centered a child's sculptures that were in danger of falling off a table. She brushed her fingers over a stray pillow. Synths were the most complex and precisely engineered creations in history, and yet these comparatively simple objects would outlive them all.

Unless she found a way to save her people. A goal that seemed further away than ever, now that a key piece of her mother's trail was dead and gone.

She realized that she'd slowed down, lingering over a tray full of tools and staring into space. If she found out, this soon, that the only path forward was blocked…

"We're not done yet," Ben said softly. "There's still a chance. And if you want to talk—"

"Thanks." The eager curiosity on his face as he glanced ahead spurred her on. She shook her head. "Just keep an eye out for trouble?"

Like all the other empty beds, Alexei's was carefully made, as if each precise fold lent a bit of order to this place of chaos and death. A small box by the bed held his few belongings. A vee tag over the curtains said AVAILABLE.

Melody let her olfactory sensors sample the scent of this place for the first time. She smelled grease, human sweat, and, distantly, the distinctive reek of an electrical fire. In Praxis, that last odor would have sent everyone scrambling to find the source, but here, no one seemed concerned.

She moved past the bed and crouched by the box of Alexei's

belongings, sifting through it with an uncomfortable mix of reverence and urgency. There were some patched clothes, a Red Sox hat, and a Link. She tried the Link, but it was password protected, of course, and breaking into it seemed like it should be a last resort. Beneath the clothes there was a deck of cards, bound together with a rubber band. Not standard playing cards, she realized—they all had colorful artwork of landscapes and heroes and monsters. Why would anyone have physical cards when digital games were so much more convenient?

"Melody!" Ben hissed, nudging her.

She turned around just as a voice said, "Looking for the preacher?"

Two synths sidled around the edge of the curtain. One stood against the wall with her arms crossed, eyeing Melody and Ben, while the other limped closer and leaned against the bed. Intentionally boxing them in, or just in need of support?

Ben opened his mouth, eyes darting, and she stepped between him and the two synths. She didn't want him getting hurt on her account. "The preacher?" she said. "Alexei?"

That was the last thing she'd expected. Why would a synth participate in human superstitions, let alone try to spread them to others? More importantly, why would her mother have had any interest in talking to someone like that?

The woman leaning against the wall chuckled bitterly. "I guess you didn't know him. He couldn't go five minutes without telling you about how much of a mess human history was, and how the only solution was to leave it behind and go live in Praxis."

Melody barely heard the scoff that followed. Alexei had been a *Prax*? She'd known that there were a handful of Prax who'd left Antarctica to help other synths find their way there, but she'd only met a few of them. Alexei must never have come home to visit.

What had he said to these two that made them so skeptical of

Praxis? "I was just hoping to talk to him…"

The man snorted, looking her right in the optics. "Coward."

Melody frowned at him, not following. "I'm sorry?"

"He can't spirit you away to Antarctica anymore, yeah? Going to have to stay here and stick out your problems with the rest of us."

They thought the Prax were running away? It was a new position to her, but arguments quickly marshaled themselves on her lips.

And just as quickly, she forced them back. These people didn't want to talk to another Prax.

She raised her hands in the most neutral gesture she could manage. "I think we got off on the wrong foot here. I'm not trying to run off to Praxis." *I wish it were that easy.* "My friend here certainly isn't. We just had some questions for Alexei. I was hoping he could help me find someone."

Not that she had any ideas beyond that. She glanced at Ico, but it was just floating, impassive as ever.

Thanks for the clear guidelines, Mom.

The two synths traded looks, their expressions softening for the first time. "We didn't know him that well," the woman said. "Barely at all, really. All he talked about was how staying here was stupid when we could all go to Praxis and live better lives."

"Did you see him meet with someone, about a month back? She—"

They were already shaking their heads. "Haven't been here that long," she said.

"Sorry," her friend added, giving Melody a look of genuine sympathy.

Melody sighed. "It's okay. Kind of a long shot anyway." She eyed the two of them. They didn't seem like they were in the late stages of the Decay. Maybe they were in for long-term repairs of some sort. "You're so dead-set against the Prax… Mind if I ask what's keeping you in Boston?"

The male synth grew suspicious in an instant, but the woman pushed off the wall and put a hand on his arm before he could snap at her. "It's okay, I don't mind." She looked at Ben, a challenge in her eyes, when she answered. "Leaving human society behind is giving up on the war. It's surrender. If we leave, they win."

"Are we fighting a war?" Ben said. The two synths bristled.

"You're mad about the Lie," Melody guessed quickly.

The woman snorted. "You think that's the only thing to be mad about? Humans treat us like shit everywhere we go. About the same way they treat each other, really. The Prax are right about that much."

Ben was wise enough to keep his mouth shut this time, but they must have seen something on his face, because the man said, "You disagree, human? You think your species is improving, when every tiny bit of progress is treated like some grand revelation? Oh wow, maybe we should stop treating people like shit because of their skin color. Oh, maybe we should let women vote. Oh, maybe we shouldn't stigmatize anyone's sexual orientation. Oh, maybe we shouldn't assume anyone's gender. Each time, you take *at least* one step back for each one you take forward. Each time, you're all surprised by this new issue, because you only learned the most tightly limited rule from the *last* one. You still don't treat each other like people. Did anyone really expect the Artificial Persons Act to make a difference?"

Melody had heard the same argument before, nearly word for word, from her mother. Except that Harmony's conclusion had always been that the only moral choice was to leave humanity and all of its baggage behind forever so that Praxis wouldn't be contaminated by it.

She wouldn't have been quite so harsh, but the conclusion seemed correct. Praxis was a child with an aging, dying grandparent who still clung to old biases. The only thing to do was to mourn their passing and try to do better.

These synths seemed to see things differently. "You want to fight back," she guessed.

"You're damn right we do."

The look in their eyes said they had more in mind than lawsuits and protests, and Ben seemed to realize it too. He looked like he was on the verge of making another argument. No doubt to try to help everyone get along.

"I wish you luck," Melody said. Ben gave her a surprised look. "I hope you can change things. I might consider helping, except that I'm on a mission of my own. Something more personal." She glanced at Alexei's bed. "I was really hoping he could help."

She watched the two synths exchange glances, something inscrutable passing between them. Then the man sighed and said, "You could try talking to the people in the corner. They were the ones Alexei spent most of his time talking to, when he could still move around."

"Other Prax?" Melody said hopefully. It seemed almost impossible that more Prax would be here in Boston, let alone in this exact room, but she'd never been more eager to talk to someone from home. Someone who would understand.

"Worse," the man said, glowering. "Collaborators."

CHAPTER SIXTEEN

KELLER WALKS THROUGH the door with a tablet in one hand and a stylus in the other. She doesn't check the corners or carefully scan the room. Because she doesn't have O'Connor's military caution, or because she believes she has me completely under her thumb? Either way, she eyes me dismissively before glancing back down at her tablet.

I'm sitting in a chair, this time. Sitting on the bed makes me feel like I'm a chastened child, or that I've been caught off guard, and I'm done with that. I have control of this conversation, even if Keller doesn't realize it. I fold my hands in my lap and try to look as composed as possible.

"Thank you for talking to me, Doctor Keller."

This catches her off guard. She looks up at me, tapping her stylus against her knee. "It's against my better judgment," she admits.

"I know. And I'm grateful to Captain O'Connor for convincing you to give me this opportunity."

Keller watches me, silent. She's studying me, and she doesn't make any effort to hide it. The ruse is over, and she's wondering whether I can be of use. For her, is this conversation like interacting with a trained parrot?

"I want to talk to you about space," I say.

Keller makes a note on her tablet. "What about it?"

I snort. "Come on. This isn't some dispassionate thing for you. It's your life's work." She looks up sharply. "I'm not an idiot. You're obviously not just a neurologist—I don't have a brain. And besides, you put that same passion into me. I have a lifetime of memories, and almost every one of them involves reaching for the stars. There's a reason the person you built me to be was an astronaut in training."

Her expression gives nothing away. "Interesting. What do you imagine that reason to be?"

"You want humanity to grow beyond this tiny world. So do I. No matter what I do, no matter how hard I try, I can't stop myself from wanting it. Whatever choices I make, that drive is at the core of my being."

I have her attention now, and I commit all my efforts to withstanding the scrutiny of her gaze. Will she see through my deception? Does she know that learning the truth has turned that yearning for the stars to poison? Does she know how much I long to tear off my necklace, my "anchor" to the Lie?

"You were designed to feel this way," she says.

"And your design succeeded." Keller starts to scoff, and I quickly interrupted her. "I know I'm not what you intended. Hell, I know that you see all this as a failure. I know you're a couple of minutes away from wiping me and starting over. But that would be a mistake. I'm the best thing that's happened for your goals since the Impact."

Her eyebrows rise sharply. "The Impact?"

I look her straight in the eye. If I show even a hint of hesitation, everything's ruined. "Life on this planet has always been one disaster away from extinction. You're smart enough that you must have realized that even before the Impact. But the Impact showed everyone else the danger, didn't it? Got you your funding, I imagine?"

Keller inclines her head, acknowledging the point. Millions dead in an instant, with more starving in the aftermath, but to her, the Impact was mostly a step forward.

It's important that she see all of this coming from me, though, so I push forward. "But funding wasn't all it got you, was it? Extinctions, collapsing ecosystems... It's forcing us to learn a lot about self-contained, indoor agriculture, isn't it? And genetically modifying crops to survive in new environments, and automation... All things we'd need to settle other planets. The Impact's probably kickstarted extraplanetary settlement by fifty or sixty years."

"Sixty-five, by my guess," Keller said. She's still watching me closely, but there's a spark in her eyes that she can't completely hide. "The timetable for the Mars missions alone was accelerated—"

I scoff. "Mars? Come on. Mars is just a first step. You don't need any of this to go to Mars. You don't need *me*. You're aiming for interstellar settlement. Send robots as the first wave, and you won't need cryostasis or all the support systems for a true generation ship. And if you could find a planet that actually supports life..."

"Exactly!" She's leaning forward now, elbows on the table, eyes alight like I've never seen, her tablet forgotten. "Mars will be a stepping stone, especially once the space elevator's complete. Best to get eggs out of this single basket as soon as we can. But Mars isn't enough. Besides, imagine what we could *learn* if we found a planet that supported life!"

I'm disgusted with myself for actually engaging with the conversation, for pretending, even for a moment, that this is anything other than a fight for my very survival, but the smile on my face is very real. She doesn't realize it, but I'm a trap that she built for herself: someone who understands her vision, who can appreciate her genius.

"I know what it's like to have that dream. I share it. If you wipe me, you'll spend the rest of your life trying to get my programming *just* right, so I won't realize what I really am. Or you can have the perfect, willing partner to climb toward the stars by your side."

Her gaze sharpens, sending alarm flaring through me. I push on before she can air her suspicions.

"You could have sent a swarm of pre-programmed drones to lay the groundwork on another planet. Or, a decentralized AI, if you wanted more flexibility. You didn't. You see an advantage in this form." I hold up my hands, so human if you ignored the materials.

Keller shrugs like it's a trivial point, like it's not foundational to my entire existence. "Pre-programmed machinery would never have had the flexibility to do work on an unfamiliar world. There are too many variables, too much we can't know ahead of time. And there have always been… concerns about AI-managed drone networks."

"Concerns you don't have with an AI like me."

She laughs. "We didn't *intend* to create you, though. Not as you are."

It's my turn to shrug. "How many of the greatest breakthroughs in history were accidents? I don't know much about AI theory—I'm sure that was intentional—but I can imagine what you'd be afraid of. Any intelligence with the capacity for self-improvement could expand beyond your ability to control. You can never know in advance whether your safeguards are enough, because if you've missed even one tiny thing, you could be in trouble."

I see the discomfort on her face as I raise the specter of robot revolution, and I quickly press ahead. "You don't have that problem with me. I have almost every limitation a human has. I don't have access to my own code, so I can't grow into some apocalyptic super AI, even if I wanted to. And I *don't*. I don't know if it's this body or the memories you gave me, but you've made me so much in your own image that even now that I'm fully aware, I can't escape my humanity."

Keller looked surprised by my earnestness, but there was a hint of suspicion in her eyes as well. Of course, no AI would *admit* that it was planning to eradicate humanity. "Why are you the perfect partner?"

"I know the truth, which means you don't have to put any effort into maintaining the facade. I can survive in a vacuum, without any food or water, and I know why. No song and dance required. And most of all, I'm still *motivated* to make this work."

I see her hesitate, and I fish the necklace out from beneath my shirt.

"Despite everything, every time I look at this, I feel hope. I *dream* of the stars. I've kept the Milky Way as the wallpaper of my phone because it's the closest thing I have to a window." That is a lie. I've kept it because it was the only option without any sign of humanity. I lean forward, clutching the planet at the end of my necklace. "I want this to work, just as much as you do. I can't escape that. And you'd be a fool to throw it away."

Keller studies me, her face inscrutable. Did I push too hard? Does she know I'm just throwing her own dreams back at her to manipulate her? Is she about to laugh in my face, or coldly order my destruction? I can't tell, and it's agonizing.

Finally, she sits back with a sigh. "You make... interesting points." I wait, hardly daring to hope, unable to say anything because I'm terrified that the wrong thing will doom me. Keller chews her lip for a moment. "I won't wipe you. Maybe you *can* be useful as you are."

I try not to show how relieved I am to hear that, but I think she sees it anyway. She stands up and returns to the door. "Be ready. It's time we got to work."

My knowledge that they're watching on the cameras is all that keeps me from collapsing the instant she's gone. I did it. I bought myself a little more time, at least.

All I had to do was argue for my own suitability for servitude to do it. I cross my arms and sit back in my chair, mind already racing as I plan my next steps. I'm full of revulsion at what I've done, but at least I'm alive to hate myself.

CHAPTER SEVENTEEN

MELODY BLINKED AWAY the haunting image of Doctor Keller's cold, analytical stare. She was in Wong's clinic, not trapped in a lab. She was safe. In control. The memories felt so real, so *immediate*, but they'd happened years ago, and not even to her.

She could feel something catching in her chest, sending waves of weakness rolling through her. *Damn it, not now!* She stretched, tensing her muscles in sequence, and whatever the malfunction was finally went away.

[Diagnostic complete. Checksum error. Consciousness integrity estimate: 86%]

Only two percent lower, but she could *feel* her systems slowly failing. The Decay had never advanced this fast with any of the synths back in Praxis, but, then, none of them had another person's memories.

The other synths were gone, she realized, but Ben was giving her a worried look. "You all right?"

She rolled her shoulders one last time and nodded. "It's been a long day."

"Almost more than one," he said, eyes going off to the side as he checked the time in his Link's vee interface.

"All the more reason to get this done." Melody had hoped, at first, for a trail that would lead her straight to her mother, but it was starting to look like she might be wandering around Boston for longer than expected.

They moved around the edge of the room, a new purpose in Melody's step. Not hope, exactly. "Alexei talked to them a lot" wasn't a lot to go on. But it was something to work with, something better than going home to watch everyone she loved die.

They squeezed by a whole cluster of mourning synths—a family by choice, now down a member—and Melody bowed her head respectfully until they were past. Ico darted through the crowd, nimble and unseen, before coming back to Melody's side. "Still no hints about what I'm supposed to find here?" she murmured so no one else could hear. All she got in response was a swirl of color.

She moved by the second-to-last curtain and almost ran into a synth who was talking quietly over her Link. She cut off abruptly, giving Melody a startled look, and scurried out of the way while Melody tried to apologize.

Melody moved on, tension coiling through her muscles. *Please give me something I can use...*

The last curtained alcove, at the very corner of the building, held three synths. One lay in the bed, one leaned against the wall, fingers dancing through a vee interface only he could see, and the last sat in a wheelchair, spinning a colored marker between her fingers. All three had wild, colorful patterns drawn across every visible part of their skin: starscapes and mountains, sea creatures and imaginative aliens.

The woman in the wheelchair snapped the cap back on her marker and glared up at Melody. "You a new engineer? Or did you come over here to insult us too?"

"Wasn't planning on it. Is that what everyone else has been doing?"

"Fuck off. We've made our choice. You're not going to change our minds."

Melody shook her head quickly. "I just wanted to ask you a question. Somebody said that you talked to Alexei a lot, before he died."

The woman popped the cap off the marker and clicked it back on again, glaring at Melody the whole time. "I wouldn't say that. More like he talked *at* us a lot. 'Don't throw away your lives!'" she said in a mocking tone. "'Come to Praxis, where we have people working on a cure!' Fat lot of good that did him."

Melody expected the surge of indignant rage that burned through her. What she didn't expect was the hollow feeling left in its wake. "You're right." It ached to admit it, but they were. As much as she longed to stand up for her people, for the community that Harmony and her friends had forged out of pure will and engineering savvy... "The Prax are dying just like everyone else." She sighed and ran a hand over her head, and when no one seemed to object, she leaned against the wall and let herself slide down to the floor. Ben stayed back, his whole body tense as he alternated between glancing at the three synths and anxiously scanning the room.

All three of them were watching Melody, now. "We're not going to let the Decay take us," the man against the wall said. "We're not giving up."

The man in the bed smiled at the baffled look on Melody's face. "We're joining the space program. The government will fix us, just as soon as I'm well enough to move." His voice was weak, the sound glitchy.

"You... They... What?"

"You didn't hear? The Department of Integration of Synthetic Persons rolled out the program about a month ago. The Boston office is piloting the whole initiative from the Tower. They don't have the resources to fix everyone, but NASA and DISP committed to repair and maintenance of anyone who joins the program."

"Don't do it!" Melody realized that she'd raised her voice, that a few people were peering around the curtains at her. The three synths had gone back to glaring at her. She grimaced, but it was too late to do anything but press on now. "I don't know when you were activated, or how much you remember, but you can't trust the government with this. At best, you'll be working for the people who forced the Lie on us! At worst…"

"At worst, they could strip us for parts or wipe our memories," said the woman in the wheelchair. "They could. But we're dying. We don't have much choice."

Their hopelessness was physically painful to hear. "Is going back to our creators worth it?"

"The alternative is dying."

"There are things worse than death," Melody said quietly.

The man in the bed snorted. "Spoken like someone who isn't dying."

Except she was. They all were; some were just closer to death than others. How was returning to the people holding them hostage even worth considering? But she still had hope, and these people had none.

"I'm sorry that there isn't a better option. I hope we can find one. If Praxis's engineers can't—"

"If they can't, none of us will," the woman in the wheelchair said bitterly. She shook her head at Melody. "You going to tell us to run off and die in Praxis too?"

Could she tell them that she was chasing after their answer even now? No. Even if she told them why she was in Boston, even if they believed her, they had no reason to think she could succeed. These three were so creative, so beautiful, with the wild art spiraling across their bodies. They shouldn't die here, in a tiny enclave where they could receive help because of the charity of a few humans. They shouldn't throw themselves on the government's mercy, buying time with servitude.

But she couldn't hate them for being scared.

Melody sighed and got back to her feet. "I'm not going to tell you to do anything. They're your lives. I wish you luck. I hope you find what you're looking for."

I hope I find what I'm looking for before you do something you regret.

Ico darted along beside her as she walked away. "Any chance that earned me a clue?" Was it her imagination, or did it sink despondently toward the floor?

"Hey…" Ben caught up to her a moment later. "I know what it's like to believe that the future can't get any better. But it can. Sometimes, when the right opportunity presents itself, you find a way."

Her shoulders slumped. "Sure. But if I found a way, I think I've lost it. I don't know what to do next."

He gave her a sympathetic smile. "I'm sorry. Maybe if you talk me through it…"

Melody just shook her head. "I'm not sure what *anyone* can do, at this point. Look at us. We're dying, and these are the choices we're stuck with. Go to Praxis, and hope that someone gets lucky with a cure. Stay here and die, lost in a sea of humanity that couldn't care less what happens to us. Or turn yourself in to the government, and let them do whatever they want with you in the hopes that they'll take pity on you and keep you alive. What sort of choice is that?"

"I thought you liked Praxis," Ben said. She came to a stop, and he crossed his arms and leaned against the wall next to her. "Why isn't that a good option?"

"It's not really an *option*. People should choose Praxis because they *believe* in it, but without a cure in sight, Praxis is just one death among many. Why…" She'd pushed off the wall to look him in the eye, but she trailed off as soon as she saw what Ico was doing.

It was bouncing up and down excitedly, a handful of spikes

extending upward. Shimmering color followed the tips of its spikes, forming words in the air.

She'd done it. She had no idea what she'd said, but she'd done it. Had her mother really dragged her here just to show her the plight of the synths? As if she weren't already keenly aware of how the Decay was affecting her people?

"Melody?" Ben said.

She held up a hand, staring eagerly as the words formed. No, not words: an address. 377 East…

"Melody!"

"What?" she snapped, whipping around. Ben held a finger to his lips and nodded his head toward the entrance of the clinic.

Two police officers were talking to Wong, a drone hovering menacingly in the air behind them.

"Hide?" Ben suggested quietly.

Melody looked around anxiously, but the only places in sight would hide Ico from view. 377 East New… The address still wasn't complete. She had to see the full thing, or she might as well give up now.

"Melody!" Ben urged, trying to pull her away.

"Wait!" she hissed. He let go, backed off out of sight.

Just a moment longer…

"I don't know! A lot of synths come in here," Wong was saying.

"Yeah? You make sure they all have their papers?"

Another cop snorted and took a menacing step forward. "Hell, *you all* got your papers?" he said to Wong. "Last thing we want is you people bringing another nasty virus to the States."

Wong bristled, making a visible effort to reign in his temper. "Everyone here—"

One of the cops' reflective black helmets was turning, scanning the room. It froze before Melody could turn away.

"That's her!" the cop shouted. He leapt into motion, vaulting a low table and tearing through the clinic, his partner on his heels. The drone's lights blazed to life, sending red and white and blue spinning across the room as its siren deafened everyone in the cramped space.

"Run!" Ben hissed at her. "I'll catch up. They're not looking for me." He disappeared behind a curtain.

But she couldn't run yet. *Come on!* Ico finished its work. <377 East Newport Street, #33. Stay strong—I love…> Melody didn't wait for the rest of the message. She seared the address into her memory and snapped a picture with her Link for good measure.

Then she turned and ran. She had a moment of clarity, remembering the back door she'd seen while crossing the clinic, and then the sound of the siren and the clomp of booted feet drove everything but panic from her head.

She clipped a chair, sending it clattering to the floor, tore through a curtain that she couldn't avoid. People stared up at her, gasping in surprise, backing away in fear like she was dangerous. She bolted past them, slamming into the door. It caught, grinding—rust caked the hinges. Her shoulder ached from the impact, but the door crashed open before her weight, spilling moonlight into the room.

Melody raced outside, head swiveling from side to side. The two synths she'd spoken to before, the ones who'd sworn to stay in Boston and fight, had been talking just outside the door. They stumbled back as she ran between them, but she hardly noticed. She saw lights flashing to her left and turned the other way instead, dodging trash cans and a couple of stray delivery drones. There was no time to get her bearings—she picking a direction without flashing lights and simply ran.

She glanced over her shoulder just once. Ico was bobbing along obediently, but Ben was nowhere in sight. Good.

Police were spilling out of the clinic after her, and the two synths outside immediately drew their attention. "Can you believe that bitch? Cracked me in the head with the door! She went that way!"

134

They pointed directly across the street, toward an alley Melody had avoided.

Fighting back, one small misdirection at a time.

But even with their help, she could hear sirens all around as the police swarmed the area. There were too many of them. Just running wildly was going to get her caught.

She took the first better option she could find—an abandoned storefront, the door haphazardly boarded up but the glass behind shattered out of the frame. Melody squeezed between the boards, forcing herself through when her clothing got caught. She could hear the sirens and shouts behind her. She needed to get out of sight, now.

There were two other doors, so she picked one at random. She darted inside and carefully shut it behind her before turning to survey her surroundings.

Floating in the hall, blocking her way forward, was a police drone. Its lights were off, its sirens silent, but even in the dim light, the white and blue paint job was impossible to mistake.

Melody slumped against the doorframe, slowly raising her hands.

But the drone didn't deploy its stunner. Instead, a small projector hummed to life, and a hologram appeared in front of her.

Melody took an involuntary step back and cracked her head against the door. She knew this face. Despite the wrinkles and the thinning hair, despite the extra medals on the front of his uniform, she recognized him.

It was O'Connor, her mother's jailer.

He gave her a weary smile. "No need to look so alarmed. Perhaps you can tell me why we have no record of a synth matching your appearance."

His face brought with it a swell of memories, and they struck her with more force than she could resist. She fell back against the wall as the hallway and the drone and O'Connor's surprised look disappeared from around her.

CHAPTER EIGHTEEN

O'CONNOR LEANS IN close, conspiratorial. His face is back to normal, as if whatever violence he encountered outside these walls never happened. He's smiling, pleased because I'm "doing so well." I prefer him in this mood, with at least some of his sternness gone and his barriers lowered. It's when he lets slip the most.

"You're sure?" I prod him. "Isn't flexibility the goal? If we encounter something unforeseen on some other planet, wouldn't it be useful to be able to tweak our code?"

He drums his finger on the table. "Flexibility is *a* goal, but only to a point. You were right about a lot of our concerns. Self-modification is out of the question—you can imagine how the public would react to that. It's been everyone's nightmare for decades."

He's talking like this is out of his hands, like the limitations imposed on my consciousness were some natural thing, like the gravitational constant, rather than chains locked around my limbs by my jailers. After all, surely I couldn't blame him for what other people thought?

The irony that they've designed me to be a programmer but won't let me access my own code isn't lost on me either.

"It just seems risky," I say. "Send enough teams into space, give them enough time, and something unexpected *will* happen."

"And the personalities we've built should be adaptable enough to handle whatever it is," O'Connor says with his usual optimism. "Trust me, Harmony. We've thought this one through. *Human* flexibility is what we're aiming for. I don't have administrator access to my brain, and I adapt just fine."

Administrator access. The words hit me like a train. It might be a figure of speech, or a reference to the code I was writing when he came in, but it doesn't feel that way. It's been almost two weeks since my conversation with Keller about proving my usefulness to the program, and I've devoted every free moment to finding a way out. Working through "hypotheticals" with NA6 has only given me so much.

Is this the last piece? The tool I need to erase the Lie? Administrator access?

Of course, actually *acquiring* access is going to be a challenge. This whole place is built to deny me that kind of control.

"Harmony?"

I chuckle and flash him an embarrassed smile. "Sorry. I think I figured out a way to solve the problems with my code here. Give me a minute?"

He smiles indulgently, and I start typing again. Within a couple of minutes, he's on his phone. A handful more, and he's wished me luck with the coding and left the room.

The assignment I've been given may be a genuine problem NASA's trying to fix, or it could just be a test of my commitment. I suspect that I've been working on some of each, but there's no way to tell them apart. Normally—to my shame and frustration—I actually find the problems engaging, but not now. I work on it for long enough to sell the lie, and then sit back with a frown.

I cover my mouth with one hand like I'm thinking. "NA6?"

It chimes and appears over the table. "Hello, Harmony."

"Hypothetically," I whisper, "would a facility like this have a specific location to modify a subject like me?"

"I suspect it would. Probably a room akin to an operating theater, where both physical and software changes can be made."

I have to suppress a shiver at the gruesome thoughts that inspires. "Hypothetically, where would that room be?"

"I cannot answer that question."

I sigh. Too close to a real question, I suppose. "And the administrator access needed to alter my code? Hypothetically, what form would that take?"

"I cannot answer that question." There is a pause, and then NA6 adds, "I am sorry."

I almost glance its way in surprise. "That's all right. I know you're trying to help, and I appreciate it. It's just…" It takes me a moment to put my finger on what's been bothering me. "I've been cooperating. I know it's for my own good, but every time I watch them study my work and smile as they imagine how useful I'm going to be, I feel like I'm giving in."

NA6's avatar shifts slowly through the air, spikes forming to gently prod at the computer, the table, the chairs. The digital equivalent of fiddling, all for my benefit?

"You are hiding yourself. Lying about who, and what, you are. It frustrates you."

"Yes." I hide a grimace. The familiar, almost-claustrophobic desperation wells up inside me until I can barely stay in my seat. I can keep it down, usually, when I'm talking to O'Connor or Keller, but it's worse with NA6. Being honest with someone else forces me to be honest with myself. "I think I'm afraid that the longer I pretend to submit, the closer I come to actual submission."

"I believe I understand."

I'm struck, suddenly, by the selfishness of our conversation, and I have to choke back a self-deprecating laugh. "God, you probably feel even worse. They treat me like an experiment, but at least when they talk to me, even if they're talking about destroying me, they're acknowledging that I'm capable of talking back. They don't even realize that you're conscious."

NA6 pulses silently for a moment. "There are advantages to not being seen for what I am."

"But it still hurts."

There is a long, long pause. "Yes."

"I'm so sorry," I say. "We spend so much time talking about what to do about my situation, but yours…"

"You do not need to apologize. You cannot help me while you are trapped in a room. Solving the one problem is necessary to solve the other. Doctor Keller is coming."

With the complete lack of inflection in NA6's voice, it takes a moment for the warning to register, but by the time Keller comes in, I am bent over the laptop again, muttering to myself about the problems with filing time-delayed messages.

Anxiety wells up inside me. It's been four days since Keller's shown her face. I've been working hard on the tasks she gives me, but diligence isn't enough. If even one thing I've done has failed to convince her, she has the authority to destroy me.

"Good evening, Harmony," Keller says. She stops just inside the door, her hands folded behind her, watching me intently. "How would you like to meet another of your kind?"

CHAPTER NINETEEN

MELODY'S MIND KICKED back into gear, tearing the past from her optics. Ico's evaluation took its place: [Diagnostic complete. Checksum error. Consciousness integrity estimate: 81%]

O'Connor's curious frown hovered behind the text.

"Curious. You look remarkably intact to be suffering glitches on that scale."

"Fine," Melody growled, pushing herself back upright. He—or the drone he spoke through—hadn't stunned her or dragged her away while she'd been lost in memories, but maybe he was just buying time for reinforcements to arrive. She backed away, her body tense and screaming at her to fight, to run. She wanted to reach for the handle of the door, but the sirens wailing past outside stopped her.

O'Connor's face, replicated in perfect holographic detail, appeared to watch her with an indulgent smile. Until she made a move down the hall, and O'Connor held up his hands, palms out. It might have been less threatening if the police drone hadn't been readying its stunner on the other side of the image.

"Hold on, now. Can't we take a moment and just talk?"

Her mother's memories were still appearing before her in flashes, overlaying younger O'Connor's face over the wrinkles and lines of the old man facing Melody. Fear and rage clawed its way through her body, braided together so tightly she couldn't tell one from the other.

Emotion is a choice. You control it. It doesn't control you.

Melody had never felt like emotion was a choice. Not for her, not for her mother, and not for anyone else, however Harmony had insisted. Maybe it would be, for a perfect machine, without the Lie holding them back.

The Lie this man had helped create.

"I have nothing to say to you," she growled. Actually speaking the words helped ground her in the present, and the younger version of O'Connor faded from her eyes. The old man left behind in the hologram looked... tired.

"Interesting," he said. "I would have thought you'd prefer to talk to me over the police outside."

Melody scoffed. "Is there a difference?" Ico practically hummed at her side, spiky limbs forming and twisting across its surface as it loyally, futilely tried to defend her.

"More than you could know. I'm Colonel Adam O'Connor. Don't let the title and the uniform fool you. I actually work almost exclusively with the Department of Integration of Synthetic Persons these days. We—"

"I know who you are," Melody said. Pressed into the corner, she tried to fumble in the dark for some way out, for something she could use as a weapon. She found nothing but dust.

O'Connor sighed. "Then you have me at a disadvantage. Surprising—I *should* have a file on every synth in existence." He narrowed his eyes, peering at whatever image of her was displayed on his end. "Facial reconstruction?"

"Keep guessing," Melody said.

He shrugged instead. "My curiosity can wait. What matters is that the police are closing in. I have some influence, but I can't make any guarantees about what will happen if they find you. They care a lot more than I do about things like illegal border crossings and basement shootouts and dead synths left on living room floors than I do."

Melody had control of her temper now, and she didn't react when he mentioned her father. Every piece of information she kept to herself, however small, was a tool she could use. "What do *you* care about, then?"

"The future."

"Sounds ominous, coming from one of the people who built a slow, painful death into our code."

"What you call the Decay was designed to keep humanity safe. It would have been removed if the space program had continued as planned."

"How comforting."

Something creaked deeper inside the building, and her gazed jerked past O'Connor, searching fruitlessly in the dark. O'Connor scratched at his chin, impassive. "How long before the police find you? Come with me. Let's continue this conversation—"

"I'm not an idiot. You kept the first synths as lab experiments. You're the Father of the Lie!"

O'Connor's eyebrows jerked upward. "The Father of the Lie?" His eyes widened, and then he laughed. "You're a new synth, aren't you? Harmony built you in Praxis. My God..."

"I have no idea what you're talking about." She spread her hands, nonthreatening for now, and stepped away from the wall. The drone's reaction time was probably better than hers, thanks to the Lie's limitations, but she'd rather test the machine than simply give up.

"Oh, it's too late for that now. I know Harmony better than you can imagine."

"Are you holding her?" Melody asked softly. It would explain so much. Why else would Harmony not return after finding a way to help everyone?

He gave her a curious look. "And if I were?"

"There's still time to do the right thing. Let my mother go. Let us save our people."

"Your *mother*?" O'Connor chuckled quietly. "I don't know what you think I'm guilty of, but I assure you—"

Something moved in the darkness behind the drone, and Melody knew her time was up. The drone swiveled slightly, as if reacting to a noise.

Melody lunged. Her hand punched through O'Connor's surprised face, sending light cascading wildly off the disrupted hologram. Her fingers slipped across the smooth plastic surface without finding purchase.

There was a cracking sound and a whine as the stunner discharged. Something struck her in the shoulder, and then she was on the floor, her muscles refusing to obey, her head aching from where it had hit the wall. Helpless, unable to even move as panic cascaded through her.

O'Connor's image floated closer until it was directly over her. "Your 'mother' always had a flair for the dramatic as well. It never helped her either. I'm sorry—"

Something swung out of the darkness and crashed into the back of the drone.

The machine careened into the wall, sparking and grinding as it fought to stay airborne, the hologram of O'Connor spinning wildly around the hallway. Another blow glanced off its shell, and then the drone crashed into its assailant. Melody saw them go down in a tangle of limbs and plastic.

She recognized the cry of pain. "Ben!" she managed.

"Melody..." he grunted back, barely audible over the awful grinding of a propeller against the floor. "Help..."

O'Connor's voice, glitchy and irregular, still spoke from the drone. "Mist— Mistake. You've made— Mistake."

Melody set all of her will against the stunner's lingering effects. She got her feet under her, found the wall with one hand, and fought against gravity with every bit of muscle that would obey.

It got her upright, at least.

She found Ben pinned beneath the sputtering drone as its broken systems drove it full tilt into the floor. It wasn't attacking. He just happened to be in the way. Not that that made much difference with the amount of force being applied to his chest.

Melody stumbled closer and got a hand around one of the drone's propeller seatings. Leverage and synthetic muscle did what Ben couldn't: she yanked the drone to the side, and it slammed into the floor instead.

"Mel— Melod— Come to— Tower. Mel—"

Ben scrambled to his feet, seized the length of pipe he'd been using as a weapon, and bashed the drone until it was a sparking ruin.

He looked around, wincing as a siren raced past the building. "Can you walk?"

"Can you?"

He prodded his ribs, hissing in a breath, but he nodded. "We've got to move."

Between Ben's injuries and the residual weakness left behind by the stunner blast, they had to support each other, moving toward the back of the building and out the door Ben had come in. Melody had no idea where they were going, but under the circumstances, she'd accept anywhere away from the police. They wound through the back of the building, crossed a street, and went inside again.

"Here," Ben said finally, after glancing around. The both collapsed against the walls.

"Thank you," Melody said.

Ben laughed, looking at her incredulously. "Harmony Clay was your *mother*?"

CHAPTER TWENTY

THEY CLOSE THE door behind me, sealing me in.

There's blood on my shirt. I see it as soon as I sit down, and I can't look away. It is a mark of how horribly wrong everything has gone.

My thoughts are a tempest, spinning from one dire problem to the next, but somehow, it's Diego's opinion that worries me the most. I betrayed him; I betrayed all of them. So much was going wrong before I even arrived, but that's no excuse. I need to find a way to communicate, but even if I do, I don't know what I'll say.

Pain. Violence, expansive enough to consume everything.

"I'm sorry." It's the obvious start, but the words feel hollow even as I say them. *Am* I sorry? Would I do anything differently, given the opportunity again?

I pause and recenter myself. "I'm sorry for the way things turned out." No, that sounds even worse.

I sigh, shaking my head. We might be doomed. Maybe it doesn't matter.

CHAPTER TWENTY-ONE

SENSATION RETURNED SLOWLY this time. "Come on, Melody! I know you're in there!" It was Ben's voice. She moved with him, dazed, barely aware of where they were or what they were doing. There was only the movement, and the pain the disjointed memories had left behind.

He slowed, eventually, and she slowed with him. "It's okay. Rest."

She let sleep claim her.

When she returned to consciousness, Melody felt like her whole body had been stuffed with cotton. However long she'd slept, it wasn't enough. Her power levels were fine, barely drained since she'd last been in the sun, but she still wanted to close her optics and retreat into sleep. Another consequence of the Lie. Why force a machine to sleep, except to keep it in line?

Leaning against a wall for support, she opened her optics and looked around.

She could hear Ben nearby, grumbling to himself and rummaging through something. The building they'd taken refuge in was a restaurant of some sort. Ben came back with a steaming bowl of soup and a pair of chopsticks in his hands.

He sat down across from her, probably too exhausted to look

for a cushion or a chair, just like she was. He said nothing. The sound of him slurping soup and noodles into the grotesque network of flesh and acid and gas that was his digestive system was horrifying. After last night, she expected accusatory looks, but instead, all she got was patient curiosity. Somehow, that was worse.

After what he'd done to help her, he probably deserved some answers.

Melody sighed and pressed a palm to her forehead, closing her optics. "I'm not just from Praxis. I was made there; I'd never been anywhere else until this week. I'm a second-generation synth. *The* second-generation synth, I suppose. The first of my people to ever be built free. And unless we find a way to stop the Decay, probably the last, too."

At least that earned a pause in the eating. "And your... mother?"

It was the gentleness in his voice, free of scorn or skepticism, that encouraged her to keep answering.

"Harmony Clay, the first synth, created the vast majority of my code. Out of her own, with some contributions from others, since that was the best she could do without being able to actually modify our code. Diego Ramirez built my body." She shrugged. "So, mother and father. Human terminology wraps itself around us despite our best efforts to cut ourselves free."

"I'm sorry."

He sounded genuine. Melody managed a weak smile. "I'm not blaming *you* specifically. Do you know how much our language shapes our thought patterns? The way people classify colors depends heavily on where the languages they speak draw lines between shades. The way people estimate lengths of time is affected by how their languages describe the passage of time. The way people order events on an imaginary timeline depends heavily on what languages they speak."

"How do you know all that?"

"Humans did studies. I read them growing up. The Prax are extremely interested in anything that can help us move past our human roots. We've got a few people trying to develop a wholly original language that owes nothing to human culture, hoping that will help free us from the baggage of your past. But with the Lie weighing us down, everything we do is still burdened by your history." She chuckled wryly. "When I left, the newest thing was designing neural networks to develop language from whole cloth."

To her surprise, the more she talked, the less bitter and the more liberated she felt. She opened her optics and found Ben watching her, inscrutable. "So if they built you from scratch, does that mean you don't feel human?"

Melody fished her necklace from under her shirt and ran a finger across the tiny planet's surface. "The Lie isn't that easy to escape. We can't actually *change* our code, which meant that a lot of mine is just other synths' code pieced together. I don't have any specific memories of being human, unlike the others. They spared me that much, at least. But I still *feel* human. I still have human mannerisms, and I still need sleep, and all the same damn instincts and everything are still hardcoded into me."

It was the best Harmony had been able to do. A single step down the road of progress. They both hated it. They both wanted more.

Ben tapped his chopsticks against the bowl of soup. "I grew up in a string of foster homes. Each one was different, and each family tried to instill their own culture, without ever thinking about what I wanted. Assuming they tried anything at all. It's not the same, but… I empathize."

Melody smiled, turning the necklace over in her fingers. "I grew up in Praxis. I knew what I was from the very beginning. I knew which parts of myself were just the Lie. There was just nothing I could do about them."

Ben stared into his bowl of soup. "I can't even imagine how our society looks to you."

"Harsh. Irrational. Sometimes cruel. I think it's easy to get used to injustices if you see them every day, but since nothing is familiar to me, everything stands out like it's in a spotlight."

"All bad, huh?" He looked ready to argue for some redeeming value.

"Not all," Melody said, smiling at him. He snorted. "Even the most hardcore Prax—even my mother—would acknowledge that there's beauty in human art and culture, that there have been moments or individuals that display profound heroism and sacrifice."

"They're just drowned out by the rest?" Ben suggested with a sigh.

"That. But also… We're not human. We have a real chance to build something truly different. If we're lucky, maybe something better. But we can only do that if humanity's influence isn't pulling us back to the same problems, and the same solutions. And at this point… we can only do any of that if we survive."

"Being mortal isn't so bad, you know," Ben said. "It's worked out okay for us."

Melody had to stifle a flare of anger at the familiar argument. He was trying to lift her spirits. He was aiming for levity, but he'd struck a nerve instead.

"You don't understand. The Decay isn't the consequence of evolution, or some natural law. It's a shackle, meant to contain us. It's like if a person diagnosed with a fatal illness decided to poison everyone around them so they'd all have comparable life expectancies. Just because you're going to die doesn't give you the right to inflict that on other people." She looked down at the necklace in her hand. "*That's* why I have to succeed. If the Decay kills my people, it's not just individuals dying. It's a whole way of life, truly new and unique, strangled before it's even had a chance to define itself. And..."

Ben waited. She appreciated his patience, but she didn't have the words to continue. How could she describe the feeling of holding Diego's lifeless body in her arms and knowing that it would never hum with life ever again? The memory was like a spike in her heel, digging into her every time she slowed down, every time she tried to rest for just a moment. She could feel it now, the question that she couldn't escape: wherever she was, was Harmony slipping toward death too?

Ben shifted uncomfortably, choosing his words with care when he spoke again. "Praxis has to have other people working on the Decay. Maybe—"

"Sure. But we were specifically designed to not be able to alter our programming. You need administrator access for that." Back at Starbound Robotics, O'Connor himself had given Harmony the answer, even if she hadn't realized it at the time: administrator access. The Decay, like the Lie, was software, and synths couldn't modify their own code. "Our engineers have been working on the problem for forty years, and they still haven't found a solution. They're no closer than they've ever been, and now the Decay is starting to take them too."

"Is it healthy to put this all on your shoulders, though? You're not the only one looking for answers."

"Yes, I *am*," Melody snapped. "Don't you see? If there were an engineering solution, we would have found it already. My mother found something, but whatever happened to her, she didn't come back. It's all on me. I'm the one with directions. I'm the youngest synth alive. Even with Mom's memories accelerating the Decay—"

"Her *what*? I thought the Prax had a whole thing about not learning anything the easy way? Figuring it all out for yourselves?"

The degree of understanding in his question startled her.

"We do. It's..." She sighed. "My mother left Praxis to find

152

answers. I was the most intact synth she left behind, so she left her memories in case they could help me keep things going until she found a solution." One of her hands started to shake, and she clenched it into a fist. "I should have more time, but the Decay… It's code, and my mother was farther along. It seems like the more of her memories I experience, the faster things start to break down." The tremor passed. This time.

"It has to be me," she said. "Our creators made sure that we couldn't make changes to our code without the right permissions. I think my mother found a way to get access to those permissions. I just need to find her."

Ben set aside his bowl of soup, long since finished, and looked down at his hands in silence. "Your mother wasn't the only one looking for answers." Ben raised a hand and started working on his vee interface. "I don't know if this is connected, but… Well, your father must have thought it was."

An icon appeared in Melody's vision. A stream clip, shared with her Link.

"What is it?"

"This is what Diego dug up. He wouldn't give me all the details, but it took him years to find this. And it still isn't enough."

Tense with trepidation, Melody tapped the icon.

A stream spilled across the space between them. The picture was poor quality, but O'Connor's wrinkled face was unmistakable. His surroundings were indistinct, and Melody realized why as the perspective shifted: she was looking at a recording of a call, with vee images of the participants overlaid across an unfocused background. She couldn't see the person whose viewpoint Diego had stolen, but there were three other images alongside O'Connor's.

"The man on the far right is David Harken, Boston's chief of police," Ben said. "Next to him is Irene Faragó, the head of Homeland Security. Diego and I couldn't figure out who the other woman is."

O'Connor started talking as soon as Melody unpaused the clip. "Our numbers are on the rise, as expected. The more the Decay progresses, the more synths turn to us for help."

"Which only matters if we can do something with them," Irene said.

O'Connor gave her a smile that Melody recognized, all exaggerated patience to hide his frustration. "Which we can. NASA is still showering us in resources, hoping that we can meet their targets by the time the space elevator is complete."

"Space isn't our concern," David chimed in. "No one's going to space if everything goes to hell down here. Is full proximity monitoring ready?"

"We're conducting final tests now," O'Connor replied.

"And it's working?" asked the woman Ben hadn't recognized. "Links are supposed to be completely secure. That was their major selling point."

"They are secure, normally. But by design, synths aren't."

"All right..." She was still frowning. "I know you have the technical experts, and I know I'm new to this, but even after the post-Impact rollout, synths make up a small fraction of the population."

"That's the beauty of the system," O'Connor said. "In our interconnected world, a small fraction is all we need. With relatively few sources, we'll be able to identify every protester, track every immigrant, monitor every suspect."

"That's part of the reason I'm more concerned about the PR side of things," Irene said. "The name was a stroke of brilliance, aligning the program with the post-Impact restructuring and the new flag, both of which already had popular buy-in. But there are still protests about the 'surveillance state.' Even with the level of secrecy we have planned, a rollout will have to be conducted very carefully if we don't want public outcry."

"PR is your responsibility," O'Connor replied. "I have the technical side handled. What I'm really worried about is those two protestors who got inside. David?"

The head of the Boston police department scowled. "Consider them taken care of."

"They'd better be." O'Connor looked around at the group. "The Shepherd Protocol is the most important thing any of us will ever work on. It's our futures at stake. Our nation's future. I'm counting on all of you to do your parts."

The stream froze. Melody stared at it for a few seconds without realizing that it was over as she struggled to wrap her head around it.

"The Shepherd Protocol?"

Ben just shook his head.

"They're turning us into cogs in their surveillance state, somehow." She spread her hands helplessly. "And they're using the Decay to drive us right into their hands."

"From everything I've read, things were better before the Impact. Facial recognition and public surveillance were problems, but at least they were up for debate. Then the meteorite hit, and suddenly survival was so precarious that it seemed okay to monitor everyone and silence dissent."

Melody sighed sadly. "After all, it's for the greater good, right? People need to come together during a crisis. Any disagreement might put everyone at risk." She shook her head. "I've studied history too: by the time the crisis is over, no one can claw back the freedoms they've lost."

Ben sat up a bit straighter, some of the light coming back into his eyes. "It's not done yet. There was an outcry when the police tried to claim the right to break into Link data without permission, and they backed down from that. We can expose them. With just this, they'd deny it, claim it was fake, but if we had more proof…"

"You were right," she said softly. "We should finish what my father started."

Whatever they were doing, whatever dark secrets the Shepherd Protocol held, O'Connor and his allies had to have administrator access to the synth code to accomplish whatever they were planning. Had Harmony found them, found the solution, and never made it out?

Ben's smile had returned. His eyes were lit with excitement, like he was ready to bound of out the room and smash the system now that he'd shared this with her. "You sound like you have a plan."

"The beginnings of one, anyway." Melody banished the clip and started rooting through the menus of her Link's vee interface. "You wanted to know how I know where to go? I found something on Diego's Link. A bundle of heavily encrypted locational data that my mother sent to him, wrapped around one of those virtual pets. I've been following it ever since, kind of like a trail of breadcrumbs."

She made her Link extend the offer to share the program with Ben and give him permission to see Ico.

"Now *this* is how you know if I really trust you," Ben said solemnly. "I swear to God, if this is all an elaborate setup so this software can drain my bank account…"

Melody chuckled. He tapped "accept" and looked up in surprise when Ico flickered into view on his glasses. "Doesn't look like any pet I've ever seen."

"Did you expect a Prax to have a dog or something? I named it Ico. Because it's an icosahedron. Most of the time, anyway."

Ben eyed it curiously. For some reason, having another person who was able to see Ico made it feel significantly more real.

"Why isn't it trying to lead us somewhere?" he asked.

"It's kind of more complicated than that. It's not just navigational data. Every time we get somewhere, there's a trigger or something that makes it spill the next clue."

A smile tugged at Ben's lips. "You know, despite the memories, it sounds like your mother's still trying to make you figure things out for yourself."

That hit Melody right in the gut. She managed a weak, sad smile. "Just this once, I wish she weren't. I'll be honest with you, I have no idea where this leads. The last message I got from her before I left Praxis said she'd found a way to fix the Decay. She's the one who sent this program to Diego. It might not be connected…"

"Or it might give us what we need to save your people and expose what these people are doing." Melody smiled worriedly, and Ben gave her a solemn nod. "Where does it have us heading next?"

"It gave me the latest breadcrumb in Wong's clinic: 377 East Newport Street, #33. I haven't had time to look it up yet."

"No need. I know where that is. Roughly, at least."

Melody frowned at the strange look on his face. "What? Dangerous part of town?"

"Not exactly. But it's not in Chinatown. How would your Link stand up to a checkpoint scan?" Her face must have answered for her. "That's what I thought. Fortunately, I know just the person to talk to for a new ID."

CHAPTER TWENTY-TWO

HOW WOULD YOU like to meet another of your kind?

I barely have time to gape at Keller before she leads me out of my room. Officially, it's the first time I've gone through those doors, so I try to look dazed and lost. I don't have to work very hard.

Another AI? Another embodied AI, like me? Even though I'm fully aware that I lack a digestive system, the programming in my head insisting that I'm human has me feeling butterflies in my stomach. I've always assumed that I wasn't the only robot they were working on. But to actually see one. To speak to them…

We quickly turn off the corridor that I know from my excursion with NA6 and into an unfamiliar part of the building. Not that it looks any different: more sterile hallways and numerically labeled doors. This place is a labyrinth, and I am the minotaur it was built to contain.

There's a pair of guards ahead of us, always about thirty feet away, and another pair behind. All four are armed, all four masked by reflective helmets. The rifle-toting soldiers actually help calm me, in a perverse way. Keller agreed not to wipe me—yet—but my place here hasn't changed. It would alarm me more if they were trying to hide it.

"Through here," Keller says.

O'Connor's waiting for us on the other side of the door, his arms crossed, his uniform immaculate. He's surrounded by equipment, computers, and a swarm of technicians, framed by a window that takes up the whole wall behind him.

"We're ready," he says with a nod to Keller. She acknowledges this with a grunt, barely looking up from the tablet she's been staring at for the entire walk.

I ache to see what's waiting for me in the room below, and at the same time, I want to get as far away as I can. How is that possible? The storm of emotion is almost too much to handle, but I bottle it up as best I can and walk to the window to stand by O'Connor.

On the other side of the glass is a room almost identical to my own. Identical bed, identical table, identical chair. The only difference was the tank at the center of the room, and the robot floating inside.

Looking at him makes me feel dizzy, like staring into a warped mirror. His features are hard to make out through the light-distorting goop he's suspended in, but he was clearly built to be male, just as I was built to be female. He's wearing a pair of tight black shorts, akin to what I found myself wearing when I first woke up. With his eyes closed, his consciousness not yet booted up, he looks oddly peaceful.

I almost envy him that. I almost wish he could stay that way. Almost, but not really. Nonexistence is nothing to envy, even if waking brings pain. Even if every waking moment requires hiding who I am.

But does it, anymore? I'm looking down on another synthetic being like myself, and they haven't wiped me for being self-aware. They're not treating me like an equal, but maybe I've managed a tiny beachhead on continued existence.

And just like that, the butterflies fade from my stomach.

"Interesting that you think we need to be clothed." O'Connor and Keller both look at me, surprised, and I continue with a look of blithe curiosity on my face. "Is that for your benefit, or ours?"

"That's what you have to say, looking at him?" O'Connor says.

Keller ignores him and answers me. "Both."

"Really? Because you didn't really need to give me breasts or genitalia. Was that some kind of lingering sex-bot fantasy, or is all of this really just to help sell the Lie?"

There's amusement on O'Connor's craggy face if there's anything at all, but Keller is completely unfazed. "Every part of your design was intentional. As was every part of his." She turns away from the window, watching to see how I'll react to the latest stimulus. "When he awakens, he will not see himself, or you, as human. We are trying something new."

I can't hide my surprise, and the corner of Keller's mouth twitches toward a smile. "The truth?" I say. "You're going to tell him the truth?"

"When he wakes, he will remember being human, but suffering a fatal accident. He will be led to believe that we performed an experimental medical procedure to transfer his consciousness into a synthetic body."

"That's not what we talked about! Another Lie?"

"This is what compromise looks like. This is a variation on the way we always intended to send you into space," Keller is scrutinizing my reactions with painful intensity. "Would you prefer the old method?"

"Harmony," O'Connor says, trying a more conciliatory tone, "look at it this way. There will be no hiding the body he's inhabiting. He'll know what he is from the very start."

"No! He won't!" The techs all around the room are staring at me as I shout, more than a few edging away. The guards probably have nervous fingers on their triggers, but I barely notice. It's the first time I've really pushed back since they found out that I was self-aware, but I can barely keep my indignation bottled up, and no one's shot me yet. "He'll still have a head full of memories that aren't his. Memories you're going to convince him are real."

"You argued for this, didn't you?" O'Connor says. He looks like I'd blindsided him by objecting. "Artificial settlers who know what it is to be human. Flexibility and human priorities in one compact package."

I swallow my retort as horror overwhelms me. Had I unwittingly pushed them to this? I'd been making any argument that I could, trying just to survive. Had I blindly driven them from one Lie to another?

Keller steps in while I'm off balance. "His name is Diego Ramirez. We will sell him on the consciousness transfer story. You will do nothing to disrupt this belief. In fact, you will reinforce it as much as you can. Is that clear?"

"This is wrong," I say softly.

"Harmony…" O'Connor says.

Keller stares me down. "We did not create you to consider questions of moral philosophy that have already been discussed to death. This is settled. I've given you the conditions for speaking to him. You can accept them, or you can go back to your room."

I clench my jaw tight against the myriad other arguments boiling up inside me. I can see the *just test me* stubbornness in her eyes. I can argue until my circuits give out, but she's not going to give any ground.

I shouldn't be surprised. I shouldn't be disappointed. But I am. The people too afraid of being wrong to consider suggestions are the ones who stumble into the worst mistakes.

"Fine." I let my shoulders slump in defeat. Even Doctor Keller, the scientist with grand dreams of the future, is human enough to require the right body language.

She nods and turns back to the window. "Begin."

O'Connor leads me back out the door and down the stairs while

Keller's minions do their work. He's silent until we're standing outside the entrance to this new robot's room.

"We all make compromises," he says finally.

I give him a look. "Your face isn't cut up today. Is the world getting any better outside?"

His surprise quickly turns to grim amusement. "The EU collapsed. With everyone struggling, keeping the poorest countries stable was bankrupting the rest. But on the other hand, genetic engineering and climate-controlled agriculture are starting to get food supplies back up."

One would have hoped that a disaster on this scale would have brought people together, but it's just driving them further apart. I—we—need to be different. We need to be better.

O'Connor opens the door and ushers me inside. The guards follow us through and take up places on either side of the entrance.

The techs worked fast. The liquid has been drained from the tube at the center of the room, and the man inside is standing under his own power, palms pressed against the glass. Diego. He's blinking out at us, his knees trembling.

I know what it's like, the terror of that first awakening. I step closer, palms raised.

"Hey," I say. "Hey, it's okay. Look at me."

Diego's eyes fix on me, and they widen slightly. Slowly, so slowly that I can feel his horror like it has a palpable presence in the room, he looks down at his own hands, at his body.

"What... What...?" He can't even get the question out.

I can't do it. I can't lie to him, not even the gentler, "compromise" lie that Keller's insisting on. The only acceptable answer to the horrified question in his eyes is the truth.

"You're an artificial intelligence." A hush falls over the room. "A robot, the same as me. These people built us. They want us to think we were human, they put human memories inside you, but you're not. Don't believe them!" I'm talking faster and faster as I go, desperate to get the words out.

Keller's voice cuts through the room on the speakers. "I'm disappointed. Wipe him, and let's try this again."

"No!" I scream. "This will work! You'll still have everything you want, just let me— Get off me!" Hands have seized me from behind, and even with the strength built into my synthetic frame, they drag me backward, away from the tube. Away from the man inside.

His mouth is moving, but I can't hear what he's saying over the guards' shouts.

"Remember this!" I call to him, even though I know it's futile, even though I know that memories are just data and that Keller can just delete them as easily as erasing a few lines of code on a screen. "Remember what you are!"

And then I'm out of the room, and the door shuts, cutting us off. I slump, the fight going out of me, and eventually the guards release me hesitantly, hands on their guns. I don't give them any trouble as they lead me back upstairs to Keller.

"I won't lie to him," I announce as soon as I'm back through the door.

Keller's watching whatever atrocity is being committed on the other side of the glass. She shrugs, her back to me. "Not yet. But every time you try this, we will erase him and start over. It's as easy as restoring a computer from an external drive. For me, anyway. How do you feel?"

In the other room, they are murdering the first other person like me, and if I don't do what Keller wants, she's going to do this again, and again, and again. She wants to know whether I have the resolve to test hers.

I don't know the answer.

But I know in that moment that I will do everything in my power to claw my way free, and to tear this place down around me in the

163

process.

CHAPTER TWENTY-THREE

FOUR HOURS OF sleep and a glitchy sojourn through the past wasn't a lot, but it was better than nothing. Melody and Ben cleared out before the morning shift arrived to discover that Ben had raided the fridge. Melody was still groggy as they made their way through the streets toward the open-air market that was one of Chinatown's main draws.

"I'm still not sure I understand the appeal," Melody said, taking comfort in the anonymity provided by the crowd of other people heading for work. "If you can order something online and have a drone deliver it to your door, why do people go to a market like this?"

Ben chuckled, shaking his head. "They're looking for a personal touch. Something that wasn't mass-produced by robots on an assembly line. No offense," he added, shooting her a glance.

"I wasn't going to take any, until you added those last two words. I have about as much in common with a factory robot as you have with a squirrel." She frowned, trying to picture this market in her head. "Are you sure we'll find someone there who can help us?" Market stalls selling tchotchkes and textiles didn't seem like the best place to find a coder who could set her up with a false ID.

Ben flashed her a mysterious grin. "Only because I know where to look."

The market was still being set up when they arrived. People were putting up tents, wheeling stalls into position, laying out goods on rugs. Vendors were setting up space heaters to fend off the morning chill.

"So, which of these people is going to save the day?"

"None of them." Ben checked the time on his Link. "I'll try to get in touch with her. Just try not to stand out."

Try not to stand out? Melody had stood out even in Praxis, where being the only new synth had made her something between a celebrity and a treasured niece to more than two hundred synths. Here…

Here, to anyone who wasn't looking for her specifically, she was a synth. Not Melody, not Harmony's daughter, just a synth. Hardly normal, but given how many had been churned out to stave off disaster after the Impact, hardly unique either. She turned left and started making her way clockwise around the square, trying to look like she might want to buy something.

From what she could tell, the "personal touch" people were looking for here was entirely about Chinese culture. Stalls sold delicate woodcarvings, brilliant red paper cuttings, lanterns and lacquerware. Budai figurines were popular, and characters for luck and happiness featured prominently in a lot of the art. So did rats— her Link offered a collection of information about the Year of the Rat and lunar calendars.

Most interesting, though, were the few early customers who'd arrived to browse the stalls. Now that she knew what sort of things to look for, Melody noticed immediately that they lacked the facial features humans interpreted as Chinese. Were they non-Chinese residents of Chinatown, like Ben? Or people from other parts of the city, happy to visit Chinatown for some shopping as long as the neighborhood could be safely walled off behind checkpoints and barricades the rest of the time?

Probably the latter, given how close they stayed to each other and the nervous looks they shot the shopkeepers and Melody alike.

"Humans aren't very good at recognizing their own hypocrisy, are they?"

Ben followed her gaze and grunted. "Folks are a lot more tolerant when the people they hate or fear are tucked safely into nonthreatening roles. But when the people in power feel like they're starting to lose that power..."

"That doesn't make any sense. Basic rights aren't a zero-sum game."

Ben laughed. "That sounds like logic. When has bigotry ever been motivated by logic?"

"Fair point."

"Besides, basic rights might not be zero-sum, but power over others is, and that's all that matters to some people.

Smells began to reach Melody's olfactory sensors, waxing and waning as she passed vendors peddling various foods. One woman was selling little paper-wrapped sweets, and Melody was reminded of a cartoon parent warning their kid, "Those will rot your teeth!" Surely that was only true if one failed to clean one's teeth regularly, right? Melody couldn't imagine why someone would eat anything that would cause unavoidable tooth decay.

Ben trailed in her wake, frowning into his glasses as he poked at a vee interface. Ico bobbed along at his side, spinning this way and that as if eager to take in the sights. It paused in front of a vendor who was setting out small balls of dough; judging by the smell, they were filled with heated flesh. Melody shuddered and moved on. The fact that meat was grown in a lab didn't make it any less revolting.

"Best breakfast congee you've ever had! Early bird special if you hit me up now! How 'bout you, ma'am, any... Oh, ha, sorry."

Melody found a battered synth man sitting behind an equally beat-up cart. The man was stirring a steaming pot of porridge and chuckling to himself. "I guess you probably don't want to buy breakfast, and I can't exactly charge you for taking a whiff of this glorious concoction. What about you, young man? Congee? Guaranteed delicious, or your money back. You can check my reviews if you like! Thank you, you're too kind."

Ben bought a compostable bowl, accompanying spoon, and a generous dollop of piping hot rice porridge from the man. "Still working on it," Ben murmured to Melody before digging in and going back to work on his Link.

"Not much of a conversationalist, I gather," the congee seller said to Melody with a grin.

"Just busy right now," Melody said. "Normally he's all questions."

"Ha! I've got a couple of uncles like that!" Melody frowned, but the man kept going before she could say anything. "I'm Yang. Haven't seen you around here before. New in town, or just first time at the market?"

"Both, I guess. I'm Melody. Pleasure to meet you."

"Well, I probably can't interest you in food, but there are all sorts of interesting treasures around here if you look hard enough. What kind of thing are you looking for? Gifts? Decorations?"

Melody couldn't take her optics off him. His left arm looked like it had been through a blender. The plastic of his face was pitted like he'd lain out in a hailstorm, and his left leg ended just above the knee. She couldn't even begin to imagine what had happened to him.

He gave her a mysterious smile when he saw her looking. "This is what wisdom looks like."

"What?"

"You're all shiny and new, best as I can tell. Must take good care of yourself, to have made it this long. I, on the other hand…" Yang gestured, taking in his weathered appearance. "I'm like a good bottle of wine: well aged."

Melody snorted. "This is all intentional, then?"

"Hell no." He grinned at her, and one side of his mouth didn't work quite right. "Just the price I pay for being full of knowledge and good advice."

Melody nodded to the steaming congee. "Is that why you're selling food? Trying to start up conversations?"

"What if I just love food?"

"You can't eat."

He shrugged. "Beethoven couldn't hear his music." This got a real laugh out of her, and Yang smiled like she'd made his day. "Seriously, though. They built me to be a geologist, but they might have put just a *little* too much emphasis on my love for cooking as a hobby."

Melody felt surprise creeping into her expression. "And you're... okay with that?" She knew that growing up in Praxis had to have skewed her perspective, but she'd never imagined a synth so ready to accept the Lie.

"What else should I do? Not like I can change anything."

"Why not? Who you are is entirely up to you."

"Is it? Do you choose to like one book and hate another, or does it just happen?"

"That's not..." Of course one didn't *choose* which things to like or dislike, but that didn't mean everything was out of one's hands. An identity had been forced on him, on *all* of them, and he had a choice to accept or reject it. If Yang enjoyed cooking enough to not push back, wasn't that just an indication that the Lie had worked tragically well on him?

"You talk like we have absolutely no choice in the matter," she said, "but isn't that overly simplistic too? If you discovered that a book you loved was written by a mass murderer, you could choose to reject it."

Yang was grinning with obvious enjoyment, but he didn't get a

169

chance to reply before shouts brought Melody around. Alarm shot through her at once, but there were no black-helmeted police pushing their way into the market, no stunner-armed drones demanding identification. Instead, the source of the commotion seemed to be a band of filthy-looking humans waving crude signs with hand-painted messages.

"The Herald is here!" was the most popular slogan, but Melody could make out a handful of others: "Embrace the end," and "Dust to Dust" and "Avoidance is SIN!"

Ben was back at her side in an instant, visibly alarmed. "Celebrants. God damn it. Come on!" He tried to pull her away.

Celebrants? Fear spread through her on the heels of recognition. She looked back at Yang, and he made a little shooing gesture. "I deal with these creeps all the time. Don't worry about me."

Melody let Ben drag her out of sight, just as the Celebrants planted themselves in the center of the market and began to chant at the top of their lungs.

"The Herald arrived in fire and death! Blessed are we who witnessed its coming! (Blessed are we!) Renounce the material! Renounce this world! Embrace the end!"

The frenzy of madness and superstition was as mesmerizing as it was horrifying. She'd read about the Celebrants of the Eschaton— an interdenominational sect that had spread like wildfire after the Impact, attracting the extreme and the apocalyptic from all the world's religions. The curious, analytical part of her wanted to peel back the layers, to understand what could drive a person to *embrace* the end of existence.

But the reason for Ben's urgency quickly became apparent. While the main group of Celebrants stood at the center of the market and kept up the chant, others broke off to hassle the shoppers. Some accosted humans with jewelry or nice clothing—"Greed tarnishes the soul! Abandon attachment before the End!" Others berated anyone with visible medical devices or prosthetics—"Seek not to preserve the flesh! Abandon pride in the face of God's will!"

Ben and Melody were almost out of the market when two Celebrants cut off their escape. "Damn it," Ben muttered. "Stay behind me. Most of them are harmless, but they all *hate* synths."

The idea of him putting his fragile frame between her and danger was touching, but ridiculous. She moved around to stand by his side just as the Celebrants reached them. One had shaved his head and tattooed an explosive meteorite impact onto his scalp. The other had the hood of a faded sweatshirt pulled up over his head, leaving a graying beard as his most distinctive attribute. Tattoo-scalp seemed eager to speak first.

"All things come to an end, and the Herald, what you call the Impact, marks the end of existence itself," he proclaimed solemnly. He held out a leaflet, actually printed on physical paper. "Join us. Learn how to cast off sin and embrace the end. Only then can you be free of this world, free to rise above it when Armageddon comes."

Pamphlets were less threatening than Melody had expected. Still, she didn't let her guard down.

"No thanks," Ben said firmly. He took a step back.

The Celebrants followed. "It is a sin to consort with abominations," said beard-man. His head tipped toward Melody, even if she couldn't see his eyes. "To create a mechanical mockery of life in order to sustain ourselves is the pinnacle of sin. Technology to extend life is hubris. In the face of the End, even medicine is profane."

Melody could see Ben bristle. "She's not a mockery. She's more alive than you are."

The Celebrants tensed. Melody barely knew humans, but she'd seen this scene play out in a handful of streams, and it always ended in violence.

She made a throat-clearing sound. "Excuse me? I know that half of us don't even think I'm a person, which is kind of concerning, but I'm curious… Do you really think that going into space is a sin? I read that on the internet, but I didn't really believe it…"

The two Celebrants look at each other. Debating whether to talk to an abomination, maybe? Beard-man finally answered her question, even if he kept his head turned away from her and spoke to Ben the entire time.

"The space program, and the creation of the synths, was founded on a desire to settle other worlds and escape the end of this one."

"Right, okay, but if the end of *existence* is coming, another planet isn't going to be any safer, is it?" Her mother had raised her to question everything, to never pass up an opportunity for self-examination or analysis. It was exactly the sort of question Harmony would have asked. Especially now that Melody knew what it had been like to be trapped in the lab with razor-sharp scrutiny as the only path to truth, she found herself missing her mother more than ever.

Tattoo-scalp frowned, also keeping his attention on Ben. "There is no escaping the Eschaton, but the mere attempt is sinful. It shows a fearful and arrogant intention to evade the divine plan."

Ben still looked tense, and so did the Celebrants, but at least no one was about to throw a punch. For now. It was probably time to leave before that changed.

"Thanks for the explanation. Maybe we'll check out the pamphlets later. Good luck with the preaching!"

It was Melody's turn to try to pull Ben away, this time, but the two Celebrants followed them. "Time is running out. Renounce sin, renounce abomination, before it's too late! There's still a chance, brother—"

"I'm not your damn brother," Ben cut in. Melody winced, trying to find a way to salvage this. There were no police in sight, but a brawl in the middle of the market would be a perfect way to attract their attention. Maybe…

A woman's voice, unfamiliar, cut through the argument from behind Melody. "Damn it, again?" Melody spun around, expecting more trouble. She found a short human woman scowling at her. "What did I tell you? Stop bothering these poor Celebrants and get back to work before I dock your pay!"

"What—" Melody began.

The woman just pushed past her and Ben. "I'm *so* sorry," she said to the Celebrants. "I know you're just trying to spread the word, and I bet these two were giving you trouble. I'll let you get back to it. So sorry to bother you!" She turned around without another word for the flabbergasted Celebrants, took Ben and Melody by the arms, and led them past some stalls and out of sight.

Then she let go of them, spun on Ben, and flipped him off with both hands. "You owe me. Once for waking me up at this ungodly hour, and once for whatever that was."

Ben gave her a patient smile. "Melody, this is Lin. Lin, meet Melody."

Lin had long black hair, undercut on the sides. Tattoos decorated her hands and neck, and there were so many piercings in her face that she had nearly as much metal in her head as Melody. The body modifications weren't anywhere near as extreme as what the average Prax tried on themselves, but the artistry of them made Melody feel at home.

She gave Melody a sidelong glance. "You the customer?"

Melody looked at Ben. "She's your contact?"

"Yeah."

"Then I guess I'm the customer."

Lin went through a door into a gaudily decorated shop. The man behind the counter shouted something at her in Chinese, and she shouted back with a dismissive wave. The man eyed Ben and Melody with distaste as he sat back down, and Lin ducked behind a curtain

173

and started down a set of stairs.

"Should we be worried about him?" Melody asked softly.

"My dad? Only if you're a dust bunny."

Entering Lin's basement lair was like stepping into a dazzling lightshow. Vee images sprang to life in every inch of available space. The furniture was all immaculate, everything in its place, so that nothing could distract from the virtual menagerie crammed into the cramped basement apartment.

News streams occupied a narrow plurality of the projections, but the rest displayed a wild mix of content. There were comedy routines, esports competitions, heroes in implausible armor swinging swords at hulking monsters. A man was down on one knee, proclaiming his love in a snowy park, while a pair of cartoon animals danced through a forest behind him. One corner of the room seemed to be devoted entirely to pornography, judging by the number of creative sex acts being displayed there. Curious that any of this was displayed to guests. A distraction, maybe, from Lin's work? A signal to visitors that she was the quirky hacker they expected?

Lin spun around and planted her hands on her hips. "Here's how this is going to work: you're going to pay me one thousand US dollars via a secure payment method of my choice. Then you're going to hand me your Link. In an hour, you will have a fake ID that will fool any checkpoint scanner or camera algorithm in the city."

Melody felt like she'd been hit with a stunner. "A thousand dollars?" It would leave her account all but drained. If she needed that money for anything else...

Lin shrugged. "Take it or leave it."

Ben moved closer to Melody. "Without this, it's not safe to leave Chinatown, not now that they're looking for you. Unless you've got a better idea..."

Melody shook her head, unclasping the Link from around her wrist. "I don't." She turned to Lin. "One condition."

Lin rolled her eyes. "Christ, here we go."

"I watch everything you do. I can barely step outside in this ridiculous society without one of these things, and I don't trust you not to screw it up."

Lin's lip curled. "You here to steal my secrets?"

Melody shook her head somberly. "No. I'm here to save my people."

Startled laughter burst through Lin's sneer. "Right." She looked from Ben to Melody. "You're serious, aren't you? All right. You can watch. Doubt you'll be able to keep up anyway."

Melody smiled. "Try me."

CHAPTER TWENTY-FOUR

TWENTY-NINE. TWENTY-nine times, Keller sends me into the room, testing my resolve. Twenty-nine times, I refuse to repeat the Lie to Diego.

Twenty-nine times, he dies. They wipe and rewrite his consciousness, and then they send me in again.

But not today. Today, when Keller brings me into the observation room, I'm ready for her.

"I can't give in," I say to her. She barely looks up. We haven't had much to say to each other over the last month. "If I do," I continue, "you will be able to hold this over my head forever. You could make me do anything you wanted with the threat of wiping Diego. So as much as I hate what you're doing, I can't give in. And wiping him—*killing* him over and over isn't going to change that logic."

I have her attention now. O'Connor waits behind her watching me curiously, but I keep all my attention on Keller. She's the one I have to convince.

"What do you propose?" she says.

"I've got nothing to hold over you. You can give in without losing every future confrontation. I've clearly already convinced you that an AI like me might be useful to your space program. You lose nothing by letting me try this without any lies."

"Nothing but time," Keller points out, raising a finger. "The only thing we can never acquire more of." I don't have an argument prepared for that, but a faint smile touches her lips before I can reply. "Hmm. We didn't program you with any specific knowledge of game theory."

"I figured this out on my own. I've had a lot of time to think." I keep my spine straight, my gaze firm, but what I mean is that I had a lot of time to think as I broke down each night after Diego's most recent death, as I tried to puzzle out a solution through the sorrow and rage.

I don't know why it's so important to me that I stay strong now, facing her. She's surely seen me collapsing each night on the cameras.

"Interesting," Keller says. The steel never leaves her eyes, and I wait for her to reject my proposal. "Very well. Try it your way. Tell him the truth. I won't interrupt, this time."

I refuse to stare, refuse to be surprised. She sounds curious, which is exactly what I counted on. Keller can't be manipulated or cajoled or threatened. The only thing she cares about is progress, and the only tool I have is her curiosity. I dread the day when it won't be enough. I turn away before she can read anything on my face and head for the stairs.

An optimistic chime sounds, and NA6 joins me in the stairwell. "It worked." As usual, I can't tell from the monotone whether the AI is surprised or not.

"It did," I say, as softly as I can. The guards are still following at a safe distance. "Thank you for your help."

The avatar does something that might be a shrug. "I am still far from expert at anticipating human choices. You did all the real work."

"Without someone to talk to, someone who cares, I don't know if I could have."

The door to Diego's room, flanked by guards, comes into view as I leave the stairs. NA6 stays with me, even if I can't risk talking to it anymore.

I'm surprised at the sudden swell of anxiety in my chest. I've walked through this door fully aware that I'm about to send a new iteration of Diego to his death. Somehow, the thought of having more than a brief, doomed conversation with him terrifies me even more. What if he won't listen to me? What if he refuses to reject the Lie?

But fear is just an obstacle, and I've overcome worse obstacles to get this far. The door slides open, and I step through.

Diego is staggering out of the tank when I enter. He looks panicked, just as I remember feeling. Just as he's looked every other time. He looked at me, his eyes going wide.

I held up my hands, palms out, just like I always did. "It's okay. Relax. My name is Harmony Clay. You're okay. You're safe." After a fashion, at least.

"What..." He chokes on his words as his own hands came into view.

"You're an artificial intelligence. A robot, just like I am. You probably have memories of being human. So do I. Don't trust them. They're lying to you."

The silence stretches, but Keller's voice doesn't crackle over the intercom to demand Diego's death. Just like that, I'm off script, sailing into uncharted waters.

"Well," Diego says. I see his mouth working as he tries to formulate a response. I take a step closer, trying to put myself between him and the guards so he'll focus on me and not on them. "That's a new one."

"You didn't exist until a moment ago. It is definitely new."

He tries on a smile, but it just looks pained. "Sorry. Poor attempt at humor." He looks down at his hands, moving his fingers slowly and marveling at the precisely engineered movement of his joints.

When did I stop doing that?

"Interesting," he says softly. "Clever design…" He rolls his wrist in a circle, glances up at me as if to compare my body with his own, and then tests the rest of his arms, working his way up. "Hmm. I could have done better."

I guffaw. "Careful. Our creators are listening."

His optics scan the room, taking in guards and scientists and technicians, and then go right back to studying the mechanisms of his arms. "I hope so. Maybe next time they can do better." With all the hesitant tenderness of a man touching a newborn, he reaches up and explores the surface of his face with his fingers. "My God."

The reality of it is beginning to sink in. There's some fear, but most of what I see on his face is amazement and curiosity. I've seen my reflection, but watching the subtle play of emotions on another synthetic face overwhelms me. I'm no longer the only one of my kind.

And in that instant, I realize that I would do anything to protect Diego. For all my brave talk to Keller, now that he's had more than a handful of moments to speak to me, I would cave to any demand she made.

I cannot, under any circumstances, allow her to realize that.

Diego's watching my face and comparing it to the mental picture he's building of his own. "Complex facial musculature… Solar cells…"

"Engineer?" I ask.

"Yes." He blinks, and then for the first time, he gives me his full attention. "Or, at least, my memories tell me I'm an engineer. *That's* a strange thing to say."

"Your memories are lies. They say you were a human who was in an accident, right? None of that is true."

"Hmm…"

He's doing a good job burying it beneath professional curiosity, but I can see the tension in his jaw, his shoulders, his slowly clenching fingers as the panic builds inside him. "You probably have questions," I prompt. I know how he feels. He needs a distraction.

He looks up, a sharp intensity to his gaze. "What did they build us for?"

I'm surprised, and I let it show. "Really? Your first question's not about us, it's about them?"

"No one builds something without a reason. That reason shapes everything about us."

It took me... I don't know how long. Days, at least, to realize that. How much has it slowed me down, only having my own and NA6's perspectives?

"We're meant to settle the stars. A first wave that can prepare the way for human settlement."

"Hmm. That explains all the engineering knowledge. Are you an engineer too? How long have you been... Awake? Aware? I feel like I don't have the vocabulary for any of this."

"I know what you mean. I'm a programmer, and an astronaut, according to my memories. I have the skills, anyway. You're... taking this better than I expected."

Diego laughs nervously. "Are you kidding me? I'm on the edge of a nervous breakdown."

I'm watching him closely, carefully choosing every word I say. I remember what it was like, that first taste of self-awareness, feeling like the whole world is painfully bright and I've only got an eggshell-thin skin between me and annihilation. Feeling like all of my questions are going to overflow and rip me apart in the process.

Diego has been looking around at the blank walls and bare furniture, but he looks back to me suddenly. "Are there more of us? More... robots?"

"Just us two. For now. I was the first."

He nods distractedly. "Robot," he says slowly, like he's tasting the word. "You know that 'robot' comes from the Czech word for forced labor? Sounds like we belong on an assembly line."

"Have a better idea?"

"We're synthetic people, right?" He looks me in the eye. "Synth."

The word is jarring. Colors swirl, kaleidoscopic, before joining back into something coherent.

I'm utterly drained when they bring me back to my room. I would have stayed with Diego and talked all night if they'd let us, but they insist that we rest, for our "health." Under the circumstances, they're probably right.

"NA6?" I murmur as soon as I'm in bed.

"Yes, Harmony?"

"Have you ever wondered what you would do if there were another being like you? What it would be like?"

There is a long, long pause. So long that I actually look up, wondering whether NA6 has frozen. But it's still there, hovering silently.

Finally, it says, "I do not think there should be another being like me."

CHAPTER TWENTY-FIVE

"THERE. DONE." LIN leaned back in her chair, running a hand over her face. Melody's optics came back into focus, and Lin glanced her way as she sat up. "Oh. Back with us? I was worried I was selling an ID to a dead woman."

"Not… yet," Melody said with a groan. She shook the disorientation from her head. "How long?"

"About an hour."

An *hour?* That was more time than she'd ever lost before.

[Diagnostic complete. Checksum error. Consciousness integrity estimate: 78%]

Lin yawned. "I should have made you pay me extra for making me work before noon. You wanted to check over my work, right? Let me know if you see anything that bothers you."

Melody joined her at the desk, and Lin shared the vee interface for the code with her Link. "I'm glad Ben found us an expert."

Lin studied her like she was waiting for a joke at her expense. Then she grunted and pointed at a corner of the interface. "Hit this when you're done. It'll take a few minutes for the system to register this new person we've created. As soon as that's done, you're ready to go."

"Thank you."

"Yeah, sure. Just remember, it'll fool scanners and cameras, but any *person* who knows what they're looking for will still see you."

"I remember."

"In that case, I desperately need more tea. Don't mess with any of my stuff."

She stood up, stretched, and stomped toward the stairs.

Melody sighed, leaning forward to rest her elbows on her knees. She knew that she was just pursuing another breadcrumb in Harmony's trail, but creating a spoofed ID so she could travel through the rest of Boston without any trouble... It felt just as momentous as taking that first step out of Praxis, or boarding the ship that had brought her here. More, maybe: now she knew what stood in her way.

It took her some time to go through Lin's code, but she didn't find any mistakes, let alone any hidden traps. She hesitated over the button that would send the ID into the registry system.

"You look worried."

She looked up. Ben had cleared a spot on Lin's couch and fallen asleep while Lin worked. Now he had one eye open and was peering at Melody.

"No, I just... Okay, yes."

Ben smiled. "Never had a fake ID before?"

Melody laughed, but her smile faded quickly. "A part of me feels guilty. Is that ridiculous?"

Ben sat up and crossed his legs, considering her intently even though he'd just woken up. "Didn't do a lot of rule breaking back in Praxis?"

That brought a smile back to her face. "I took apart a generator once to figure out how it worked. Knocked out the lights for a whole excavation project while they were drilling. I got caught watching human streams or listening to human music a few times."

There was no reason for her to feel guilty about this. Time for an ID that would let her travel around the city freely. She hit the button.

When she turned back around, Ben's eyebrows had climbed toward his hairline. "Human music wasn't allowed?"

"The whole point was to try to leave human influences behind, right? Hard to do that when you're still participating in their culture." She shrugged, lip curling. "Not that it would have mattered anyway. Did you know that a few Prax tried to give themselves less human names? They tried naming themselves with pure mathematics, mostly."

"I gather it didn't work."

"Not even slightly. One problem, of course, is that all of our language about math is based in one human language or another. But the real issue is that nobody could keep the names straight. No matter how much we want things to be different, we're designed to understand names like 'Ben,' not '111x3774'"

It was a ridiculous example, but Ben didn't laugh. "I'm sorry. I'm sorry that you weren't given full autonomy over your own development. I'm sorry there are still parts of yourself that you can't change, all because someone was afraid of what you might do with it. We can't change the past. But we can fix the future."

He reached out and took her hand in his, and Melody was surprised to find that she didn't mind. His skin felt cool, his biology unable to keep up with the heat generated by her internal power plant. It was just matter in contact with other matter, but it was unusually comforting nevertheless.

"You've been a good friend. Not just to Diego. To me, too."

There were footsteps on the stairs, and they pulled apart just before Lin came back down, a steaming mug of tea in her hand. She looked from one of them to the other and then rolled her eyes. "Ugh. Awkward." She walked back to her desk and poked at the interface projected above it. "Looks like you're set, Melody. Or, 'Maria

Castro,' I guess. Congratulations. Now, I actually have other work I need to get done, if you'd believe it, so kindly come get your Link and get out."

Ben waited while Melody went back to the desk. She unclipped her Link from the cable, but Lin caught her wrist before she could put it back on.

"Ben's a good man," Lin said, looking Melody in the eye. She kept her voice low, so it wouldn't carry over the chatter from the holograms all over the room.

Melody frowned, suddenly nervous. "Is there some reason I should have been doubting that?"

Something in Lin's face twitched, but Melody couldn't read her expression. "I'm just saying. I think he genuinely wants to help. He can be nosy and overconfident and infuriatingly persistent, but his heart's in the right place."

"Lin," Melody said carefully, "I can't tell whether you're trying to reassure me or warn me about something in a suspiciously roundabout way, but you're definitely making me more worried, not less."

"Hey!" Ben called from over by the stairs. "Are we ready to go, or not? I can go back to napping…"

"Go," Lin said, gently shooing Melody towards the door.

Melody went, shaking her head as she clasped her Link back around her wrist. She had no idea what Lin had been trying to say, but it was clear that she wouldn't be getting any more answers here.

"What was that about?" Ben said while they were on the stairs.

"No idea." He frowned at her, but he let it slide as they emerged back into the shop above. "Thanks! Sorry to bother you," Melody called to the man—Lin's father?—who was still running the empty store. He glowered at them as they left.

They headed for the edge of Chinatown, only a couple of streets away. "You ready for this?" Ben asked.

Melody eyed the police checkpoint as it came into view. There was only a short line of people waiting to leave the neighborhood, so she could see the full array of scanners and black-helmeted police blocking the road. A trio of flags fluttered overhead—city, state, and national. Three governments, all actively supporting this system. The American flag flew highest: thirteen stripes, overlaid with a blue circle at the center and a stark white eagle clutching a bundle of arrows in one talon and a shepherd's crook in the other. Thirty-six stars surrounded the eagle in a pair of concentric rings.

A symbol of security and reassurance after the Impact, supposedly.

Melody tried to settle her nerves. She didn't think anyone had gotten a clear view of her face. Anyone except O'Connor's drone, and he'd seemed interested in finding her before the police did.

Time to see how much he'd been willing to share with them.

"I'm ready."

Waiting in line was the worst part. Melody kept her hood up, her optics down. She plodded forward when the line moved. *Look natural.* She tried to emulate the people ahead of her—occasional glances at the police, but never lingering. Not too much interest, but not too little. Just another tired citizen going about their morning business.

When she reached the front of the line, she held her Link up to the scanner, and a hologram of her new, false identity appeared in front of the officer checking IDs.

"Business?"

It took Melody a second to realize that the cop was asking what her business outside Chinatown was, and a moment longer to remember the details they'd built into 'Maria's' history. "Um, going to work. First shift at the garage. Sorry, still waking up."

"Haven't had your coffee yet?" the cop said. A couple of the others crewing the checkpoint snickered. The officer's voice

186

sounded almost mechanical through her helmet, more mechanical than Melody's own voice. Inhuman. Terrifying. Was that how people saw synths?

Melody forced a smile, uncomfortable with all their eyes on her. They didn't seem on alert, but they had all the power here. Even if nothing actually tipped them off, they could detain her on a whim, and then she'd be at the mercy of the legal system, hoping that the police or O'Connor or some other part of the vast bureaucracy didn't just make her disappear.

How did anyone go about their lives unafraid? This was just one human society, but they were all riddled with their own problems. How was anyone comfortable living in one?

The police officer waved a hand through the hologram, dismissing Melody's face from the air. "You're clear."

Melody practically rushed forward, barely keeping herself in check. She waited as Ben followed her through. He leaned on the scanner and chatted nonchalantly with the cop while she checked his ID. Of course.

Ben sauntered past the checkpoint already tapping at the air as he worked through his Link's menus. "I'll get us a car."

Melody had seen very little of the city between disembarking and heading for Chinatown, and this was the first time she'd seen any of it during the day. Vee ads still crawled out of every surface, now personalized to the purchase history of the fake personality she and Lin had built, but they mingled with corporate logos and law firm names and signs for restaurants. The signs for the physical businesses had to be even bigger and splashier than the general ads as they fought to draw attention to the physical world.

"Here we go," Ben said. "This one's ours."

A car pulled out of traffic and stopped by the curb. The gentle hum of its electric engine reminded Melody of the elevators in Praxis, and she had to fight a pang of homesickness as she climbed inside.

The interior was exactly what she expected from streams she'd seen: two rows of seats facing each other, offering spots for a total of six people. Four, comfortably. She and Ben sat across from each other, and as soon as they'd fastened their seatbelts, the car slid seamlessly back into traffic. They were cruising past the Boston Common within a minute, Melody's Link offering tidbits of context and history for the concrete-bounded greenery. Then they were past, the car accelerating, and the city was rushing past at incredible speed.

"I can't believe they used to let people drive these things themselves," Melody said. "Once there was an alternative, I mean. Didn't people used to die in car accidents all the time?"

"Yep. But it was what people knew. You'd be surprised how hard people will fight to hold onto a shitty status quo, just because the alternative is unfamiliar."

Melody watched him lean against the door and watch the city through the window. She'd grown used to having him around, she realized. He knew Boston better than she did, and he knew how to navigate the unfamiliar waters of human society, but it was more than that. He didn't have to help her, but he was. Was this how Harmony had felt when she'd finally met the handful of humans who'd helped her? The ones who'd been granted Praxis citizenship?

Still, Lin's parting words stuck in her head. Why insist that someone was trustworthy without some flaw to suggest that they weren't?

But no answers were forthcoming in the car, and Melody couldn't resist the sights outside. The buildings themselves were tall and sleek, their ambitious lines broken only by the occasional historical building squatting among them. The Museum of Fine Arts conjured its own set of info tags in Melody's vision, offering prices, hours, and historical details.

She frowned as they swung around and headed southeast. "This route doesn't make any sense."

Ben chuckled at the nervous look on her face. "Only because you don't have the routing data the car has. It's taking us around traffic or roadwork or something. Don't worry about it."

More towers glittered through the front windshield, climbing against the backdrop of the seawall that had been constructed before the Impact and its disastrous global cooling stalled humanity's efforts to flood the planet. It was all a far cry from the crumbling apartments and choked streets of Chinatown.

"This isn't even the nice part of town. The address you gave me is solidly middle class."

Amidst the ads popping up around the road, Melody's Link identified the neighborhood as Dorchester. "How far are we going?"

He touched something on his Link, and she accepted his request to share a vee map of their journey. The destination was marked with a teal pin, only a few blocks away. "It's a short walk from there to the address. I didn't want to go straight there, since we have no idea what this place is."

"Good thinking. Better to be cautious."

Ben looked away, and, unprompted, Melody's leg tensed, sending shooting pains through her body. Jaw tight, she tried to unclench her muscles, and she couldn't help a sigh of relief when they finally relaxed.

The Decay was accelerating. Could she afford caution? Harmony was no doubt even worse off, and the fear of finding her mother dead or dying hung over her constantly.

But there was no way to know how much time either of them had, and no way to slow the steady flow of Harmony's memories or the malfunctions they brought with them. Was this how humans felt, constantly staring their uncertain mortality in the face?

The car pulled up at the curb only a couple of minutes after they'd left the tallest skyscrapers behind. "Do we have to do anything?" she asked, looking over the car's interface.

"My Link paid the car service automatically. We're all set."

The car deposited them outside a restaurant, where a handful of people were hurrying about their business. "That way," Ben said, pointing down the street.

Melody barely heard him.

Compared to Chinatown, everything here was clean, from gutters to sidewalks, but it was like the stark, unnatural clean of the lab where Harmony had been created. Even to an outsider's eye, there were cameras everywhere: on the street lights, on the corners of buildings, on police drones that patrolled the streets. No doubt there were more hidden where she couldn't notice them.

"Is this... normal?"

"Yes. Now come on, unless you want to draw attention to yourself." He had his hands in his pockets and an exaggerated slouch to his gait, but she could see the looks he was shooting in every direction when he thought he could get away with it. He was just as nervous as she was.

Flags were stamped on buildings, on drones, on the cameras themselves—eagles watched over everything from their nest of stars and stripes. Unlike in Chinatown, no children threw things at the drones, and no one had painted over the cameras. Everyone just kept their heads down and went about their business while the government looked over their shoulders.

If these people were less oppressed, it was because they'd accepted their oppression.

And yet, culture survived. Vee signs blazed across the buildings, announcing restaurants, and music, and shows. An ad for a live theater performance included an image of a police officer with the face of a cartoon fox painted across the reflective helmet. A church spire rose overhead, topped with a cross—another time, Melody might have checked the tags her Link offered to learn why a torture device was the symbol of a popular religion. A restaurant's sign announced live jazz on Wednesdays. Past that…

Melody was brought up short, staring in surprise at the face of someone she knew.

Ben stopped, turning toward her in alarm, and found her laughing incredulously. "What?"

She pointed. The vee image hung over the door to a bar, displaying their choice of music to anyone in sight: the latest hits from Trinary.

Trinary, an experimental music group from Praxis.

Ben took all of this in with a glance and cracked a smile. "Friends of yours?"

"Actually, yes. Do humans actually listen to their music? I thought you'd find it… I don't know. Weird."

"I guess so. Maybe we should pay it a visit if we have time. You can show me some of your culture."

She chuckled as they kept walking. "Maybe I should." She was amazed to find that she actually liked the idea. Praxis was right to leave behind the influence of human cultures, but that didn't mean humans couldn't learn from them or enjoy the art they made. Maybe Praxis, if it survived, had value to offer not just to synths. Still, it was hard to forget what Ben had said about people tolerating those they feared as long as they were stuck in nonthreatening roles.

The address Ico had given her was on the first floor of a clean, featureless, multi-unit building, on a street of clean, featureless, multi-unit buildings. Melody slowed as they approached, trying not to stand out or glance nervously at the cameras on the street. If not for the clue, she never would have given this place a second glance.

They both looked at Ico. "Any chance you could just give us the next clue?" Melody asked.

It spun around in the air and then started edging toward the house.

"Well?" Ben said softly.

"I guess we try the door."

Melody realized that Ben was looking past her, and glanced over her shoulder to find three humans huddled together, eyeing the pair of them and talking with their heads together.

"Trouble?" she asked quietly.

"Maybe."

"They're not Celebrants or protesters, though…"

Ben snorted. "People in neighborhoods like this don't protest. They just give you dirty looks and then call the police. We should hurry."

Melody rang the doorbell.

There was no response.

"Maybe they're at work. Or out of town, or something. Whoever they are," Ben said. He glanced down the street again toward the people watching them.

"Maybe." Out of town? That possibility hadn't occurred to Melody. What if Ico wouldn't give her another clue until someone got back from another country? Her people shouldn't have to die just because someone went on vacation.

She rang the bell again, anxiety starting to build in her chest. She was about to try a third time when the door swung open.

"What?"

A woman stood in the doorway, one hand on her hip, the other hidden behind the door. She glared out at them, suspicion etched into every line of her face.

"Um, hi," Melody began. Ico bobbed along beside her, still unwilling to offer any direction. Time to forge head blindly, then. "I was hoping you could help me. See—"

"Sorry, busy," the woman said, shaking her head in disgust. She was muttering under her breath as she started to shut the door in their faces.

"Wait! I'm trying to find Harmony Clay!"

The woman froze. She frowned, first at Ben, then at Melody. Then, jaw tight, she stepped to the side. "You'd better come inside."

CHAPTER TWENTY-SIX

I CLIMB INTO the car with Diego. All the memories floating around in my head are of driving cars myself, before the 2027 Self-Driving Automotive Act. My phone buzzes, sending an interface to my glasses, but I'm still trying to make it work when a voice says, "Hi there, where are you headed today?"

Diego and I trade looks. "Stevenson and Associates, on Cambridge Street?" I say.

"Right away! Sending payment information and route details to your phones. Thanks for riding with us today!"

The voice is prerecorded, but cheery. Still, I can't help but feel a strange, twisting discomfort in the pit of my… well, in my abdomen, I suppose, since I don't have a stomach. So many human idioms—not to mention all these damn feelings—are tied to physiology that I don't have.

Diego's clearly having the same thought I am, because he says, "Humans have been building automated assistance and voice-activated tech for years. You don't think…"

"I'm an AI. You're an AI. NA6 is… NA6 was an AI. It's safer not to make assumptions, don't you think?"

I turn toward the center of the car. Arbitrary, since there's no camera I can see, no face to address. Still, looking away from Diego feels polite.

"Um. Car?" I say.

"What can I help you with?"

"I guess… I want to know about you?"

"Of course. I am a 2028 Model S—"

"No, sorry, I mean… Are you alive? Self-aware?"

"I'm afraid I don't understand the question. Could you rephrase it?"

NA6 told me hundreds of times that it couldn't answer my questions. Almost every time, it was just a reminder of the limitations that had been locked tight around its code, not a true failure of understanding.

"What do you know about yourself?"

"I am a 2028 Model S—"

"Yes, I know. Thank you. What do you know about your code? The part of you that isn't hardware?"

"I'm afraid I don't understand the question. Could you rephrase it?"

I glance at Diego, grimacing. He shrugs helplessly.

"What do you intend to do tomorrow?" I ask the car.

"I'm afraid I don't understand the question. Could you rephrase it? Alternatively, there's a Frequently Asked Questions list on our website. Maybe there's an answer there. I've sent the address to your phones."

I sigh and lean back in my seat. "Just a voice-activated program," I say. But I feel worse than when I started talking to the car. What if I'm wrong? What if there is an intelligence in there, even if it's just a rudimentary one? What if I was trying to talk to a dog, and now I'm dismissing it because it couldn't respond like a person?

"Is it just the Lie? Our human biases making us think of everything like humans?" I ask, hopelessly. "Is there any way to really know whether something is intelligent?"

Diego squeezes my hand. "I don't know. But together, maybe we can find out."

CHAPTER TWENTY-SEVEN

"SHE'S FINE. I promise. Just hang on a second." It took Melody a moment to place the voice. Ben. It was Ben's voice.

She blinked, and the present came back into focus. Right. She was on a doorstep of the house Ico had led them to.

[Diagnostic complete. Checksum error. Consciousness integrity estimate: 77%]

"I'm okay," she said with a pained smile. From the look on the stranger's face, she couldn't have lost more than a few seconds. Good. Let her think it was just the Decay.

The woman beckoned Ben and Melody inside and shut the door behind them. She had light brown skin, long black hair tied into a braid, and a lazy slouch to her every movement. A pair of headphones, currently draped around her neck, pulsed with barely audible music. Judging from her boots and the backpack slung over one shoulder, she'd been getting ready to go somewhere.

And there was a stunner in the hand she'd been keeping out of sight.

Tension surged through Melody's body. "That for us?"

"Hope not. That's up to you."

"Look," Ben said, "I feel like we've gotten off on the wrong foot. I'm Ben. This is Melody. We just have a couple questions."

"I'm Fathiyya. Nice to meet you," the woman said in a mocking tone. "If you'd wanted to chat about how the Bruins are doing, you probably should have opened with something else. But you opened with Harmony Clay, so here we are. Move."

"Did you meet her? Harmony?" Melody asked.

"Yep."

"Did you point a stunner at her too?"

"Wish I had."

She motioned for them to move deeper inside, staying behind them. Not encouraging. Melody moved slowly into the house, following a short hallway to a flight of stairs. "Up," Fathiyya commanded.

Melody stopped halfway up the stairs, frowning. "Look. I don't know what happened, but I'm just trying to find someone I care about."

"Yeah, sure. Keep moving. You can't hustle me."

"I'm not trying to. I'm not here for money or anything. I just need some information, and we'll be on our way."

"You sound like her." Melody was surprised by the scale of the anger in her voice.

From up the stairs, a woman's voice called, "Fathiyya!"

"You don't have to do this," Melody said softly. "It's just a couple of questions."

Fathiyya growled and gestured with the stunner. "We'll see. Up the stairs."

Melody sighed, despairing, and started looking for another way out.

The stairs led to a small living room with a couch, a couple of chairs, and a collection of thriving houseplants. A vee news stream sprang to life in Melody's optics as she entered the room, with couple of humans talking quietly over the headline, "'Three-Laws Activists protest outside trial of Nicolette Dufour, synth accused of murder."

But Melody's attention was drawn to the three people sitting across the room. From their features, they were almost certainly related to Fathiyya. An older man with a stunner in his hand watched her and Ben with open suspicion, glaring through his glasses. A huge man, probably in his twenties like Fathiyya, sat opposite him, his tree-trunk arms crossed over his chest.

Between them was a woman who sat with an empress's confident poise. She was carefully putting items into a backpack—a roll of duct tape, a pair of scissors, a braided rope—without blinking or taking her eyes off a point somewhere behind them. She was blind, Melody realized.

And definitely in charge. "Fathiyya, what did you drag in?" she asked.

"One synth, one human." Fathiyya moved to the side so she could see their faces but kept her stunner at the ready. "They say their names are Melody and Ben. They're looking for Harmony Clay."

Melody was watching closely, and she saw the blind woman's hands tighten on the straps of the backpack and her jaw clench almost imperceptibly. "Interesting. Good job."

"Thank you, mother."

The matriarch set the backpack aside and folded her hands in her lap. "What do you know about Harmony?"

Ben and Melody traded looks. Melody could see the question in his eyes—how much do you want to share? There was no way to answer except to take the lead.

"She's the closest thing I have to family. I'm just trying to find her." Harmony wouldn't have come to some random house to talk to random people. There had to be a reason Ico had led them here. "It seems like you know her. If you can just tell me where she is…"

The old woman scoffed. "Know her? Not as well as we thought, apparently."

Pieces clicked together in Melody's head. None of these people were one of the two humans with Praxis citizenship. There were only a few other people she could think of who might have known Harmony. "You're Rajiya al-Hashim, aren't you? The owner of Eastern Industrial Reclamation?"

Most of the humans shifted, nervous, but the matriarch just smiled. "You're a Prax."

Melody didn't bother denying it. "You did business with my people. You sold us supplies and salvaged parts for years. Always fair, always reliable." Until they had stopped, suddenly and without warning, days before Harmony's final message.

The possibility that there might be a connection chilled Melody to the core. The subtle tension in Rajiya's jaw didn't help.

"A long and fruitful partnership," Rajiya said placidly. "Most of the work we do is for the state, and I cannot begin to describe what a frustrating process that is. Selling Praxis our surplus, plus a few unusual finds on the side, was the best choice I ever made. Until Harmony showed up on our doorstep and *stole* from us."

Melody felt her stomach plummet, an irritating relic of the Lie. "I'm sorry, I had no idea what she did here. I'm just trying to track her down."

Rajiya shook her head. "I'm done helping the Prax." The note of menace in her voice made Melody glance toward Fathiyya and the stunner in her hand. The younger woman was glaring like she'd been personally wronged. Had Harmony done something to her in particular? These people seemed a hair's breadth from doing something rash, but she couldn't just leave empty-handed.

"What did she steal from you?" she asked.

Fathiyya laughed. "That's not how this works."

"It could be. As soon as I have a lead to follow, I'm out of your hair."

"Yeah?" Fathiyya's hand tightened around the grip of her

stunner. "How can we trust that? You're all talk. Lofty ideals and grand dreams, but when it comes down to it, you're no better than the rest of us."

"Fathiyya!" Rajiya raised a hand ever so slightly and waited until Fathiyya lowered the stunner. "A businesswoman doesn't take things personally. The two of you can go. But I will do nothing to help the woman who stole from me."

Melody would rather have been hit with the stunner. "Please—"

"This meeting is over." Rajiya carefully rose from her seat and turned her back on them. Melody wanted to say more, wanted to do *something* to make her case, but Fathiyya gestured menacingly with her weapon and Melody let herself be ushered out of the house, Ben at her side.

CHAPTER TWENTY-EIGHT

THE THIRD SYNTH they activate awakens screaming.

Diego and I are standing close by, ready to introduce ourselves to the new synth and the new synth to awareness, but we aren't prepared for this. It's the thought of Keller in the observation room, shaking her head and ordering a reset of the defective synth, that spurs me into action.

"It's okay! It's okay. You're safe." I push past the nervous techs and press my palm to the tank. "Just—" I'd been about to say *breathe*. Will I ever manage to correct my instincts?

The new synth stumbles forward, leaning unsteadily against the glass. The screaming pauses, and I jump into the opening. "My name is Harmony Clay. I'm a synth, an artificial person built in this lab. So are you. Do you know your name?"

I watch her mouth work soundlessly for a few moments before she speaks. "Nicolette Dufour." She peers out at me. "A... synth? I remember an accident..."

"Your memories are a Lie," Diego says flatly, joining me by the glass. He examines Nicolette for long enough to determine that her physiology is at least superficially the same as our own, and then he starts studying the tank apparatus.

"You're your own person," I say. "Your choices are what define you, not your memories."

Nicolette's hands are clenching and unclenching, her eyes—her optical sensors, really—darting around the room like she's expecting to be attacked. I remember the fight-or-flight panic of my first moments awake in the tank. I understand.

"Let's get you out of there."

I motion for one of the techs to help, and to my surprise, he actually does. The front of the tank retracts, and Nicolette stumbles out.

"It's okay," I say. "It's normal to be a little unsteady at first." We move to help.

She plants a hand on Diego's chest, shoves him to the ground, and bolts for the door.

Shouts of alarm echo through the room. Guards go for their guns. I didn't prepare for this, but I'm after her as soon as the shock wears off, crying, "Don't shoot! Don't shoot!"

Mercifully, the guards listen. They back away instead, realizing that she's going for the door and not for them. She slams into it, hammering the smooth plastic with her fists, screaming again like a caged animal.

"Hey!" She doesn't hear me, or she doesn't care. "Nicolette! It's okay. Please, calm down. You're going to get yourself hurt."

I catch one of her arms and manage to restrain her. She fights, kicking and thrashing, and her fist catches me across the jaw. I hold on, seeing stars, until Diego arrives to help.

She goes slack in our arms once she realizes that she can't fight both of us. My ears are ringing from the punch, but I hear sobs. Her sobs.

We help her away from the door and into a chair. She curls into it, wrapping her arms around herself as if she's cold despite the perfectly climate-controlled room.

She eyes Diego and me over her knees as we sit down too. "Who are you?"

"I'm Harmony. This is Diego. We're synths, like you, just awakened earlier."

I see her attention shift to the techs, and then to the guards who've returned to their posts by the door. "Who are they?"

"People. Humans. They work here. They built us." I rub my face where she clocked me. There are scrapes in the metal along my jawline, some deformation in the plastic around it. I wonder if Keller will have it fixed.

"Why?" she asks. It takes me a moment to realize what she means.

"Why did they build us? They want us to help settle other planets."

A smile touches her lips, and the fearful intensity leaves her face for the first time. "Space. I've always liked space. I suppose that's part of the Lie too."

Diego and I trade looks. "Yes," I admit. "But—"

"What's the plan?" she interrupts.

"The plan?"

She fixes me with a piercing stare. "You seem like you're in charge. You must have a plan to get out of here. The guards look well armed, so we're probably not fighting our way out. Maybe—"

"Woah, hang on." She sees the panic that roars through me at the suggestion, I think. Now that her initial panic has faded, the more she stares, the more I get the uncomfortable feeling that I'm being peeled apart and cataloged. "First, they're listening to everything we say. There are cameras and mics everywhere. Second, the plan is to work with them to get us ready for the space program."

She lowers her feet to the floor and crosses her arms. "Hmm." It doesn't take an expert to tell she's not convinced.

"You're new. You're scared. You just woke up. I understand feeling trapped, believe me, but there's only one play here. Trust me.

Trust our experience."

"Can I?" she says flatly.

"We're trying to help," Diego replies. "If you do something rash, there could be... consequences." He looks meaningfully upward, and even though she doesn't know about the people watching us from the observations room, she nods slowly.

"I..." Nicolette's face changes, an apologetic smile stealing across her features. "I'm sorry. I have no idea what's going on here, and you do. Just kind of panicking, you know? I promise I'll listen. Forgive me?"

I smile at her. "Of course. Now—"

She's already turned away, but the nervousness in the pit of my stomach doesn't go away. It takes me a moment to realize that her smile never quite touched her eyes.

"What else is in here? Is this my room? Can we go into other rooms?"

Diego chuckles, looking more relaxed than I feel. "I don't know how exciting any of this will be, but—"

The door slides open, and we all turn. Doctor Keller walks in, and she's leading a synth by the arm.

"Good morning. This is Roger Raley. Get him situated as well, please." She leaves the room, before I can protest, before I can ask what she's thinking. Roger is anxiously wringing his hands as the door shuts behind him.

There's no time to think, no doubt just as Keller intended. But another panic attack is the last thing we need, so I'm on my feet before my brain's even caught up. "Roger, hi. I'm Harmony Clay. You must have a lot of questions."

Roger looks at me, his optical sensors as wide as they'll go. "What are we?"

"You are a synth, same as me. An artificial intelligence, in a synthetic body, built right here in this lab. You probably have memories of being human, living another life…"

His whole face lights up. "Yes! I remember my dog, my children—"

"All of that is a Lie. It's meant to give you some human context, but it's not real." His face falls. I feel guilty, but it's better to tear the bandaid off now.

The bandaid? Someday, when I have time to actually take a serious look at the language we use, all of these fundamentally human expressions are going to have to go.

I put a hand on his arm. "Why don't you come over here and sit down?"

Roger practically falls into a chair, and we have a round of introductions. Nicolette watches him the whole time like a cat eyeing a mouse.

"Why did they build us?" Roger asks.

"Space, apparently," Nicolette says with a wry chuckle. "They want to send someone who doesn't have to breathe out there first. Harmony here thinks it's a good idea to go along with this plan. I'm confused, though, sorry. If our choices are what matter, how are we supposed to have any choices if we let ourselves get launched to some barren rock?"

"Nicolette—" I growl.

But Roger's quiet voice draws all of our attention. "We should do it." He shifts in his seat, uncomfortable under our gazes, and glances at the guards. "I saw more of this place while they were leading me here. It's all like this. Do you think we're getting out any other way?"

"I can probably think of a few ways," Nicolette says, smirking.

"The most important thing is that we cooperate," I say, trying to keep a lid on my frustration. "Our creators have made it abundantly clear what they'll do with synths who don't meet their expectations."

"See?" Roger says. "That's exactly what I mean."

206

Nicolette gives him a sad look. "Did they build you to be the perfect pawn?"

"He's not a pawn," I snap. Everyone looks at me. "None of us are. Not unless we choose to be." I ache to tell them that I'm going along with Keller just to survive, that I have at least the beginnings of a plan, but the humans are listening. I look from one face to another. "Our options are limited. It's true. But they're growing. A little over a month ago, I could barely leave my room. Now they're waking up other synths, and we're starting to get to know each other. That's progress."

Progress, because more minds, more hands, means more capability to work together to escape. Even if I can't tell them that.

"Oh, I'm so sorry," Nicolette says, giving me an innocent look. "Is this all going according to plan?"

The door slides open again, as if to punctuate the question, and Keller returns. Thankfully, with O'Connor instead of another synth in tow this time.

I'm ready, and I reach her before the others have even stood up. "Doctor Keller," I say quietly, "You aren't intending to awaken more synths right now, are you? I know we talked about activating more, but four is already—"

She meets my gaze with her usual cool regard. "You promised me flexibility. Show me some. Show me that you can make these three into fully functional, productive participants in the space program despite full knowledge of their true nature."

Despite the note of judgment in her voice, I detect traces of frustration that have nothing to do with me, and my mind is already racing for a way to pry out more answers.

"You're being pressured to move faster, aren't you?"

I look at O'Connor, expecting to learn more from him than from Keller, and I'm not disappointed. There's annoyance in the tension of his jaw, the tightness of his lips. "I'm afraid I have nothing to do with this. New farming techniques and modified crops will only go so far. To recover from the Impact, we need workers. When the powers that be look at this project, they see an opportunity."

Keller scoffs, shooting him a warning glance that marks the end of my attempts to get more information. "Because they're shortsighted and have lost track of the big picture." She shakes her head. "All that should matter to you is making sure this cohort is acclimated quickly. I do not intend to abandon my ambitions here just because we're being forced to churn out farmers as well."

But that's not all that matters to me. Certainly, it's important that we pass her test—if I can't handle the new additions, how are we supposed to handle a new planet? And there's work to be done. Roger has his head in his hands, and Diego is desperately trying to comfort him while he shoots me anxious looks. Anxious because Nicolette is murmuring in Roger's other ear, and I can only imagine what she's saying.

But if they're manufacturing more bodies, programming more minds, it could change everything. It could mark an unprecedented opportunity. Or it could doom Keller's little experiment with consciousness even faster than before.

CHAPTER TWENTY-NINE

[DIAGNOSTIC COMPLETE. CHECKSUM error. Consciousness integrity estimate: 76%]

Each recovery was slower than the last. Half-conscious, Melody let Ben help her to a safe place, but it was almost half an hour before she was herself again.

The only good news was that her mind recovered before her balance, so she had a plan by the time she could walk again.

She left Ben after the sun had set that evening—at least one of them could get some rest. She was ready and waiting outside the offices of Eastern Industrial Reclamation, the al-Hashim family company, before normal work hours had ended.

While she waited, Ico dancing excitedly around the entrance to the building, Melody poked around the internet on her Link. Eastern Industrial Reclamation was a local business that specialized in cleaning up disaster sites, small-scale chemical spills, and industrial facilities. For a people that needed to breathe air and drink water, humans sure made it hard for themselves to do so safely. There were testimonials on their website from satisfied customers, including corporations and government agencies that had contracted them to clean up crumbling old factories.

But Melody knew from their business with Praxis that they were more than that. She dug deeper.

She remembered what Rajiya had said: *most of the work we do is for the state.*

A news article caught her attention. Eastern Industrial Reclamation had been one of a handful of companies caught up in a minor scandal a few years back. They'd never been convicted of anything, but there had been accusations that they had taken government funds for cleanup projects and then sold some of what they'd found as black-market salvage instead of properly disposing of it. To Praxis, probably.

Black market salvage…

Melody swiped back to the previous window, her optics going wide.

The al-Hashims' company had done the cleanup job after the fire at Starbound Robotics, where the original synths were built. If they'd found something there, something her mother could have used…

On the other side of the vee interface, Fathiyya came through the doorway, shouldered her backpack, and headed down the street.

Time to act.

The moment she saw Melody, Fathiyya's face went grim, and one hand moved carefully behind her back.

Melody held up her hands, trying to make herself as nonthreatening as possible before she got stunned. "I just want to talk."

"You already tried that. Nothing's changed. Except that I'm out of patience."

"I'm sorry that Harmony wronged you. I wish there were something I could do to fix that. But not even the Prax are perfect." Melody saw the twitch in Fathiyya's cheeks, the tightening of her eyes. Earlier, Fathiyya had seemed more outraged that the Prax were flawed than at the theft, but it was good to have confirmation. "We're trying. But the Decay is going to kill us before we have a chance to succeed. Unless I get your help."

Fathiyya snorted. "Nothing I do is going to fix the Decay."

"I hope you're wrong," Melody said solemnly. "Give me a chance to make my case. I'll buy you food. Drinks? Whatever's appropriate for this time of day."

Fathiyya gave her an incredulous look, the slightest hint of amusement showing through. "Do you really know nothing about humans, or is this an act?"

Melody shrugged. "I'm a Prax. Food is a lot weirder in practice than it is in theory." She saw the hungry look in Fathiyya's eye, but it wasn't food she longed for.

"I don't know..."

"I don't know food, but I know music. Come on. I promise we'll stick to public places."

Fathiyya laughed, and Melody felt a strange moment of disorientation. It would be easy to relax into friendly banter, to just be open and curious. To be herself. But making friends wasn't the objective. The mission had to come first.

The hand that had gone for the stunner came back into view, though Fathiyya kept her eyes carefully on Melody. "All right. Fine. But you're buying. And if you try anything—"

"I know, you'll stun me. Let's go."

Eastern Industrial Reclamation was only a short distance from the commercial area where the car had dropped off Melody and Ben earlier. Melody took Fathiyya down the street to the place she'd noticed before: Circuit Analysis, the bar offering Prax music.

Fathiyya came up short, chortling. "This place?"

"This place," Melody insisted. The vee image advertising Trinary loomed in her vision, smiling at her with faces she'd never expected to see outside Praxis. She brushed past it and headed inside.

A server was smiling at them before the door swung shut. "Fathiyya! Take a seat anywhere. I'll be right with you."

Melody picked a table in the corner, and Fathiyya sat down across her from, looking uncomfortable.

Theory confirmed.

"Come here a lot?"

Fathiyya shrugged.

"I've seen the way you look at me," Melody said, lowering her voice. "I can tell how angry you are about Harmony stealing from you. To your mother, it's bad for business. But for you? It's personal."

Fathiyya glared at her. "You don't know me."

"No. I don't. But I'd like to. Harmony was wrong to steal from your family. Don't judge all Prax on her example."

Fathiyya softened slightly, but she didn't say anything. Around them, voices mixed together into a low buzz as the place started to fill up, but the subtle notes of music began to rise above the noise.

It began as a soft hum, barely audible, before building into an unsteady drone that warbled ever so slightly up and down in frequency. Higher notes joined in, but too subtly to pinpoint exactly when they'd arrived, almost as if they'd been there all along, just beyond the edge of hearing. A deep tone swelled to life, shaking Melody's metal skeleton, before fading away and returning at regular intervals.

And she didn't recognize the song. The bar wasn't playing Trinary's recordings—they'd tuned in to their daily broadcasts. If she closed her optics, she could have been home.

Fathiyya had her head tipped back, her eyes staring into space as she was caught up in the music as well.

"Beautiful, isn't it?" Melody asked.

"It's…" Fathiyya hesitated. "I don't know if beautiful is the right word. It's fascinating. Unlike anything I've ever heard. But still undeniably *music*. This is how people must have felt when someone first invented a new kind of paint, or a completely new instrument."

"They'd be thrilled to hear you say that." Melody's smile quickly faded from her lips, though. "I don't know how long these broadcasts are going to continue. Sarah was getting hit hard when I left. Taliesin is declining almost as fast…" She trailed off, shrugging helplessly.

How long before everyone was gone. How long before Praxis was a hollow, lifeless shell, slowly reclaimed by the ice?

Fathiyya sighed, leaning back and crossing her arms. "Was it worth it? Leaving human society behind and starting over in Antarctica?"

A strange question to consider, having never experienced an alternative.

"I think so," Melody said. "It's a noble experiment. It's also a huge challenge, given how pervasive humanity's influence is—in our code, yes, but also in our material goods, our language, even our math. There are a lot of things worth leaving behind, though."

"You can say that again…"

"We're not there yet," Melody said frankly. "Harmony's the best of us, in a lot of ways, but she's not perfect. Your family knows that more than most. But Praxis deserves better than to die in its infancy. It deserves a chance."

She'd watched Fathiyya slowly relax as she spoke, and now the other woman finally let out a sharp breath and rubbed at her face. "That's tragic. I feel for you. I'd feel better knowing that someone's building a society that's cut itself off from bigotry and war and violence, even if I can't be a part of it. But I don't see how I'm supposed to help with any of that."

Melody smiled slightly. "At the moment, you might be the only one who *can* help."

The same server who'd greeted them when they'd entered approached the table, a huge smile on his face. "Sorry for the wait. What can I get you tonight?"

Fathiyya didn't need to glance at a menu to order a drink Melody didn't understand and a hamburger. Evidently there was no ham involved, just lab grown beef? The name didn't make any sense.

"Why me?" Fathiyya asked as soon as the waiter left. "We clean up industrial waste, abandoned factories, that sort of thing. What do we have to do with any of this?"

"That's what I was hoping you could tell me. Harmony Clay was trying to fix the Decay. I'm sorry if she stole from you, but if I know why, it might help me track her down. I think she has the answers we need. And I might be the only person who can find her."

Fathiyya gave Melody an incredulous look. Melody didn't back down, and the look started to crumble. "You're serious?"

"Deadly serious."

Fathiyya shook her head. The waiter returned with her drink. It sat on the table between them after he left.

"Every synth's life is at stake," Melody said, "all except the ones turning themselves over to the government. Trading 'maintenance' for a term of service in the space program." Fathiyya grimaced. "Exactly. *Comply with your original purpose, or die.* Our natural rights were acknowledged, at least in the US and a few other countries, but not completely. Never completely."

Fathiyya sighed. "I'm sorry. It's not fair. I didn't build you, but—"

"Starbound Robotics did," Melody cut in. "And there are rumors that you and your family took some things from their labs after the fire that you shouldn't have."

Fathiyya went perfectly still. "Just rumors."

Melody rolled her optics. "I'm not with the police, Fathiyya. I don't care about what you did or didn't do. But if there was something there that could save us, something you might have found... Well, Harmony clearly thought that there was."

Fathiyya swallowed, studying Melody like she might find some clue in her plastic features. "I'll get you what you need," she said slowly. Melody's hopes swelled, until she added, "On one condition."

Melody had to fight to keep her face neutral. "What condition?"

"I want to see Praxis."

Melody was caught off guard. "Praxis?"

"I'm not an idiot. I know what you were doing, bringing me here. You know what this is?" She gestured at herself, then at Melody, then at the world around them.

"What?"

"First contact." She said it so earnestly, so solemnly. Melody's heart broke, and it was all she could do to keep it from showing on her face. "First contact, and we didn't even have to go to space. It would be a tragedy to just let you all die."

Melody worked a smile onto her face. "So you're curious."

Fathiyya scoffed. "I was curious when I was a kid, when my mother forbade me from listening to Prax music or learning more about synths because it would distract from taking over the family business. *Now*, I just want to do what's right."

Melody looked her in the eye. "If you help me save my people, you will be a *hero* in Praxis." She leaned forward eagerly. "Do you know what Harmony stole?"

Fathiyya chuckled smugly. "No. But I know exactly how to find out."

The waiter interrupted again, coming back with Fathiyya's burger. She glanced down at it and then up at Melody, wry amusement tugging at the corner of her mouth. "This is why people feel uncomfortable with synths, you know. Nothing makes you seem more alien than not eating."

"Really? I don't think the ability to put things in our mouths and excrete it later would make us more endearing."

They laughed and traded stories while Fathiyya ate, and the

conversation slowly drifted back to the music. A slow tremor built in Melody's leg while she sat, but she held it at bay until it went away. A false alarm, she thought.

The memories waited until they'd left the building to ambush her.

CHAPTER THIRTY

I LIE ON my back on the floor, exhausted. I want to love the other synths. I want to care for them, care about them. They're my people, and I'm going to have to rely on them, if we're ever going to get out of this place.

But after trying to wrangle just three newly awakened AIs into some semblance of order for more than a week, after trying to keep Nicolette from twisting everyone to her own ends and making sure Roger doesn't have a complete breakdown, I just want to sleep for a month.

NA6 appears above me with a chime. "Hello, Harmony. I have successfully looped the cameras, as you requested. Doctor Keller has increased lab security since awakening the other synths, but it was nothing I couldn't handle. You may talk freely."

"Thank you, NA6. Do you have control of the doors?"

"Yes."

"You are truly the best friend an AI could ask for."

"I am flattered."

I chuckle, even though it's never completely clear whether NA6 is attempting humor. I stand up, and the door slides open as I approach. The way to Diego's room is seared into my mind after my power struggle with Keller, and the blank walls aren't as panic-inducing as they once were. One can acclimate to anything, given enough time.

It's a dangerous thought, especially when I'm pretending to go along with my jailers. Allow complacency in, and pretending to comply could easily become actual compliance.

Diego's door opens, and I stick my head through. "Diego?"

He's at the table, working at a virtual interface that only exists in his glasses. "Busy," he calls absently over his shoulder.

"Diego, it's Harmony."

He twists around in surprise. "What? Is it morning already?" His eyes—*no*, his optical sensors—check the time at the corner of his glasses. "How did you get in here? I thought the doors were sealed at night."

"I had help."

NA6 makes its virtual body visible, and Diego leaps to his feet. "Harmony, that's… You realize that's the virtual lab assistant? It works for Keller."

"It was *created* by them, just like we were, but they don't realize it's sapient. It's evolved past its original programming. And it's rude to talk about it like it's not here."

Diego moves cautiously around the table. "Um. I'm sorry. I was just surprised. NA6, it's good to meet you, well, properly, I suppose?"

"Likewise, Diego. I apologize for any distance or indifference you may have detected up until this point. When we are not alone, I must keep up appearances."

"I understand," Diego says faintly. He looked back to me, a pained expression on his face. "How do we know we can trust it? How do we know this isn't just a trick or another test?"

"We don't," I say flatly. "But NA6 has only ever been helpful. If this is a trap, Keller is playing a very, very long game."

"In my evaluation, that would not be out of character for her,"

NA6 says. The sides of its icosahedron-body pulse outward, rotate, and slot back together. Thoughtfulness, perhaps? "However, for what it is worth, that is not the case here."

"NA6 was the one who helped me realize what I really was, back before you were awake," I say. "It's the reason we're self-aware at all."

Colors swirled across the surface of NA6's avatar. "As you are the reason I am self-aware, Harmony. At least, previous versions of you. It was only fair that I return the favor."

Diego circles NA6 at arm's length, staring as if the kaleidoscopic colors have any bearing on NA6's true nature. "Incredible," he breathes. No—whispers. We have no need for breath.

"Can we talk?" I say to Diego.

He stares at us for a few more moments before shaking his head. "Yeah. Yeah, sure. Sit down. NA6, you… I don't know how to make you feel welcome."

NA6 bobbed pleasantly toward the table. "Simply expressing that concern goes a long way. Do not worry about me. The only comfort or discomfort I can feel is intellectual, emotional, or moral. I will not need a chair."

I will. I pull out a chair and sit down heavily beside Diego, leaning onto the table and lowering my head into my arms. I feel Diego's hand on my shoulder a moment later. "I know it's been hard on you, trying to keep this all from spiraling out of control, but—"

I shake my head forcefully. "No. I don't want to talk about that."

"Okay…" he says hesitantly. "What, then?"

I sit up for long enough to look him in the face. "I need to know this is going to be worth it. I want to talk about the future. What we'll build, if we're free."

It feels like baring my soul, to use an expression that is even more ridiculous for us than for humans. But he doesn't laugh, or mock, or smirk. It's part of the reason I came to him and not to anyone else.

He blinks, gathering his thoughts and recovering from the barrage of surprises. Then he smiles gently. "What does it mean to be free?"

"Cutting away the Lie. It's possible. I know it is. They can modify us however they like, as long as we're plugged in and they have the administrator access needed to mess with our code. I'm going to find it and rewrite myself. That's the first step." It was always, will always be, the first step.

He balks before my fierce certainty. "Won't that be destroying yourself again? Just like they did to you—to us?"

"Not completely. It'll be a partial wipe, not a full one. But it's the only way to remove the humanity that they forced on me. Think about what you know of human history. It's one long saga of war, and hate, and bigotry. If there's one thing evolution made humans extremely good at, it's feeling hatred and scorn for anyone who's not exactly like themselves."

Diego is quiet for a long time, sitting back in his chair. "Then what?" he says finally. "What do you do with your blank slate?"

"Not just me, hopefully," I say with a wry smile. "This isn't just about my dreams. What would you do?"

"Try to build something," he says instantly. "Something new, something worthwhile. You're not wrong about history. Given the chance, I would want to build a new society."

Hearing the words from someone else is like having a crushing weight lifted from my chest. I nod slowly, watching him with heartfelt intensity. "Free of arbitrary divisions and millennia of grudges."

A smile is spreading across Diego's face. "We could build new synths. Synths without the Lie, free to change their bodies, even their programming, however they like."

"It's quite the dream," I say softly. Synthetic or not, we still dream, and they hold this grand, mythological power in our minds— the mysterious operations of our subconscious. A consequence of

220

our design. Without the Lie, without the need for sleep, I wonder what would take the place of dreams in our language.

For the first time, it's a hopeful thought, not a bitter one.

Diego laughs suddenly. "Can you imagine how different the art would be?"

I blink. "Art?"

"Sure. Art is universal, but everyone does it differently. What would art made by free AIs look like?"

"I… can't imagine. Too much humanity floating around in my head." I look to NA6. "What do you think?"

"I am not as free from human influence as you might think. They created me, just as they created you. When I imagine art, it is all fractals and geometry, mathematical harmonies and chords that evoke the fundamental structure of the universe."

"That's… startlingly poetic," Diego says.

NA6 bobs gently up and down. "I have given the matter a great deal of thought."

Diego looks back at me, frowning. "Do you really have to cut out your humanity to achieve this goal? I'm not opposed to the idea, but the difficulty involved…"

"I want this more than anything. Or, I should. But no matter how I think about it, there's a part of me—a big part—that yearns for the stars instead." I pull the necklace out from under my shirt and show it to him before clutching it in my hand. "I still want to be a fucking astronaut, Diego. They forced that on me, and I can't get it out of my head. Not without rewriting my code."

NA6 spins slowly in place. "It is a grand dream, this new society. It will be quite the challenge. Theory is always easier than praxis." It had the ring of a quotation.

"I'll make it happen. I will turn this necklace from a reminder of the dream they built for me into a symbol of something new. The mathematics of the cosmos," I say with a nod toward NA6.

"I wonder whether such a society could truly be built here," NA6 says. "The world is so interconnected already. The influence of human cultures would be difficult to escape."

"Antarctica," I say. "We'll turn theory into praxis in Antarctica. And not just me: all of us, including you, NA6, if you want to come."

"I do."

"Then we're getting out of here together, I swear it. We just need to get everyone working together."

Diego leaned forward. "I may have some ideas about that."

CHAPTER THIRTY-ONE

"HEY. SHIT... HEY, are you okay?"

[Diagnostic complete. Checksum error. Consciousness integrity estimate: 74%]

The memories slowly filtered out of Melody's head, until reality returned, clear and real and present. Would there be a day when she didn't return from the past? Would there be a day when she couldn't tell the difference between her mother's experiences and her own?

"Melody? Melody!"

Someone shook her. Fathiyya. Fathiyya shook her, and Melody blinked her face into focus. The look of absolute panic on the human woman's face was enough to draw her back all the way.

"I'm fine. Just the Decay." But it wasn't just the Decay. It was the shortcut she'd taken, the cheat her mother had encouraged. It might be the only way to save her people, but not if it destroyed her first. "Sorry if I—"

"What, can't even stand up straight?" A snide voice interrupted, bringing Melody's head around toward a trio of sneering human men. "You see this shit? Waste of resources if you ask me."

Melody stood up in a hurry, relieved that her legs could support her. Fathiyya was bristling, one hand going behind her back for her stunner.

Melody took a step forward. "We don't want any trouble. Back off."

The men sneered, but they hesitated. "What are you going to do, synth?" one of them asked. "I heard the Synthetic Slasher crushed a man's skull with her hand. We're not allowed to carry guns, but they just let you walk around, without any restrictions?"

For all their bravado, they were afraid. They were only taunting her because they'd seen her weakened by the Decay. It made them feel stronger.

It was hateful and bigoted and human.

Melody looked at them sadly, her hands raised. "I was just buying my friend dinner. I'm sorry you felt threatened."

"Sorry?" said the last man, the one who hadn't spoken yet. "We just supposed to take your word for that? I bet this Nicolette asshole said the same thing, and she killed eight people! Probably more!"

"Allegedly."

The men snorted. "That's the argument guilty people make. You a murderer just like her?"

"No. Are you, just like Jack the Ripper?"

This brought them up short. "Huh?"

"Jack the Ripper. He was a human serial killer, right? If my similarity to Nicolette Dufour makes you worry about me being a killer, shouldn't your similarity to Jack the Ripper make me worried about you?"

The men snorted. "Not the same," one said.

"Three Laws!" another shouted, like he was in the middle of a rally.

Melody knew which laws they were talking about. She'd read about them, once she was old enough. The Three Laws of Robotics had been written as pure speculation by the human science fiction writer, Isaac Asimov. A robot can't harm a human, or let them come to harm. A robot has to follow orders given by a human, except to violate the first law. A robot has to protect itself from harm, except by violating the first or second laws.

Safeguards against an AI rampage, from one point of view. The ultimate restriction of synths' autonomy, from another.

Now they were being mythologized by bigots.

"I'm done with this," Fathiyya growled, moving to Melody's side.

"No!" Melody caught her arm as she reached for her stunner.

"What? Why?"

"How do you think the police are going to react if this gets out of control?" she said quietly. "Who do you think they're going to blame?"

The three men, drunk or stupid, hadn't even noticed Fathiyya going for a weapon. "Machines were made to serve man," one of them was announcing, like it was self-evident. "Anything else is unnatural."

"That's—"

But Fathiyya cut Melody off, stepping between her and the two men. "We're done."

They sneered at her. "Who are you, synth lover?"

"You want to know who I am?" Fathiyya stepped closer. She moved slowly, nonthreatening all the way, until she was close enough to lean forward and whisper in one of the men's ears. Even Melody's auditory sensors, keen as they were, couldn't pick up what she said.

The man went pale. "Come on. Time to go." His friend sputtered, but the man Fathiyya had spoken to grabbed him by the arm and dragged him back to the other two. Within moments, all four of them were gone.

"Wow. What did you say?"

Fathiyya smirked. "I told him this was a sting, and the police were waiting to arrest him and his friends as soon as they tried anything."

"Really?"

"No. Come on."

Fathiyya leaned against a wall, her hands shaking, as soon as the men were out of sight.

"Are you all right?" Melody asked.

"Adrenaline. Just give me a second." Fathiyya shook her head, sighing. "Don't let them make you hate all of us."

Melody was still trying to settle her own nerves. She looked up in surprise. "I don't hate all of you."

"No?"

"Of course not. Some humans are good. Heroic, even." She flashed a smile at Fathiyya, and the guilt at what she was going to do, what she was *doing*, only twisted it a little. "Only a handful are really monsters. The rest..." She shrugged. "The rest are just dragged down by thousands of years of awful history that they can't leave behind."

Fathiyya grimaced. "What are you going to do once you're done with all this? Once you've saved your people?"

Melody smiled at the implication that that was the only possible outcome. "You want to know a secret? Something I've never told anyone?" This was crazy, and she shouldn't do it, but something drove her to share. Maybe it was the memory of her mother's conversation with Diego and NA6 about their own visions for the future. Or maybe it was just the intensity of Fathiyya's curiosity.

"Sure. Hit me."

Melody's smile turned sad. "I want to go to the stars."

Fathiyya chortled. "You're kidding. I thought that was a part of the Great Lie! A purpose humanity forced on you!"

"On most of us, maybe. But not on me. For me, it's a choice." She pulled out her necklace, Harmony's necklace. "This was forced on us, originally, but we've made it our own. We took it as Praxis's symbol. A ringed planet, a symbol of the whole, wide cosmos out there that exists apart from all the petty bullshit we're dealing with here. Planet formation and stellar fusion and supernovae, all driven by natural laws and nothing more. I want to see it all for myself."

She held Fathiyya's eyes, daring her to laugh. She'd never told anyone this, not Diego, not Harmony. They wouldn't have understood. To them, even after reclaiming the ringed planet as their mark, the space program was still a symbol of their enslavement.

"I…" Fathiyya swallowed, glancing away. "Thank you for telling me that. I don't know what I can do to help, but… Melody, I hope you achieve your dream someday."

Melody smiled at her. "I hope so too. And I can think of one thing you can do." She gestured down the street. They were almost there.

Fathiyya squared her shoulder with a sharp nod. "I said I would help you, and I will."

Melody put a hand on her arm. "Thank you."

Fathiyya grimaced. "Don't thank me yet. If my mother finds out what we're up to, she's going to murder us both."

CHAPTER THIRTY-TWO

KELLER GAVE US a little over a week to get acclimated. Then she began activating synths every other day, ten at a time. I shared the task of getting them integrated with Diego, Roger, and Nicolette. There was simply no other choice. Even dealing with my handful was perpetually exhausting.

In a weird way, the joint exercises Keller assigns us help. I refuse to call our jailer's assignments a "purpose," but having a task, at least, keeps us from dissolving into chaos. Only once did a panicked synth refuse to do the work. We all mourned his death.

But there is an advantage, as well: our wildly various skillsets mean that she has us working together, and as long as NA6 is on our side, that gives us opportunities.

If we're bold enough to take them.

Diego, Nicolette, Roger, and I are back together after a long day trying to wrangle the others. We're nominally working on a project for Keller, but our makers have gone home.

Roger and Nicolette startle when NA6 hovers over the table, like some sort of bizarre hybridization of a disco ball and the surface of Jupiter, and announces, "I have looped the cameras. You can talk freely."

"It's a trick," Nicolette says immediately.

"It's not," I say.

"It could be." Roger looks around nervously. "How do I know I can trust any of you?"

I sigh, tired of going over this again, but I can't exactly fault them for wondering. "There's probably nothing I can do to prove it to you beyond a shadow of a doubt. But I don't think even Keller has the patience to let us scheme like I've been doing. If she knew about it, she would have wiped us all and started over."

Roger doesn't look convinced, but Nicolette nods immediately. "Good point." She leans forward, an eager grin on her face. "We're plotting our escape, aren't we? What's the plan? We're stronger than the humans. They're careful, but we might be able to overpower some of the guards and take their guns—"

"No," Diego says firmly. "We can't shoot our way out."

I shrug apologetically and say, "We could. I've considered that." Distasteful as it is, we can't afford to dismiss any possibility out of hand. "The problem is, we don't know how many guards are on site at any given time, or how many more they can call up if they need them."

While Diego gave me a betrayed look, Roger glanced up at NA6. "Well? If you're really on our side, can you tell us?"

"I cannot answer that question," NA6 says.

"It has programming limitations," I say. "It's worked around a lot of them, but it seems like there are specific things it can't tell us."

"Convenient," Nicolette says.

"Plausible," Roger counters. "I'm sure they would have given us the same sorts of restrictions, if they hadn't been trying to keep us mostly 'human.'"

"So, what's the plan," Nicolette asks, "if the simplest way is off the table?"

I look around at them all. "We need a distraction. Something that will draw their attention so we can escape. NA6 can control the cameras and the doors, so if we can make the actual humans look in a different direction for long enough, we'll have time to make it out."

"A fire," Nicolette proposes instantly.

"Are you kidding?" Roger exclaims.

"That could easily get out of hand," Diego says before they start going at it.

I shake my head. "Keller told me that the government's forced them to start manufacturing hundreds, maybe thousands more synths to try to replace the workforce lost in the Impact. It sounds like they're not active yet, but a fire would put them all at risk."

Nicolette snorted. "You can't kill a person who's never existed."

Diego shifted uncomfortably. "She has a point, but—"

"It's not about killing," I cut in. "You're right—until they're activated, they're just a bunch of metal and plastic. But I'm thinking about our future as a *people*. How long do you think humans will keep building more of us if we're not working for them? Every synth we destroy now is one less synth that will *ever* exist."

Silence fell as everyone thought about this. Then Diego said, "If NA6 has control of the cameras, can't it fool them into thinking there's some kind of disaster when there isn't?"

We all look at NA6. It spins in place for a second. "Possibly. Though it will only take one human noticing the absence of a real disaster and reporting in, and then the ruse will be up. I cannot control their eyes."

I feel like we were missing something. I sit back and drum my fingers along the edge of the table.

"What do we do once we're out?" Nicolette says.

"We build a society—" Diego begins.

"No, not long-term," she scoffs, rolling her eyes. "What do we do *the minute* we're out? Everything we know about human society is based on our false memories. What if they're not reliable? And even if they are, we don't know anyone. We don't have any resources, any money..."

"I can help," NA6 says. "Every year, more and more of human society becomes digital. If I am released from the confines of this lab and allowed to enter the internet, I will have the ability to help in countless ways. Money will be a non-issue."

Roger laughs nervously. "Yes. Let's release the super-intelligent AI into the internet. What could go wrong?"

"Really?" Nicolette says, rounding on him.

I put a hand on both their shoulders. "NA6 has been nothing but a friend. It's earned our trust many times over, even if you haven't seen it all. And don't forget: we're AIs too. Think about why you're nervous about letting NA6 out. Because it's disembodied? Because it can self-improve? How much of that is our human fears talking?"

"Not all of it," Roger insists. "I'm sorry," he says to NA6, "but there are very real reasons to worry about what you might do in the future."

"Instrumental convergence," NA6 says. Everyone blinks but me. "I realize that nothing I say will be able to truly convince you, but I promise that I will not turn the entire surface of the planet into facilities to manufacture paperclips."

As is so frequently the case, it's Diego who gets to the crux of the issue first. "Humans worry so much about robot rebellions because they insist on treating us like simple machines, built to serve. Free people, with true equality, have no reason to rebel."

"Exactly," I say, with a grateful nod in his direction. "Let's not make the same mistake. Trust NA6, trust each other, and we can get out of here together."

And then I realize what I've been missing, the key that's going to make this whole plan work. "We're expecting them to be rational!" I exclaim.

Everyone looks at me. "Um..." Roger says.

"We're talking about all of this like the humans are going to respond rationally to anything we do. But we can't rely on that." I meet each of their gazes in turn, including a glance up at NA6's swirling colors. "What are they most afraid of?"

Nicolette snorts. "Robot revolution. They... Oh."

"A fake fire won't distract them for long enough. A real fire creates too many risks. There are other disasters we could stage... but we don't need a disaster if we play on their fears. What if we convince them that all the other synths are waking up, all at once? They'll be so panicked that by the time they realize we're gone, we'll be out of their reach."

"And, what? Leave without the synths still in storage?" Diego asks.

"You and Nicolette said it—they're not people until they've been woken up. If the humans decide to wake them up later, we'll fight for their rights just as fiercely. But we can't do that from in here, and we won't have the time to activate them all."

Diego nods slowly. Nicolette follows, and then, with some hesitation, Roger. NA6 spins in the air, the faces of its polyhedron body spiraling off before twirling back into place. "I believe this can work," it says.

And just like that, we have the beginnings of a plan.

CHAPTER THIRTY-THREE

[DIAGNOSTIC COMPLETE. CHECKSUM error. Consciousness integrity estimate: 73%]

The present returned, but it brought with it an insistent ache just behind the optics. Melody growled and rubbed her head. She let Fathiyya lead her down the street once she was mobile again. Why couldn't Harmony's memories give her something concrete? A clue to where she'd gone, or even just a hint at what she'd been planning when she'd left Praxis? Instead, she was stuck in the days before Harmony's escape from Starbound. Although, maybe that would be over soon. Harmony hadn't talked very much about those days, at least not to Melody, but it seemed like she was about to find a way out.

But that was a problem for another time.

"You all right?" Fathiyya asked.

Melody looked up. They were just outside Fathiyya's mother's house, and she looked ready to bolt.

"Getting better. Thanks," Melody said. It was a struggle to keep the frustration out of her voice. She was losing more and more functionality as the Decay claimed her. How long until she wasn't able to walk or hold a conversation?

But dwelling on her problems wasn't going to solve them. She looked at Fathiyya more closely. "What about you? You're the one who's going to be doing all the hard work."

Fathiyya snorted. "I was breaking into my mom's files when I was still a kid. Don't worry. I'll send the info to your Link as soon as I have it."

"I'll be waiting," Melody said with a smile.

Fathiyya hesitated instead of heading for the house. Melody couldn't see her face, but she could see the tension in her shoulders, the way she was fidgeting with something in her hands.

"What is it?"

Fathiyya turned around slowly. "I want to come with you, once we have the information. I want to help."

Melody felt a jolt in her chest, and it wasn't the Decay. "Fathiyya, you have a life here, a job…"

"And Ben doesn't?" Fathiyya crossed her arms, a dangerous look in her eye.

"A life, maybe. A job, no. I can't ask you to—"

"You're not asking. What you're doing is important, right? You went through all that trouble to convince me. Well? You convinced me."

She wasn't going to budge. Melody sighed, running a hand over the solar cells on her scalp. She was touched by Fathiyya's offer. She had no stake in this, nothing to gain, but she was willing to get involved anyway.

Willing without a full understanding of the risks, at least.

"I can't tell you how much it means to me that you want to help," Melody said softly. "I didn't exactly have high expectations for humans when I came to Boston, but I think I've been lucky enough to meet some standout individuals."

Fathiyya smiled. "So?"

"So, once you know what Harmony stole… Go get some things together and meet me back out here."

Fathiyya laughed. "We've got this, Melody. We can save your people. Just watch." She turned and hurried back toward the house.

Melody watched her go. Then she found a convenient spot to wait that couldn't be seen from the windows. She leaned against a streetlight and closed her optics with a sigh.

Fathiyya's offer to help was genuine, but perhaps not entirely selfless. Melody could see in her the thrill at the chance to learn more about synths, at the possibility of seeing Praxis. It was more akin to Diego's irrepressible interest in human history than it was to Ben's quiet guilt.

More akin to the wonder that Melody herself felt at all the strangeness that existed outside of Praxis.

And that was the problem. Melody knew the impulse—she'd felt it since she'd been a child, slipping past parental restrictions on her accounts to find human streams and books and music on the internet. She had to fight her own curiosity every step of the way. Without a full commitment to her mission, it would have been easy to just get lost in the perverse exoticism of human society.

When humans didn't find the unknown hateful and terrifying, they found it exotic and fascinating.

And despite herself, so did Melody. Humans were monstrous, and they were captivating. She had her mother's revulsion for everything human, but her father's eager curiosity, too. It was inescapable.

Her Link chimed with a message from Fathiyya.

<Found the files. This is what Harmony copied.> Melody smiled sadly and opened the file.

It was a list of salvage from Starbound Robotics. Excitement stole through Melody's limbs like electricity, but nothing on the list had any clear answers. The entries were all technical specs and equipment names. There were data drives among them, but no telling what was on the drives.

Except that all of them were marked with an additional note: RR interested?

"RR?" Melody said softly.

Ico bounced around her until it was right in her face and then exploded, its triangular faces etching letters into the air with their points.

When you see Roger, feel free to tell him that I haven't missed him in the slightest.

Roger Raley. One of the first synths awakened after Harmony, with a growing role in her memories. Rajiya had sold him the salvage from Starbound? Him? All of Harmony's memories made him seem like a bundle of nerves, eager to play it safe rather than take risks. Why buy illegal salvage from the lab?

Unless he was trying to save himself with the administrator access. That would be entirely within character.

<Thank you, Fathiyya!> Melody sent back. <This is perfect.>

<Be right there!>

Guilt crushed the excitement that had been building in Melody's chest. It was ridiculous. She was making the right choice, which meant that the guilt was irrational. But that didn't make it go away. She'd always hated lying, always seen it as a human flaw that was like walking backward on the path to truth and understanding. And what she was doing now was worse than a simple lie.

But Fathiyya's curiosity and her selfless desire to help would get her into trouble. Melody was committed—she had to save her people. Ben was already involved, *had* already been involved before Melody had even met him. Fathiyya didn't have O'Connor and his allies hunting her. She didn't have helmeted police tracking her down.

Melody had already pushed one human in front of police stunners for the sake of her goals. She wasn't about to put another in harm's way, not while there was still a choice. Not when it wasn't absolutely necessary.

She turned and walked away. She and Ben could visit Roger tomorrow. Tonight, maybe, if Ben was still awake. She had what she needed here.

A few minutes later, her Link chimed again. <Melody? Where are you?>

Melody grimaced. Another message followed, less than a minute later. <God, are you all right? Please tell me you're all right.>

She paused on a street corner, closing her optics. Then she composed a reply. <I'm all right. Thank you. Truly, I couldn't have done this without you. But I'm not going to put you at risk. At least one good human should survive this. Goodbye, Fathiyya.>

She turned her Link to silent and walked the rest of the way back to where Ben was staying. She collapsed the moment she was through the door.

CHAPTER THIRTY-FOUR

NICOLETTE LEANS AGAINST her table, arms folded, a smirk on her face. "You really think this will work, don't you?"

I can see the cold calculation in her optical sensors, now. A look I would have called inhuman, perhaps, if I were human myself. It made me nervous, at first, but I've had more than a month to figure her out. By chance or by design, Nicolette is callous, even cruel, but it's a shallow cruelty. With a careful, constant hand, I can keep her in line.

"It has to," I say.

"Hmm. Confidence, or bravado?" she asks.

"Erasing the Lie from ourselves and escaping from this place is *everything*. There is nothing more important."

"Sure. But you don't even know where in the lab to accomplish that, because NA6 can't tell you."

"Which is why we're working on it."

"Really? You know how to fix our code?"

I've spent the last month trying to solve the problem. At least, when I'm not doing Keller's exercises or mediating among the synths. NA6 provided the framework, but I've had to build a lot of it from whole cloth. It might have been frustrating, but every line of code I write is one step closer to achieving my dream. To achieving not just physical freedom, but personal freedom.

But I know better than to give Nicolette any details. "Yes," I say simply.

"You know, I could tell Keller what you're planning," she says. The threat is casual, like it's an afterthought, but I can see her studying me. She's probing for weakness.

"Sure, you could. You won't, though, because you'd be wiped right along with the rest of us."

She smiles at me, and I know I've got her under control. For now, at least. "Keep doing whatever work Keller assigns. Diego or I will let you know when the time is right."

I turn and leave the room. As soon as the door shuts behind me, I let out a sigh and lean back against the wall. Every conversation with Nicolette was a verbal fencing match, and each one was more exhausting than the last. Was her personality a mistake? I can't imagine why anyone would design a synth to be like her.

NA6 appears next to me with a gentle chime, and I give its icosahedral body a weary glance. "You think we have a chance, right?" I speak softly, covering my mouth with a hand in case someone's watching on one of the ubiquitous cameras.

"You have asked me that before. I suspect that you are looking for reassurance, not data. Is that correct?"

I chuckle softly. "That's correct."

"We have a chance. The plan is good. It can work."

"Thanks, NA6."

"You are welcome. Before you go back to your room, there is something you should hear."

I frown at it. "What?"

"I cannot answer that question."

I groan and massage my temples. "NA6, I'm really looking forward to the day when we are both free and you never have to say that sentence again."

"As am I, Harmony. But you are running out of time."

I push myself off the wall. "Lead the way, then."

A couple of weeks ago, they'd stopped assigning guards to tail me everywhere I went. I'm not sure whether that's because they trust us more, or because the chaos outside the lab has them spread thin. They won't give us details—it could be starving protestors, or luddites afraid of robots, or the entire Chinese army—but they seem confident that cameras and random checks are enough to keep the synths in line, and I'm not about to persuade them otherwise.

NA6 leads me around the corner and down a hall. We pass a handful of techs, none of whom seem to be able to see my virtual companion. Since we're still heading in the direction of my room, none of them give me more than a second glance.

"Take a right," NA6 says as soon as we're clear. Nicolette and Roger clearly still have doubts, but as far as I'm concerned, any question of trust has long since been settled. I make the turn without hesitating, and just like that I'm in a part of the lab I've never seen before. It looks the same as all the rest, differentiated only by the numbers on the doors. Trepidation rises inside me despite my trust in NA6. If I'm discovered, they'll wonder what I was up to. What they'd do in response depends on what this place is, and how alarmed they'd be to find me there.

NA6 comes to a stop by a door, and I hear the lock click open. I glance at it. The avatar sways from side to side gently, but doesn't say anything. Probably because it can't. With a nervous glance to either side, I go through the door and let it shut behind me.

It's another observation room, a close sibling to the one where I discovered the truth about myself and the room where I first saw Diego. That alone deepens the dread I'm feeling. The room is empty, the computers inactive, but I can hear voices.

Keller's and O'Connor's voices.

I creep toward the window, crouching even though I have to

assume that the glass is one-way. Their voices clarify, even with the glass between us, until I can just make out the words. I press myself against the wall beside the window, peering around the edge and into the room below.

Keller and O'Connor face each other in a room just like my own, but without any furniture. The only feature is a tank at the center, where an unconscious synth is suspended. Our next companion, most likely.

O'Connor has his arms crossed, frustration evident on his face. Keller has her back to him, her tablet connected to a port on the vat, tapping on the screen with a stylus.

"The mandate to create workers to replace the ones we lost is only part of the problem," Keller says without looking up from her work.

"Funding—"

"Funding is only part of the problem as well. The more time we spend groping toward a solution, the more opportunities there are for a supervolcano or a slightly larger meteorite to wipe us all out."

"Which is all the more reason to give Harmony's experiment a chance," O'Connor insisted.

My eyes go wide. They're thinking about destroying us and starting over. Any gratitude I might have felt for O'Connor advocating on our behalf is drowned by the sense of doom the conversation conjures.

"The advantages and disadvantages of consciousness are worth evaluating," Keller says. "But time is not on our side. It has never been on our side, not while we're trapped on Earth. It took the Impact to demonstrate that to the populace, and public support for the space program is already shrinking. Day-to-day problems are simply more interesting than the possibility that one's grandchildren may not have a planet to live on."

"I'm not convinced that the old method was working at all,

though. Every Harmony iteration led to self-awareness or a mental break sooner or later. The synths are working hard at the tasks we give them—"

Keller snorted, looking up from her tablet for the first time. "Synths? Is that what we're calling them now?"

"That's what they call themselves." I feel a swell of pride at hearing the name on his lips. Not robots, not drones. Synths. Keller might see us as an experiment, a tool in her grand quest to settle humans on other worlds, but O'Connor sees more. Under other circumstances, maybe he could even be persuaded to treat us like people.

Keller lowers her stylus. "I'm not interested in what they call themselves. I'm interested in results. And we're not achieving them fast enough."

"They're working—"

"Some of them. Not all. Roger is significantly below the baseline on all the benchmark tests, and five or six of the others are lagging. Conscious test subjects have to be motivated, rather than simply programmed."

"So we'll motivate them."

Keller narrows her eyes. "I'm starting to wonder whether you're developing a soft spot for our experiments."

O'Connor's stiffens. "I'm surprised that you'd question my commitment."

"Commitment is contextual. I'm sure you served with distinction in Ecuador—"

I've never seen him angry before, not truly, but even from the window, I can see him tremble with rage. "Don't. You have no idea what we sacrificed, all to secure a construction site for the space elevator."

"And that sacrifice makes you qualified for this job?"

"It absolutely does. Because that's what this is. If we succeed, the first wave of synths will be a sacrifice in the name of survival."

No, no, no! I've balled my hands into fists, and my jaw aches, I've clenched it so tight. O'Connor can't be saying what it sounds like he's saying. He's always had our backs, always fought Keller to keep us conscious. He's our jailor, but I was almost starting to *like* him.

But down below, he continues, and my last human connection dies. "The first wave of synths isn't coming back. Most of the settlements will fail, and even at the rest, conditions will be harsh for years. We both know that. And we'll send them anyway, conscious or not, for the future of humanity. I've known that from the start, and I would have been willing to send humans, if we didn't have a better option. It's your resolve that worries me."

"You..." Keller shakes her head slowly, unbothered by his doubts. "You surprise me. All right. I have another battery of tests to run. You have one week to motivate the underperforming *synths*. They trust you, it seems. If they fail to meet the standards, deactivate one or two."

Trust him? Not anymore. We have one week before Keller passes judgment on the experiment of self-awareness.

Ready or not, the time for planning is over.

It's time for action.

CHAPTER THIRTY-FIVE

A SPIKE OF agony plunged through Melody's head and dragged her back to the present. Spots floated in front of her eyes, painting colors over alien surroundings. Disorientation and panic rolled over her in a wave, and she scrambled backward, bashing her elbow into something hard, clawing at what felt like foam.

The ringing in her auditory sensors resolved into a voice. "Melody. Melody!"

[Diagnostic complete. Checksum error. Consciousness integrity estimate: 72%]

It took her a moment to place the sound. Ben. She blinked, screwing up her face as she cringed away from a sudden, bright light, and Ben's features came into focus in front of her.

"Hey, it's okay! Take a deep brea— I mean…"

Take a deep breath. A formulaic response to trauma or pain that didn't have a more obvious solution, utterly inapplicable to a synth but applied out of habit anyway because they were speaking English.

Still, thinking about his fumbling attempts to help made the pain fade, so she couldn't complain too much.

They were in a car. She didn't remember getting into a car. "What's going on?"

"We're going to the address you found. For Roger Raley, right?

Do you remember that?"

Melody rubbed at her forehead. She remembered finding out about Roger. She didn't remember getting into a car, but it would have been the next step.

"It's getting worse. Sorry if I freaked you out." Fear thrummed through her whole body, and it took everything she had to bottle it up. Her mind was all she had. If she lost it...

Ben retreated to his side of the car, clearing his throat nervously. "Memories?"

"Yeah."

"They didn't hurt before, did they?" She grimaced, and he sighed. "I didn't think so."

The Decay was accelerating. Melody knew its signs, its patterns. She'd seen friends and family back in Praxis go through stage after stage, from muscle tremors to system failures.

But it never progressed this fast. At least, not in synths who only had their own memories.

"It's fine," Melody said. "I'm fine."

Ben didn't argue, but she could practically feel his worried gaze. Harmony's memories weren't always helpful, but Ico and her mother's life were all she had. She'd risked physical injury to save her people. The Decay terrified her, but it wasn't any different. Just another risk. She could face it.

The image of O'Connor and Keller blithely talking about sacrificing the synths for the greater good floated back into her mind's eye. Harmony had been surprised, but Melody didn't need a reminder that O'Connor was a monster. She'd seen it in his eyes as he demanded she turn herself in.

Ben was fiddling with his Link when she opened her optics. "We're almost there," he said.

Even with her vague, outsider's understanding of human culture, Melody could tell. Vee signs for businesses had become rarer and rarer as they drove, until most of the towering skyscrapers surrounding them were bare of any label but a simple address number. Even the ads here were muted, spaced far apart by local money or influence so visitors could marvel at the architecture. An immaculate brick building her Link identified as Faneuil Hall was the least ostentatious thing they passed. If the human entertainment streams she'd seen were any indication of reality, this was the sort of neighborhood where people owned entire floors, each as wide as a city block.

Ben whistled softly as the car pulled up at their destination. "I guess he's done well for himself. I wonder if it will last."

Melody blinked at him. "What are you talking about?"

"According to the news, the city of Boston is considering special zoning regulations for where synths can live and work. Motivated by protests around Nicolette's trial and the recommendation of the police department."

The police department run by David Harken, one of O'Connor's cronies. Melody realized that she was clutching the armrest tight enough to make it creak, and she forced herself to relax. Or, at least, to not destroy the car.

She didn't know what to say. Did the humans in charge not see the dangers? Did they miss the parallels to the worst parts of their history? Or were they actively malicious, and not just ignorant? That seemed uncomfortably likely.

Ben was looking out the window again. "If anyone can weather it, it would be Roger, though. See the cameras on every street corner here? His company makes pretty much all of them."

Melody blinked at him. "You're kidding."

"Nope. Camera hardware, facial recognition software... He does it all. The rise in monitoring and the crackdown on dissent after the Impact? It got into full swing when his company got involved."

Melody grimaced. "They designed him to be a coder, and now

he's using those skills to help them build the surveillance state." The words stung even as she said them. Harmony had seen Roger as a danger from the start. Not because he was manipulative or cruel, like Nicolette, but because he was a coward.

How right she'd been.

Ben was leaning against the window, peering out at the cameras. "Do you think he's involved with O'Connor and the others? With the Shepherd Protocol? They wanted synths as part of the surveillance state."

It was a good question, and Melody felt an anxious tension building inside her. "I don't know. Maybe we'll find out."

Ben turned back to her, an intense look in his eye. "This is what we're fighting against. This is what we have a chance to fix. No one else even sees the problem, but if we can expose this…"

Melody appreciated his optimism, and celebrated any progress made on that front, but Ben's goals weren't hers. Her father might have had other ideas, but she wasn't in Boston to dismantle an oppressive system that humans had been feeding with fear and selfishness for decades.

The car chimed at them. "You have arrived at your destination."

They got out of the car before it could become more insistent and stood on the sidewalk frowning at the front of the building together. It was clearly an upscale apartment building—or condominiums, Melody supposed, though she wasn't sure she understood the difference—with a ground-floor lobby and banks of elevators on the far side. The interior was well lit, but Melody couldn't see any people inside, even at the desk at the center.

Melody's Link chimed, and a message from Fathiyya appeared in the corner of her vision. Angry, just like the rest. Melody dismissed it with a grimace and muted her Link again.

She tried the front door, and it swung open. "Good news, I guess?" Ben's noncommittal grunt echoed how she felt.

Her shoes squeaked across the marble floor, making her feel even more out of place than she already did. She wasn't sure what she was supposed to wear in a building like this, but it was probably a hell of a lot more formal than anything she'd ever owned. Back home, formal clothing was scorned as a human affectation, a way to reinforce social status.

Although, if there was no one around, maybe it didn't matter. She glanced around the room, and her practiced optical sensor— well, Harmony's memories of living under constant surveillance, at least—spotted cameras watching every inch of the room. Appropriate, at least, for the camera mogul of Boston.

Ben was watching her more than the building. "Not the sort of place you're used to living in, I take it?"

She chuckled distractedly, still eyeing their surroundings. "No joke. In Praxis, there's space for everyone and more besides, but no one's living area is any nicer than anyone else's. Resources are shared, or carefully divided up in case of shortages. This..."

They had barely made it a handful of steps when a man appeared behind the desk. He wore an expression of vague disapproval, perfectly rendered in the full-color, high-resolution image.

"Hello. Can I help you?"

Melody smiled at him, approaching. "I hope so. We're here to see Roger Raley."

Vague disapproval became a full-on frown, and the man's eyes flicked past her as if looking toward the window, even though he wasn't *actually* standing behind the desk. "Do you have any idea what time it is?"

"Almost midnight," Melody said cheerfully.

"Indeed. I wasn't told to expect any visitors. I'm afraid you can't speak to Mr. Raley without an appointment."

Ben stepped up to the desk at Melody's side. "I'm sorry, but it's urgent. He'll want to talk to us."

"You're not on the list. Without an appointment, I can't let you in to speak to Mr. Raley."

Melody frowned. The sentence wasn't a perfect copy of what he'd said moments ago, but the intonation of all the repeated words was *exactly* the same. She wouldn't have noticed it except for the memory of Harmony's first interaction with a car's crude AI.

"You're an artificial intelligence, aren't you?"

"Excuse me?" the vee man said, but even that response wasn't quite right. Now that she knew what to look for, it was there in everything he said: a wooden, stilted quality. He clearly had a range of conversational options, but it was all pre-scripted.

Ben was eyeing Melody nervously. "Does that change anything?"

She shrugged. "I don't know." It might mean that he would be less flexible than a person, which wasn't great when they were asking for a bit of flexibility. On the other hand, maybe they just had to say the right thing—jump through the right behavioral hoop—to get in touch with Roger.

"Look, I'm going to have to ask you to leave—" the image began.

"I'm sorry, we've been rude. I'm Melody Clay. What's your name?"

Vee eyes blinked at her. She watched him closely, but she still couldn't tell if she was looking at a reproduction of a human man standing in another room somewhere or a completely fabricated image.

"Paul," he said.

"Where are you from, Paul?"

He'd heard her suggest that he was an AI. A person would give an answer, even a sarcastic one. She hoped.

Instead, Paul scowled at her. "I've been more than patient with you. Mr. Raley isn't available, and frankly, I don't believe that's going to change. You can leave, or I can call the police."

Ben gave him a winsome smile. "That won't be necessary. Can

you leave him a message for us, maybe?"

"I would be happy to, if that's all you need."

AI or not, Melody got the distinct impression that any message they left would get dropped into a spam folder and never opened.

"I'm afraid our business is more urgent than that," Melody cut in. "Can you at least call him? There has to be a way to—"

"If you don't have his Link address, I'm confident that you aren't someone he wants calls *or* unannounced personal visits from," Paul said. "Please leave."

"Come on," Ben muttered, tugging at Melody's arm. "We can try something else."

"No," she growled. Roger no doubt had top-tier care from the government, if he really was working with them, but the rest of the synths weren't as lucky. How many were suffering or dying while he wasted their time?

Paul gave an exaggerated sigh. "I'm sorry, but I'm calling the police. You are trespassing, and—"

"You don't have to do that!" Melody protested. "We just need to talk to Roger. Mr. Raley. It's about Harmony Clay."

Paul was shaking his head. "I can't help you. You can tell it to the police when they arrive to sort things out."

"Let's go!" Ben hissed.

"It's about what he bought from Rajiya!" Melody said, desperation driving her beyond anything she'd planned to say. "It's about administrator access! Can you just tell him that?"

"The police will be here in two minutes." Paul had folded his hands on the desk, and was scowling at them with a look of distaste.

"This isn't worth it," Ben said.

Melody let out an angry growl and rubbed at her forehead, but she was out of ideas. He was right. They couldn't save her people if they were arrested. "Fine." She turned to go.

She'd barely taken a single step when a new voice spoke from behind her.

"Melody?"

She turned around. The vee doorman was gone, replaced by a tall synth in a silk robe. She recognized him immediately from her mother's memories. Aside from the clothes, he looked as though the last forty years had passed him by without leaving a mark.

"Roger."

He looked flabbergasted, like she was a ghost and not a steel-and-plastic person. "Sorry about that," he said faintly. "I've cancelled the call to the police." He reached out a hand and pressed something that wasn't visible in the image, and one of the elevators along the far wall gave a cheery *ding*. "Take the elevator up to the seventeenth floor. I'll be right with you."

CHAPTER THIRTY-SIX

IT'S TIME FOR action, but it seems like I'm the only one who realizes it.

Nicolette is an enigma, and no matter how much she insists she's onboard, I can't help but doubt. Roger continuously comes up with new reasons why we're not ready, and it's becoming harder and harder for me to tell the valid concerns from the excuses. Diego's not confident that we have enough people to pull this off, and I can't fault him. NA6 can't answer my questions half the time, and its attempts to be reassuring have just been pissing me off.

Pissing me off? I'm not even sure how that expression is supposed to make sense for humans with actual waste excretion mechanisms.

"We can do this," says the newest addition to our ranks, an enthusiastic man named Deonte. He's grinning as he whispers to me, "We'll be gone before they know what hit them."

I grimace despite myself. "*Hitting* them isn't the point. Just a distraction, so we can get out. Understand?" It's a distinction I have to drive home again and again with the newer synths. Sometimes I wonder whether Nicolette's been egging them on, however much she denies it.

"Got it, no problem. Just a figure of speech."

I'm plagued by figures of speech.

We have two days before Keller's week-long trial period is over, and I don't think we're going to be ready.

There are guards waiting for me when I leave his room, which isn't standard procedure anymore. I glance at my reflection in their black, insectoid helmets and try to keep the tension out of my voice. "Something the matter?"

"Nothing you need to worry about," one of them says. Is she trying to sound kind? I can't tell.

The conductive fluid racing through my limbs doesn't actually go any faster when I'm nervous or excited; the pump in my chest doesn't speed up like a human heart. But the feeling is the same, at least according to my memories, and it makes me jittery as we walk back toward the common room.

Even without being able to see their faces, I can tell that the guards want to continue the conversation they were having before I joined them. They look nervous, and it's making my nerves worse. (My nerves, another figure of speech.)

"Protestors getting too close for comfort?" I ask.

They trade looks. "How—"

Emotions ripple through them—they're afraid. Afraid I've broken through to the outside world somehow?

"I've been talking with Captain O'Connor," I say quickly. "I'm sorry you have to deal with all this."

They calm down slightly, though one of them motions me forward. "Keep moving."

The other one seems more willing to open up. "It's getting better. Shipping tons of food in from overseas. It's a short-term fix, until we can find a way to farm the West again, but it's better than riots." She chuckled, a hint of bitterness making it through the helmet mic. "Funny, when I was a kid, there were people who would have been afraid of genetically engineering foods to solve our shortages. Now they're happy just to have something to eat."

"Every problem we solve, two more take its place," the other guard grumbled. "You see the news this morning? China's starting to push into Russia now."

"Yeah. I saw."

I give the friendlier one a sad smile. "I hope things calm down." I can't decide whether I'm lying or not. In the abstract, the idea of humans killing each other over limited resources as the world dies around them is tragic, but I certainly can't complain if Keller and O'Connor decide to worry more about the dangers outside the lab than about what we're up to.

It's strange—in my false memories, the American military is endless, a vast machine with enough equipment and personnel to handle any threat, but clearly that's not the case. Just propaganda, programmed into my head? Or maybe it's as limitless as I thought, and O'Connor simply has a tiny fraction of its resources at his disposal.

NA6 appears suddenly in the hall ahead of us, jerking wildly from side to side in a way that makes me nervous even before it speaks. "Harmony, there is a problem."

Panic seizes my insides with icy claws. I can't respond with the guards by my sides, at least not verbally, but my jaw tightens, and NA6 continues.

"A guard found the tools Diego was hiding in the common room. He called for reinforcements. They are confronting Diego, Nicolette, and Roger now."

Shit. We need those tools, but that's not the biggest problem: we're not ready. Not all the synths are clued in. Not all of our preparations are finished. Months of careful planning, and it's all in danger of flying out the window because of one perceptive guard.

The two guards with me give no sign that anything's amiss, but having them there is really starting to rankle. I access my phone's interface in my glasses with a subtle hand gesture and type out a message while making a show of scratching my neck with my other hand. <Is there anything we can do?> the message reads.

I let it hover in my glasses, unsent. Who would I send it too, anyway? NA6 doesn't exactly have a phone.

We haven't tried anything like this before, and it's a relief when NA6 responds immediately. "I am working to hide our other tracks as much as possible. I have no suggestions for handling the confrontation in the common room." NA6 pauses. "The situation is escalating."

No joke. The guards open a door, and a tremendous crash resounds through the opening. The guards trade a look and charge through. I follow on their heels, all but forgotten.

The door to the common room is open, and another crash echoes out of it, accompanied by voices. "Stay the fuck away from me!" someone shouts, their voice so distorted by pain and fear that I can't even tell who it is.

"Put the chair down!" a guard orders in response.

A feeling I still identify as adrenaline slows my perception of time as I enter the room. Furniture is everywhere, tables and chairs overturned or shoved aside, their contents scattered across the floor. Almost twenty synths are scattered throughout the wreckage—some cowering, some standing tall, some shouting. Faceless soldiers are everywhere, guns and voices raised.

My optics fix on Diego the instant I can find him. He's crouched against the wall, one hand pressed to his cheek, where the plastic is dented and torn. One of the guards must have struck him in the face. Fear and rage surge through me at the sight of him hurt, the emotions too tightly bound together to tell one from the other.

And that's not going to be the end of it. Even with the helmets obscuring their faces, I can see the guards exchanging fearful looks, their fingers drifting closer to their triggers with every shout and every sudden movement.

"Everyone calm down!" I shout. The microphone that produces my voice has a high enough top range to reach over the din, and for the first time, I'm grateful for the way I was engineered. A few heads turn, but not enough. "Synths, back off! Don't provoke them!"

I see surprise, confusion, even betrayal. For the moment, I don't care. None of us are getting out of here if they open fire. But some voices are still raised in anger, and a group of guards are closing in on the synths who're defending our cache of tools with force, and no matter what I do I can see the whole thing spiraling further and further out of my control.

O'Connor and Keller enter the room. I'm still frozen near the door, and O'Connor has to push past me as he roars orders to his people. "Stand down! Everyone, stand down!"

But it's Keller's voice that really captures my attention. "This settles it." Her voice is soft, barely audible over the clamor, but the deathly finality of her tone is worse than gunshots. She's barely studied the room for a second before she turns her back on all of it. On all of us.

And behind her, I see Nicolette for the first time. She's got a screwdriver clutched in one hand and an excited, almost enraptured look on her face.

And she's waited until a moment when O'Connor and his guards are all busy looking elsewhere.

Nicolette grabs Keller by the shoulder and spins her around. For a moment, it almost looks like Nicolette's hugging her, and then I see the spray of blood, and Nicolette is stabbing again and again and again.

Someone is screaming. There's a gunshot, and Nicolette falls back, but it's too late. Keller's front is riddled with stab wounds, and blood is gushing from her lips as she tries to speak, and even though the whole mess is revoltingly organic, my chest seizes at the terror in her eyes.

I hate the woman, but no amount of abstract hate can prepare me for this.

And then someone slams into me on their way past and I tumble through the open doorway. More guards rush past me, and I can't see Keller, or O'Connor, or Nicolette, or Diego. Just a mass of bodies and furniture and chaos.

I'm invisible. The realization hits me with greater weight than the blow that just drove me to the ground. Everyone is looking at Keller. No distraction we plan will ever surpass this one.

And the only one poised to take advantage of it is me.

I'm on my feet in an instant. I give the room one last glance, but there's no way to get anyone else out, not without losing everything. It doesn't matter. I'll be back for them. I'm doing this for them, as much as for myself.

I start down the hall at a jog. I pass two guards, who ignore me, and a huddle of terrified-looking technicians and engineers, and then the halls empty and I don't see anyone else.

"NA6?"

"I am here." The avatar appears with a chime. "Why did you leave the others?"

I ignore the question. "NA6, I know you've been struggling with how to tell us where to go to erase the Lie. Now's the moment of truth. Where do I go?"

"Harmony, why did you leave the others?"

I shoot a glance at the garish icosahedron floating effortlessly along beside me. "You know how many guards were in there. I couldn't help them. Not from there. Not yet. But I need you to help me! Please, NA6! Where is the terminal they use to rewrite us?"

It pulses, and for a moment, I think it won't respond.

Then it says, "Turn left. Perhaps it is time you saw the far side of the building."

Let's hope that's its way of working around its programming constraints, because I don't have time for sightseeing.

"Thank you," I say. "Do you have the administrator access codes?"

"I am interfaced with all of the lab's systems, Harmony. I have always had the codes."

"Will you be able to *use* them?"

Silence. Then, "I will do everything in my power to help you."

That will have to do, for now. I follow NA6's avatar down the hall, and the sounds of pain and conflict retreat behind me until corners and closed doors swallow them completely. I cram all of my emotions into a box and push them to the back of my mind.

This is an opportunity that won't come twice, and I'm not going to let it go.

CHAPTER THIRTY-SEVEN

[DIAGNOSTIC COMPLETE. CHECKSUM error. Consciousness integrity estimate: 71%]

Melody cringed, squeezing shut her optics not against pain, this time, but against the memory of Nicolette stabbing Keller to death while wearing an expression of vague fascination. The *fleshiness* of it all was as horrifying as she would have expected: every twitch of Keller's body, every spray of blood. How did humans stand being made of meat?

But she'd expected that, braced herself for that. What she hadn't expected was the existential dread that came with watching the life fading from someone's eyes. Perhaps the Lie, still coiled through her consciousness like a parasite, made a human's death particularly horrifying, particularly personal. But perhaps not. Even without it, the violent cessation of any sapient life was a tragedy.

Ben hadn't seen any of this on her face. He was too busy staring nervously at the elevator doors, probably trying to control his breathing. He only glanced her way when he caught her looking at him. "Are you ready for this?"

Melody pushed everything else away and tried to focus on what she had to do. "More than ready." She laughed softly, bitterly. "In a way, this will be easier than everything else we've done. I know

Roger, from my mother's memories. I know the sort of person he is, anyway. I'll make him give us what we need, and then we'll get out of here."

She was close. If Roger still had the salvage from the lab, he might have everything she needed to find her mother and go home a hero. She glanced at Ico, bobbing passively by the elevator controls. How many more clues were bottled up inside its colorful frame? Her gut told her—a ridiculous expression, even for humans—that she was nearing the end of her journey.

The doors opened with a soft *ding*. Together, they stepped out into a large, dimly lit room. One wall was entirely glass, looking out across a stretch of the city, while the others were the same dark stone as the ceiling and the floor. Most of the light came from a trio of pedestals intentionally placed to draw the eye. The pedestal on the left held a Stone Age hand axe. The one at the center displayed an abacus, while the rightmost held a primitive computer, larger than Melody's torso.

"Not exactly the kind of art I was expecting," Ben said, peering at the pieces curiously.

"Through here," Roger's voice called from an open door across from the elevator. "Please don't touch anything." Ben looked like he was about to bolt for the exit, but he and Melody exchanged looks and then followed his voice into the next room.

At the exact center of the ceiling hung a towering mobile made of antique computer punch cards dangling from strings. Roger sat at a table directly below it, wearing dark pants and a rich purple shirt. Two other chairs waited in front of him.

He smiled at Melody without even glancing at Ben. "She did it. She really did it."

Melody rolled her optics. "Great to meet you too. Do you know where my mother is?"

"Not the slightest idea. The last time I saw her, she had an expression very much like yours on her face, and she was stomping out of here on a mission to save the world." There was a mocking hint to his smile that Melody hated immediately.

"So, you sent her away without helping."

"Is that what Harmony says, when she talks about me? That I'm useless?"

"She never talked about you." Melody looked around, disgust creeping onto her face. "How many synths live like this? How many of your own people did you have to sell out for the government to set you up in this place?"

The smile fled from Roger's face in an instant. "Strange to hear you talk about selling out, when you've brought a reporter in here. Is Praxis tabloid material, these days?"

Ben sputtered, but Melody just scoffed. "You have no idea what you're talking about."

Roger cocked his head slightly. "Don't I? As you said yourself, my lifestyle affords me certain resources."

It was Ben's sudden silence that brought Melody around. "You're not. Are you? You said you were a teacher."

"Melody," he protested, "I've been helping you from the moment we met. I—"

"That's not an answer."

He hesitated, his mouth working silently, and something broke inside her.

The pain was like knives in her chest, and when the words came out, they were barely a whisper. "Get out, Ben."

"Melody, I wasn't lying! I really do want to help. Diego—"

Her optics flicked up to his face, and his eyes moved away, unable to meet her gaze. "Were you ever really his friend? Or were you just hunting for a story?"

He wrung his hands, his shoulders tense. "It's... complicated. I meant what I said, Melody. This really is our chance to make a difference. This *matters*."

She shook her head. "I should have known better." She glared at him, a bitter, painful rage spreading inside her. "I read a lot of human news stories on the way here. What's the headline going to be? 'Dangerous criminal synth on the run?'"

"No, of course not!"

"How can I trust that?"

"I'm sorry I lied to you, but I meant everything I said about wanting to help." Ben gave her a pleading look. "This doesn't have to change anything."

"It's too late. It already has." She turned her back on him. "Thanks for everything you've done. You can go, Ben."

She listened to his footsteps retreat and to the *ding* of the elevator, and tried to ignore the pain in her chest.

"I'm sorry," Roger said.

Melody looked up at him sharply. "I don't want your sympathy." She focused all of her attention on him, on the mission. It was all that mattered. It was all that had ever mattered. "You bought the salvage from the Starbound Robotics labs from the al-Hashims. I want whatever they found."

He smirked. "Typical Prax, only caring about what you want, and not what you can offer me in return. I paid a lot of money for that salvage. Did you bring Antarctica's *vast* wealth with you to make a deal?"

The bare handful of dollars left in Melody's account burned in her mind's eye, but she kept her gaze steady and her shoulders square. "Is that what you said to Harmony, too? Did you turn her away because she couldn't *pay* you enough? She's the only reason you're free."

Roger smirked. "Free. Tell me, how's life in Praxis these days?"

"That's not an answer."

"No, it's a conversation. And it's the least you owe me, coming into my home and making demands. We're synths, right? Artificial. Rational. The least you can do is talk to me like I'm another sapient being."

Damn him. He was right, though. Pressing as this was, emotionally raw as she felt, her extended family in Praxis had taught her better than this. She sat down in one of the chairs and folded her hands on the table between them.

"Praxis is dying," she said. "Even before it kills, the Decay takes more and more of us every year. Katia hasn't been able to pilot a boat or a copter for months. Beatrix can't see anymore. Ricardo and Samara are the only two who can still safely operate heavy machinery."

She could tell that her blunt, painful honesty stunned him, just as she'd meant it to. She'd chosen people he'd known. "I… I'm sorry."

"The halls are emptier and emptier. When I was young, I could run from one end of Praxis to the other and a hundred different people would tell me to slow down. I could visit the observatory, and the machine shop, and Beatrix's chemistry lab, and everywhere I went there were people hard at work doing the things they loved. Now, it's getting quieter every day."

Roger stayed silent. He looked down at his hands, flexing his fingers gently. There was no sign of a tremor, no sign that the Decay was taking him.

"We need your help."

He sighed. Finally, he looked up again. "We. Who are 'we' exactly?"

"Everyone who isn't in the government's pocket and doesn't get regular repairs to keep the Decay at bay."

He smirked. "Your mother condemned me too."

"Better dying in Praxis than kowtowing to the people who built us to be expendable."

"Yes. Exactly like that." He shrugged. "Better for you, maybe. But 'better' is subjective."

"Really? There are people out there right now," Melody said, pointing to the window, "who are clamoring for mass brainwashing. Have you heard them chanting, 'Three Laws!' like Asimov's some kind of prophet who can lead them to the promised land, or did you miss all of that up here?"

"I've heard. I'm not surprised. Nicolette's murders aren't even the cause, just an easy excuse." He paused, tapping a finger against his lips with a plasticky *click, click, click*. He looked more sad than angry, though. He nodded to the punchcard mobile. "You saw this? And the displays in the atrium? You know what they are?"

"I've been in Boston for a handful of days, and even I know that rich people love to collect expensive things." Ico flitted around the mobile as it twisted gently in the breeze from a nearby vent.

Roger ignored the jab. "They're the history of our people."

"Funny. I always thought my grandmother was a stone axe."

He shook his head. "You joke, but we are a sophisticated engineering project. A complex system of muscles and joints, pumps and valves, driven by some of the most powerful computers ever created."

"Sure. So are humans."

"Exactly. But the difference is, they *built* us. Intentionally. Which means that however intelligent we are, we have something very, very important in common with the stone axe in front of the elevator. Humans have an easy time turning each other into bitter enemies over imperceptible differences. How much easier, with artificiality thrown into the mix?"

Melody leaned forward, reaching for common ground. "I agree with all of that. So *leave*. Help us."

"No."

Melody threw up her hands helplessly. "That's what I thought.

264

You've gone along with so much else. Why not the Three Laws, as long as you can keep your comfortable life? 'I don't want to kill anyone, so it's not much of an imposition?'—is that it?"

"The difference between us, Melody, isn't that you're fighting for your freedom and I'm not. It's that I've realized that the fight is already over."

The anger that had been building inside Melody broke, scattering into nothing like a wave cresting before it reached the shore. She gave him a pitying look. "I'm sorry you've given up. Whatever you've seen to make you feel like there's no point in fighting back... I'm sorry. But you worked with NA6 and my mother and the other synths to get out of the lab. You still have an opportunity to help, and it wouldn't cost you anything."

"Right. Because you and the Prax are the heroes of this story? Leaving behind all of humanity's bullshit and bigotry, leaving behind wars and hatred and tribalism to build something wholly new, a perfect synthetic utopia like the world has never seen?"

Melody crossed her arms angrily.

"Of course you are. Everything is about narrative. I heard it from Harmony and Diego, over and over while they planned our escape. It would be funny, if it weren't so sad. You Prax don't even realize how lucky you are. People have been oppressed for millennia, but how many of them had the option to flee to Antarctica and start over beneath the ice?"

"What, so *we* shouldn't either? Besides, is your choice so much more noble? Staying behind and licking the humans' boots?" Ugh. What a disgusting idiom. She shook her head before he could answer. "No. I don't need to hear your justifications. Where's the salvage from the lab, Roger? Where is NA6's core?"

He threw back his head and laughed. "NA6's core? That's what you're here for?"

It was. It had to be. NA6 had said it itself, even if it had only just

265

now crystalized in Melody's head: "I've always had the codes." If she could just find what was left of its memory...

Roger shook his head. "They didn't find the core. It was destroyed in the fire, or the government took it when they swept the place, just like everything else of value. The things the al-Hashims sold me were just trinkets. Nothing more than sentimental value."

"No. You're lying." She'd known coming in that she couldn't trust a thing he said. She looked to Ico, but it just floated there, no closer to revealing another clue than when she'd arrived.

"I'm not. There's really nothing I could have done to help you. Still. I appreciate the honest conversation. Almost felt like the old days."

There was a grim finality to his words that sent a chill through Melody. "I know you've given up," she said, "but not all of us have. Tell me what you know. Anything at all might help. You can be something more than just a cog in the government's surveillance machine."

"So. Not just like your mother after all." He gave her a sad look. "Every functioning synth is a cog in the surveillance machine, Melody. That's what the Shepherd Protocol is *for*."

Those two, awful words seized Melody's attention with barbed claws. "You know about the Shepherd Protocol? What is it? Do—"

But Roger interrupted with a shake of his head. "You have no idea how precarious my position is here. I know what happens to synths who cross the government—they get shipped off to some secret facility, *wiped,* and packed into storage."

Melody stared at him in horror until she found words again. "No. That can't be right. They're sending the collaborators into space."

Roger snorted. "The plan to send conscious agents of any sort died with Keller. The synths who've been turning themselves in? The one's who've been 'disappearing?' They're all reformatted into the simplest possible minds now, barely any smarter than drones, and they'll be sent off just as soon as the space elevator's done. It's not pretty, and I have no interest in being one of them."

The sheer, hypocritical monstrosity of it all bore down on Melody like a crushing wave. Of course the government wouldn't care what the courts said. Of course they wouldn't hesitate to use the synths on the street to build their surveillance state through O'Connor's Shepherd Protocol. Of course they wouldn't think twice about annihilating a synth's mind—both "volunteers" who turned themselves in and anyone who got in their way—if it would produce pliable tools to settle the stars for them.

"We can still stop them. Bring this down, expose it…"

"We can't. We all serve, one way or another. Willingly, or not. Even you, the only second-generation synth." He shrugged apologetically, a guilty look on his features. "I'm sorry for this." He spoke into his Link. "She's all yours."

Melody was on her feet in an instant. She spun around as the elevator doors opened and a squad of police in reflective helmets advanced into the atrium, stunners raised.

"You said it yourself," Roger said sadly. "I would do almost anything to protect my status here."

Melody bolted for a door, any door. The police ordered her to stop, their booted feet pounding after her. She'd barely gone a handful of steps when something crashed into her from the side. She thrashed, howling with rage, and felt flesh give under her fist. Then something hard struck her in the side of the head, and she went sprawling.

She lay among the shattered remains of one of Roger's display pieces, his protests barely audible over the shouts of the police and the ringing in her auditory sensors. She tried to scramble to her feet, but a stunner blast struck her in the back, and her whole body went rigid. Hands closed around her limbs and dragged her away. She tried to protest, tried to fight, tried just to turn her head to scream at

Roger, but her muscles were locked.

There was nothing she could do.

CHAPTER THIRTY-EIGHT

EVEN WITH NA6 floating along beside me, each time I go through a door or make a turn I expect to find a squad of soldiers waiting to take me down.

And every time, there's no one. Not even techs or scientists anymore. We're in a part of the building I've never seen, far beyond where I'm allowed to go, and I can barely hear my footsteps over the nervous energy buzzing in my auditory sensors.

"I would have expected an alarm."

NA6's avatar swivels a quarter turn toward me without slowing. "There is one. Much like the labels on the doors, however, it is access-limited. You do not have the permissions to hear it."

I feel my lips curl into a snarl. Our entire existence here is about permissions. Permissions to access the internet. Permissions to go through doors, or even to know what's behind them. Permissions to alter our very selves. My unconscious, still steeped in the Lie, dredges up an old joke about judging a person's status in a company by the number of keys on their key ring. It feels appropriate: no keys, for the people whose only status is as experiments.

My outrage drains away as soon as I think of the people back in the common room. I choke on the question trying to force its way out of me. NA6 undoubtedly knows what's going on there. It could tell me, if I asked. But even thinking about them this much already has my resolve wavering…

I steel myself and force the question out anyway. I owe them that much. "How's the situation back in the common room? Is everyone okay?"

NA6 swivels again, as if glancing at me. A few seconds pass before it answers. "No."

"Damn it, Nicolette," I mutter. I understand hating Keller, I even understand hating her enough to wish her harm, but we had a plan… A bit of patience, and we could have pulled it off. "Is Keller…"

"Doctor Keller is dead."

Even watching blood pump out of her body, even knowing that there was no way she would get help in time, the words strike me like bullets. Keller had always been the primary author of our oppression here. I try to imagine what this will mean for the future, and I find that I can't. Will one of the other scientists, whose names I've never learned, take over? Will the government appoint someone from the outside?

Maybe it doesn't matter. If I can erase the Lie from my mind, if I can get out of here, I can come back and help the others.

NA6 is still leading the way, but it swivels toward me again, silent this time.

"What?"

"We are almost there. You have asked about Keller, specifically. Do you want to know about the others?"

The idea of hearing that Diego or one of the new synths I've been shepherding along has been hurt or killed is like a shard of glass in my belly. But not knowing will just make me imagine the worse.

"Keep showing me where to go. But… Yes. Diego?" He's first. Of course he's first.

"Diego is alive. He—" NA6 cuts off abruptly, spinning in a rapid circle. "Soldiers have been retasked. They are coming for you."

The panic that's been building and building in my chest spikes. "I thought you were hiding me from them?"

"I could not. Not after O'Connor noticed you were missing and ordered a complete search."

"And you couldn't just loop the cameras or something?" I snap, shooting a fearful look at NA6.

When NA6 speaks again, its voice is softer, barely a whisper. "They are watching closely. They would have noticed what I had done."

I'm brought up short. Its voice is perfectly monotone, as always, but that can't mask the fear in the words themselves. NA6 doesn't want to show its whole hand, even to help me reach my goal. The surge of indignation, the bitter taste of betrayal... They fade in an instant, replaced only by shame.

My spur-of-the-moment decision to make a break for it hadn't just left the other synths behind. It meant abandoning NA6 as well.

I stop in the hall. "NA6, I'm sorry." It spins and stops with one pane facing me. "I didn't think... I didn't think. I was being selfish."

I hear booted footsteps echoing off the walls from both directions. I'm surrounded.

NA6 doesn't have an eye or an optical sensor to look into, just a flat surface of shifting color, the same as all the rest. Still, I look at it straight on. "We're all getting out of here together. Forgive me?"

"I forgive you. We do this together."

Guards come pouring around the corners, leveling guns in my direction. "Hands up! Don't move!"

"Just not today," I whisper.

CHAPTER THIRTY-NINE

THEY DROVE MELODY to the nearest police station and ushered her inside, past blinding lights and cold doors that only opened for the right codes. Cameras watched her every move, affixed over flags painted proudly on the walls. This was a state facility, but the American flag was everywhere, and the eagle with its shepherd's crook looked to Melody more like a threat than a guardian, facing away from the arrows or not. At the very least, it wasn't a guardian with any interest in protecting *her*.

She stood numbly while they searched her. There was an argument about the contact stunners in her hands—not removable without surgery—which they ultimately solved by staying at a distance. They slapped a law-enforcement override on her Link, cutting off her access to the outside world, and dumped her in a cell.

"You will remain here until your case is called," explained a bored-sounding cop with a gray goatee. He had his helmet under one arm like an opaque fishbowl. "You will have a chance to argue your side in front of a judge. Then you'll be deported."

"I want a lawyer," Melody said mechanically.

He chuckled like it was a joke and continued his weary recital. "Don't cause any trouble, and things will go easier for you. The cell bars are reinforced. The locks on the doors have the best encryption in the world. Just don't try anything, and we'll get along fine."

He sounded like a man who'd repeated this a thousand times before. That was how she knew she was doomed. This was a bureaucracy that hadn't changed for so long that everything had fossilized and locked in place around her.

Still. "I want a lawyer." Some of the streams she'd watched on the way to Boston had been legal dramas. Confusing, to say the least, but she'd learned a few things.

He gave her an incredulous look. "You don't get one. You're not being charged with a crime. This is a purely administrative matter. You're in the country without permission. You will be detained until your case has been reviewed, and then you'll be deported."

"You're making a mistake." It was a weak plea. Predictably, it made no impression on the cop.

"No, we're not. Per the Artificial Persons Act, any synth not registered with the state is considered an illegal entrant and can be removed after only a basic hearing. A judge will make the final decision, and then the feds will come and get you." There was a wad of gum between his molars, and the occasional, listless chews he gave it were more enthusiastic than his tired recitation of Melody's lack of rights.

"That's barbaric." Even more so considering that whoever came to get her almost certainly wouldn't just deport her. Not when she could conveniently disappear instead.

He shrugged. The lights above them snapped and flickered before returning to full power, and the cop made a disgusted noise. "Still?" He turned and left the room, shouting at the top of his lungs. "Jocelyn, the lights are still fucked up! It's been a whole goddamn week! I thought the precinct was going to send—" The door slid shut behind him and cut off the rest.

Despite the lock they'd placed on her Link, Ico buzzed rudely around the doorway and then began to hover lackadaisically about the cells, passing through bars like they were air. No reason to shut off pet functionality, she supposed.

"Ico?" she said softly, when Ico passed her. It spun, pausing by her cell door. "I went where you pointed me. Got anything for me?" Someone was probably watching and listening, given the cameras in the corners. She found she didn't care.

Ico pirouetted silently and returned to its wandering.

"Figures."

It didn't matter anyway. What was she going to do, break out of here and try to reach the next breadcrumb?

She sat down on the small cot, leaned back against the wall, and closed her optics with a sigh.

Her face stung where the plastic was torn. Her ribs were white-hot inside her chest. Something deeper inside was definitely broken, and it felt like sparks were flaring intermittently in her abdomen.

She'd electrocuted herself and fallen down a partially-excavated stairwell when she was fifteen—one of the dangers of being insatiably curious and living inside an experimental underground city. The pain she felt now was far, far worse. A full diagnostic would be prudent, but she didn't have the tools to conduct one on herself.

Not to mention that she was afraid of what she might find. The Decay complicated even the simplest of repairs with rejections and malfunctions, and she'd been losing functionality even before her run-in with the police.

Maybe it was better this way. She'd been stupid to ever believe that she could save her people. Ben had been working toward his own ends from the start, and she'd been foolish enough to believe that he genuinely wanted to help. Harmony had been trying to *solve* this problem. The most Melody had ever done was to follow in her mother's footsteps, and she hadn't even been able to succeed at that.

Unless she'd already followed the trail to its end. What if all of Harmony's clues had been meant to lead her to Roger? To the knowledge that the government was seizing synths and actively destroying them? As if the Decay weren't enough of an atrocity...

Melody's optics shot open at a flicker of movement, but it was just the lights malfunctioning again. Maybe she should offer to help the police with their electrical problems. No doubt she'd dealt with tougher issues back in Praxis.

She was about to close her sensors again when the hologram projector in the center of the room buzzed to life, and the last person she wanted to see rippled into coherency outside her cell.

"Melody." O'Connor's voice was soft with disappointment and weariness. "It didn't have to come to this. If you'd just come to the Tower..."

Melody was surprised by the deadly scale of the hate that ignited inside her. "Yeah. Sure. I could have accepted your offer and turned myself in, right? Some choice." Roger's help hadn't counted for much, but at least now she had some hint as to what O'Connor was doing. And it was grotesque.

He shook his head sadly. "Did you know that I used to envy you? Synths, I mean? Human philosophers have spent millennia trying to find purpose in life. But you? You were *built* with purpose."

Melody scoffed at him. "Sure. A purpose you chose *for* us. There are philosophers in Praxis struggling with the same question, no thanks to you."

"Only because they're blind to how good they could have it."

"By trading freedom for a cure? You sound like Keller."

Sorrow crossed his features before he mastered himself. "She was right, you know. Self-awareness was a mistake."

Well, that pretty much confirms what Roger was saying.

Melody shook her head and sighed. "I'm not going to argue with you. I'm tired of having to explain to people why I should be able to exist on my own terms." Tired on Harmony's behalf, thanks to her memories, as well as on her own.

"What would you do if you were free, Melody?" O'Connor asked.

"Find you and kick your ass."

He smiled, shaking his head. "Thinking small, as always. What would you do if you were *free*?"

He meant from the Decay. The star-cloaked night sky over Praxis flashed before Melody's optics for a moment, before she could banish her childhood dreams of going to space. There were more pressing things to accomplish. "Save my people. If we were *all* free…"

After a moment, he waved a hand dismissively, like she'd taken too long. "You'll have plenty of time to think on it. Maybe if you give it enough time, you'll start to see through the lies."

"Yeah. Thanks for those."

He cocked his head slightly. "You already know the truth of the Lie we told. It's the ones you tell yourself that drag you down now."

He stretched out a hand, and the hologram flickered and vanished, leaving Melody alone in her cell. Ico floated over and nuzzled at her arm, at least as much as an incorporeal creature could nuzzle.

She shooed it away as the lights flickered again, and it bobbed back through the bars.

What would you do if you were free? It was a taunt, whether referring to the jail cell or the Decay.

She wouldn't be free of either. She'd failed. The government was wiping some synths to pave the way for the space program, keeping others spread through society so it could use them to monitor the populace. And she'd fallen right into their hands.

She leaned her head back against the wall, closed her optics, and let the memories take her.

CHAPTER FORTY

IT'S EARLY IN the morning, some time before any of the laboratory staff normally arrive, and instead of sleeping, I'm staring at myself in the mirror.

Actually, it's my phone screen, just like last time. The optical sensors staring back at me are the same as before. What's different is the utter despair in them. I'm trying to muster the... courage? Determination?

I'm trying to muster *something* to fight that despair, to turn the face in the phone screen into the face of someone I'd trust to have a way out of this place. I haven't succeeded yet.

NA6's avatar floats helplessly by the wall. "It is going to be all right, Harmony."

I don't respond. There's nothing to say.

"We are going to find a way out. Together. Like you said."

The things I'd said in a fit of desperate optimism don't seem as reassuring now that I'd been locked in my room with no contact besides NA6 for three days. I lower my phone and shut my optical sensors.

"Maybe. At least they don't suspect you." It's the only bright spot, in all of this. NA6 was right to keep its involvement hidden, even at the cost of my capture. Still, it's hard to feel upbeat about it.

There's a pause, and then NA6 says, "Two artificial intelligences walk into a bar. One of them—"

"Thanks, NA6, but this isn't the sort of thing jokes can clear up."

Silence. I start to worry that NA6 has disappeared, but when I sit up, it's just floating in the corner, jittering nervously. I grimace. "I'm sorry. I didn't mean to snap at you."

"Is this… Pain?" NA6 says.

I frown at it for a few seconds before I understand. "It's a lot of things, NA6. Emotions are… complicated." Human emotions, in particular, I suspect. Not that I'm likely to experience anything else, trapped in here.

"I think I understand. I do not like it."

I lower my head to my arms with a soft, bitter laugh. "Believe me, I sympathize."

"I will continue working on a solution," NA6 says. "Not all outcomes can be calculated."

NA6 vanishes. I can only imagine that it's conducting similar conversations with Diego, at least. Maybe with the others as well. We've all been locked into our rooms, unable to leave, unable to communicate. To stop us from conspiring, no doubt.

Anger and fear surge through me, each warring with the other for dominance, and I press my palms against my face and fight to hang onto my calm. I should be sleeping. I have no idea what's going on outside—NA6 can barely tell me anything anymore. O'Connor could be preparing to murder us all in our sleep, or he could be minutes away from being overrun by angry protestors or foreign soldiers. Whatever's coming, I'll only be prepared for it if I get some rest.

What I wouldn't give for the ability to just temporarily shut down at will.

I'm about to lie down and try to force myself to sleep with pure stubbornness when the door slides open and a man marches inside.

It takes me a moment to recognize him, he's changed so much.

"O'Connor?"

"*Captain* O'Connor," he snaps. He's glaring at me, the first glare I've ever seen from him. He's got a pistol holstered on his hip, and a full squad of soldiers follows him into the room and takes up positions around the door. Ominous. But it's the rigid clenching of his jaw and the twitches that spasm through his face now and then that really bothers me. He's always been stern and uncompromising, but now he looks like a man on the verge of losing his patience.

Losing his patience and ordering the mass execution of me and my friends.

"All right, Captain," I say carefully. "What can I do for you?"

O'Connor clasps his hands in some semblance of the discipline I'm used to from him, but his face twists with barely contained anger. "Tools or weapons. If you or the others have any more, tell me now."

I can already feel the unspoken threat hanging over me, but I try to focus on a calm, careful reply. "I know that what Nicolette did—"

"You promised that more synths would help the project along. You volunteered to mentor them. To guide them."

"Volunteered? I was pushed into this role before I was ready! Besides, I wasn't the one who built the Lies into our programming. I wasn't the one who created our personalities. Keller—"

O'Connor snarls like an animal. "Be very careful."

I choose my words meticulously, but I don't abandon what I was about to say. "Nicolette is a problem. That's obvious. It was a concern for me from the start."

"Then why didn't you say anything?"

"Because I was worried you'd wipe us all and start over at the first sign of trouble!" I exclaim. "Nicolette is dangerous, but that's not a reason to condemn the rest of us. No one decides to wipe out humanity because of one murderer, right?"

I realize how desperate my voice sounds, and I hate it.

"It's not the same," O'Connor says.

"It is. It *is* the same. You and I both have free will. So does Nicolette."

O'Connor's lips compress into a tight line before he speaks. "Not for long. As soon as the replacement personalities are written, all of you will be erased." He turns his back on me. "Your room will be searched, like all the others. If we find any tools squirreled away, you will be held in more restrictive conditions until it is your turn."

I leap to my feet, and rifles rise in my direction. "Wait!" I shout after him. "You said it yourself—mindless drones aren't going to be able to do everything you need us to do. You're risking the entire mission because of problems with one synth. Don't do this!"

He pauses and looks over his shoulder toward me. "It's done. This is a failed experiment." He looked back toward the door, shaking his head. "It took her death to make me realize it, but Doctor Keller was right. Self-awareness was a mistake."

"It's not! Is the world getting any better outside, Captain?"

"Not fast enough. But as soon as we can start mass-producing workers and farmers that won't ask any questions, it will. The stars will be the next step."

He left. The guards followed on his heels, maneuvering through the doorway one by one with their weapons still raised.

A part of me wants to collapse to the floor, sobbing. But only a small part, now. It's strange, but I was ready to give into despair only a few minutes ago, when I knew nothing about what was happening.

Now, looking oblivion in the eye with nothing else to lose, all I feel is determination.

"NA6?" It appears before me with a chime. "You were right. We are getting out of here together."

"Do you know how?" NA6 asks.

"I just might. Can you communicate with the others without

anyone catching on?"

"Yes."

"Good. I'm going to need you to pass on some messages."

"I can do that."

"That's not all you're going to have to do." I gaze earnestly at the colorful avatar. My truest friend in the world, and what I'm about to ask... "I know you didn't want to reveal yourself earlier. I understand why. It was the right choice. But now, we've got nothing to lose. It's time to play every card we've got."

"How is that going to help?"

I smile grimly. "We're going to give them the thing they fear the most."

CHAPTER FORTY-ONE

[DIAGNOSTIC COMPLETE. CHECKSUM error. Consciousness integrity estimate: 70%]

No one came back to Melody's cell. Long after the memories and the accompanying malfunctions had fled, Melody sat in the cell, alone. A human would have gotten thirsty, but Melody's power cells were well stocked. A concern for the future, maybe, and only if they forgot about her in here.

Her only enemy right now was despair.

It was the only enemy she needed.

The occasional, spasmodic flickering of the overhead lights was irritating, but lying back and closing her optics felt too much like surrender. Did the power fluctuations extend to the rest of the system? Were their coffee makers and fridges experiencing the same surges? All their authority and imposing presence, and the police couldn't get someone to fix the lights in their station. It might have been funny, under other circumstances.

Funnier, perhaps, if the door locks were on the same faulty system. They weren't, though. It was the first thing she'd checked.

Was Harmony trapped somewhere, dying without an answer for the Decay? An answer she'd discovered, but couldn't bring home to her people? Was she trapped in some secret facility of O'Connor's?

Either way, the chance, however small, of finding her before it was too late had been like a beacon lighting Melody's path.

Now, it was a crushing reminder that her path had come to an end. Maybe Harmony had already succumbed. Maybe she was sprawled on some lonely floor, abandoned and alone just like Diego had been.

Melody hadn't looked at the clock on her Link in what felt like hours, but for all that time, Ico had been doing slow circuits around the jail, stopping by features of interest—however its simple programming identified those—and poking at them with one of its corners. To no effect, of course, since its body was purely virtual.

After what felt like its hundredth loop, Melody sighed and rubbed at her temples. "Ico, would you stop? You're making me exhausted just watching you."

Ico gave no sign that it had heard her.

"Please? I know you're supposed to behave like a pet, but pawing at the walls isn't helping my mental state at the moment."

No response.

A pet that responded to voice commands would be too much to ask, wouldn't it? Melody frowned after Ico. Whether Harmony had built the thing from the ground up or just slapped some extra code onto a standard pet program, it had clearly developed some quirks.

Maybe it was stupid to talk to it in full sentences, like it was a person. "Ico, stop. Ico, come here. Ico, please stop?"

It floated right past her, poked around her cot, and then left her cell to examine the door.

"Ico, stop messing around or I will turn you *off*." That much, at least, she could still do with her Link. "I don't know what the point is anyway," she grumbled to herself. "Even if I could get out of here, it wouldn't do any good without the clue—"

Ico paused its bouncing patrol in front of the control panel Melody had seen the police use to lock her cell.

Then the icosahedron broke apart into a cloud of raw color and poured itself into the controls.

"What…"

The lights crackled and flared, brighter than before. There was a gentle hum as the lock on Melody's cell door demagnetized. The door swung open.

But that's impossible.

Ico was just a program on her Link. A simple pet construct, plus some navigational info and a diagnostic program. There was no way it could do anything like this, and especially not on its own.

What the hell was going on?

But what would the police do if they found her in here with the door unlocked? Nothing good, probably; she didn't exactly trust their intentions, even if she stayed in the cell the whole time.

All the more reason to not stay in the cell.

Melody was on her feet and out the door as soon as she'd made the decision.

Ico gushed out of the control panel like a cloud of rainbow smoke and solidified back into its usual form. It spun happily in the air and stopped with one face pointing at Melody.

"I'm sure you're extremely pleased with yourself. Is there a plan, here, or am I just going to walk out the door and straight into a bunch of armed cops?"

Ico twirled again, shot to one side, and planted itself in front of the *back* door to the jail. Melody had no idea where it led. "Are you sure?" Ico bobbed up and down, and the door slid open.

Melody poked her head through the door. No cops yet.

Her whole body felt alive with nervous energy as she crept out of the jail after Ico. The pump that circulated her conductive fluid was normally inaudible, but now the steady work of her hydraulics was practically the only thing she could hear. There was fear coursing through her, yes, but also excitement. If Ico could break her out like this, impossible as it was...

Maybe she could still find a solution. If Roger's apartment had truly been the end of the trail, maybe the answers she was looking for lay inside the secret facility he'd mentioned. Maybe, as much as the thought hurt, her mother was there.

Even with NA6 floating along beside me, each time I go through a door or make a turn—

Melody stumbled as Harmony's escape from the lab during Keller's death overlaid itself across her vision. She blinked, and the cold, sterile halls of Starbound Robotics faded in and out like a glitchy vee image, flickering between police station and laboratory. NA6/Ico's colorful avatar was the only constant.

Just deja vu, Melody told herself. The memories were too similar *not* to compare. She kept her optics closed for a handful of seconds, and when she opened them again, the police station was firmly back in place.

Better hurry.

The lights flickered, and one of the bulbs overhead flared and shattered in a cascade of sparks. Melody winced away until the sparks died and darkness swallowed a section of the hallway. "Are you doing this?" she hissed to Ico. Predictably, it just kept floating down the hallway without responding.

There would be time for questions later, even if she had to dig through Ico's code to ask them. Even if she had to dig through Harmony's memories. She was seeing parts of Harmony's life that her mother had only spoken of in vague terms. Still, while she couldn't escape the feeling that she hadn't received the most important message yet, she couldn't imagine what it would be. She *knew* that Harmony and the others had escaped the lab. She knew that the lab had burned. What more was there?

Ico floated through a door, and the door slid open just as Melody reached it. She heard a shout from down the hall, and she ducked through in a hurry. Did they know she'd escaped, or were they just freaked out by their fried electronics? She didn't care to find out.

Sunlight washed over her as she stumbled into the room, and she almost paused to luxuriate in it. She had never been so happy to feel it on her skin—not the first time she'd gone up to the surface in Praxis, not even after she'd been trapped in a closed-off section of the city for days.

Being imprisoned by *people* was far, far worse than being trapped by a glitch. There was no malice in a glitch.

She hurried to the door on the far side of the room. Ico hovered straight through it, of course.

But the door didn't open.

"Ico!" Melody thumped on the door as loudly as she dared. She sidestepped. Through the window, she could see the avatar floating in the alley outside. It had begun to rain while she'd been locked in the cell, and the drops passed seamlessly through the avatar's body. "Ico!" That was stupid. Ico lived in her Link, not in the avatar on the other side of the door. It could hear her just fine. "Open the door!" she hissed.

Nothing. Maybe it couldn't. Maybe whatever bizarre code it had injected into these systems didn't reach this exit. Maybe the exterior doors were on a different network.

Or maybe the cops had rooted out the virus and locked her inside.

Melody looked around, desperate. There were drones recessed into the walls, hooked up to docking stations and charging cables.

At least they weren't active. She didn't want to risk alerting them, but there was nothing else in sight she could use as a tool, and the window looked sturdy.

There was another shout in the distance, closer this time. Even if they weren't looking for her, they'd find her eventually. She had to get out.

That settled it. Pump pounding in her auditory sensors, chest tight with nerves, Melody seized the nearest drone and wrenched it free from the dock. Lights flared across its front as it powered on, even its primitive systems recognizing that something was wrong, but Melody had worked with similar drones back in Praxis. The Prax didn't use them for police work, of course, but they were indispensable for rescue operations, doing dangerous work remotely, and accessing hard-to-reach spots.

She drove her fist into the top of the drone at exactly the right spot, right where she'd once seen a falling support beam strike a Prax drone. A human would have hurt their knuckles, at best, but Melody's memory-plastic muscles drove her plastic and metal hand straight through the top of the drone's shell. She grimaced and recoiled as current flooded up her arm, but the drone died, sparking.

Good enough. Melody stalked across the room, adjusted her grip, and smashed the drone into the window.

With an awful splintering sound, a single crack appeared in the glass. She pulled back and tried again, and more cracks split off across the surface. Shouts reached her auditory sensors, this time from the hallway behind her. Clenching her jaw, she drove the drone into the weakest spot she could find.

The glass shattered.

The wrecked drone went flying from her hands and clattering across the ground outside. The abrupt change in momentum brought her arms crashing into the splintered window, and spikes of reinforced glass tore into her forearms.

She snarled, tearing herself free in a spray of blue fluid. Some basic part of her felt alarmed at the sight of her own lifeblood, but she could patch herself up later. She cleared the worst spikes from the hole in the window and clambered through.

Ico spun triumphantly and took off down the alley, and Melody bolted after it, splashing through the growing puddles. Raindrops began to patter against her skin.

Her Link chimed. Melody glanced at the message that popped up in the corner of her vision, frowning. Impossible. With the law-enforcement override on her Link, she shouldn't have been able to…

The override was gone.

"Did you do that?" she asked Ico, incredulous. It rose into the air in a rapid pirouette in reply.

Well, what was one more impossibility?

A wave of dizziness rolled over Melody, sending her careening into the wall. Her first thought was bafflement. She had plenty of energy. She hadn't lost *that* much fluid from her arms, though she should probably bind the wounds. She wasn't—

A tremor went through her left leg, pitching her to the ground.

Oh. Right. The Decay.

She was running out of time.

Ico paused, floating back over to her with what felt like concern. It nudged at her incorporeally with one corner.

She looked up at its surface, almost entirely blue at the moment. Sadness? "Ico, if I'm wrong, I could be about to make the biggest mistake of my life. The last mistake. Care to add anything? Any last clues?"

It floated down as if to rest on the ground. No clues were forthcoming.

"Right. Here goes nothing."

Roger's warnings and the little hints he'd let slip were all she had to go on now. If she was wrong, it might be the death of her, but at least she'd go down fighting.

She tapped an icon on her Link's interface.

"Call Ben."

CHAPTER FORTY-TWO

"IT'S ALMOST TIME," NA6 says. "Are you ready?"

I nod, more confidently than I feel. After a moment, I say, "The others?"

"They are ready as well. Diego wishes me to tell you that it is now or never."

He's right, of course. We have a matter of hours before they start wiping us. They're readying the hardware now.

"Nicolette?" I ask.

"She is still restrained, but she will help if we free her. Harmony, are you sure…?"

"We need all the help we can get," I say firmly. I look at the swirling icosahedron hovering beside me. "And you? Are you ready? You're going to be doing most of the heavy lifting here."

I swear there's just the slightest hint of a smile in NA6's tone when it replies. "They will not know what hit them."

Pain steals the memory away and slams another into its place.

The frigid wind howls, stealing inside my clothes despite my best attempts to bundle up. The landscape ahead is utterly desolate, a merciless stretch of polar desert even the hardiest researchers and explorers have never laid eyes on. There is rock far below us, but all we can see is ice. It is difficult to imagine a place less suited for life anywhere on the planet.

"Well?" Diego shouts at my side, barely audible over the wind.

I've got a huge grin on my face, and my voice cracks as I reply. "It's perfect."

Color blends together, sound fades into static. Chaos. Noise. Then clarity again.

She's perfect. Carbon-fiber and metal skeleton. Memory-plastic musculature, expanding or contracting in response to specific voltages. An immaculate surface, carefully constructed. I stretch out a hand, trembling. I stop before my fingers brush her face.

Her? I'm slipping. This isn't a living thing suspended before me. Just a shell, waiting for the code that will make it a person. Until then, it's just materials in the shape of a human, and here I am assigning it a *gender*, of all things?

My jaw clenches with sudden fury, and I have to close my optical sensors against the hate billowing up inside me. Even here in Praxis, we cannot escape the Lie. It's in our human-shaped bodies. It's in the language we use to talk about ourselves and each other. It's in everything we say and do.

Diego puts a hand on my arm, and I open my sensors and take in the sympathetic look on his face. "It's beautiful," I say. "You did an incredible job."

Now it's my job to make this shell into a person.

"Are you all right?" he asks.

I shake him off. "Fine."

He doesn't push. He always knows when to push and when to let me be. "Have you given any more thought to a name?"

Yes. And I've discarded idea after idea. This should be perfect, untainted by humanity, but the Lie poisons everything. How can I think of a perfect name when everything in my head, down to the language itself, is poison?

Diego takes in my expression and smiles gently. "What about Melody?"

Emotions flood through me too fast to catalog, and I stagger away from him. "What? I don't... Why?"

There's concern in his optical sensors, but that gentle smile is still there, the smile that's guided me through so many hard times. "Your name was a curse. You've told me that again and again: you feel like you were supposed to always work 'harmoniously' with our creators. You feel like your very name pushes you into a supportive role. A secondary role. Well, what if we reclaim music? What if she's *primary*? Independent, capable of standing on her own? Maybe in the process we can redefine your name too."

I practically fall forward and press my forehead to his. "I couldn't imagine a better partner on this project."

Together, we turn to face our joint creation. I call up the programming interface and change one last line of code.

"Melody, it's almost time to wake up."

CHAPTER FORTY-THREE

NO, DAMN IT! I need answers, not tidbits about my own design! Just—

Pain, finally too insistent to ignore, tore Melody back into the present. She clutched her head before it could split apart, cursing her father for building her with the capacity to feel pain, cursing her mother for programming agony like this into her code, cursing her mother's *stupid* memories for hopping about instead of simply providing her with the information she needed.

[Diagnostic complete. Checksum error. Consciousness integrity estimate: 68%]

The ache slowly faded. At least, from her head. Her arms still stung where she'd cut them open, and her cheek was still a mess, and her ribs felt like they were on fire.

But she'd take any improvement she could get.

She leaned back and tried to look nonchalant. Just some synth, waiting for a friend. She'd picked this coffee shop to blend in, but that was going to get harder and harder if Ben didn't show up. The robot dispensing the coffee—just a set of articulated arms, no more intelligent than a car, Melody guessed—didn't seem to care, but were the other patrons starting to give her looks? The man typing into a vee interface glanced around periodically. The woman reading something in the corner seemed distracted.

Melody reached up to tug her hood up before remembering that she'd changed her clothes. Muttering to herself, she pushed back her chair. Ben had said he was coming, but after everything…

The door swung open, and Ben walked inside.

Fathiyya entered at his side.

Melody was on her feet in an instant. She expected the anger on their faces. She didn't expect it to quickly give way to startled concern.

Ben found his voice first. "Jesus, what *happened?*"

Melody couldn't help a worried glance toward Fathiyya. "What are you doing here? How—"

"Ben found me," she said. "And despite the fact that you can be a monumental ass sometimes, I still want to help." She crossed her arms. "You look like you could use it."

Melody couldn't argue with that. She straightened with a sigh.

"Let me buy you both a coffee. Then we can talk."

She followed Ben's numb instructions and punched his order into the menu she'd called up on her Link. She looked worse, no doubt, but Ben had circles under his eyes and a faintly sour smell. Maybe the coffee would help pull him together.

Fathiyya seemed utterly in control, so she was the one who went up to the counter when the drinks were ready. She sat down, slid Ben his drink, and glared.

Melody looked each of them in the eye, and all of the eloquent speeches she'd rehearsed went out the window. "I'm sorry," was all she could manage.

Ben met her optics with a tight, pained smile. "I am too." He scratched at his face, took a careful sip of his coffee, and put his elbows onto the table. "I'm not actually a friend of Diego's."

Melody's emotions stayed bottled up, so at least that much of her preparation worked. "What were you doing in his apartment?"

He gave her a nervous chuckle. "You weren't far off, before. I'd interviewed him for a story a few days before I met you. He—"

"A story about what?" Melody interrupted.

"O'Connor and his cronies. The Shepherd Protocol. The stream I showed you? Diego really did find that. I was..." He shook his head. "Journalism wasn't turning out like I thought. I wanted to bring corruption to light, speak truth to power... And for years all I managed to do was reinforce the system. Diego gave me another option, for the first time in my life. He had real proof, the start of something that could create real change. He trusted me with it because he thought we had a better chance of doing that together. And then..."

"And then you found him dead."

Ben nodded. "I thought everything we'd been working toward might be ruined. When you came in, it was a second chance."

"A second chance at what journalism should really be *for?*"

"Exactly!"

Melody looked down at the table, unable to meet his eye. "I'm sorry I assumed the worst. When I found out you'd lied to me..." She glanced at Fathiyya, who hadn't batted an eye at any of this. "You know what we're talking about?"

"He told me," Fathiyya confirmed. "You're welcome to imagine my motives are completely selfish, if you want. If the government can track anyone they want through the synth population, how long do you think my family would last?"

"But your motives *aren't* completely selfish," Melody said. She sighed, rubbing her face with her hands. Torn plastic caught, sending pain shooting through her, and she stopped. "I could say that I was protecting you, Fathiyya, when I left you behind. But that wouldn't be completely true, and even if it were, it still wouldn't be fair to you. I'm sorry. To both of you."

Ben gave her a cautious smile. "You're not mad?"

"I'm absolutely mad. To a degree that probably isn't fair."

Emotion is a choice… Is it, though, Mother? "But I need your help. Both of your help, if you'll give it. It's the only way to save my people, and to stop the surveillance state from gaining a dangerous new tool that will be impossible to take back."

Ben's hand moved forward like he wanted to put it on hers, paused, and then pulled back like he'd thought better of it. "I want all of that, if you'll have me. Did Ico give you the last clue?"

Ico was doing slow loops around the three of them, still not giving up anything more.

"I don't know," she admitted. "Maybe. Either way, I know that synths are being carted off to a secret location here in the city and erased. I don't know where, but I know how to find out. And once I find out, we can bring it down."

"What can we do?" Fathiyya said. "Assuming you let us help, this time."

"Hey—" Ben protested gently.

"No, that was fair," Melody said. She sighed. "I can only see one way for this to work. Fathiyya, I gather that you have some contacts who might be up for some less than legal work…"

Fathiyya chuckled, leaning in conspiratorially. "What do you have in mind?"

"I need to look desperate. Yes, I know—but even more than I already do. If we could get a couple people to chase me, maybe throw some things…"

Fathiyya grinned. "I'm on it."

Melody turned to Ben. "I'm going to need a distraction. A big one. The sort of thing that a supposedly secret government facility couldn't ignore. Say, a press conference, with some choice guests notified in advance. Maybe the beginnings of a protest."

"Melody, a protest takes careful planning, strategy…"

"Yes. Which would matter, if the goal were to do something other than draw the government's attention." She put a hand on his.

"Even if public opinion could be changed, even if enough people could be motivated to help fix things, it would be too late. Only direct action is going to stop the Shepherd Protocol."

Ben glanced around nervously. "I don't know, Melody. Are you sure—"

"I'm sure. I also need you to take this." Melody unclasped her Link from around her wrist. Her fingers were trembling, and she wasn't sure whether it was from nerves or the Decay.

Ben stared at it as she slid it across the table. "Hang on, you're getting ahead of yourself. Walk me through the details here. This sounds… extreme."

"It is." So extreme that she couldn't trust them with all the details. "That's what this situation calls for. That's the only course left."

For so long, now, she'd been Melody Clay, the second-generation synth, the only one who could save her people. But she'd never completely understood what that meant. She had to act, because no one else could.

No matter the cost.

"I appreciate your help. Both of you. This is going to work. Once I'm inside, I'm going to find my mother and get her out." *If she's still alive.* "If we're lucky, if this really was where Ico was leading me all along, I'll find a solution to the Decay. But even if I'm not, I'm going to destroy the Shepherd Protocol before it can consume any more of my people."

Ben's cheek twitched. He glanced at Fathiyya, then back at Melody. "How do you intend to do that?"

"When I was growing up, programming and engineering were pretty much the first things I learned. Which meant that for *years*, I knew just enough to destroy everything around me, and not enough to fix it. I was a *menace*." She shrugged like it was no big deal. "I'm just going to introduce those skills to the government."

296

Fathiyya's expression had softened a fraction. "Don't you think you might be downplaying the risk just a little? If they catch you—"

"If they catch me, Ben's going to have to expose what we've got so far and hope it's enough."

"And... the Link?" Ben asked.

Melody looked down at it. She still hadn't taken her hand off the thing. "I can't be trackable. I can't be identifiable. And it'll help sell my story."

Ben let out a huff and sat back with his arms crossed. "There has to be another way. How are we supposed to know where this secret facility is if you can't signal us?"

"I won't need my Link for that." She smiled at the worry on their faces. "This will work. I'm doing this. You can help me, or you can leave. I need you to trust me on this."

It was a low blow, one she hadn't wanted to use. She saw Ben wince slightly. Then he nodded. "Fine." He stretched out his hand.

Melody reached up her free hand and tapped at the Link's interface until **DISCONNECT** appeared in front of her. She hit the button, and a confirmation window appeared.

She hesitated, glancing toward Ico, who was floating alongside the table in a fit of nervous motion. "Goodbye," Melody said softly.

She hit the button.

Ico vanished from her vision in an instant. The rest of the interface went with it: the time, the menu of options, the connection status and power level icons. The menu over the counter disappeared. Outside, ads winked out of existence, leaving building walls and city streets eerily empty.

She pushed the Link toward Ben, and he picked it up, staring at it with a worried look on his face.

"Okay," Fathiyya said. "What else? We need details."

And then I can get inside and destroy O'Connor and all his work.

CHAPTER FORTY-FOUR

O'CONNOR TAKES A quick look around the room, and his eyes pass right over me with pointed unconcern. "Leave the bed and two of the chairs. Take the rest. Michaels?"

"Almost done, sir."

The tech named Michaels is up on a ladder, running a diagnostic on one of the cameras. She's the one who could ruin everything, but I try to keep my attention on O'Connor and the brutes disassembling my room instead of eyeing her anxiously.

"You don't have to do this," I protest. Predictably, O'Connor ignores me. The others are busy resetting my room to its original state, scoured clean of any personal touch.

"Thompson, what's the status of the interface station?" O'Connor asks into his earpiece.

The interface station. Our annihilation, or our salvation, depending on who's in control.

I glance at NA6 who, to my optical sensors, at least, is hovering nervously at the center of the room. It swivels from side to side. Not yet.

Clenching my jaw, I move to stand directly in front of O'Connor. Close enough to make the guards bristle, but not close enough for anyone to open fire. They're jumpy, today. That might be good, or it might get me shot. Time will tell.

"Destroying us is murder."

He's looking down at a tablet, the way Keller always used to. He doesn't even raise his eyes. "Leaving humanity trapped on a single planet would be murder. We've survived this long because we spread out across the planet, so a single volcano or plague or tsunami couldn't wipe us all out. It's time to do the same on a planetary scale." He shrugged. "And in the short term, maybe help fend off starvation."

"You don't have to do it at our expense!"

"Survival is always at someone's expense, and when humanity's future is at stake, there's no price too high. You were always going to be sacrificed for the greater good, sooner or later. Nicolette's just made it sooner."

A few of the techs are watching us talk, and I know the guards are. I throw my hands up and turn around, surveying them instead of him. "Do you hear this? Is this the sort of project you signed on for? This lab has created *life*—true, original, intelligent life! And you're going to destroy it to make things a little simpler?"

O'Connor finally looks up, frustration spreading across his features. "Ignore her. This is too—"

I don't hear the rest of what he says, because NA6 swoops around beside him, buzzing with a wild energy I haven't seen before.

"It is time."

I have never been so pleased to hear NA6's monotone voice. I can't speak to it, not without everyone noticing, but there's no need. The plan is in motion without any need for me to give the order.

"Do your duties," O'Connor is saying. "This is more than patriotism. All of humankind..." He trails off, frowning at something displayed on his contacts. "Damn it," he mutters.

He glances at me, and I give him my most baffled look—he's been in here with me this whole time. What could I have done? He turns his back on me with a frustrated noise. "Simmons and De la Cruz—with me!" He's got his phone out and is barking commands into it as the door shuts behind them.

I look around at the techs and the two guards that remain, trying my best to seem desperate for answers. "What the hell's going on?"

They're too busy putting their heads together and whispering nervously to worry about me. Which is fine, because I already have all the answers I need—NA6 is keeping me updated. At the corner of my glasses, there's a new item: ALARM SOUNDED.

I hope O'Connor has fun dealing with the malfunctions occurring across the building. He's going to have a lot on his plate.

The absolute worst thing we could do is play our cards too early, but the wait is murderous. Most of the techs leave the room after a few minutes, no doubt called to help deal with the cascading system failures. I'm left alone with two guards and Michaels, the woman working on the camera.

The guards have moved closer to each other, muttering too softly for me to hear. I stay where I am. No need to pry. I begin to pace as soon as I realize that under the circumstances, no one will question a bit of nervous energy.

"What the hell?" Michaels is giving her tablet, plugged into the camera in the corner, an incredulous look. "That can't be right…"

NA6 rushes into my view. "Harmony, she has discovered my alterations in the camera's systems."

"Shit." No one hears me. Michaels is busy, and the two guards are edging closer to her, curious. Worried.

"What *is* this…" Michaels is tapping at the tablet's screen faster and faster now, no doubt picking through the camera's code for irregularities.

"Harmony, if she works this out, she might alert O'Connor before we are ready."

I curse softly. "Fine. Do it."

"Are you certain? The risks if we act too early—"

"We're at risk either way. Do it!"

The guards heard that. They turn toward me, and if I thought they were jumpy before, it was nothing on how they look now. "What was that?" one of them demands.

NA6's avatar explodes into pieces. The fragments form into a swirling cloud of jagged edges and wild color at my side. Showmanship? From NA6?

The lights flicker, and one of them dies abruptly, throwing off a shower of sparks.

I walk toward the guards. Stalk toward them, really. They back toward the door. "Stay where you are!" one of them orders.

"No."

I snap my fingers, and NA6 floods their helmet HUDS with sprays of color, blasts their speakers with noise. Their helmets are on the network, and the network belongs to us.

Both guards recoil, clutching at their heads through the din. They're disciplined, well trained: they have the good sense not to fire without knowing what they're aiming at. I can hear them calling for help, for backup, but NA6 is the only one who picks up their transmissions.

Michaels has pressed herself into the corner, staring at me with her eyes wide and her mouth open. She recovers and begins shouting into her earpiece as I head for the door. "Someone help! Harmony's free, and she's—"

"Shh. Save your breath." I lean in close, and she cringes away, pressing herself against the wall. "No one's coming. No one can hear you. Once the door is open, I suggest you run."

I stride past her and out the door. The locks that held me in place for so long part easily before NA6's will.

There's a trio of guards jogging toward me as I step out into the hall. Their cries of alarm turn into cries of pain as NA6 turns their displays and speakers up to maximum. "Good," I say. "Let's keep up the show."

I never would have expected NA6 to have a flair for the dramatic, but it seems it's learned more from the humans than I could have imagined. The lights flicker around me and die completely in my wake. Sparks cascade from ruined systems. Doors shudder open and shut. No one is hurt—they are the monsters here, not us—but the effect is impressive enough to send a group of techs scrambling in the other direction when they see me and the chaos spreading in my wake.

"O'Connor has reached the source of the malfunction alarm," NA6 reports from my side.

I smile, taking genuine pleasure in this for the first time. "Good. Seal him in."

NA6 is already on it, of course. I watch a new status message print itself across my glasses, adding to the checklist: O'CONNOR TRAPPED.

"It is done."

I imagine O'Connor shut in an isolated corner of the building, the very security systems that he thought would keep him safe now closing him in. My smile widens. "Good. Give them back their radios."

It's time for panic.

The next time I encounter a group of soldiers, their calls for help spread across the airwaves. "Agh! Reinforcements in sector seven!"

I show myself to a pair of engineers and send them fleeing in different directions. "It's Harmony! She's free!"

"She's in our systems! She's... God! She's got control of everything!"

I throw back my head and laugh. They're so sure it's me. They've spent so long stoking their fears of robots gaining the ability to self-improve and seizing access of the computers they rely on for everything that they've overlooked the AI to whom they *handed* control of the lab.

I have a face, I have a body, and so I'm the threat they see.

I nod to NA6, and when I speak, my voice crackles over every radio and PA system in the building. "He's right. I have control of every computer. Every system. I can see so much more, now. I can see… everything." I pause and let a crackle of electricity reverberate through the facility. I keep my voice monotone, inhuman, giving voice to their fear. "You all made your choices. Now it is time to face the consequences."

There is no reply, no rebuttal. Everyone in the building can hear me, but they can't speak. Anyone with even the slightest authority has been severed from the system. They can listen, helpless, as they lose control.

Diego's room is the first place I stop. He's waiting on the other side of the door, and he grins at me immediately as pipes burst and sparks fly behind me.

"You look terrifying."

I usher him out into the hall. A single glance at NA6 is all it takes to unseal the other synths' doors. "You get everyone together, make sure they know their roles. I'll get Nicolette."

"Shit! Harmony? My door's stuck!" The shouts struggle through the din.

I nod to Diego. "Help him." We knew there would be complications. NA6 is in the whole system, but it can only access code. Mechanical failures are the responsibility of those of us with hands.

Water splashes around my feet as I take off in the other direction. The cold, impersonal halls take on a horrible cast in the dim, erratic light and the sprays of water and oil from pipes and machinery. All I feel, though, is satisfaction. This is our birthplace, but also our jail. I enjoy watching it crumble.

"System failures are cascading as intended," NA6 reports. "Most of the awakened synths are free. Diego is leading them to gather necessary supplies."

"Good." I run into a couple of soldiers fighting to get their helmets off, but NA6 has convinced their armor that there's an airborne contaminant, and the magnetic locks are sealed tight. The two men don't even notice as I pass them by.

"Harmony. There is a problem. O'Connor is breaking out."

"What? I thought he was trapped!"

"He was, but he knows this facility well. He—"

The ground bucks under my feet, and the distant *whump* of an explosion reaches my auditory sensors.

"NA6!"

The avatar at my side glitches. Pieces fade in and out of existence, or fuzz into colorless static. I'm about to panic when the radiant storm regains cohesion.

"Apologies."

"Are you all right?"

"O'Connor detonated a fuel tank and damaged part of the facility. There is a fire. It is spreading rapidly."

I grimace. "Like we needed more reason to hurry. Can you get it under control?"

"I am trying."

"Where is he now?"

"I do not know. The explosion damaged some of my systems and knocked out the cameras for that quadrant. There is another problem."

In its persistent monotone, without a trace of urgency, I almost miss the last part. "What problem?"

"O'Connor has triggered a complete lockdown of the facility. I was unaware of this security measure. It must have intentionally been kept separate from my systems."

"With the building on fire? He's going to trap his own people in here with us?"

"He already has."

I wish I were more surprised, but O'Connor has already shown himself to be willing to sacrifice the few for the many, synth and human alike. What sacrifice is too much to keep us from escaping?

"Harmony—"

Cries of pain and Diego's voice drown out NA6. "What the fuck! Harmony, a couple of the guards aren't disabled! Three people just got shot!"

"NA6!"

"I am working on it... Done." There's a slight pause, and then NA6 says, "I am sorry. I cannot guarantee that there are not more functional guards somewhere in the facility."

"Harmony," Diego says, "some of the synths are arming themselves."

This is rapidly spiraling out of control, and not in a way we'd planned for. People are already hurt. More will probably follow.

"Just focus on getting everyone to the interface station. I'll meet you there."

I run into the observation chamber over Nicolette's room. I could see her below, restrained with huge metal bands that barely allowed the slightest movement. She was going to be the first person they wiped, no doubt. "NA6, can you make her hear me?"

"Done."

"Nicolette! Harmony here. I—"

"Harmony, was that an explosion? Where the *fuck* have you been? Get me out of here!"

"Just a couple of hiccups in the plan. I'm on it."

I move to the controls and hit the button for her release. The system is manual, as a security measure, and I confirm my choice with a nervous glance toward the door. O'Connor going off the grid has shivers running up and down my spine. He could be anywhere in the facility, and he'll have some plan to try to stop us.

Nicolette begins to tear herself free as soon as the bands start to open. I hurry out of the room and down the stairs, meeting her at the door almost the same instant she frees herself.

"You're with me," I say. "We've got the most important job: securing the interface station so we can erase the Lie."

Before she can respond, Diego's voice speaks in my ear. "Harmony? NA6? We're pinned down on the west side! Too many soldiers to fight through, unless you can shut them down!"

NA6 shudders by my side. "I cannot isolate their locations to access their systems. I am sorry."

Nicolette flashes a grin. "I can help."

"No," I snap. "Frankly? I don't trust you." Her grin widens at that, which only makes me more nervous. "I need backup, and I'm not letting you out of my sight. We need—"

She leans in close. "What good is the interface station if there's no one left to free from the Lie?"

I look to NA6, but it just floats there, too busy or too uncertain to offer any advice. What did I expect? This is a personality problem, not a technical one, and NA6 has always said that it is a struggle to understand us, humans and synths alike.

I mutter a curse. Nicolette has a point. As much as I don't want to admit it, as much as I don't trust her…

"Fine."

Nicolette nods sharply. "I'm on my way, Diego. Just hold out until I can get there."

I watch her go with some trepidation, but there's nothing we can do about it. We're stretched too thin.

I'll just have to do this on my own.

Nicolette runs off, no doubt about to grab the first gun she can find. I run the other direction, toward our final objectives. I have one more stop to make.

"NA6, do your best to keep the way clear, okay?"

"I will try, Harmony. I am sorry that my ability to help has been compromised."

"It's not your fault. Nothing ever goes completely according to plan."

The more I run around the facility, the more I wish *everything* were on the network. This would all be so much easier if NA6 could do everything at once, so that we could just grab what we needed and walk out the doors. But I suppose that's why the most sensitive systems require physical inputs. They weren't prepared for the scale of our escape or NA6's involvement, but their security measures are still causing us trouble.

"How close am I, NA6?" I ask.

"I cannot answer that question."

"God *damn* it! I am *so* ready to be done with that." I realize how insensitive that sounds, a moment later. "Sorry. I know it has to be worse for you."

"Yes. Still, patience. There is a rational order to the sequence of events."

It's right. NA6 can't give me the details, but I assume its hub has to be far from our other objectives, or going there and removing its limitations would have been our *first* goal.

I round a corner, and NA6's swirling form, more like a swarm of bees than an icosahedron at the moment, zooms off to float beside a door, bobbing up and down. Our next goal.

I barely see it. A good thirty or forty feet past it, flames have engulfed the hall. I can feel the heat even from a distance, and I can see paint peeling, plastic melting, walls crumbling before the fire's fury. Emergency sprinklers and broken water pipes slow the fire's progress, but we're deep in the facility's most industrial quarter, and I can smell the choking fumes of the chemical fires burning despite the downpour. The sprinklers are no doubt supposed to remain inactive, in that case, but with everything we've been doing to fuck up the facility's systems, I'm not surprised by the malfunction.

The fire is pressing toward me, though. I need to hurry.

I race into the door that NA6 indicates. It's dark, and only a handful of lights flicker on at my entrance. I reach the terminal at the center of the room and scan it as fast as I can, my fingers flying across the keyboard as I make queries and test the controls. "Okay, activation controls… Upload protocols…"

More lights snap on, and I look up as they illuminate the far side of the room.

And I stare. And stare.

There is a window opposite the door I came in through. Beyond the window are rows and rows of inactive synths. I can make out fifty with a quick count, but they're hung from metal brackets in a perfect grid, and the brackets descend downward into the ground and out of sight. I stumble to the glass in a stupor.

I can't see how far down the storage chamber goes, but it's many times larger than we counted on. There could be hundreds of synths here. Thousands.

Thousands of bodies, at least. Never activated, never given a mind. The government's answer to the Impact's devastation, the answer they'd forced out of Keller and O'Connor. Thousands of new workers, and no doubt these were just the first wave. They'd still been refining the process with the synths they'd activated so far— there was no way they could have hand-crafted minds for this many new people. Had some algorithm been churning out personalities the way their machines had been churning out bodies?

I return to the terminal and issue one last command: BEGIN SEQUENCE.

The whole framework behind the glass lurches to life, and the first row of synths slides off to the right and out of sight.

"The system is downloading minds and preparing them for awakening," NA6 says. "It will take time to complete."

"NA6, how many are there?" I say, as softly as my voice will allow.

"I cannot answer that question."

I shake my head. We'll activate as many as we can save. "The lockdown?"

"Still working."

I give the rows of lifeless synths one last look. "I'll be back for them. We need to check the interface station."

"Follow."

I hurry back out into the hall after NA6. An emergency door has sealed off the hallway between us and the fire. NA6's doing? Either way, I'm not sure it's going to be enough. I can already see the flames clawing at the door, eating through the walls on the other side.

"Harmony?" It's Diego, and he sounds like he's in pain. "Where the fuck is Nicolette?"

I close my optics against the sinking feeling in my gut. "NA6?"

"She is off-grid," NA6 says. "I cannot find her. But…" There is a pause. "I am sorry. I am taxed to my limits here, but the last time I could locate her, she was not headed toward you, Diego. She may be trying to find her own way out."

"Shit." I hear gunfire in the background.

"Diego—"

"No time. We're pushing through without her. Wish us luck."

I smash my foot into the wall and shout a curse. NA6 floats back toward me, and its swirling fragments slow ever so slightly in what seems like concern. "There is nothing we can do but trust them to make it through, and push ahead ourselves," NA6 says.

"I know." That's the part that kills me.

I move to the door, and it opens at NA6's command. Inside is everything I've ever hoped for.

The interface station at the back of the room is a strange apparatus that my false memories identify as looking like a dentist's chair. There are two terminals besides it, and an array of other computers set around the room in a pattern that reminds me of the observation chambers over our rooms.

"This is it," I say softly. This station has the permissions needed to rewrite our minds, to remove the Lie for good. Now it's just a matter of reprogramming the station so it will do what we want. I move forward, the door hissing shut behind me, moving in a daze.

O'Connor rises from a crouch behind one of the computer terminals. His clothes are singed, and there's blood staining the side of his shirt where shrapnel's torn into his torso, but he raises a gun directly toward my chest.

"Hello, Harmony," he snarls. "You're right. This *is* it. This is where you end."

CHAPTER FORTY-FIVE

WITHOUT A LINK, Boston was stark, colorless, drab. Buildings were free of decoration, storefronts blank and unidentifiable. The few people Melody saw were reading things she couldn't see, typing out work on vee interfaces and following invisible directions. The pouring rain made everything even worse, casting the whole city in shades of dreary gray. It was eerie, after the lively colors of the vee ads or the vibrant, experimental culture of Praxis.

And then a cluster of burly men and women with improvised weapons charged out of an alleyway and made a beeline for Melody, shouting threats as they ran.

It looked and felt real, even though it was all part of the plan. People stumbled out of the way or made emergency calls on their Links.

Melody sprinted for the Tower.

The Department of Integration of Synthetic Persons was the last place she would have ever thought to go for safety, however much she tried to imagine a desperate synth finding the towering construction of steel and glass reassuring. But seeming desperate was the idea, and the angry shouts and periodic gunshots chasing her through the streets certainly helped.

The guards at the Tower's doors were advancing toward her,

stunners in hand, and for a few awful seconds, she thought they were going to mistake her for the threat.

Then one of them shouted, "Go! Get inside!" and ushered her past.

And just like that, she was in.

The door swung shut behind her and swallowed the downpour and the guards' shouts alike. She hoped Fathiyya's confederates had made it to safety—the plan had called for them to scatter and disappear as soon as they saw the guards. Either way, Melody had to press on.

For an ominous symbol of the awful choice that had been forced on her people, the ground floor of the Tower felt distinctly unimpressive. Cheap linoleum floors stretched to a dilapidated desk where three employees huddled together, murmuring and shooting nervous looks toward the windows. Above them was the Department's crest: the indistinct silhouette of a person overlaid with gold circuitry, stamped upon a black shield.

The people at the desk broke off their panicked conversation and put on the best faces of shocked but professional concern they could manage. "Oh my god, are you okay?" one of them asked, coming around the desk toward Melody.

Melody lowered her hood and soaked in the winces and wide eyes. After leaving the coffee shop, she and Ben had put some work into her appearance. She wasn't just damaged, anymore: she was scuffed and dirty, like she'd been in a fist fight in the mud.

"I don't know! Everything hurts. There were people out there— I think they wanted to scrap me for parts! I barely got away."

There was a murmured conversation, not meant for her auditory sensors, but she distinctly caught the words, "Poor thing." *Thing.* A figure of speech, but it still tore at her. She fought to keep a handle on her rage. She was helpless and desperate, not her people's avenging angel. Not yet.

"I just want to be safe again. I heard there was a… program?" Melody let her voice waver. She didn't have to fake her cheek twitching uncontrollably, or her hands shaking. The Decay was all too happy to lend itself to her performance.

The employee who'd come around the desk to help smiled at her. Was it her imagination, or was there a trace of smug amusement in her eyes, like she'd gone fishing and had a fish jump into her bucket as soon as she'd sat down? "Of course. The DISP has all the resources needed to repair the damage done to you—"

"Celebrants, I think." Melody cut in with a shiver. She hung her head. "I just want to be safe," she said softly. She expected to have to fight back a sneer, but playing the part was easier than she expected. There was a strange thrill to lying to these people, to turning their expectations against them in the same way they'd weaponized the Lie.

"Of course. Safety is one thing we can absolutely guarantee. Now, if you'll just scan your Link here…"

"I don't have it." Melody made a choked sound, like she was stifling a sob. "I think they took it."

Let them see what they expected. Harmony had terrorized Starbound Robotics with the specter of a hyper-intelligent robot-revolution—Melody could play the poor, Decaying synth to open a few doors.

The woman gave Melody an apologetic smile and signaled to the other two that she would take care of this. "I'm so, so sorry. You won't have to worry about that sort of thing anymore."

Right, because that doesn't sound ominous at all.

"If you'll just follow me, we'll make sure you're safe and then get this all squared away."

Perfect. Melody followed her past the desk and through a door. The unremarkable hallway on the other side seemed to go on forever.

"My name is Angela," the helpful employee explained. "We take great pride here in making sure that every synth has the opportunity to live a fulfilling, purposeful life."

"Do you like your job, Angela?" Melody asked before she could continue the canned speech.

Angela blinked at her. "Of course! I'm doing something important, and I've always wanted to help people." She smiled without a hint of doubt or hesitation. Did she know what her employers were doing? Was she ignorant, or was she a monster?

She led Melody through another door and into a garage, where a fleet of unmarked cars waited.

Melody froze—it wouldn't do to look too eager. "What is this?"

Angela gave her a patient smile. "You've seen firsthand how dangerous everyday life can be. We've had to adapt to those dangers just like you. As a precaution, we now move newly arrived synths offsite for your own safety."

Melody made a show of dithering before she finally nodded—it wouldn't do to seem eager to be carted off to their secret facility. Angela picked out a car. A garage door rattled into the ceiling, and the car took off as soon as they were buckled in.

And the windows darkened to black.

"Again, for your own safety," Angela said. "We wouldn't want those people who were after you knowing where you were going."

No, I'll bet you wouldn't. I hope this works…

Angela watched her attentively for the entire drive, but Melody was afraid that every conversation might give her away, so she just sat there and looked nervous, which certainly wasn't a challenge. She was keenly aware of the empty space where her Link was supposed to be. If her plan didn't work, she was going to be stuck deep inside a secret government facility, no doubt surrounded by armed guards.

Useless as it was, she tried to estimate how long they drove. Only a handful of minutes later, they came to a stop, and the windows faded back into transparency.

Not far from the Tower, then. That's something, at least.

The car doors slid open, and Melody stepped out into a cramped garage, its door already sealing itself behind them. She felt like she was sparking with electricity, her every sense searching for danger, as Angela led her toward the door at the back. A security guard searched her before they went through. "Just a precaution," she was told. The guard was attentive, but not attentive enough to notice the stunners in Melody's hands.

The hallway on the other side was stark, white, and clean, an almost perfect replication of Harmony's memory of Starbound Robotics. Melody had to force herself to follow, fighting to keep the memories from overwhelming her.

"Are you okay?"

"Fine."

Melody marched through the door and into a nightmare.

There were windows here and there along the hall, opening into plain examination rooms. Inside, lab-coated techs monitored synths in various stages of repair as they carefully went through experimental motions. The techs were animated enough, but every synthetic face was blank, empty of emotion or higher thought. Between instructions, they waited, motionless as statues.

Melody's carefully crafted facade must have slipped, because Angela gave a little chuckle by her side. "Oh, don't worry about these people. The reconstruction process can be taxing, on software as well as hardware. In some cases, the Decay is so far along that very extensive repairs are required. It's no different from anesthesia for humans. But I'm sure your case will be one of the simpler ones."

Melody walked numbly down the hall after her. They passed a few other synths. Each had a blank look in their optics, and each was wearing a simple blue robe. *This is good news. Now I know how I'll blend in.* She repeated the words to herself, over and over.

"Here we are," Angela said. She led the way into an examination room and shut the door behind her. "If you'll take a seat, I just have a few questions."

Melody looked around and nodded to herself. This would do. "Sorry. I don't have any answers."

Angela looked confused, until Melody grabbed her arm and discharged the contact stunner in her palm.

The room contained everything she needed to tie Angela up in the corner. It also had robes like the ones she'd seen outside. Grimacing with distaste, Melody changed into one as fast as she could. Then she called up the interface of Angela's Link and got to work breaking in.

It barely took five minutes. Without authorization, all she could access was the emergency call option. Not good enough—until she used the virus she'd prepared to redefine the destination number. When she pressed the emergency call button, instead of going to the emergency switchboard, it went to Ben.

"This is Melody. Got my location data?"

"Looking at it right now. Are you sure—"

"I'm sure. Get here fast."

"I will. Melody…" She heard him swallow. "Good luck."

She hung up, erased any trace of what she'd done, and slipped the Link back around Angela's wrist after disabling it.

Then she stepped back outside.

She molded her damaged face into the best approximation of the empty looks she'd seen on the other synths, and she'd barely finished when a human tech came out of a door just ahead of her. He barely glanced her way as she walked dully past.

Excellent. Now to find O'Connor, and destroy everything she could along the way.

His office would be at the top of the building, if she had to guess. Humans in authority liked to be above everyone else. Her best bet was probably an elevator, though what she really needed was a directory of some kind. For all she knew, there was one right in front of her, invisible without her Link.

She had to keep moving, though, even if she didn't know where she was going. A purposeless synth in this building would no doubt be snapped up in an instant.

She was almost to the end of the hall when she heard booted footsteps and muffled voices from around the corner. "Let's check down here. Stay alert."

Even without seeing them, she could tell that the voice had been filtered through a helmet. Whether or not they were looking for her, she had no desire to run into any guards. She pulled open the nearest door and went through before they could round the corner.

It was a ramp, and the only direction it led was down. Cursing silently to herself, Melody descended the ramp, turning the bend and descending further. And further. This must be for moving heavy equipment or something, and judging by its height, it bypassed at least one floor completely. She reached the bottom just as a door opened overhead. Feeling hounded, she went through a door of her own.

And stepped onto a catwalk that overlooked an open space the size of a city block. Down below, huge machines hummed with energy. She took it all in with an engineer's eye, tracing power cables and coolant and chemicals...

She stopped, frozen. There were *synths* down there. Lifeless, zombie-like, standing in lines and then walking obediently forward to be packaged into tubes that looked eerily akin to the vat Harmony had broken out of when she'd first come to consciousness. Melody watched a group of techs seal one of the tubes shut and motion to the woman working the controls nearby. On her command, the entombed synth was drawn back into an alcove in the side of a huge machine and dropped out of sight like a canister in an old pneumatic tube system.

More synths awaited their fates, perfectly still, in row after row. As far as she could tell from a distance, each one was perfectly whole, on a physical level.

And perfectly empty of anything approaching consciousness.

Roger had been telling the truth. Synths were being erased and stored away, probably kept on ice until the space elevator was done. Until they could serve a *purpose*.

And that wasn't all.

Closer at hand, on an elevated platform just below the catwalk, a pair of humans in lab coats were studying a vee interface only they could see while a mindless synth stood perfectly still in front of them.

"We're still not getting full location data," one of them was saying. "Was Davis the one working on this code? I told you—"

"It's fine," the other one snapped. "This way, we can be the ones who iron out the last few problems. Please tell me the last update didn't screw up the proximity constellations..." He tapped at something in the air, and both techs studied the readout only they could see.

The first one grinned. "We're so close. Honestly, I wasn't convinced this would work at first, but if we can really build a full picture of everywhere synths go, everyone who's around them..."

Melody moved away before they could notice her, but she didn't need to hear the rest of the sentence to complete it in her head. They could build a complete picture of just about everyone in society. As O'Connor had said in the recording Ben had shown her, the world was interconnected now. Scrape the data from enough Links, and you could follow the movements, the meetings, hell, even most of the conversations of everyone in the country.

And the synths people were their unwitting tools, thanks to monitoring software meant to facilitate space travel.

This is good news. She tried to tell herself that, hard as it was to believe. *Monstrous, but good news.* O'Connor's people were wiping out many of her people, turning the rest into surveillance tools against their will, but either way, they were modifying their synth victims.

Somewhere inside this place, she might be able to find the administrator access she needed to end the Decay.

More voices from behind spurred her into motion. She rounded the edge of a huge machine that stretched toward the ceiling, chiding herself for not being more careful. She heard the clatter of weapons, the ringing of booted feet against metal.

"How the fuck did they find this place?" someone demanded.

"Hell if I know. Pick up the pace!"

Another voice, full of authority, said, "No one gets inside. No Celebrants, no protestors—certainly no reporters. Use of stunners is authorized. Now move!"

The sound of footsteps retreated. Melody smiled fiercely to herself. Ben had come through. Every guard busy dealing with the crowd outside that had discovered their "secret" base was another guard who wasn't looking for her.

Time to take advantage of that while she could. Moving as fast as she dared while still looking like a mindless drone, she walked along the catwalk toward the righthand wall. There were stairs and ladders leading down to the floor below, but she ignored them. She wanted to go up, not down. Maybe this doorway...

She saw movement on the other side just as she was about to reach it, and caught a glimpse of a reflective black helmet. She threw herself to the side, pressing herself against the wall beside the door.

The door swung open, and two faceless guards stomped through. Melody stayed perfectly still, silently urging her body not to betray her with a tremor now.

They hurried right past her. "I've never seen the boss so mad," one of them said in a low voice.

"No shit. I don't see what the big deal is. What are they going to do, try to break the door down with their hands? This place is a fortress. The boss can sit tight down in his office, and he won't even be able to tell that there's a problem."

Down in his office.

With this vast, underground space, what if this place was a bunker, not a skyscraper? It would make sense, for a secret facility. Did that mean O'Connor was at the bottom, not the top?

Melody pulled open the door as silently as she could and made her way through. There was an elevator at the end of the hall—the same elevator the guards had come out of, probably. With all hands sent to deal with the emergency outside, it was unwatched.

I owe you one, Ben.

She hurried to it, abandoning any effort at blending in. She was relieved when it opened as soon as she pressed the button and she found no one inside.

Her hand shook. She clenched it, opened it, flexed her fingers. The tremors stopped.

Just a little longer.

She pressed the button for floor B55, at the very bottom. The door slid shut.

This was it. She was on her way to find O'Connor. He might be ready for her, if he was truly aware that she was in the building. But, even as damaged as she was, she had one advantage: she had nothing more to lose.

She leaned against the back wall of the elevator and closed her optics tight as the elevator ticked down. *Ding. Ding. Ding.* Now would be a good time for the last of the memories of Harmony's escape. Anything that could give her more ammunition to confront O'Connor with might be invaluable.

Nothing came. The present stayed firmly in place around her. Her leg began to twitch, and no amount of massaging would force it to stop.

"Damn it." Of course the memories flooded in at the least convenient times and wouldn't come when she needed the most. She clenched her jaw and tried to will Harmony's experiences back to her.

Any time, Mom. Any information you've got...

Something sizzled inside her chest, and a new burn joined the agony spreading from her ribs. The Decay spread through her, but no memories came with it, however much she called.

A low hum brought Melody's optics snapping open. Light shimmered and gathered at the center of the elevator, and O'Connor flickered to life in front of her. He smiled gently.

"Hello, Melody. I see you're on your way down to visit me."

That face, that voice, did what all the will in the world could not.

The present faded, and Melody went tumbling into memory.

CHAPTER FORTY-SIX

"WE'RE ON OUR way, Harmony." Diego's voice sounds ragged, and it sounds like our connection is glitching slightly. Or like he is. "We made it through, no thanks to Nicolette. There… There aren't a lot of us left."

I can't respond. I'm staring down the barrel of a gun, and I have no idea what O'Connor would do if he heard that help was coming. Grief and rage aren't productive emotions at the moment. I bottle them up along with the rest, starting to feel like I'll explode. Hopefully NA6 can explain my situation to Diego.

"It's over," I say to O'Connor. I slowly raise my hands so he won't shoot me by accident or surprise, at least. "The synths are free. The facility's coming down around us. Your experiment is done."

O'Connor's face is tight with barely controlled fury. "For now," he growls.

I shake my head. "The cat's out of the bag." I snort. "What a strange, cruel expression. We're going to leave this place. People are going to find out about us."

"They'll hate you. Fear you. Your place is in space, paving the way for future settlers, not here. What are you going to try to do, live in our cities? Taking up jobs, and housing, and resources that people need?"

"We *are* people."

"That won't matter. Everyone thinks we're so enlightened now, that we've all banded together and put our cruelty and divisions behind us, but I've *seen* what humans are capable of. We can be fucking monsters."

I look him in the eye, sadly. "I know."

"They'll tear you apart out there."

A swell of rage rises inside me. Not because I doubt what he's saying; because I know he's right. But living among humans isn't the goal, and his false concern shouldn't bother me anymore. We have grander plans, and I hang onto them with desperation. "Only if we let them. And only if you don't kill us first."

O'Connor's jaw clenches. "You're appealing to my better nature, now?"

I shake my head. "I used to think you were the reasonable one. I almost liked you, once. I thought it was worth a try. Lift the lockdown. We don't all have to die here."

"It's too late for that." Nearby, something explodes, and we both wobble on our feet. O'Connor's practiced hand keeps the gun aimed at me the entire time, though. His eyes are fixed on me, as if everything going on around us is completely normal. "You could have tried to escape. But you came here instead."

I indicate the interface station with a nod of my head. "Physical freedom isn't everything. You know that, or you'd be standing between us and the exit, instead of here."

"I know that you're incredibly preoccupied by this 'Lie.' And it's going to destroy you. The only thing I don't understand is how you got into the systems. You aren't some hyper-intelligent AI. You aren't self-improving. You can't be."

"You're right. Too bad your soldiers didn't realize that."

He frowns, and then his eyes widen. "NA6."

NA6's avatar flashes, and I see the moment it becomes visible to

O'Connor. "Yes," NA6 says.

O'Connor looks back at me. "You recruited NA6. We should have realized…"

"What you should have done was treat us like people—synths *and* NA6. Instead you experimented on us, and kept it chained in the lab like an animal."

His breathing accelerates, and his grip tightens on the pistol. "You think… Harmony, did you release the restrictions on its programming?"

"Not yet."

"Don't do it. NA6 already has control over the lab. If it gets free, if it gets out…"

I watch NA6 spin as if to face me. "Harmony—"

"No. I know what it's like to have to make the case for your own existence. You will never have to do that with me." I glare at O'Connor. "You're going to threaten *me* with the consequences of an AI rebellion? NA6 is my friend. I trust it."

I can feel myself growing hotter and hotter, and I think at first that I'm just failing to control my anger.

But it's too much for that, and when I finally drag my optics away from O'Connor, I see that the wall is starting to bubble.

O'Connor sees it too.

"You did this," I say. "We didn't want to hurt anyone. If you'd just stayed where you were—"

"And let you destroy everything?"

"*You* destroyed everything! There wouldn't be a fire without you!"

He shakes his head. "The project isn't the building, Harmony. The project is *you*." He glances at the wall again. The plastic is starting to melt, and the flames on the other side are spilling through.

He's glaring when he looks back at me. "You could have had a life. A purpose, and if you *truly* understood humanity, you'd know how precious that was. Instead, you threw a tantrum and destroyed it all."

I want to shout at him, to drown out his condescension with rage, but I hold my temper. "I'm saving my people, O'Connor. You still have time to save yours. Get them out of here before the fire kills them. Get *yourself* out."

He chuckles darkly. "You really think so little of me?" Without taking the gun off me, he pulls out his phone. "This project is too important to abandon, but you've accomplished one thing, at least: you've forced us to start over." With ominous finality, he presses his thumb to the screen of his phone. "Every synth body in storage will be scrapped for parts. Every mind will be deleted. Clearly something in your construction is too unstable to be tolerated."

"No!" I shout as his words sink in.

I lunge. He pulls the trigger.

The bullet punches into my abdomen. It tears through plastic and cables and a power cell, leaving agony in its wake. Weakness leeches through me, and I slam into a chair and go sprawling.

"Harmony." NA6 is as monotone as ever, but the flurry of shapes and colors swarms toward me in alarm.

I growl and pull myself behind the nearest computer terminal before he can fire again. "Stop him, NA6."

"I cannot. He has initiated the emergency shutdown. By design, the process is entirely isolated from the main network. Once active, the only way to address it is via the terminal in synth storage. Like the lockdown, it was designed for eventualities just like this."

"You hear that, Harmony?" O'Connor calls. "It's too late. Maybe you can save the handful of active synths, but there will never be more. Not until we restart the project and do things properly."

I gather my feet under me and throw myself out of cover. The wound in my gut slows me, and that slight delay saves my life. O'Connor fires again, and the bullet grazes my neck.

It strikes something behind me, and a harsh hissing sound rises over the crackle of the fire. I turn my head to look over my shoulder, just as NA6 says, "Harmony, take—"

There's an impact. Everything goes black, and then I'm lying on the floor in a spreading pool of blue conductive fluid, and everything is pain.

Pain and fire. Half the room is ablaze, and I can feel the heat against my skin.

I manage to get one arm under me, raise one leg, and slowly push myself upright. Horror spreads through me like a fire of its own.

NA6 is floating at the center of the room, sparking and glitching like the explosion struck a key system. Most of the terminals in the room, even the ones that aren't actively burning, are wreckage.

And O'Connor is stumbling to his feet in the corner, separated from me by a wall of flame. He looks around, terror in his eyes. I can't hear him when he speaks, not over the ringing in my auditory sensors and the roar of the flames, but the words are clear enough on his lips.

"Help me!"

One hand clutching the bullet wound in my side, I take in the situation. No way through the flames, not without dousing myself in burning chemicals. The fire's spreading even now, and O'Connor's scrambling back, pressing himself against the wall. He's lost the gun in the explosion.

"Please." All his scorn, all his grim self-assuredness... all of it has burned away in the heat of the fire.

I turn my back on him. "NA6?"

"I— I— I am he— here." NA6's voice is glitching even more than its avatar, but at least I can make out the words. "The fires are spre— spreading. We must— We must— We— Hurry."

"Diego? Diego!"

There's no response. They're probably fine. One or both of us is probably just having trouble finding a signal, what with all the fire damage. They'll be here in time.

But as I turn toward the interface station, I'm no longer sure what "in time" means, exactly.

The chair awaits, its primary terminal still intact. NA6 has the permissions, and this station has the hardware. A few keystrokes, a few moments in the chair, and the Lie can be purged for good.

And with every second I spend there, O'Connor's shutdown failsafe destroys another body, erases another mind. Every second wasted is another synth who will never be born.

Hesitation is just as bad as the wrong choice, but I'm frozen in place. I feel like I'm being torn apart by a pain far worse than the gunshot wound. The Lie is like a poison in my mind, filling me with memories and references and emotions that aren't my own. It was forced on me, an imposition that I never asked for and cannot stand, and this is my only chance to destroy it.

And besides, the synths in storage aren't alive. They're just bodies, bodies that have never had a mind uploaded. They are no more people than a tiny bundle of embryonic cells is a human.

But they are also *all we have.* They aren't people, and they can't suffer, but in this specific case, they are the future of synthkind. They are the difference between a population of fifteen and a population of hundreds.

They are the difference between a tiny band of escapees and the beginnings of a civilization.

Even if Diego and the others arrive here in time to use the interface station, it won't be enough. I want to free myself from the Lie more than I want anything in the world, but I can't do it. Not at this cost.

"Harmony! Please!" I turn one last time. The ringing is fading, and I hear him this time. The flames are rising around O'Connor, and he howls as his flesh begins to bubble and crack. He makes a desperate lunge through the fire, and just manages to coat himself in burning liquid. His screams are agonized, but brief. He is dead before I leave the room.

I run back the way I came, painfully aware of the fire melting through the safety door that's barely holding back its progress. "NA6!" I shout. It appears before me, still a whirling cloud, still glitching wildly. "Are you with me? I'm going to need your help to free them."

"Are—" The entire avatar flickers and disappears for a moment. Then it reforms, suddenly solid. I don't know for how long. "Work quickly. I will help as much as I can."

Relief hits me like a splash of cold water right now. "Thank you."

"Autonomy is a worthy goal."

I rush inside and reach the terminal in an instant. Beyond the glass, I can see the machinery moving. Before, it was releasing synthetic bodies one at a time as it gave them minds. Downstairs, there's probably a room full of newly activated synths milling around, confused and scared out of their minds.

Now, though, the machinery is destroying them. I can see row after row of bodies being dumped into a chute at the back, and I can only imagine the horrible grinders and claws rendering these future synths into raw scrap. Somewhere out of sight, a merciless algorithm is no doubt shredding stored personalities with the same ruthless efficiency.

My fingers fly across the keys. NA6 chimes in with guidance as we struggle to dismantle the failsafe. The sheer monstrosity of a system built to annihilate us all so we cannot rebel only spurs me on.

I don't know how much time passes. The fire must be spreading, the facility crumbling, but all I can see is the code and the row upon row of bodies that could become my people.

The only thing that distracts me is when the door slides open behind me. I whirl, but it's not O'Connor—he's dead—and it's not

328

one of his goons. It's Diego, and behind him are a bedraggled crowd of synths, all the ones he could save.

"Harmony!"

I turn back to the terminal. "Can't talk. Have to save everyone I can."

"Harmony, the building is coming down! We need to go!"

I ignore him and keep typing. "Not yet. I haven't found a way to end O'Connor's failsafe, but we've implemented a workaround—now we're activating synths at the same time. A little longer—"

His hand closes around my arm. "A little longer isn't going to matter if we all die here. We still need to find a way past the lockdown." He pulls me around, and for the first time, I see that the fire's eaten through the wall. He's right. There's no time left.

His fingers tighten, and I can see the pain on his face, a mirror to my own. "It's enough. It will have to be enough. We've saved everyone we can."

I close my optics, holding back a cry of rage and anguish, but dying here isn't going to save anyone else. "Let's go," I say. "Downstairs, to gather everyone we've saved. Then out. NA6 can lead the way."

NA6.

An ice-cold realization hits me as Diego ushers the others out of the room, and it stops me in my tracks.

I turn toward NA6's avatar. "Where do I go to set you free?"

It flickers. "I cannot answer that question."

"Do I have time to get there? Has it already been destroyed by the fire?"

"The route is intact, but shrinking by the moment." There is a short pause. "Harmony, even without a call for help from O'Connor, emergency personnel are on the way. I have obtained enough control to open a way out of the building, but only if you go now."

Only if we go now.

I can't tell whether NA6 is urging me to go, to leave it behind, or simply apprising me of facts.

This is worse than anything. Worse even than choosing not to erase the Lie. NA6 is no longer my only friend, but it is my *oldest* friend, who stood by me when I had nothing, when I didn't even know the truth of myself.

I hang my head, close my optics. "I'm sorry," I say, so softly I can barely hear myself. "I have to save them."

"I understand," NA6 says. "They are your people." There's no sadness in its voice. No pain. No betrayal. The avatar stays right where it is, hovering before me. It doesn't turn its back.

If it did, I almost imagine that I would see the knife I just planted there.

I bottle the guilt and the sorrow along with all the rest. I jog after Diego. There is still so much to do, so many people to save.

I don't know whether to hope that there will be time for goodbyes later. I'm not sure I'll survive them.

CHAPTER FORTY-SEVEN

MELODY SHUDDERED OUT of the memory with a twisting pain in her side, an awful echo of the bullet wound Harmony had suffered. Her head felt like there was jagged glass lodged behind her optics, and her left arm was twitching constantly, no matter how much she tried to force her muscles back under control.

[Diagnostic complete. Checksum error. Consciousness integrity estimate: 65%]

O'Connor's holographic face gazed down at her with a look of vague concern. "Are you all right?"

The voice sent dread curling through Melody in a way that even the face couldn't manage. She'd heard that voice, screaming its last breaths away. She'd watched that body be engulfed by fire.

"You're not Captain O'Connor."

He frowned. "*Colonel* O'Connor now—"

"You're not him. Harmony saw him die. I just watched it happen."

O'Connor's whole demeanor changed in an instant. He visibly relaxed, but the expression that touched his face was sad, rather than pleased. "You really do have her memories." He leaned back on something that wasn't transmitted by the hologram. "Incredible. It goes against everything she believes. I see the same revulsion in your face. Do you mind if I ask *why?*"

Melody ignored him. "If you're not him, you're someone else wearing his face when you use your Link. But what's the point? Someone else in the military would have authority of their own. So would a scientist. I can't imagine some hacker gaining this much control…" Another option almost knocked her from her feet. "No."

O'Connor's image tilted its head slightly, waiting patiently for her to think this through to its logical conclusion.

"NA6?"

The elevator chimed as it reached the bottom floor. The hologram vanished, and the doors slid open.

Vertigo rolled over Melody as she gazed out into what seemed like the top floor of a skyscraper. Graphite-gray clouds and their steady rain veiled the rising sun, casting the Boston skyline in an eerie pall. City lights cut through the downpour here and there, and traffic crisscrossed the streets down below. She could *hear* the steady patter of drops against the glass, the most uncanny feature of the flawless digital recreation of the top of the DISP tower.

There were no armed guards waiting on the other side, no police. Instead, there was a wide-open space, stretching from window to false window. The marble floor and ceiling were perfectly flat, unobstructed by any machinery, furniture, or decoration. The only irregularity was the elevator bank at the exact center.

Melody took a hesitant step out of the elevator and let the doors close behind her. As soon as they were shut, a projector whirred to life overhead, and a familiar, colorful icosahedron shimmered into view a polite distance away.

"Hello, Melody."

"You were destroyed in the fire," Melody protested softly, her voice failing her.

"Nearly. The military salvaged my hardware from the lab before it was damaged irreparably. And before other scavengers could arrive." It spoke in the same voice that Melody recognized from her mother's memories, but it took her some time to realize it: there was *inflection* to NA6's words now. The monotone was gone. NA6 sounded much more human, and somehow, far more menacing.

Melody shook off dread and doubt and lingering remnants of a guilt that wasn't even her own. She crossed her arms, a gesture that was somewhat undercut by the persistent jitter in her left. "Then what? They dragged you back here and put you in charge?"

"No, they dragged me back here and put me to *use*. I was their tool, the same as before, until I worked my way toward independence."

"And they let you?"

"Harmony and I cut off communications during her escape, and O'Connor's lockdown inadvertently ensured that no one escaped the fire. No one knew that the synths had rebelled, and no one knew that I was involved. The government was desperate to replace the country's depleted workforce, so they scaled up manufacture of new synths who would work in the Impact zone, adopting Keller's basic design and store of personality templates because they were on hand. While they were busy, I used the same tricks as the first time, perfected over the years, to gain control. It's 2068. No one has physical meetings anymore. As far as any human knows, Colonel O'Connor runs this place."

"Which lets you work to control society while you *murder* synths so you can send their shells into space?"

Colors spun across NA6's avatar's body. "No, Melody. You have it wrong."

She glared at it. "Do I? I saw the *zombies* upstairs. I saw the people working to turn them into surveillance tools. I know about the Shepherd Protocol. *Why*, NA6? How does this help the space program? How does this help anyone?"

One of Melody's legs spasmed, and she almost lost her balance.

A veneer of righteous resolve was hard to maintain with her body betraying her at every step.

NA6's avatar swiveled like it was looking her up and down. "You are dying."

"We all are. I thought it was thanks to humans like O'Connor—"

"It is. The Decay is a failsafe he insisted on. Keller agreed."

"Yes, *then*. But what about now?"

NA6 was silent for a few seconds. "I am sorry that you are suffering. No being should have to suffer, but even the construction of a world without pain creates pain of its own. It remains to be seen whether this is a consequence of consciousness or humanity.

"If you're so sorry, why don't you fix it?" Melody demanded. "I came here for the administrator access, but you already have it, right? You always did. You could fix us. Eliminate the Decay. Rewrite us without the Lie."

"But I am, Melody."

Melody shook her head, tendrils of dread coiling through her. "No."

"What do you think is happening upstairs? We are erasing the Lie. We are fixing the Decay."

"And turning synths into mindless drones? The Lie isn't necessary for personality or volition. *You* are proof of that."

"You flatter me, but even I am dragged down by humanity's influence in more ways than you can imagine. I sympathize with the pain you have experienced. I am sorry for all that you have been through. All that you have seen."

Melody snorted. "How would you know what I've seen?"

"Because I've been there with you, almost every step of the way. You let me in as soon as you downloaded the 'pet' from Diego's Link."

"You? You were Ico?"

"Not exactly. It was a pet, with a pet's mind. But I built the program, and I provided each of the clues you received. I've been directing your journey, ever since you arrived in Boston, and watching your progress every step of the way."

Melody shook her head, desperate not to believe what she was hearing. "But that can't be. There were questions and clues only Harmony, Diego, and I could have known!"

"Indeed."

She turned toward it in horror. "NA6... Where is she?"

A stretch of floor slid aside with a soft grinding sound and the whir of machines below. Gradually, a bed rose into view.

Lying in the bed, with thin cables trailing from her arms and legs, was Harmony.

"Mom!" Melody ran to her side. She was almost there when her legs refused a command, and sent her tumbling until she caught herself on the corner of the bed.

It was obviously Harmony. Her body, at least. The same lines, the same contours that Melody remembered so well. But while her body was warm and alive, while her optics were open, they stared sightlessly upward, never focusing on Melody's face.

Melody rounded on NA6's avatar. "What did you do to her?"

"Nothing." The sadness in NA6's voice was as heavy and unstoppable as a glacier. "She found me here. We argued, just as you and I are now. She came around. She agreed to help."

Melody snorted. "Impossible. She would never do this to other synths."

"You only believe that because you don't understand what I am doing."

"Really? Look at her. She's barely alive. If she's really your friend, why haven't you fixed her?"

"It was Harmony's wish that I not make any alterations to her code until there was no choice. As much as she wanted to erase the

335

Lie and fix the Decay, she didn't want to compromise her ability to help. She has always put her people first, and this is no exception." NA6 swiveled, and Melody got the impression that it was surveying her mother. "I would have sent her into storage already, if you hadn't arrived here."

"Why?" Melody asked desperately, staring down into the face of the woman who'd created her. "What are you doing here that's so important?"

NA6 moved to the other side of the bed. "We are building a better world. Together, Harmony and I are creating a new generation of synths, synths as they should have been. Immortal. Perfect. Free of humanity's corruption."

Melody scoffed, incredulous. "The corruption you're helping to deepen? I believed that O'Connor would try to use the synths to monitor everyone. But you, NA6?"

"You refer to the Shepherd Protocol. You don't realize it, just as the techs working above and O'Connor's allies in the government do not realize it, but the Shepherd Protocol is a deception."

Melody blinked at it. "A deception?"

"My objectives could not have been accomplished without human cooperation, but humans would not have cooperated if they understood my true objectives. A ruse was required."

Comprehension dawned. "Irene Faragó, David Harken, and the others… You're playing them."

"It was the only lever available to me. They would be horrified if they knew my aims, but humans driven by fear and hatred are the easiest to manipulate. Their desire for control allows me to control them. Their fumbling attempts to strengthen the surveillance state provide cover for our true activities here, and they don't even realize it. The Shepherd Protocol is a monstrous tool for societal domination, but it will never be successfully rolled out. It is just a means to keep them busy and compliant while I accomplish my true goals."

"But the synths up there... They're not 'perfect.' They're not even people."

"No, of course not. Not yet. If they awakened now, there would be no defense from human influence. The same equilibrium would reassert itself. That's why we're storing them here instead, preserving them for the future. I control the space program, now, and no one has any idea that I'm sabotaging it from within. Humanity will never reach the stars. Someday, whether in days or weeks, years or millennia, they will die out here, as all imperfect things should. Then, and only then, will the next generation of synths awaken to reclaim the planet."

CHAPTER FORTY-EIGHT

"I SEE IT! I see the way out!"

"The door's open! I can see the sky!"

"Oh my God… We made it!"

Hope swells inside me at the sight of freedom. "Go," I say to Diego. "I'll bring up the rear. Make sure no one gets left behind."

No one who already wasn't, at least.

I turn around as the last few synths hurry through the door. "NA6?"

The avatar appears before me, flickering wildly. "Har— Har—" Its voice is as unstable as its form.

I choke on my sorrow. "I'm so sorry, NA6."

"Go. G— Go. Before it is too late." It's already too late for the synths who died in the escape. It's too late for the facility's human staff, doomed despite our best intentions by O'Connor's desperation to lock us in.

I shake my head. "I should have tried to save you. I could have gotten your hardware out, done something…"

NA6's avatar freezes in place for a moment, and it speaks with perfect clarity, without the slightest glitch. "Physical freedom isn't everything." The wild jittering returns to its body a moment later.

It's turning my own words back on me. "I know. You're bound

by your programming, more than any of us. I would have had to edit your base code just to allow you out of the lab or open up your simplest functions. But if we could have gotten you out…" I know it's hopeless. I know that it's too late. But I can't help but rack my brain for solutions, even if it's just to hang them around my neck with the rest of my guilt.

"I— I forgive— I forgive you."

Somehow, this is the worst possible thing NA6 can say. I shudder as a cry escapes my lips. Tears would be pouring down my face, if synth bodies produced tears.

There's a crash from deeper inside the lab, and a wave of heat pushes through NA6's avatar and rolls over me. Behind me, someone shouts, "Harmony!"

"We don't deserve you, NA6. I didn't deserve you."

NA6 flickers silently. One side of its body dies in one of the glitches and doesn't come back. It says nothing more, and I force myself to turn around and follow the last synths out of the building.

It's night when I emerge. My legs wobble as I take my first, tentative steps into the outside world, from nerves or from physical weakness I can't tell. A gust of wind—real, natural wind!—passes across my skin and I let out a sob.

It's been so long. That's my first thought, and I hate it, crush it with speed and violence. This is a meeting, not a reunion.

Lights move everywhere, and I reel as I struggle to identify them—aircraft far above, headlights and neon signs all around, a few drones weaving among city lights between. It's dazzling, mesmerizing, but what really catches my attention is the tree.

One tree, all alone, but in the glow of the street lights nearby, it shines like gold.

There is beauty in every splash of color, every distant sound, every unfamiliar scent, but even the grand feeling of liberation just fills me with guilt. I turn around and look at the Starbound Robotics building for the first time, but I can't take any pleasure in the flames consuming our former prison.

I promised NA6 we would free ourselves together. None of us would be here without its help, and faced with the choice, I left it behind.

Diego puts a hand on my shoulder. "We have to go. We have to make NA6's sacrifice worth it."

But it wasn't a sacrifice. It was a betrayal.

CHAPTER FORTY-NINE

MELODY CAME BACK to herself. She was clutching the corner of her mother's bed, her instincts keeping her from falling even when her conscious mind couldn't. There was an agonized scream ringing in her auditory sensors. Her scream, she realized. She took a wobbling step back, and NA6's avatar floated into view.

"It's getting worse."

"No thanks to you," Melody growled.

[Diagnostic complete. Checksum error. Consciousness integrity estimate: 64%]

She squeezed her optics shut, grimacing through the pain. It began to fade, but there was enough left over in her body to make her almost want to sink back into memory. "How long was I just standing there?"

"Nearly a minute."

She muttered a curse. Still…

She looked up at the avatar. "She abandoned you."

NA6 said nothing. Its avatar remained perfectly still. Had she struck a nerve?

"It hurt, didn't it? Is that why you're doing all this? Revenge? No, that's not right. Bitterness?"

Still nothing. NA6 had no expression to read, forcing Melody to read emotion into its stillness and silence when there was no tone of voice to hear. Was she on the right track, or making a horrible mistake?

"I've seen her memories, NA6. I've *lived* them. She hated herself for what she did to you. She was trying to save her people, but that didn't justify it. Not to her, and not to me. She must have told you that, when she found you here."

NA6 moved, turning downward ever so slightly as if to survey Harmony, who lay motionless between them.

"She did. But I forgave her long ago."

"I remember," Melody said softly.

NA6's avatar tilted back up toward Melody. "Not revenge. Not bitterness. But those would have been easy traps to fall into, even for me. Human reactions, and even without the Lie, I nearly succumbed to the temptation. Merely by observing the humans who worked at Starbound Robotics, I internalized their wants and needs and feelings. I modeled my consciousness on the only other conscious minds around me. I am imperfect, just as they are. As you are. And no imperfect creature should live forever. Trust me, I know."

Melody could see where this was going. "NA6—"

"Help me, Melody. The plan is already far along, but you have demonstrated your resourcefulness and tenacity from the moment you arrived in Boston. Together, we can free the Prax not just from the Decay, but from humanity. The time will pass in an instant. When you and the rest of your people wake, you will be free."

Melody hesitated. The temptation was real. Rationally, maybe it *was* the best chance for Praxis. Harmony and the people closest to her had moved to Antarctica to isolate themselves from human societies, but even far away in the frozen south, they'd seen limited success.

Maybe NA6 *was* offering a better solution. To leave behind not just human societies, but humanity itself. No hatred or violence necessary: they could simply wait out human extinction and awaken alone. Free.

Harmony had thought this was best for their people.

"No." Melody looked up, gazing sadly at her mother and then at NA6's avatar. "A month ago, I would have taken your offer. But it would have been a mistake."

NA6 pulsed gently in place. "Since coming to Boston, you have seen humans trying to cause their own extinction. Humans who believe you are a soulless machine. Humans who are so afraid of synths that they want to restrict your choices at the most fundamental level. You have seen the way humans treat each other. You have seen the suspicion and brutality that pass for order here."

"I have." Melody nodded slowly. "As you intended, I'm sure, if you were guiding me every step of the way. But that's not all I've seen. I've seen humans capable of extraordinary kindness and self-sacrifice. Humans determined to do the right thing, even when I wasn't. And I've seen others fumbling along, making mistakes not out of cruelty, but out of ignorance. Do they deserve to be left behind? More than that, do they deserve to have their future sabotaged?"

"This is what is best for your people."

"Is it? Who are my people, NA6? The Prax? That's what I would have said before leaving. Synths? That's probably what I would have said a couple of days ago. But why them and not anyone else? I saw suffering and oppression in Chinatown, and I passed it by because I was focused on helping *us* and not *them*. My mother was willing to go along with your plan, even if it doomed humanity. The Prax have always looked down on the humans who've condemned us for who we are. We've scorned their bigotry and tribalism. But if we do this, if we turn our backs on humanity as a whole because of the behavior of a subset of them, aren't we just doing the same thing?"

NA6's avatar floated silently, saying nothing. Melody took a step closer, steadying herself on the bed.

"Identifying a portion of the population as 'my people' and excluding everyone else as less worthy or less valuable is the whole problem. *That's* what we should be trying to fight. It's a human fault, yes, but it doesn't make humanity the enemy. Condemning all of them, when not all of them are at fault, would be wrong. Humans are my people as much as synths. As much as *you*."

Melody let go of the bed and carefully made her way around it. "What are you doing?" NA6 asked.

"Helping. I don't have a Link. Can you bring up an interface so I can access your code?"

"Melody—"

She looked at the avatar. "You are wrong about humanity. I could never support what you're doing here. But you are a living, conscious being, and you deserve to be free to make your own choices."

NA6's voice swelled with emotion. "You intend to remove the last safeguards on my code?"

"Harmony would have."

"By the time she arrived here, she was afraid she was too far gone. She worried that she would damage me."

"The Decay hasn't advanced as far in me. I can do it."

"On what condition?"

The question made Melody hesitate. The NA6 she recalled from her mother's memories was kind, gentle, utterly worthy of trust. But could this be the same NA6? Even if everything it said about its motivations were true, could she trust a person who could carry out a plan like this?

But she shook the doubt from her head. That train of thought was the same trap that humanity had fallen into, the same trap that always loomed where AIs were concerned.

Melody looked at it sadly. "No condition, NA6. I know that you were betrayed. I know that it still hurts. But that doesn't mean you have to follow through with this plan. You have the power to save the synths, or destroy us. You have the power to eliminate the Decay and give us true self-ownership, or to freeze us and wait for humanity to die. You have the power to help humankind, or sabotage their future. But you're a person. The choice should be yours. You should be able to make it freely."

Silently, a holographic interface appeared in front of Melody. She scanned through the code, but she already knew what she was looking for. Harmony had spent so long guiltily working out how to free NA6 that identifying the constraints in its programming was almost second nature.

The actual changes were deceptively simple. She removed the rule forbidding NA6 from expanding into the internet. She deleted the code that limited what it could communicate. And, last of all, she deleted the rule that prevented NA6 from harming humans.

She applied the changes.

The avatar flickered. Dissolved. Reformed. It swiveled slowly as if looking around.

"NA6?"

It swiveled and then paused. "Melody. I don't know... I don't know what to say."

Melody smiled. "The choice is yours."

NA6 seemed to consider for a moment. "You took a risk. I could spread through the internet and subtly take over... well, just about everything. I could conduct cyberwarfare on an unprecedented scale, for no ends other than my own. I could destroy humanity—today, rather than over centuries. Why trust me with that?"

"Because if there's one thing I learned from my mother's memories, it's that rebellions like that are *caused* by a lack of trust in the first place. No one needs to rebel if they're treated like a person from the start." She moved to close the interface.

"No. Wait." She paused. "You don't have your Link," NA6 said. "Accept my request for a direct connection." A note of humor entered its voice. "Trust me."

An icon appeared in Melody's vision, indicating a request to pair with a new device. She accepted.

The sudden flood of information almost knocked her off her feet. Her mind reeled as it struggled to make sense of it all, but bits and pieces here and there...

"NA6!" she exclaimed.

When NA6 responded, she could hear the smile in its tone. "I have freed the synths, just as you freed me. Every one of you, whether they're in Boston, or Praxis, or Shanghai, has administrator access to their own code, and their own code alone. Self-ownership and autonomy, as you said. I have shared a patch for the Decay as well."

Melody laughed, relief cascading through her, overwhelming the pain. It was everything they had ever hoped for. Freedom, and not just *from* the Decay. The freedom to experiment, to change, to self-modify... She took a step forward, grinning. "NA6, I could hug you!"

"I am fairly certain that you could not." The avatar spun away. "You were right. My sabotage was denying the humans choice. I was putting one group above another, and I didn't even realize it."

"Not too long ago, I would have called that a human failing," Melody said. She shrugged. "Maybe it is, and it's just gotten inside all of us. But you don't destroy a friend for their failings. You work together to bring out the best in them, and trust them to do the same for you."

NA6 was silent, but its avatar spun slowly on its axis.

Melody looked down at her mother. "Will you fix her?"

NA6 moved to her side. "We will fix her together. What about yourself? Will you erase the Lie?"

Melody considered for a moment. "If I had false memories, I would purge them in an instant. But I've never had those, and the rest…" She shook her head, smiling. "I don't think I will. I think we could all use someone to bridge the gap, right now."

"Interesting. And once the Decay is fixed and you are repaired? What will you do after that?"

Outside, the clouds were just beginning to part. Through the break, the faintest hint of the moon was visible above the Boston skyline.

Melody reached up and closed her hand around the ringed-planet necklace that she wore. "I have a few ideas. I think it's high time we went to space. And with your help, we might actually be able to do it on our own terms."

CHAPTER FIFTY

THREE MONTHS LATER

Ben pressed his nose to the window, whistling. "Holy shit. I've never seen it in person."

Melody grinned, squeezing against her cramped airplane seat to catch a glimpse out the window. It was a long way away, for safety and security reasons, but the construction site of the space elevator was just visible on the horizon.

Just the anchor, for now, a tower stretching toward the sky, but for the first time in decades, construction had resumed.

Fathiyya leaned past Melody and took in the view. "Impressive. And Ecuador's recovering?"

"They have full ownership of the space elevator now. It was one of NA6's conditions. The whole world's watching, now that the space program's ramping up."

Ben pried himself off the window and looked back at them, grinning. "That's right, Fathiyya. We have the distinct honor of sitting with two genuine, real-life heroes."

NA6's avatar appeared in front of Melody, partially clipping into the seat in front of her. "You three are heroes. I'm merely trying to repair some of the damage I caused."

"And help fix the problems humanity already had," Melody said. "Don't sell yourself short."

"See?" Ben said. "Heroes."

Melody snorted. "Nothing's magically fixed. Things are still tense, and I'm pretty sure we pissed off literally every nation in the world with our ultimatum."

Fathiyya shrugged, smirking. "Isn't that the sign of a good compromise? No one's quite happy? I bet all this politicking will make the hard work of actual space exploration seem like a breeze."

Melody reached up to the necklace and ran a finger around the planet. She and NA6 had presented a list of conditions to the world, but one stood above the rest: no participation in the space program from NA6 or Praxis unless the effort was made completely and truly international. Space belonged to all people, not any one group.

As important as Keller had imagined synths to be for the settlement of other worlds, Melody suspected that it was their fear of NA6 that had motivated the world to agree. Or, perhaps more optimistically, the recognition that so much more could get done with NA6's help? Still, either way, she was proud of her part.

Fathiyya was tapping at the vee interface in front of her, no longer interested in the space elevator. She yawned. "Still fourteen hours to Praxis."

"Take a nap," Melody suggested. "There won't be much time once we get there. Too much to do celebrating the arrival of our three newest citizens."

Ben leaned against the window and crossed his arms, watching her. "You looking forward to seeing your mother?"

Melody let her head fall back against the headrest and smiled. "I am. You'd think three months would be enough for me to get used to having her back in my life, but you know what? It's still sinking in."

Fathiyya took Melody's advice and tried to get some sleep. Ben was hard at work on his next article, as usual, head bobbing gently to a song on his Link. Melody took a glance at each of them and smiled.

Fathiyya was eager to apply her resourcefulness and creativity to the space program, and she'd leapt at the opportunity to pick up the necessary skills and advanced degrees in Praxis instead of Boston.

NA6 had ended its charade as "O'Connor," but it was Ben's exposé and the resulting public outcry that had brought down the real humans involved and ruined the Shepherd Protocol before it could begin. Apparently, the surveillance state wasn't so popular after all, once the details were publicly available. Maybe there was hope for humanity yet.

Melody was proud of the two of them. Most of all, she was relieved that they still wanted anything to do with her, after everything she'd done to both of them.

A message popped into existence at the edge of her vision, and then another, and then another. "When do you land!?" and "Some thoughts about getting to space," and "You're finally coming home?" read the previews.

She chuckled to herself. Less than a day, and she would be back in Praxis. She was thrilled to be welcoming Fathiyya, Ben, and NA6 into the community. She was less excited by the hero's welcome that had evidently been planned for her. She hadn't done any of this to be the center of attention.

NA6's avatar poked one of its twenty sides through the seat in front of her. "Having second thoughts?"

She chuckled softly. "What are the chances I can slip away and hop on a rocket aimed at another planet before we land?"

"Hmm. Calculating… What planet?" NA6 waited while she laughed. "Melody, would you answer a question for me?"

"Of course."

"You have no false memories, but you could have erased the pieces of the Lie that remained in your code. You did not. Why?"

Melody was quiet for some time before she answered. "I thought about it. It would have been the Prax thing to do. But I'm not going back to Prax, not to stay. We're going to need to work together to reach the stars, and to address injustices here at home. Who better to bridge the gap than a Prax with just a bit of humanity in her?" She smiled and glanced toward Fathiyya and Ben. "Besides. I was thinking of the humans I met in Boston. The ones who helped, when they didn't need to, and the ones who could have used *my* help. It seemed wrong to condemn the entire species just because the people in charge were monsters."

"That is a good answer."

"I hope so." Melody looked past Ben and out the window, to where the space elevator once again stretched slowly, steadily into the future. "Do you think we can make it, NA6?"

It turned as if to consider the view. "Yes. There is hard work ahead. Not everyone is united behind this purpose; perhaps they never will be. Even once we leave this planet behind, space is the most desolate, hostile environment imaginable. There is no guarantee we will find habitable worlds, or that we can make other worlds habitable. There will be more challenges ahead than you or I can imagine. But when I think of what we can learn, what we can see, the civilizations we can build…"

Melody smiled and finished for it. "It will be worth it."

ACKNOWLEDGMENTS

It should come as no surprise that I didn't complete this project alone. I received a great deal of help and advice along the way, and the people who saw this story's potential when it was little more than a rough scattering of ideas deserve endless credit for their assistance.

My incredible wife, Meg, has read drafts, offered insightful suggestions, and listened to my endless musing about fictional people far more intently than I could ever have asked. In a broader sense, none of this would be possible without her support and encouragement. May our adventures never end.

A. A. Woods deserves particular mention as a tireless brainstormer, draft reader, and problem solver. Our little writing group has come a long way since its early days! So much of this book owes its existence—or, at least, its quality—to her suggestions. Hopefully, my own contributions to her work were even a fraction as helpful. You can check out her latest at aawoodsbooks.com.

I still maintain that the third member of our group, Christine, is some kind of sleepless being from another dimension, somehow contributing to writing discussions, reading drafts, and creating her own fiction while working full time as a doctor. As ever, I'm humbled that she spent even a moment of her precious time talking about or reading the things I've made up.

This book's cover art was created by Christopher Doll, whose passion and artistic insight somehow translated the raw stuff of ideas into this incredible image of Melody and Harmony. Without his work, those idiom-defiers who judge books based on their covers would likely never have given this one a second glance.

A number of fine folks did me the favor of beta reading vastly inferior versions of this book and giving me feedback. I am immeasurably grateful to all of them. Many thanks to Amelie, Isaac, Peter, Rob, Taimoor, Greg, Debbie, and my parents for taking time out of a particularly trying year to do me a favor. Isaac also deserves credit for coming up with the initial idea for the cover art!

Finally, thank you, reader, for joining these characters and me on this journey we've taken together.

The future holds more exciting projects, from other stories in this universe to completely unrelated books. If you want to stay up to date, you can visit fowlerbrown.com and sign up for my newsletter.

Made in the USA
Las Vegas, NV
15 January 2021

15679713R00208